THE WAKEFIELD DYNASTY

3

GILBERT MORRIS

The SHIELD of HONOR

TYNDALE HOUSE PUBLISHERS, INC.
Wheaton, Illinois

Library of Congress Cataloging-in-Publication Data

Morris, Gilbert.
     The shield of honor / Gilbert Morris.
        p.   cm. — (The Wakefield dynasty ; 3)
     ISBN 0-8423-5930-3 (sc)
      1. Great Britain—History—Charles II, 1660-1685—Fiction.
   I. Title.   II. Series: Morris, Gilbert. Wakefield dynasty ; 3.
     PS3563.08742S495   1994
     813'.54—dc20   94-45604

Printed in the United States of America

99   98   97   96   95
5   4   3   2   1

To Paul and Vangie Brendiar
Most things in this world are breakable, but true friendship
formed within the body of Christ stands the test of time.
Johnnie and I feel you two have given us a part of yourselves
. . . and we are grateful for this gift.

CONTENTS

GENEALOGY OF THE WAKEFIELD DYNASTY
[THE MORGANS]

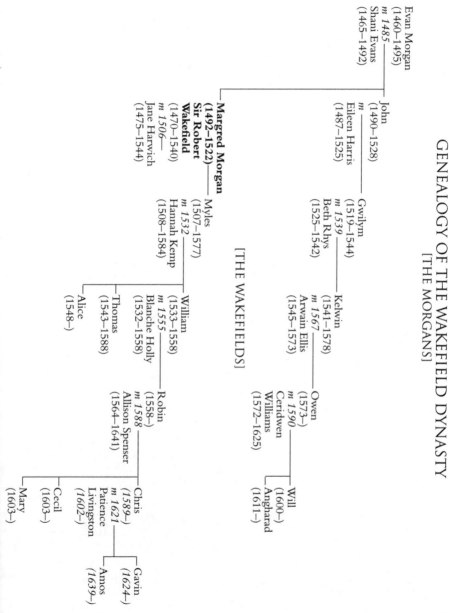

[THE WAKEFIELDS]

Evan Morgan
(1460–1495)
m 1485
Shani Evans
(1465–1492)

John
(1490–1528)
m
Eileen Harris
(1487–1525)

Margred Morgan
(1492–1522)
Sir Robert
Wakefield
(1470–1540)
m 1506
Jane Harwich
(1475–1544)

Gwilym
(1519–1544)
m 1539
Beth Rhys
(1525–1542)

Myles
(1507–1577)
m 1532
Hannah Kemp
(1508–1584)

Kelvin
(1541–1578)
m 1567
Arwain Ellis
(1545–1573)

William
(1533–1558)
m 1555
Blanche Holly
(1532–1558)

Thomas
(1543–1588)

Alice
(1548–)

Owen
(1573–)
m 1590
Ceridwen
Williams
(1572–1625)

Robin
(1558–)
m 1588
Allison Spenser
(1564–1641)

Will
(1600–)
Angharad
(1611–)

Chris
(1589–)
m 1621
Patience
Livingston
(1602–)

Gavin
(1624–)
Amos
(1639–)

Cecil
(1603–)

Mary
(1603–)

Saints &

1 6 0 3 **Part ONE** 1 6 2 1

Strangers

THE LAST TUDOR

A p r i l   1 6 0 3

Come to see the old queen buried, 'ave you now?"

Christopher Wakefield started as a hand touched his arm. Mindful of the danger of cutpurses, he whirled instantly, and his hand closed on the hand of a tall man who had come to stand beside him.

"'Ere now! Yer don't 'ave to break me fingers!"

"Oh, I'm sorry—!" Chris apologized, his face burning.

The man grinned at him and raised his eyebrows. "Yer new to London, ain't you? And all alone?" He had a pair of frosty blue eyes under black brows and wore clothes that were rather better than average.

Chris was impressed with the man's seeming ease and assurance. "Well—my family—we've come to the funeral."

"Yer family? Not a wife, surely. Why you're not more than eighteen, I'd wager." He examined him boldly, seeing a lean young man almost six feet tall. He noted the wedge-shaped face, wide mouth, and very pugnacious chin. He knew the ladies would like the lad's hair, which was auburn, and his dark blue eyes, which were surprisingly shy.

Since Chris was only fourteen—though tall and strong for his age—he felt a burst of pride at the man's words. To be taken for a *man* was a fine thing! He swelled, saying, "I meant my parents, Sir Robin Wakefield—"

"Why, I saw right off you was a lord! Now, my name is Harry Jones. What's yours, sir?"

"Chris Wakefield."

"Been in London often, I takes it?"

"No, this is my first time. By myself I mean."

"You tell me that?" Jones opened his eyes wide and clapped Chris on the shoulder in a friendly fashion. "Well now, there's a lot to see in this town. But you 'ave to be careful, you know."

"Careful?"

"Why, the place is crawling with cutthroats, sir!" Jones shook his head with disapproval. "And bad women, I'm sad to say. Many a young fellow I've had to save from going bad."

"Very good of you, Mr. Jones, I'm sure."

Jones waved his hand in a deprecating gesture. "What are we put here for but to help our fellowmen? We're all brothers, and the Scripture tells us that two are better than one!"

Chris stood there listening to Jones. The fellow was so entertaining that he forgot his loneliness. Finally Jones said, "Look now, why don't you and me 'ave a little walk? I can show you some of the town."

"Oh, I can't," Chris said quickly. "My father warned me to be back—"

"Why, a noble young man can walk with a friend for a few minutes, can't 'e? The funeral don't start for *hours!* Come on now, we'll just see a bit o' the town."

Chris tried feebly to protest, but Jones seized his arm and pulled him along the busy streets. *Just for a little while,* he promised himself. *I've got plenty of time before the procession. . . .*

For the next hour Harry Jones guided the young man through the teeming streets of the city. After the narrow, quiet streets of his village, it seemed to him that London ran on wheels! Carts and coaches made such a thundering that his ears hummed. At every corner men, women, and children met, jostled, talked, laughed, pushed, shouted. And what a beehive of activity! Hammers beating in one place, kettles whistling in another, pots clinking in a third!

He saw chimney sweeps wearing sooty rags, while some of the aristocracy swaggered about arrayed in gold and gaudy satin. Porters sweated under their burdens, chapmen darted from shop to shop, and tradesmen scurried around like ants, pulling at the coats of prospective customers.

"Watch yerself, Sir Chris!" Harry Jones cried out sharply, pulling Chris back just in time to avoid a deluge of slops that someone threw out of an upper window. "Can't get them fine clothes all filthy, can we now?"

As the pale incandescent sun of April 1603 spread its golden rays over London, Jones drew Chris Wakefield through the streets of the vast city. Mesmerized by the sounds, the colors, the whirling activity of this world, the young man lost himself in it, completely unaware of the passing of time.

The two men stopped to watch the antics of some trained monkeys and apes who performed on a high rope. The beasts were dressed in the mode of lords and pulled their hats off to the applause of the crowd who had gathered to watch them. "As good as lords, ain't they, Chris?" Jones laughed. The fascinated boy watched as the monkeys turned heels over head with a basket filled with eggs without breaking a one—then a lithe Italian girl performed a series of tricks on the rope.

"Come on, now!" Harry Jones whispered. "Don't yer be lookin' at that foreign wench! They mean nothing but trouble. Now I know a young lady who'd appreciate a lad like you. . .!"

They made their way through the streets, and Jones said, "Look, there's a bullbaiting over near the Red Horse. Do you like that?"

Jones led him to the spot where the affair was to take place. He paid for two seats, which had been placed on two sides of a large courtyard. They arrived just in time, for as they took their places a young ox was led in and fastened by a long rope to an iron ring in the middle of the yard. "Watch now!" Jones said, his eyes snapping with excitement. "'Ere comes the dogs!"

Chris watched several poorly dressed men enter the open space, leading a pack of dogs. Two of them loosed about six of the dogs, which at once plunged at the tethered ox, uttering ferocious snarls. They tore at the poor beast, who fought back as best as he could, but it was hopeless. The ox kicked wildly with his rear hooves, managing to strike—and even disembowel—several of the dogs. But the men merely loosed more dogs. These beasts, now driven wild by bloodlust, covered the badly wounded ox. One of the larger dogs caught the bellowing animal by the nose, and others slashed at his legs.

The crowd was loud, cheering certain dogs on, yelling with excitement when one of the dogs went down. When the ox at last was overcome, Jones said, "Now they've got 'im! He was a good 'un, weren't he, Chris?"

He didn't answer. The heat and the smell of blood had overcome him so that the sweetmeats he'd devoured earlier now rose in his throat. Fighting the sickening waves of nausea, he turned and left the courtyard. Valiantly holding himself erect and refusing to give in to the need to throw up, he paused when he was in the clear. Harry Jones came to him saying, "Aw, yer feelin' a little sick? Come along, now. We'll go to a place I know and have a drink."

As Chris followed Jones through a labyrinth of streets, he was torn with indecision. *I'd better get back to the inn,* he told himself. But the lure of London was on him, and Jones was an amusing fellow. The two of them reached an inn with a blue eagle on the sign that swung over the door, and Jones was greeted by two men playing cards. "Here's a fine chap just come to London," he announced, then gestured at the men. "This here is James, and this ugly chap is Henry." The two greeted Chris warmly, and soon he was seated with them, enjoying the ale that the innkeeper kept flowing to the table.

The three men seemed to know everyone in London. Chris listened to their tales with avid interest, drinking several tankards of the warm, amber ale. Before long his thinking seemed to slow down. He felt warm and thought with satisfaction, *What a fine time I'm having!*

"'Ere now, let's have a bit o' me special stuff," Jones insisted. He signaled the innkeeper, who brought a brown bottle at once with four glasses. "Now this is the real thing. I don't waste it on most people, yer see. Just for me good friends!"

The fiery liquid bit at Chris's throat as he swallowed it, but he managed to down it without choking. "Fine!" he announced, his voice coming out faint and raspy. He cleared his throat and held his glass out. "Let me buy the next round!"

The bottle went around, and then a card game began. Chris found his tongue getting thicker, and his fingers seemed numb. He was aware that he was laughing too much, but could not seem to stop. "Godd—to go—soon—!" he muttered, then finally stood up saying, "Got to—get home." But then a wave of nausea hit him.

"Aw, now, a little sick again, are you, Chris?" Jones said. His voice sounded far away, and Chris had to focus to make out his face. "'Ere, now, come along. You lie down a bit. You'll be all right. . . ."

Chris stumbled to a room, guided by Jones, and fell onto a bed. It seemed to come up and hit him in the face—and he felt himself falling into a deep pit. . . .

❦

Chris felt as though he was trying to climb out of some sort of hole, a very deep one. His head was spinning, and when he tried to open his eyes, a pain ran through his head. It was as though someone had driven a red-hot spike through his brain. He closed his eyes quickly and lay still. The sun blinded him, and he coughed and rolled over on his side. Something smelled terrible, and he suddenly began to vomit. He was so weak he could not lift his head. Finally the retching stopped, and he sat up and looked around.

He was in a kind of an alley filled with refuse. He was half lying in a pile of garbage, and even as he looked around, a huge brown rat with a white muzzle scurried by his feet. He kicked at it and frantically pulled himself to his feet. His mind was whirling—and he was stunned when he looked down to see that he was wearing only his underwear.

A trembling seized him, and he wanted to cry out, but there was no one to ask for help. Looking wildly around, he saw some old rags piled against the wall. Fumbling through them, he found some rags of clothing. They stank and were covered with filth, but he had no choice. With trembling hands he put them on, then turned and left the alley on rubbery legs.

What will Father say—and Mother?

He longed to find a dark place and hide himself, but there was no hope of that. People laughed at him as he stumbled along the streets, but he paid them little heed. All he could think was, *I've done it now! They won't ever let me forget this!*

⌐━☼⌐

"I still think you shouldn't have come, dear." Robin Wakefield held his wife's arm carefully as they made their way down the crowded street. "It's too near your time."

"I can have a baby in London as well as I can at Wakefield." At once Allison regretted her sharp response. Robin was worried sick about her; she knew that. *He was the same when Christopher was born,* she thought, then reminded herself, *It's even more worrisome now—I'm thirty-nine years old. Too old to have a child, perhaps.* Quietly she took her husband's hand, drawing his quick attention. Her ash-blonde hair framed her oval face, and her violet eyes were as clear as they'd been the day she'd first seen him. "I'm all right," she said quietly. "Hasn't God promised us that all will be well with me and the child?"

Robin Wakefield looked into the eyes of the woman he loved more than any other thing on earth. As she met his gaze, Allison thought how much he still looked as he had on their first meeting. He'd been but a boy, older than she but a boy nonetheless. In adulthood he had grown straight and tall, and his blue-gray eyes were warm as he said, "Yes, he did. I guess you have to keep reminding me of that. I'm as nervous as a cat!"

"Come now, let's be going." She slipped her hand into the crook of his arm and they walked slowly through the packed streets. They had not gone fifty feet before she said, "Oh, look, Robin. There are the Cromwells."

"So they are." Robin lifted his voice, calling out, "Robert— Robert Cromwell!" A tall man who was walking with a woman and several children halted, looked toward the pair, then waved.

"Let's go see the new baby," Allison said. She led the way and, when they reached the group, said, "Good day, Mr. Cromwell, Elizabeth, and all you young Cromwells."

A mumble of greetings from the youngsters piped in return, and Elizabeth Cromwell spoke cheerfully. "I didn't expect to see you here—so close to your time, Allison." She shifted the baby she carried to her other arm, adding, "I'll be able to come and help when the child is born."

"Let me see her." Allison held out her arms, and when she held the baby, she touched the fat, red cheeks. "How pretty she is!"

"She's a girl!" The small boy who stood close beside his father spoke with disgust. "I wanted a brother." He looked around with a frown, adding, "Who wants another old girl?"

"I do, Oliver," Allison said at once. "And you'll see—you'll love this little one like you do all the rest of your sisters." Her gaze lingered on the sturdy boy's still-mutinous face. Though only four years old, the lad was very strong willed—like his mother. Allison smiled. "Perhaps I'll have a boy, then you two can be friends."

As the two women talked, Robert drew Robin aside. "Well, she's gone, the queen. What will come now?"

"Nothing as good as she, Robert," Robin said soberly.

"You always had a high opinion of her, didn't you? But then, you knew her rather well. I thought she did some foolish things in her old age."

Robin's clear eyes grew sad and thoughtful. "She was the last of the Tudors. For over a hundred years, with a handful of bodyguards, they maintained their sovereignty, kept the peace, baffled the diplomacy and onslaughts of Europe, and guided the country through changes that might well have wrecked it."

"Aye, that's so." Cromwell nodded. He was a tall, thick-bodied man of stern character and humorless views; a conscientious landlord and justice of the peace. Robin had learned he was a man to be trusted. "What comes now, think you?" he demanded again.

"Elizabeth named James IV of Scotland to succeed her."

"What sort of man is he?"

"An honest man, I think—but he is not a Tudor. He won't find ruling England as simple as ruling Scotland."

"Well, it's in God's hands." A staunch Calvinist, Cromwell accepted the new sovereign as he accepted the sun in the sky: Both were ordained by God. He shrugged his heavy shoulders. "Come now, it's time we found a place to stand."

"Aye, but where's that boy of mine?" A touch of anger ruffled Wakefield's voice. "I gave him leave to explore London, but he gave me his word to be back by one."

Robert stroked his beard and studied his friend. He knew Robin Wakefield to be an excellent man, but he feared that, somehow, those fine qualities had not been passed on to Christopher, the only son of the family. He thought carefully, then said slowly, "You're too easy on that boy, Robin."

The younger man looked up with surprise. It was a thought he'd had himself, and it shook him to hear a man with such steady judgment voice it. "I—wanted to be a good father," he said in a low tone. "But Chris has no sense of—of what it means to be obedient." This was the bitter truth that seldom left Robin's mind—nor Allison's mind, he was sure. Their son's birth had been a time of rejoicing, of great plans for the child who would one day be lord of Wakefield. But from his childhood, Christopher had been rebellious and willful.

Robin looked quickly toward Allison, his face growing stern. "He's got his mother twined around his little finger. And I've been too lax." His lips grew thin, and he nodded shortly. "He's got to learn what it means to be responsible."

"Well, he'll show up." Cromwell shrugged. "But if we're to have a place to see the funeral go by, we'll have to hurry. Everybody in London is here—and from the country, too."

The two moved toward the women, and the small group began to push their way along through the throngs. "This is impossible!" Robin snapped finally. "You can't stand this sort of thing, Allison."

"But I must see the procession!"

Robin thought, then nodded. "We'll have to take a cab to Westminster. I can get us one, I think."

"Oh, Robin, could you?"

At once Robin hailed a cab, then when it came to the curb, started to help Allison in. But even as he took her hand, he heard Elizabeth Cromwell exclaim, "Why, Christopher—!"

Both Wakefields turned at once and saw their son—but in such a condition that for an instant neither of them could speak.

Chris Wakefield had left their rooms attired in a fine suit of plush and silk. His hair had been carefully combed, and he had jangled some gold pieces in his purse.

The boy they saw was clothed in filthy rags that stank to heaven! His hair was matted. Worst of all, when he came toward them, he staggered slightly, and as soon as he was in front of them, they both smelled the sour odor of drink.

"Christopher!" Allison whispered, reaching out to touch his pale face. "What happened to you?"

But there was none of his wife's gentleness in Robin. He had allowed his son to come with them only after extracting a firm promise of good behavior. Now this! He was aware of the covert laughter of those who drew close to watch, and a streak of anger ran through him. When he spoke, his voice was low and cold.

"So this is the way you keep your promise?"

Chris's eyes flew to his father's face as a dull red filled his cheeks. "I—I couldn't help it!"

"Anyone can help getting drunk!"

Chris had wandered around the streets, not even conscious of the disgusted looks he'd received. When he'd seen his parents, he had gone to them with shame. Now he knew he should have avoided them and gone back to the inn and cleaned himself up.

"Get out of my sight, Christopher," Robin said. "Go to the inn and stay there."

"But—the funeral—!"

"You're a pretty sight for the funeral of a queen!" Bitterness was not something that Robin Wakefield possessed as a rule, but this was a time when he'd wanted to show his respect and love for his sovereign. Harsh disappointment filled him, and he turned from his son, taking Allison's arm.

"Robin—!" Allison protested as he handed her into the cab, but he shook his head. She gave Chris one agonized look, then the door was closed. As the cab moved away, neither of them spoke. Allison knew the heart of her husband as well as she knew her own. She knew the love that he had for Chris, but she'd seen for years how the rebellious spirit of their son had built a barrier between the two—and even between Chris and herself.

She placed her hand on Robin's, and when he turned to face her, she saw that his jaw was corded with tension, his eyes tormented with grief. "I can't understand him, Allison!" he whispered. "I'd die for that boy—but he cares for nothing!"

Allison felt tears sting her eyes, and she blinked them back. "I know, dear," she whispered. "But he's young. He'll change." As the coach rolled along, she prayed, *O God! Give us more love for this boy! He's hurt us terribly, but no more than we've hurt you many times! Let us love him as you love us.*

❦

Back on the street, Chris stood watching the coach until it disappeared. A sick shame filled him, and he was suddenly aware that the Cromwells were watching him. He turned away, unable to face them, but Elizabeth Cromwell said quietly, "Go to the inn and wait for them, Christopher. After the funeral, you can explain how it was."

Chris turned to her. She was holding Oliver's hand, and the boy's eyes were fixed on him steadily. Somehow the boy's gaze unnerved Chris, and he shook his head. "No," he mumbled. "They won't understand."

Chris had always been fond of Oliver, had spent much time playing with him when his father and Robert Cromwell met for business. Now without warning, young Oliver came over and took Chris's hand. Looking up, he piped in a clear voice, *"I'm* not mad at you, Christopher!"

Chris blinked at the boy, then whispered, "Aren't you, Oliver?"

"No!"

"That's—that's good."

Then Chris pulled his hand back and walked rapidly away. As he disappeared, Robert gave his wife a sad shake of the head. "Too bad! He'll break their hearts—he already has." Then he said heavily, "Come along. Let's find a place to watch the procession."

Chris walked blindly down the streets, ignoring the taunts several people threw at him. The effects of the liquor had been driven away by the shock of his father's words . . . and by the sight of his mother's anguished face. Now it was like a very frightening dream—only it was not a dream. He would not wake up—as he had done on other occasions—and heave a sigh of relief that it was not real. *I'll never forget what Mother's face was like when she saw me!* he agonized. *Why did I do it? Why?*

But Chris had no answers. He never had answers for his bad behavior. Grief, at times, but he never knew *why* he could not resist the temptations that came at him. He stumbled down the street, asking why he had paid any heed to Harry Jones, tormenting himself. *You knew what he was—why in the name of heaven didn't you just walk away from him?*

But no answers came. None at all. He had been through this self-recrimination many times in his fourteen years and knew that he would spend long nights agonizing over what he had done. Long ago he'd learned to cover this foolish side of his life, to never let anyone else see him showing grief over his bad behavior. But it was there, even now, twisting like a knife!

Finally he slowed down and looked up to watch the crowds all headed for the street where the procession would pass. Keen disappointment shot through him, replaced almost immediately by a stubborn decision. "I'll see it for myself. How could that be more wrong than what I've done already?"

A perverse spirit took him, and he joined the crowd that surged forward. The streets were packed, but he moved to an alley and climbed to the top of an inn, the Prancing Pony. There he sat, perched on the sharp pitch of the roof, waiting for the procession to come.

Below, the crowd surged and fought for space, but Chris felt alone in his high perch. The crowd seemed to be far away, the sounds of their cries drifting up to him all muted. He liked to be alone and felt somehow that he was enclosed in a clear bubble. He could see and hear what was taking place—but it had little to do with him. A thought came as the first horsemen appeared down the street: *I wish I could be alone like this all the time!* But he knew he could not. Nobody was alone. Everyone had to be in their place—and Chris had never learned what his place was. As the long line of nobles mounted on beautifully groomed horses moved beneath him, he thought, *I'm the son of Lord Robin and Lady Allison Wakefield. Lots of boys would like to be rich and have a title. Why can't I be good?*

Guilt burned inside him like a fire, searing his heart—but he had learned to live with that. Stoically he clutched the tiles, staring down as the procession continued below him. He had met the queen once, very briefly, and when the carriage bearing her body appeared, he fastened his eyes on it. A group of black-clad mourners flanked the carriage, holding high flags of the empire. The stillness of the air was filled with the dirge they intoned, but Chris's eyes were fixed on the coffin. He tried to picture the queen's body, but could not.

"She's dead," he muttered, trying to think of death. "Where is she? In heaven or in hell?"

Somehow the thought frightened him, and he slid down the tiles and descended to the pavement. The thought came abruptly, *I can run away! Go far away—and never see Father or Mother again! I can't ever be good, so they'll never love me!*

Then he lifted his head and stared at the sky—which seemed to be the color of gravestones. A loneliness seized him, and he knew he had no choice. Slowly he turned and made his way out of the alley, then plodded along the streets of London toward the inn.

T w o

A TURN OF THE KEY

June 1620

London had been submerged in torrential rains. Every morning low-lying clouds, dark and swollen with moisture, would gather over the city, dumping fat drops that splattered in the streets and on the roofs. And every afternoon, the denizens of the city endured floods of seemingly biblical proportions.

Chris Wakefield had risen at noon on Tuesday morning, thrown on his clothes, and forgone breakfast. His head throbbed mightily as he left his lodgings and made his way to Lincoln's Inn, one of the four ancient lodging houses used as a base for senior lawyers. The cold rain poured over his hat, ran down his neck, and soaked his clothing as he splashed down the streets. The sidewalks were swimming with the overflow, and Chris had to wade through six inches of water as he crossed the street. Cursing under his breath, he shouldered his way through the men who crowded the narrow entrance.

"Good day, Mr. Dollarhyde," he said when he had entered one of the offices that branched off from a dark, narrow hallway.

"Ah! Here you are, Mr. Wakefield!" An extremely tall man with a face almost painfully thin looked up from a battered desk that was covered with papers. He had a pair of faded blue eyes filled with disillusionment—the result of years spent in observing people caught up and mangled by the machinery of the court. Leaning back, he flexed his long, bony fingers, which were stained with black ink, and studied his visitor.

At thirty-one, Chris's dark blue eyes were cynical—and reddened from late hours. *And probably drink,* the older man thought. *He's looking into the bottle every day, from the looks of him. A shame—he's not going to make it, I fear.* But he said only, "You're, ah, looking for Mr. Cromwell, I take it?"

"Yes—is he here, Silas?"

Weaving his skeletal fingers together in a convoluted pattern, then releasing them, the tall man shook his head and spoke in a regretful tone. "Ah—you forget the time, sir."

"Time? What time is that?"

"The time of Mr. Cromwell's marriage." A slight smile creased the narrow lips of the clerk as though a humorous thought had struck him. "Ah—you have forgotten, I see. Your business has kept you too busy, I suppose." *It takes so much time and energy to get drunk and chase every wench in London!* he thought disdainfully.

Chris stared at Dollarhyde blankly, then grimaced. "Aye, you're right. He's gone then?"

"Ah—yes, he left Lincoln's Inn a fortnight ago, sir. He'll be at his home now, I believe."

"Blast!" Chris struck his thigh with his rain-soaked hat, sending a spray of water on the worn boards of the floor. He jerked his head forward in an angry gesture, which sent the hammers pounding against his temples. He grimaced again. "He didn't—leave anything for me, I don't suppose?"

Dollarhyde opened his lips enough to ask, "Something for you, Mr. Wakefield? Ah—no, I don't believe so. Were you expecting something?"

Most likely a loan—or a handout! Dollarhyde knew the intimate details of Oliver Cromwell's business, as he knew the details of dozens of other young men who resided at Lincoln's Inn. Although his face showed nothing, his razor-keen mind called up the page in one of Cromwell's ledgers—the clerk had the phenomenal ability to "see" pages with his memory as though they were held before his eyes—and considered the series of "loans" from Mr. Cromwell to Mr. Wakefield, which stretched back over the past three years.

More than once Dollarhyde had warned the youthful Cromwell against such dealings. *"That Christopher Wakefield is just no good, Mr. Oliver—nothing like his father, or his great-grandfather Sir Myles! You know he throws all you give him away on liquor and wenches."*

But Cromwell had always shrugged and given the same answer. "He's got good stuff in him, Silas. I hope he'll wake up one day and discover God."

Dollarhyde let none of his thoughts appear on his face, but said thoughtfully, "Aren't you going to the wedding, Mr. Wakefield? I know Mr. Cromwell is expecting you."

Chris slanted a glare at the clerk. He knew Dollarhyde, despite his polite manner, had little use for him. "I expect I will, Silas," he mumbled. He *had* to see Oliver. He was desperately trying to get money to stave off his creditors. Another glance at Dollarhyde's expression told Chris that the clerk probably knew this. *Blast him!—He's got a pair of eyes that see right through a man!* "Well, I'll be going."

"Ah—give the bride and groom my best wishes, sir," Dollarhyde called as Wakefield left the room. The door slammed loudly, and the clerk chuckled. He picked up his pen, but the door swung open again and a short, fat man with a jolly red face popped inside.

"Wakefield again?" he asked. He dumped a load of papers on the mountain of documents that rose from Dollarhyde's desk. "Come to sponge off Cromwell, eh?"

"What else does he come for?"

"Don't see why your boss puts up with it!"

Dollarhyde snapped, "It's none of your business, James!" Then he relented and shrugged his scrawny shoulders. "It is, ah, *strange*. Mr. Cromwell is a sharp man—but he's got a fondness for the Wakefield chap that I've never understood. Of course, they grew up together, and Wakefield was more or less an older brother, I think. Cromwell's got mostly sisters, and Wakefield took him hunting—things like that. And he always brought something back for Mr. Cromwell from his travels. I suppose that's it, though I wish he'd cut the man loose. He's going to prison for debt soon enough. Either that or he'll get stabbed in a tavern brawl over some wench!"

"How much does he owe Mr. Oliver?"

"*That* is certainly none of your business! Now—off with you!"

Outside Chris plunged into the driving downpour, slogging along the cobblestone pavement.

Got to find cash—can't dodge my creditors much longer!

Overhead the clouds grew even darker, and finally he found himself in a narrow street in front of a tavern. He drew his lips together muttering, "No! I've got to raise enough cash to last me until I find a good berth on a ship."

He stood there uncertainly, the rain pouring off the brim of his hat. Despair covered him as darkly as the sooty clouds covered the skies overhead. He thought of his past, of the times he'd come back from a voyage with his pockets filled with gold . . . and soon bitter memories flooded him of the way the money had slipped through his fingers like water. How many times had he resolved to hang on to what he'd made? How many vows had he made to pull himself out of the cycle he'd fallen into—making money, then throwing it away on wine and gambling and women?

The rain made a dull patter on the stones. Chris ducked his head, staring at the swirling water that carried bits of straw, small sticks, paper, and other refuse past his feet. The City of London had a simple method of ridding itself of filth. Garbage and trash were simply dumped in the street—and when the rains came, they were washed away, down the single ditch in the middle of the street.

Why can't something wash away all the garbage I've piled up in my life?

Christopher Wakefield was a man of action, not given to a great deal of introspection. Give him a task, a blade in his hand—why, he'd know what to do! But now as he stood drenched in the rain, he was filled with an abrupt sense of how hollow and useless and wasted his life was. He'd felt this before, but always had sought forgetfulness in drink and activity.

He thought of his family—how he'd broken his parents' hearts with his wild living—and a great pain swept through him. He thought of his younger brother, Cecil, who at the age of seventeen had all the qualities that he himself lacked.

Abruptly the misery of his headache, the crisis that loomed before him, and knowledge that he was a failure in every sense of the word washed over him. The door of the tavern swung open as a man exited—and Wakefield caught the scent of ale and heard the laughter of those inside. Hating himself for giving in, he vowed as he entered, "Just one drink—got to think what to do, but what harm can come of only *one* drink?"

No matter how brightly the sun shone outside, the interior of the Black Dragon Tavern was always dull and gloomy. Even the sign that bore this ferocious title was weathered to a dusky gray, and the paint on it had faded so badly that the beast for which the place was named resembled a contorted pig rather than a dragon. The nameless lane where the Dragon was squeezed between other taverns was murky even during the blaze of noon, thanks to the protruding second-story levels of the wooden structures that effectively cut off the sun's rays from the narrow street below.

Inside the tavern, though, there was a fuliginous feel about the place, a fire crackled merrily in the large fireplace that dominated one end of the tavern. Candles dotted the darkness with yellow incandescence, and a cheerful hubbub of voices rose as pewter mugs were slammed down on the oaken tables occupied by myriad drinkers.

Chris sat down at the single vacant table, and a woman came to serve him. "Well, now, we ain't seen you in a while, Chris." She was a lush-bodied woman with a pair of sharp black eyes. "Been on a voyage, 'ave you now?"

"Hello, Maude," Chris said. She was a common woman, not pretty, but she was always ready for a good time, and she liked the presents he brought her. She owned the Dragon, inherited it from her husband, who had been taken off by the plague. Now she filled a cup with ale and set it down before him, saying coyly, "I 'ope you got some time afore you sails again, eh?"

Chris felt that he'd gone through this scene many times. He drank the ale, gulping it down, and tried to be resolute. He started to rise, saying, "Got some business—"

"Oh, you can't run off *now*, Chris!" The woman cut him short, shoving him back and filling his cup with the amber liquid. She squeezed his shoulder and smiled smugly. "You and me—we got some talking to do. A woman gets lonesome, don't ye know? Now, you sit there and I'll bring you something to eat."

The hours passed in a blur, and the last desperate thought Chris had just before becoming completely drunk was, *Got to get out of here!* But the liquor took him, and it was noon the next day before he left the Dragon—drained and sickened. Echoing in his ears were the screams of the woman who had discovered he was penniless and so had driven him out with curses and a warning never to come back.

When he arrived at his room, he washed his face and noted that his hands were shaking. Even as he stared at them, trying to think of a way out of his predicament, a heavy knock seemed to shake the door. He blinked with surprise, then moved to open it. Two men stood there, their eyes cold and hard. "Christopher Wakefield?" one of them demanded.

Chris knew at once who they were. He'd been expecting them. "I'm Wakefield. And you're here to arrest me for debt."

The taller of the two grinned, exposing blackened teeth. "A wise one, 'arry, ain't 'e?" Then he nodded abruptly. "Come easy now. No trouble, is it?"

"No trouble."

The shorter man had a simple face and seemed troubled. "Sorry to 'ave to do this, sir. But orders is orders. And you've got friends who'll 'elp you out, ain't you, now?"

Standing before the two men, Chris ran over the men he knew in his mind—then said quietly in a voice of despair that matched the dullness in his eyes: "No, I don't have anyone. I'm ready now."

"Aw, it can't be that bad, sir!"

"Shut up, 'arry," the taller man snapped. "Ain't you seen enough fine gentlemen loike this one in the Tower to know better?" He gave one contemptuous snort, then said, "Get your stuff, Wakefield. Yer new 'ome is a waitin' for you!"

St. Giles Church was not a cathedral by any means, but was a fine old structure, well-built and dignified. Elizabeth Bourchiers's family were solid members of St. Giles, and the church was filled with family and friends as she came down the aisle to stand beside her bridegroom, Oliver Cromwell. He smiled as he took her hand, and the two turned to face the minister.

As the ceremony went on, Robin Wakefield studied the pair from his seat on a pew halfway back. Elizabeth was a pretty thing—petite and rosy cheeked. Her eyes were huge, and two dimples appeared in her cheeks as she smiled at the minister.

A good young woman for Oliver—sensible and reasonably pretty.
Robin nodded slightly, then a smile tugged at his lips as another
thought struck him: *After having lived with six sisters, Oliver should
know something about women!* He thought of how Oliver, at the age
of eighteen, had been forced to become the head of the family
after the death of his father. Everyone had noted the young man's
tenderness toward his mother and his kindness to his sisters.

*A patriarch at eighteen—that's quite a load for any young man, but
Oliver's stood up to it.* The image of Robin's own two sons flitted
through his mind: Cecil, who was somewhat like Oliver, and Chris,
who was quite the opposite. Shifting away from the thought, he
studied the bridegroom, taking in the tall form and rather stern face.
There was something mystical in Cromwell's eyes, and a determined set to his lips. He was not handsome, having several small
warts and a prominent nose—but the strength of his countenance
was undeniable. When he spoke, his voice carried clearly over the
church, high and slightly raspy. It was, Robin knew from having
spent time hunting with the young man, a voice that could rise like
a trumpet when Oliver wanted to be heard. *I hope he doesn't shout
at Elizabeth,* Robin mused, but when he saw the tenderness in the
young man's expression, he knew this would never happen.

At last the ceremony came to an end, and the bride and groom
met with the guests in a large anteroom of the church. Robin led
Allison and their daughter, Mary, to the pair, saying, "Congratulations, Oliver! You got a better woman than you deserve, but then
so did I!"

Cromwell took his new wife's arm and smiled broadly. "Aye,
you have me there, Robin. She'll have a job teaching me to be a
good husband."

"I'll give you a few secrets on that, Elizabeth," Allison said as
she moved forward to kiss the bride's smooth cheek. "But you
can only have the *second* best husband in England. I have the
prize!"

"Well, now!" Oliver nodded and laughed aloud. "That gives me something to aim at—the second-best husband in the entire country!"

The party went well, and finally it was Mary who looked up from where she was sitting with her parents to see her twin brother, Cecil. He had entered the room and stood looking around for them. "Cecil! Over here!" she called out. When he came and stood beside them, she said, "You missed the wedding! Shame on you!"

Cecil Wakefield was small, not much over five feet seven inches. He had the same fair hair and blue eyes as his sister. Giving her a reproachful look, he complained, "It wasn't my fault, Mary. I had to—" Suddenly he broke off and gave his parents a doubtful look, as though he had bad news.

At once Allison asked, "What is it, Cecil? Is someone sick at home?"

"No, not that I know, Mother."

"Well—out with it, boy!" Robin said sharply, rapping out the words. "I can see that *something's* wrong."

"Yes, sir, I'm afraid there is. . . ." Cecil hesitated slightly, then shrugged his shoulders. "It's Chris. He's in trouble."

A shadow fell across Robin's features, and he shot a quick glance toward Allison. "Let's get out of here," he murmured. "I'll go make our apologies to the bride and groom."

Making his way through the crowd, Robin came to stand before the couple. "Much happiness to you both," he said. He spoke with them briefly, then added, "I fear we must leave at once."

Cromwell fixed him with an alert glance. "You're disturbed, Mr. Wakefield. Is there trouble?" When Robin hesitated, Cromwell said, "I suppose it's Christopher?"

Robin bit his lip and nodded. "I'm afraid so. Cecil's just come with the news, but don't let it trouble you, Oliver."

Cromwell's deep-set eyes grew moody. "I remember the day good Queen Bess died . . . you mind how he came, all filthy and drunk from some sort of a brawl?"

"I remember."

A smile touched the younger man's lips. "I told him I wasn't angry with him. How many times have I told him something like that since?" Shaking his head, he said thoughtfully, "Chris is a man without a star, I think. He can navigate a ship to some impossibly small dot of an island across the ocean, but he can't even find his own way!"

"Don't let this spoil your wedding day," Robin said quickly. He hesitated, then added, "I've always bailed him out of trouble—or *you* have, Oliver. I know how much you've tried to help him. Mayhap it's time for such help to stop."

Cromwell's glance grew sharp. "I've thought of that, too, sir. Perhaps it is time Chris was forced to stand on his own. But let me know if I can help."

"Thank you, Oliver. That's kind of you." Robin smiled, then took his leave of the wedding party. He joined the others in the shadow of the bell tower as Cecil gave them the details. "He's in the Tower," Cecil said briefly. Seeing his mother's hand go to her throat, he said quickly, "Don't be afraid, Mother, it's not a capital offense."

"Thank God for that!" Robin said with some relief. He'd thought for one awful moment that Chris had killed someone. "What's the charge, Cecil?"

"He's in for debt, sir."

The shadow that had come to Allison's face left. "Oh, well, we'll have to take care of it."

But Robin's lips had grown stern. He shook his head angrily. "No, we will *not* take care of it. Not this time!"

"But, Father," Mary protested, "you can't leave Chris in the Tower!"

"He's thirty-one years of age," Robin said grimly. "He's thrown away everything I've ever given him. How many times have we had to get him out of a scrape of some kind?"

"But the *Tower!*" Allison murmured, distress in her fine eyes.

"He won't die of it," Robin snapped. "My great-grandfather was there and survived quite well. Though Chris isn't the man Robert Wakefield was, mayhap this will stir some of his great-grandfather's fire in the boy. No, we'll not bail him out. This time he can learn the hard way!"

"Will you at least go see him, Robin?" Allison asked.

Robin looked down at her, and the roughness left his face. After so many years of marriage, he loved her more than ever. "I might have known you'd make excuses for him," he finally said, then smiled slightly. "All right, I'll go see him, but . . ."

Allison caught the pause. "What is it, dear?" she asked.

"Just an idea," he said slowly. "Cecil, take your mother and sister to the inn. I'll be back as soon as I can." He watched as they got into the carriage, then said aloud, "All right, Mr. Christopher Wakefield. Let's just see what you'll do to get out of jail!"

⁂

The grating of the key in the lock brought Chris out of a half-sleep. He sat up on the cot at once, then stood as the door opened. At the sight of his father, he stiffened, but waited until the door clanged shut before saying, "I suppose Cecil gave you the glad tidings?"

Robin looked around the cell without answering. It was a small room with only a cot and a small table for furnishings. A bucket in the corner sent forth a penetrating odor—but the entire prison smelled so strongly of unwashed bodies, spoiled food, and human waste that it was hardly noticeable. There were no windows in the room, and the single candle cast out a feeble pale light.

"Sorry there's no chair to offer you," Chris said with a shrug. "You can sit on the cot."

"I won't stay long."

Chris blinked at the stern tone in his father's voice. He should have expected as much, but it took him aback nonetheless. "I didn't ask for you," he rasped. He had developed a case of "jail fever," and his throat was raw from coughing. "If Cecil said that—"

"Your brother told us only that you'd been imprisoned for indebtedness." Robin studied Chris' face, thinking what a fine-looking young man he'd been. *Still would be,* he thought, *if he'd give up this wild life!* "Your mother is worried, of course."

The words brought Chris pain, but he said only, "She ought to be used to it. Tell her to give up on me."

"She'll never do that, you well know."

"What about you, sir?" Chris stared at the clean lines of his father's face. "I take it you've not come to get me out of here."

"You don't know that."

"Don't I? I see no written all over you!"

Robin blinked in surprise. He was always a little shocked to find that this wayward son of his had a sharp mind and often could read faces as easily as a scholar reads a book. He frowned, then spoke slowly, choosing his words carefully. "I've—got an offer for you, Chris."

"An offer? What kind of offer?" Chris's face stiffened suddenly and he spat out, "Oh, let me guess! You'll get me out of this hellhole if I'll come home and be a good boy."

Robin said nothing for a moment, only looked at his son. Chris had the urge to fidget uncomfortably, but refused to give in. He was what he was, and it was nigh time his parents came to grips with that fact.

His father finally shrugged. "I'm not so foolish as to think you will do that, Son. But we can't go on like this. It's too hard on your mother . . . and on me, too, whether you believe it or not."

Chris felt a stab of remorse, for he knew that somehow—after all the grief he'd brought their family—his father still loved him. "I'm—sorry, sir," he said gruffly. "I—I'm not in very good spirits." He gave an inquiring glance at his father. "Please, tell me about this offer of yours."

"I'll pay your debts and get you out of here if you'll sail under the command of a friend of mine," Robin said slowly. "And you'll stay under his orders until he tells me you've become a man who is trustworthy."

Chris stared at his father in surprise. It was not what he'd expected. "Who is he, this captain? What sort of ship does he command?"

"He has the same first name as you, his last name is Jones. He commands a merchant ship."

"How big of a ship?"

"That doesn't concern you, Chris. It's the *man* you agree to, not the ship." Robin thought for a moment, then went on slowly. "You have no command of yourself. You've developed the habit of just walking away when you didn't get your way, from the ship you're sailing or whatever job you were doing. If you agree to my offer, I must have your word that you'll stay with Jones until he feels you are ready to leave him."

"You would take my word on this agreement?"

"I don't believe you've ever lied to me, Son. You've done everything else that's bad, God knows—but not that."

This was true enough. Even as a small boy Chris had told the exact truth to his parents—and as a man he had done the same. It was some sort of symbol to Chris, that he *could* do a right thing if he wanted to!

Chris was thoughtful for a while, then he met his father's gaze. "I—can't do it, sir." Chris shook his head stubbornly. "A captain can make life hell on earth for a seaman. This Jones might be a terror as a captain. And he could keep me for years on a bad ship."

"All right, I take that as your answer." Robin knew there was no arguing with this son of his. He'd made up his mind to give the offer, to take whatever answer Chris made. Now he turned and banged on the door, calling out, "Jailer, let me out."

Chris was taken aback. He had expected his father to at least *discuss* the matter. But now as the door opened, the elder Wakefield said, "The key's in your hand, Chris. Write me if you want to turn it and get out of here, but know that it will be on the terms I've mentioned."

And then the door slammed shut, and he was gone.

Chris stood staring at the heavy wood that shut him off from freedom. Anger ran through him, and he shouted, "I won't do it! You hear me? I'll rot before I'll give in to you!" He stepped forward, struck the door with his fist, then whirled and threw himself on the rank mattress, his lips compacted into a thin line.

"We've a letter from Chris."

Allison dropped her sewing and rose at once, her face tense. "Is he sick? What does he say, Robin?"

Robin had entered the sitting room with a piece of parchment in his hand. It had just come from London, and he held it out. "Read it for yourself," he offered.

Allison took the paper and scanned it avidly. It was only three lines:

> Sir, I will accept the terms you offered me. You have my word that I will serve under Captain Jones until he is satisfied that I am capable of behavior acceptable to you.

Allison looked up with bewilderment, for Robin had told no one of his discussion with his son. "What does it mean?" she asked, her eyes hopeful.

Robin stepped forward and put his arms around her. "I know you think I was unfair to Chris, but I did offer to help him. He refused, so I had to wait until he agreed. Now . . . now, for the first time in a long while, I have hopes for him, Allison."

"I should never have doubted you," Allison said. She pulled his head down and kissed him firmly. "Now, tell me what this is about!"

She listened avidly as Robin explained the terms, then asked, "What sort of man is Captain Jones?"

"A hard-nosed merchant captain, but as good a seaman as I've ever known. Tough as a boot, smart, and fair. I talked to him before I went to Chris and asked him to do me the favor. I've done him a turn once or twice, so he agreed." Robin smiled as he added, "He gave me to understand that once Chris was under his command, though, I could keep my opinions to myself!"

Allison asked, "Will it be good for Chris?"

"All he's ever needed was to learn to control his passions. Now Captain Jones will teach him that. It will no doubt be a hard lesson, but it's better than the Tower."

"Oh, Robin, you've done so well!" She kissed him again. "When do you suppose I shall learn what a brilliant husband I have? Will Captain Jones be sailing soon?"

"Yes. He's agreed to take a load of Pilgrims to the New World."

"What's the name of his ship?"

"The *Mayflower.*"

Three

SAINTS AND
STRANGERS

The August sun cast great bars of pale light on the ships that lay in the Southampton harbor. Great skeins of diaphanous clouds floated lazily across the sky, making flickering shadows on the vessel that Chris Wakefield approached. He took little note of the fishermen unloading their catch of cod, stopping only long enough to ask one of them, "Would that be the *Mayflower?*"

"Aye, that it is," a stubby sailor said, nodding. He regarded Wakefield carefully, then offered, "Take you aboard for a shilling."

"All right." Wakefield placed his sea chest in the small dory, took his seat, and, as the sailor rowed the boat over the still surface of the water, studied the ship that would be his home. When they drew near, he saw that the *Mayflower* was not more than eighty feet long. Being a typical apple-cheeked boat of roughly twenty-five feet across in the beam—only a little over three times as long as she was broad—she had a stubby, awkward appearance.

Crew of twenty-five, maybe—and she'll be a wet ship, that low in the waist. He noted the usual three masts, the fore and main square-rigged in the simplest manner, while the short mizzenmast behind on the poop deck was rigged to fly a lateen sail. Built across the foredeck was a roomy forecastle, like a small house that had been forcibly jammed forward. A set of wooden steps were rigged on the sloping side, which Chris grabbed and climbed as the small boat touched the side of the ship.

He gave the man a shilling, saying, "Toss my chest up, will you, when I get on board?" With that he climbed aboard, then turned to catch the small chest. As he came about, he found two sailors watching him. One of them, a short, muscular man, exposed a mouth of blackened teeth in a grin. "Look 'ere, Coffin," he said. "Looks like another one of them psalm singers."

The other man, tall and thin as a reed, studied Chris then shook his head. "Don't reckon so, Thomas. He don't look holy enough to me. Reckon he's a Stranger."

Chris examined the pair carefully. On any ship getting along with the crew was important, and in this case it was critical. He had no idea what his position would be, and until he did know he was determined not to make any enemies. If he offended either of these two and it turned out either of them was over him, he'd be in for a miserable time. "Nobody ever called me a saint," he said pleasantly. "I am a Stranger, I guess. Is Captain Jones aboard?"

Thomas gave Wakefield a careful glance, his small eyes taking in the strong shoulders and large hands. He was obviously tempted to question the visitor, but shrugged, saying, "'E ain't in no good mood today." Jerking a dirty thumb toward the stern, he muttered, "In the Great Cabin."

Nodding at the pair, Chris put his chest down, made his way up a short stair to the poop deck, then knocked firmly on the heavy oak door that led to the captain's cabin.

When a voice bade him enter, he opened the door and stepped inside. The man seated at a desk gave Chris no more than a brief glance, then began writing, ignoring him completely.

Chris took the opportunity to examine the Great Cabin, which was shaped to fit the rounded swell of the ship's side. A row of windows along the stern allowed the rays of the sun to light up the low-ceilinged room. A brass lantern hung from one of the ribs overhead, and he saw that there was a spartan simplicity in the furniture. A single bed occupied one corner, two chairs and several stools ranked along one bulkhead. Pegs driven into the sides of the inward sweep of the ribs served as a wardrobe for shirts, oilskins, and various items such as a highly polished sextant and a broadsword of the old style.

The captain was seated at a mahogany desk, the top of which was covered with charts. The man was solid, tightly built, with bronzed skin and a full head of brown hair that needed combing. Chris guessed he was somewhere in his late thirties.

"Well—what is it?" The captain jammed his quill into an ink bottle as he spoke briskly. He glanced up, revealing a pair of alert brown eyes.

"I'm Christopher Wakefield, Captain Jones."

His words caught Jones's full attention, and he leaned back, studying Chris carefully, his eyes watchful. "I've been expecting you, Wakefield," he said. "You're late."

"It's not easy getting out of the Tower, Captain, even if you're only in for debt. I came as soon as I was released."

His words seemed to displease Jones, who rose and went to stare out the window. He apparently found something interesting on the shore, for he stood still for what seemed like a long time. Finally he turned and rested his gaze on Chris. "Not much of a man, are you, Wakefield?"

Anger rose in Chris, but he quelled it. His fate lay in this man's hands, and he had determined to please him. "Not much, sir," he said quietly. "I suppose my father's told you about me."

"He said you were a worthless rascal," Jones snapped. "I've known your father a long time—a fine man, he is. From what he tells me, you've done all you can to go to the devil as fast as you can. What's your side of the story?"

"I haven't got one."

Jones's eyebrows lifted with surprise. "Just as well you think so," he snapped. Then he began throwing questions at Chris—technical matters concerning the sailing of a ship.

Chris answered them all easily, and when he saw the surprise on Jones's face, he smiled slightly. "I'm a worthless son to my parents, Captain, but I'm a good sailor."

"Can you navigate this ship? Stand a watch?"

"Yes, sir."

"Well, we'll soon see about that! But you'll serve as a common sailor until I see what you've got in you." He peered at Chris closely, then demanded, "You understand the terms of your duty here?"

"I serve under you until you can report to my father that I'm worth letting live."

Captain Jones grinned unexpectedly. "Right! And there'll be times, Wakefield, when you'll wonder if it's worth the effort!" He sat down in his chair and looked at the charts, then back up at Chris. "Do you know our cargo?"

"No, sir."

"We're hauling a shipload of settlers to Virginia. There'll be two ships, this one and the *Speedwell.*" He shook his head and a disturbed light came to his eyes. "I see trouble with them even before we weigh anchor. Saints and Strangers, indeed!"

"What does that mean, Captain? Saints and Strangers?"

Jones shook his head impatiently. "Fool thing started when a group of religious fanatics from Leyden decided Holland was getting too worldly for them to live in. That group is the Saints. They decided to go to the New World—which won't be all that holy, if you ask me!—but they didn't have enough cash to hire a ship. So they've joined with others from London, the Strangers they call them." He snorted and slapped the desk with a hard palm. "By Harry, I can't tell which are the Saints and which are the Strangers! But we'll see what's in them before this voyage is over!"

"I guess I'll fit in with the Strangers, sir," Chris said with a smile. "Not much of a saint in me."

"Don't matter a lick to me. You just mind your work and keep your hands off the women," Jones snapped. "And if I catch you drunk, I'll have you keelhauled!"

"When will we be sailing, sir?"

"As soon as the supplies are aboard. In a few days, I fondly hope. Now, come with me. I'll hand you over to Mr. Clarke. . . ."

Clarke, the bosun, proved to be a hard-bitten sort—something Chris had found true of all bosuns. Clarke was skeptical of the new member of the crew and put him to work swabbing decks with holystone and serving as the cook's helper. This was standard procedure for new hands, and Chris made no complaints. He suspected that Captain Jones had instructed the bosun to put him over the jumps—which was correct.

"Give him the rough side of your hand, Clarke," Captain Jones had commanded. "See if you can make him cry."

Clarke had been surprised at the captain's interest; the man usually left the business of breaking in a new hand to him. "You've got a special interest in the man, sir?"

"I was a cabin boy for his great-uncle, Sir Thomas Wakefield, on the *Falcon.*" Jones nodded. "I was on deck when he took the shot that killed him. A fine sailor! And the lad's father, Sir Robin—he's another good one." Rubbing his jaw thoughtfully, he'd added, "I'm not in the business of reforming prodigal sons, Clarke, but I owe those two a turn. We'll see what we can do with this one."

"Aye, sir." Clarke smiled grimly. "I'll cure him or kill him, one or the other."

⸻

Few on the shore paid any heed to the two ships that sailed down the Solent, that narrow body of water between the Isle of Wight and England. The *Speedwell,* a mere sixty-ton pinnace, bobbed like a cork while the larger brown-and-gold *Mayflower* led the way.

"They're fools to put such big masts and sails on a small ship like that," Chris remarked. He had helped set the sails of the *Mayflower* and now stood at the rail watching the smaller ship wallow in the bulging gray swells that undulated hugely.

Clarke nodded his agreement. "I'd not like to sail aboard her, Wakefield. She's a wet ship." Chris had sailed aboard such a ship once. Between the vessel's age and the pounding of the seas, the planks of the deck had separated so far that no amount of caulking could keep the water out.

The bosun snorted and uttered an old sailor's platitude. "A man who goes to sea for pleasure would be likely to go to hell for pastime!"

Chris laughed. He'd come to admire and respect Clarke. "Well, I'd like to put all the Saints in the *Speedwell,* where they could do their psalm singing and preaching without disturbing the rest of us."

"Oh, they're not a bad lot." Clarke shrugged. He looked up at the sky, studied the sails, then added, "They'll get some of their religion blown out of them by the time we reach Virginia."

But the *Speedwell* fell into difficulties only a few days out of Southampton. She began raising and lowering one of her sails, the signal of distress. When her captain, a dour man named Reynolds, came on board for a conference with Captain Jones, he gave the grim news: The *Speedwell* was leaking so badly that the pumps had to be worked continuously to keep her afloat. There was no choice but to return to land. The two ships returned to Dartmouth, a few miles down the coast from Southampton.

After four days the two ships put to sea again, but when they had sailed three hundred miles, once again Captain Reynolds came aboard to inform Captain Jones that his ship was leaking so badly that it would be suicide to go on. The grim decision was reached, and the two ships limped into Plymouth.

Shortly after the *Mayflower* let down her anchor, Captain Jones gave an order to the bosun. "Mr. Clarke, see that we replace the stores consumed."

"Aye, sir." Clarke looked around and, seeing Chris and a sailor named Amos Prince standing idly at the rail watching the skyline, snapped, "Wakefield! Prince! Come along with me."

"What's up, bosun?" Chris inquired.

"Ashore to get supplies."

Chris winked at Amos, who whispered, "Shore leave!" and the two of them loaded some empty casks and large barrels onto the ship's small boat and rowed to shore. When they reached the main part of town, Clarke found that the beer needed to fill some of the casks had to be brought from a warehouse, and some of the other supplies could only be obtained by waiting until the next morning. "I've got to get back to the ship," he said with considerable irritation. "You two stay and load the beer this afternoon. You can sleep ashore with the supplies we've already got, then pick up the rest in the morning." He handed a slip of paper to Chris, saying, "It's all paid for—here's the receipt, Wakefield."

"We'll take care of it, bosun."

Clarke gave him a dubious look. "Stay out of the taverns and don't get into trouble, or I'll have you flogged. Understand?"

"I thought we'd spend the night in prayer and meditation," Chris said, adopting what he assumed was a pious expression.

Despite himself, Clarke grinned. "That I doubt, but mind what I say! Prince, you see to it that the two of you stay out of trouble."

The bosun whirled abruptly and stalked back toward the docks, and Chris grinned at his companion. "You heard the bosun, Amos. Watch me and be sure I don't get into any mischief."

Prince, a cheerful young man of twenty with apple-red cheeks and a pair of knowing blue eyes, nodded at Wakefield. "But who's going to watch me, Chris?" he demanded. The two of them laughed and moved at once toward the tavern.

It was a long, hot afternoon, so the two kept to the relatively cool interiors of several bars. They sat drinking beer and ale, leaving the cavelike darkness only long enough to make their way to another alehouse. Chris was enjoying himself, for the short trips of the two ships had been vaguely irritating. He listened as Amos, a talkative young man, droned on and on about his past experiences. Most of the tales the young sailor spun were about his conquests of beautiful women, and once Chris protested, "You're too young to have had that many woman, lad!"

"I loves 'em and I leaves 'em!" This declaration amused Chris, and Amos repeated it at regular intervals. By late afternoon, both men were pleasantly half drunk. Chris had to roust the young man out of a bar called the Lost Lamb to get the remainder of the ship's order of beer. They saw to the filling of the casks, stowed them in the wagon Clarke had rented for hauling the supplies, then drove idly along until they found a stable, where they paid a small fee for stabling the horse.

"Now, let's get back to serious drinking," Amos said with alacrity.

"Somebody's got to stay with this load of beer," Chris said. "I'll toss you for first watch." He extracted a coin, tossed it, and Amos called out, "Tails!"

They bent over, and Chris laughed. "Heads! Take over, Seaman Prince!"

Prince slumped down on the hay, warning, "You'd best be back by dark, Chris. I can't lose too much time with those black-eyed lasses at the Lost Lamb!"

"I'll stop by and tell them what a terrible fellow you are, Amos," Chris teased. Laughing, he left the stable, and for the next hour he moved along the streets of the harbor, watching the sun drop slowly into the pale gray ocean. The tang of the salt air was sharp as he thought of the many lands he'd visited. *The sea's always the same,* he thought, *no matter how different the land or the people.*

As the heat of the day began to seep away, he savored the cool breeze and finally turned from the docks and walked along the cobblestone streets. When the boredom finally became too much, he stopped in at a tavern, staying for over an hour. He felt no joy in the thought of sleeping in a stable, standing watch over a load of beer kegs, so he drank rather heavily.

As he laid down a coin and lifted the cup to his lips yet again, the disturbing thought that this was his father's money he was using came to sit heavily on him. He recalled how he'd received a small purse with several gold coins from the keeper of his cellblock at the Tower. With it had been a note that said, *May God keep you in the days to come, Son. Your mother and I—and your brother and sister—will be praying for you. You might find a little cash necessary until you get your pay. It would be good to write your mother.*

Chris looked down at the purse, which was still in his hand. He sat a long time, staring at it. A bitter thought rose in him: *Here I am—thirty-one years old—and I don't have a cent except these few coins. And even those are a handout from my father!*

Abruptly he rose and ordered the small silver flask he'd brought from the ship filled with brandy. He paid the bill, moved outside, and stared down the street. It had been a tremendous relief, coming out of prison, but as he plodded along the street he thought of the days and months—yes, even years!—to come, and muttered, "What's the difference? I'm still in a prison! It's just not as unpleasant as the Tower!"

Night was coming, and he dreaded going to the stable. Turning aside, he walked slowly to the wharf where the ships were lined up at anchor offshore. From time to time he sipped from the silver flask, flinching as the strong liquor bit at his throat. When he looked toward the *Mayflower*, he could make out her lines, and he pondered the idea of being confined to her for what might be an interminable time. He leaned against a round pier, aware of the harsh anthem of the gulls as they fought over scraps thrown over the rail of a schooner by a sailor. The waves lapped at the wharf, making a sibilant symphony. Looking overhead he saw a frigate bird appear and watched as it sailed majestically on the wind, a graceful outline in the quickening shadows.

As the creature soared over the earth, Chris thought it looked like a clipper ship, but when the bird landed it lost all grace. It suddenly seemed transformed into a clown with a ragged suit and an absurd face—though with a cruel and feral eye! Chris waved his arms and the frigate bird flapped his wings frantically and lifted off, quickly gaining altitude until he flew in a sweeping circle overhead. As Chris watched, he heard a voice so close behind him that he was startled. He whirled, lifting his hands in defense.

"What sort of bird was that?"

A young woman wearing a light brown cloak stood watching him. The hood of her cloak was back, and he saw that she had an oval face with large eyes, a wide mouth, and a crown of light brown, curly hair. At first Chris thought she was one of the tavern wenches, but seeing the clearness of her eyes and the clean lines of her face, he knew she was not.

She regarded his raised hands without comment, and he dropped them quickly. "That? A frigate bird." When the woman looked up and gazed at the bird in question, he added, "Not a very nice fellow, I'm afraid."

"Not nice? How can a bird be bad?"

She was quite tall, and there was an openness about her that Chris could not quite explain. She was pretty and well formed, and he at once categorized her as he did all young women: a possible conquest. Speaking easily, he said, "Why, your frigate bird is a pirate. He steals, that is to say."

"I don't understand."

Chris stepped closer to the young woman, studied her, and asked, "Do you live here in Plymouth?"

"No, I don't." Her voice was quite deep and husky, and Chris tried to think of another question to ask her, but she evidently was rather methodical, for she went back to the issue of the frigate bird. "How could a bird steal?"

"He waits until another seabird gets a fish, then he dives down on him and takes it away from him." She really was *quite* pretty. Chris stepped closer and spoke of the habits of the bird. Though she didn't seem the least bit afraid of him, he also noted that there was no air of boldness about her. She simply seemed at ease.

She listened carefully, watching as the frigate bird wheeled overhead then finally disappeared into the darkness. "I suppose he must get by the best way he can," she remarked.

"That might be said of all of us." Chris grinned. "But men and women who take from others, well, they get hanged for it. That fellow won't ever have to face a jury or a rope! Doesn't seem right, does it? That a bird has more freedom than a man."

Just then the sound of a fiddle floated to them, carried on the wind from one of the ships that bobbed with the tide. The music made a plaintive sound, and the woman turned her head to one side and stood in the falling darkness, listening hard. Finally she said, "That man is very good. I know that song. It's an Irish melody." She gave Chris a quick look, then glanced around, noting with some surprise how dark it had grown. "Good night," she said and turned to go.

"Don't go," Chris said. He took her arm and held her, adding, "Stay and talk a bit."

"No, I must go now." She tried to pull away, but he held her fast. Her eyes met his, and he saw no anger or fear there. Only decisiveness. "Let me go, please," she said in an even voice. When he continued to hold her arm, she stated quietly, "I'll have to call for help, and I believe that will get you into trouble."

His judgment numbed by too much to drink, Chris decided her passive attitude piqued him. What would it take to shake the composure in which she wrapped herself? With a rakish grin, he pulled her close and, before she could cry out, put his lips on hers.

She remained in his grasp, immobile and stiff. It was like holding a stick of wood.

When Chris finally released her, she only remarked, "You're drunk. Let me go."

Chris frowned. Where did such control come from? Surely most women would be screaming their heads off. He found himself admiring her coolness as he smiled again. "Yes, I am drunk," he said with a congenial nod. "Now, get away from here and thank the stars that I'm not a bit drunker. For then you'd not get off so easy."

She stood where she was, not moving for one moment, then nodded. "Good night. And you might want to consider going to bed. I daresay you could use a good sleep." With that, she turned and walked away, her back straight and her steps precise and even.

"Well, I'll be——!" Chris whispered. "By heaven, she's a cool one!" He laughed silently, watching until she was out of sight. Then he made his way to the stable, where he found Amos almost jumping up and down with impatience.

"Where you been, Chris?" he demanded, then shook his head. "I was about to come after you meself, and the supplies be hanged!"

Chris sat down on a keg of beer and said quietly, "I think you and I are the ones who would suffer that fate, my friend. Now get yourself off. The black-eyed lass is waiting for you."

Prince stared at him suspiciously. "You didn't get the wench for yourself, eh, Chris?"

"I decided she was more your sort," he said, grinning. "But there was one woman you cannot have. I met her on the wharf, where we had a brief but meaningful exchange. But then, who needs words when there is moonlight?"

"Aw, you're drunk, Chris!" Prince dashed out into the night, and for a long time Chris Wakefield sat on the keg, an image dancing in his mind of a clear-eyed girl who wore a brown cloak and appeared out of nowhere. Finally he stretched out on the straw and said to the horse, who gave him an inquiring look, "Yes, horse, I did indeed have a few words with a young woman. All quite innocent, I assure you."

The horse, a dappled bay, snorted at this information and resumed chomping on wisps of hay.

<hr/>

Plymouth was famous for its shipbuilders, and a full supply of experts examined the recalcitrant *Speedwell*. As the Saints watched anxiously, masters, master's mates, boatswains, quartermasters, coopers, and carpenters crept along the ribs, examined the sides of the vessel, and searched every inch of timber and decking.

After every test, the verdict was that the new masts were too large and that running in the heavy Atlantic swell would open the strained timbers wider and wider.

"Nothing to do but abandon her," Captain Reynolds announced to an assembly of Saints and Strangers.

William Bradford, leader of the Leyden group of Saints, exclaimed, "But Captain, how can we get to Virginia? If we have no ship of our own in America, after you leave us, we'll be cut off from all help in England!"

Indeed, the *Speedwell* had been the cornerstone of all their plans—but Bradford was a man of strong faith. After much discussion and debating, Bradford finally said, "Captain Jones, we will take as many of the passengers as we can in the *Mayflower*. The rest will have to come later."

There was much anguish and grief, but in the end twenty of the passengers had to be sent back to Leyden. The supplies were all transferred from the *Speedwell* to the *Mayflower*, and on September 6, 1620—after a delay of seven weeks—all was finally ready for the voyage.

As the passengers from the *Speedwell* came aboard the *May-*

flower, Chris was ordered to help the women. He shared the duty with Prince, and as he reached down to help a young woman, she looked up into his face. A shock ran through him as he recognized the woman he'd kissed on shore!

She recognized him at once, and he half expected her to call out to accuse him. *If she does—I'll get the cat!* he thought, and clenched his jaws.

But when she was on board and he had released her hand, she said only "Thank you" in quiet tones, then stood with her blue eyes fixed on him. Shaken, Chris turned to help the next woman aboard, this one obviously expecting a baby. As Chris helped her to gain the deck, she said, "Well, Patience, this is home, is it?"

"For a while, Susanna," the young woman said. "Come along, and I'll help you get settled." She paused, then fixed her clear eyes on Chris. "What is your name, sir?"

Uncomfortable, he answered shortly, "Christopher Wakefield."

"I am Patience Livingston, and this is Mrs. Susanna White. We thank you for your assistance."

Chris found it difficult to meet her steady gaze. He felt his cheeks flush—something he couldn't remember happening since he was a child!—and stammered, "Why, it was nothing, Miss. If you need anything during the voyage, just let me know."

Later when the passengers, all 102 of them, were on board, Chris helped man the sails. As the *Mayflower* sailed out of Plymouth into the open sea, he looked down from the crow's nest at the passengers who lined the rail. He found his eyes drawn to Patience and grinned at his own foolishness. *You're acting like a callow boy!* he jibed at himself. *Just what you don't need, Christopher Wakefield—getting intrigued with a psalm-singing woman!*

England took no heed of the small ship as it nosed into the deep waters and headed for the New World. In London, the talk was all of King James and his display of weakness in dealing with Spain. With England about to go up in flames of war, who would

stop to notice a handful of tattered exiles sailing west in a
weather-beaten freighter under the absurd delusion that God
would take care of them in a savage wilderness? Had anyone even
paid them a thought, it would have been to call them fools.

But John Bradford, the leader of the Saints, knew differently.
He had summed up the quality that drew this small number from
the safety of their homes to face dangers and death. In his journal
he wrote of the Saints: "They left Leyden, that goodly and
pleasant city which had been their resting place for nearly twelve
years—*but they knew they were Pilgrims!*"

Four

Two Kinds of
Storms

The *Mayflower* was divided into strata, the passengers staying rigidly in clearly defined groups. The ship was packed to the gunnels with the passengers' goods and supplies. Of the 102 passengers, a little over a third—41—were Pilgrims who had fled Europe seeking a new world where they might worship God.

The others, the great majority, were "Strangers," largely from London and southwest England. They were not fleeing any sort of persecution, religious or otherwise. On the contrary, they were good members of the Church of England, not from strong conviction, but simply because they had been born and baptized into that faith.

All the passengers, however, had one bond in common: They were of the lower class, from the cottages, not the castles, of England. There was not a drop of blue blood to be found among them. Among these common people were three Strangers that history would make most famous: Miles Standish, John Alden, and Priscilla Mullins.

Miles Standish was an older man, a hardened professional soldier, known sometimes as Captain Shrimp because he was short in stature. He had red hair and a florid complexion that flamed crimson when he flew into a rage, which was often.

Priscilla was in her late teens, probably not half so prim as some love to think. Her future husband, John Alden, was a hopeful young man of twenty from Essex. He was tall, blond, and very powerful in physique—one of the strongest men in Plymouth.

The Saints and Strangers were not the only distinct and often antagonistic groups on board the *Mayflower*. A third group consisted of hired men, five in all, who were to work for the more affluent members of the group. And a fourth and much larger group was sharply set off from all the others: the indentured servants. These were not servants in the modern sense of the word. They were brought along to do the heaviest kind of labor: to fell trees, hew timbers, build houses, clear and plow fields, tend crops during the harvest, and do whatever their masters required them to do. Eleven of these servants were strong young men, others were young women, some barely out of childhood.

Another group, of course, was the crew, the ship's officers being led by Captain Jones, who, at almost forty years of age, was a hard, rough sea dog. Under him were four mates and a master gunner. The first officer, Daniel Clark, a man of many adventures, proved to be a good friend to the Pilgrims.

September had come and gone under fair skies and with a fresh wind blowing, and the *Mayflower* was now making headway in the mid-Atlantic. Christopher Wakefield had fallen into the routine of sailing the ship, proving himself to be an apt hand— even better at navigating than any of Captain Jones's other officers. He was standing one morning in early October at the prow of the ship, watching a group of porpoises as they followed along, admiring the curve of their backs and the sharp dorsal fins as they seemed to cleave the water. Jeff Thomas stood beside him, big and burly, a look of disgust on his face.

"I've had about all I can take of them psalm singers."

Chris looked over to where John Bradford was standing on the afterdeck, bringing a sermon to the group that had gathered to listen. It was a common enough event for a Sunday: the Saints having a service at which all who were able joined to sing together and to listen as Bradford preached.

"I guess they're harmless enough, Thomas," Chris responded with a shrug.

"I wish the whole lot of them could be chucked overboard to the sharks." Chris looked at his companion thoughtfully. For some reason Jeff Thomas had developed a steadfast hatred for Bradford and lost no opportunity to curse him behind his back. He dared not do more than this, for the captain had given strict orders that the passengers were to be left alone. Now, however, as Thomas looked over the group, his eyes fell upon several of the young women that were turned in his direction. A lustful grin turned the corners of his mouth up and he grunted, "Now, that one there, that Mullins girl, I'm bettin' she ain't half the goody-goody she makes out. I'll catch her one day when none of them preachers ain't around and find out."

"Better leave her alone. You know Captain Jones—he'd have you keelhauled."

"He'd have to catch me at it first, and I can tell you right now that won't happen." He rattled on, talking lewdly of the young women, until Captain Jones crossed the fo'c'sle and came toward them. At the sight of the captain, Thomas clamped his mouth shut and walked away.

Jones came to stand near Chris. "Listening to the sermon, are you, Wakefield?"

"A man can't help but listen if he stays on deck." Chris grinned. "Bradford's got a powerful voice, hasn't he?"

"Yes, he has." Jones studied the preacher then turned abruptly, and his light blue eyes fixed on Chris. "What do you think of all this, these psalm singers, these preachers? I know your great-uncle and father are Christian men. What about you?"

"I guess you know where I stand, Captain," Chris retorted.

"I've never had much use for all that. Not that I have anything against these folks. I've seen enough in my family to know that there's such a thing as real religion, but I've seen quite a bit of the other side of it, too."

Jones was quiet for a moment—Chris had learned that the captain was a man who liked to think things over—then the man's square jaw grew firm and he nodded. "Of course, there are hypocrites, but I'd hate to think I let such as them scare me out of finding something that is real." He hesitated, then inclined his head toward Bradford. "There's something real about these people, Wakefield. I don't know what it is, but it seems to be something real and dependable."

The two men stood there, listening as Bradford spoke. Chris was impressed at the minister's skill in covering his subject. He had not listened to sermons much, but now, as Bradford spoke of the love of God and of the mercy and long-suffering that God had extended to men, he found himself believing this man was genuine. *He really believes what he's saying,* Chris thought, *and I guess that's what makes the difference between a real minister and some that I've seen who just took their money and ran.*

"I'll have a good report to give to Sir Robin," Jones said suddenly, breaking into Chris's thoughts. He smiled as he saw the look of surprise on young Wakefield's face. "I must admit I was expecting less of you, but I begin to think I was wrong. You've done a good job, lad. I think you could sail this ship by yourself if something happened to me." He hesitated, then said, "I can't understand why you haven't gone up in the world, Christopher." Chris was warmed by the man's use of his first name. "You've had all the advantages—good education, good family. Why haven't you done something with yourself?"

Chris had asked himself that very question more times than he cared to remember, yet still he had no answer. He shook his head, and a bitterness crept into his voice as he answered, "Nobody knows the answer to that, Captain. I've as much as wasted my life. . . . I've nothing to show for it, but I don't know why. Some men, like you, have got what it takes to go on and be a success. Then there are fellows like me who just wander around, taking the easy way all their lives, and finding no peace or satisfaction." He looked over to where Bradford was ending the sermon and listened as they started singing a song, one of the Psalms. He wished there was more he could say in defense of his life, but knew there was not.

"Well," Captain Jones said with some hesitation, "I'm not so sure that I'm such a success. I own a ship, but there's more to life than owning a ship." The *Mayflower* suddenly rose high on a crest, and the two men settled their feet automatically, and as it went down into the trough, sending a crash of a wave over the prow, the drops sparkling like diamonds under the sun, Captain Jones shook his head. "We'll be converted, you and me, if we keep on listening to that fellow." He turned and left Chris standing there until finally, he too moved away.

Patience moved carefully down the ladder that led to the waist of the ship. The wind had picked up, and the ship rolled as she swung along in the troughs of the waves. There were only the crudest kind of conveniences available: the traditional bucket comprising the only sanitary facilities. The air in the narrow, crowded quarters below deck was nauseating. The cool breeze helped a little, making the stench not quite as staggering as usual.

But while the cool air served to help in that area, it was a trial in others. The North Atlantic, always cold, was beginning to lay its harsh hands upon the passengers, who found it almost impossible to keep warm and dry. Except for an occasional hot dish, they subsisted on a monotonous and upsetting diet of hardtack, "salt coarse," dried fish, cheese, and beer.

For the last few days, Patience had been concerned about Dorothy Bradford, John Bradford's youthful wife, and she made her way into the tiny cabin where the woman lay on a plank bunk. "Are you all right, Sister Bradford?" she said.

Dorothy Bradford's face was pale and her eyes wide. She moaned slightly, saying, "Oh, Patience, I'm going to die."

"Nonsense," Patience said cheerfully. "You're just seasick. When we get to land you'll be all right."

"No, it's not that. I'll never see my home again. We'll all die in that howling wilderness, or this ship will sink." Dorothy Bradford was a fragile young woman at best. The hardships of the voyage had taken a heavy toll on the woman both physically and emotionally. As Patience sat beside her, the woman began to weep. Patience spoke to her in a calm voice until the tortured patient fell into a fitful sleep.

Patience got up and left to go to her own mattress, but walking was far from easy. The great width of the *Mayflower,* in proportion to her height, made the young woman subject to the push and pull of the waves. With every change of wind the ship waltzed with a thunderous flapping of canvas—and Patience had to struggle to keep her balance.

The *Mayflower* was built for roominess and carrying capacity. Below the deep hold and the upper deck was a gun deck, twenty-six feet wide and seventy-eight feet long. It was here that most of the passengers were settled. Patience had to step carefully, for most of this deck was covered with quilts and bedding. As she progressed, she came to a dark passageway and suddenly encountered one of the crew—a large sailor who blocked her way, grinning at her broadly.

"Well, lookee here what I done found." The man put out his fingers to touch her face, and Patience ducked away. She had seen the man before—Jeff Thomas was his name—and she did not care for the way he spoke and acted. She moved to run away, but he grabbed her by the wrist. "Now, you can't run away from Jeff. None of the gals run away from him. No, they don't."

Patience was not afraid—the ship was so crowded there was little possibility that the man would attack her or harm her—but she was disgusted by him. She tried to pull her hand away, but his massive fingers closed on her wrist. He laughed and pulled her close and, before she could stop him, seized her head and placed his rubbery lips on hers in a slobbering kiss. She wrenched her head away. "Stop that! Let me alone! Stop!"

Ignoring her cries, Thomas started to pull her close again, but suddenly a hand closed on his wrist. He whirled and found himself facing Chris Wakefield, who had evidently come down the aft ladder. Thomas scowled.

"Get out of here, Wakefield! I found her first!" He tried to wrench his hand away from Wakefield's grasp, but Chris's fingers suddenly contracted on his wrist like bands of cold steel. Anger leapt into Thomas's eyes. Few ever challenged him, for he used his brute strength to rule the lower part of the deck. Though few men liked him, most feared him.

"Better leave it alone, Jeff. You know what the captain says about the passengers."

Thomas released Patience's wrists, but only that he might throw a sudden, unexpected blow at Wakefield. His fist caught Chris high on the forehead and sent stars before his eyes as he fell backward. He barely had time to get his feet under him before Thomas came roaring in, intent on smashing him. Wakefield planted his right foot firmly on the deck and fended off a mighty blow straight at his face, countering with a driving, crushing right straight into the man's mouth.

It was as though the larger man had run into a timber. The blow stopped him dead in his tracks, but he was only dazed. After a shake or two of his head, he went at Wakefield again with a roar of fury.

Patience moved back, her eyes wide as the two men fought. Thomas looked like a huge animal, bearlike in his strength. *O Father,* she prayed as fear for Wakefield swept over her, *protect him!*

Suddenly a voice barked out, drowning out the grunts of the two men. "What's this? What's this?" Wakefield and Thomas froze, and Patience was overjoyed to see the first officer, Daniel Clark, standing there, displeasure on his face. "Brawling again, Thomas? And you, Wakefield, I thought you'd know better! Come along, I'll let the captain settle this."

The two men followed the first mate and soon were standing in front of Captain Jones, who looked with displeasure on the pair of them. "I've warned you before about your brawling, Thomas. A taste of the cat, maybe, will teach you a lesson." His eyes fell on Chris. "Wakefield, I'm surprised at you. What was it all about anyway?"

Chris was tempted to tell his side of the story, but he knew the voyage ahead was long and he was not one to tell tales out of school. "Just a disagreement, Captain Jones," he said. He didn't beg, but stood there waiting for his sentence. The captain's eyes narrowed. "The first officer tells me Miss Livingston was involved. I've heard you make remarks about her, Thomas. I assume you were annoying her."

Thomas's face screwed up into a fierce scowl. "You always think the worst of me, Captain." He threw a glance at Wakefield, adding, "Why don't you blame him?"

The captain shook his head and was about to speak when suddenly a knock came at the door. "Come in," he said brusquely. When the door opened, he stared at the woman and said, "Miss Livingston, come in. I may want you to help me with a judgment I must make."

Patience entered the room, and Captain Jones was impressed with this tall, well-formed woman. She had been a great help to the sick members of his own crew, and he had gained great confidence in her. Now he said, "I'm going to ask you to tell me what happened down below, Miss Livingston. Did either of these men accost you or insult you in any way?"

For one moment Patience held the captain's eyes. She was sober, yet there was an attractiveness even in this sobriety. She had bright blue eyes, and they glanced once at the two men standing to one side of the captain's desk. "I wouldn't want to be any trouble, Captain. If there was any misunderstanding, please let me bear the blame for it."

Chris shot a quick glance at Thomas and saw shock run across the blunt features of the big man. Then he glanced back at Patience and met her eyes. He listened as the captain entreated her, for Jones was sure there was more to the incident than she had admitted, but when Patience stuck to her story, the captain shrugged, saying, "Let that be the end of it then. You two are dismissed."

Chris led the way out of the door, and when he and Thomas were clear of the captain's cabin, he said, "She saved your neck, Thomas. If she hadn't come in, the captain would have had both of us tied to the grating."

Thomas's anger had subsided, and a puzzled look came to his muddy brown eyes. "Whot did she do it for?" he mumbled. He scratched his mat of brown hair and shook his head. "Never saw a female act like that before."

Chris said no more, but later on when he encountered Patience alone, standing at the deck, he said, "Thanks for getting me out of trouble. I didn't expect it."

"Didn't you?"

He was surprised at the brevity of her words. "Captain's hard on sailors who molest the passengers. You knew that, didn't you?"

Patience was looking out over the sea and suddenly cried out, "Look! Look there!"

Chris looked and said, "Why, it's a flying fish! Haven't you seen one?"

"No! Look! There are others—a lot of them!"

She appeared to have forgotten the argument, but Chris suspected that she was simply trying to change the subject. He would not let it go, however. "I owe you for what you did, Miss Livingston, and so does Thomas. I always try to pay my debts."

"They're so beautiful, aren't they?" The young woman was looking out over the sea, but after a moment she turned to face him and smiled slightly. "I would hate to see either of you get hurt over a foolish act," she said quietly, then she turned and left the deck, swaying slightly with the roll of the ship.

⸙

Sickness was not an uncommon thing aboard the *Mayflower*. The food was bad, and the opportunity to do any genuine cooking was practically nonexistent. The galley was barred to the passengers, and there was only one cook to feed officers and crew, so it was all but impossible to undertake feeding a hundred passengers. The women managed to serve an occasional pea soup or a lobscouse—a thick soup or stew containing chunks of salt meat. For a treat, once in a while, there was oatmeal sweetened with molasses, or doughboys—dumplings of wet flour boiled in pork fat—or, best of all, plum duff, a suet pudding containing raisins or prunes.

But the passengers were unused to the rigid and meager diet, and sickness came without warning. Two of the ship's crew fell desperately ill. Peter Maxwell, a servant of Samuel Fuller, went down with a bad stomach that he could not shake off, and, two days later, Jeff Thomas—for all his bulky strength—was laid low with a mysterious malady that none could identify.

Samuel Fuller, the physician, stood over the sick sailor as Chris and Patience sat beside him on boxes. "How do you feel, Thomas?" he asked quietly.

Thomas's eyes opened and he mumbled something. Chris saw

that the man's eyes were yellow, and he had lost so much weight that the flesh seemed to have dropped off his bones. "Sick—sick—help me!" the burly sailor gasped.

Fuller shifted his glance and met Chris's eyes. He gave his head a slight shake but said only, "I'll make up some medicine. Wakefield here can give it to you. You'll be better directly."

Chris got up when the physician nodded to him.

"Don't leave me alone!" Thomas said frantically, and Patience leaned forward, taking the large hand that reached out to Chris. "I'm with you, Mr. Thomas. You're not alone."

Calmed for the moment, Thomas closed his eyes with a groan as Chris followed the doctor outside.

"What is it, Dr. Fuller?" he asked. "I've never seen anything like it. A big, strong man like Thomas has been on fifty voyages, and he said he's never been sick a day in his life."

"I don't know. I've never seen anything like it, either. It's kind of a cross between malaria and scarlet fever. And it's that fever that is eating him alive."

"Can't you do anything for him?"

Fuller gave him a direct look. "I can pray."

Chris bit his lip in disgust. "I thought you were a doctor."

"So I am, but I'm not a miracle worker. I don't know what's wrong with the man. Most of us doctors don't know much anyway. We can set a broken leg, bleed a man, but I can't say about Thomas. He's a sick man, I know that."

The ship shifted abruptly and Chris looked up suddenly. He had forgotten the weather, and now he saw clouds rolling in from the north. "We're in for a blow," he said. "I'd better go tie Thomas down. I'll have to man the sails. Now, what about that medicine?"

"I'll go with you, Chris, to give him something that'll make him sleep. But that's about all I can do for now."

They returned to the cabin, where the doctor mixed some medicines, then Patience held Thomas's head as he drank it down.

Within minutes, the suffering man was in a deep sleep. Chris stood watching him for a moment, then looked up to meet the doctor's gaze. "Will he last the night?"

Sam Fuller was a good doctor, but he had learned long ago when to resign himself to the inevitable. Now, as he stood looking down into the face of Thomas, he raised his eyes and said, "I've done all I can do. I don't think he'll see the morning."

Patience lifted her eyes to his and studied the face of the physician. Finally she said, "He can't die. He's not ready to meet God." She reached down and put her hand on the sick man's forehead, then shook her head. "He's got to know Jesus before he goes into eternity."

Contrary to the doctor's prediction, Thomas made it through the night, though he continued to grow steadily worse. Chris had been busy helping keep the ship on course, then going about his duties. Though he was no real friend of Thomas's, he did what he could for him. There was something pitiful about the man who had so prized his strength but now lay as helpless as a mewling baby, with his very life seeping out of him. Chris had seen death often enough to know that Thomas had little chance of surviving much longer.

Throughout Thomas's last days it had been Patience Livingston who had come to be the ailing man's most faithful nurse. Time after time, Chris had descended into the hole where Thomas had been placed, on a special section reserved for the sick, and found Patience sitting beside the emaciated sailor, washing his face with fresh water. Once Chris had come upon her and, upon hearing her voice, he stopped and stood there in the murky darkness as she prayed fervently for the man's soul. He had wondered how she could pray for someone like Thomas after what he'd tried to do to her. He had not yet arrived at an answer.

Once again he made his way to Thomas's side, and as he looked around, he saw the physician, the girl, and Captain Jones.

"Nothing you can do, Doctor?" the captain said solemnly.

"Nothing any human being can do." Fuller shook his head. "If I were you, Captain, I'd get the minister in here."

"All right," Jones said, "I'll go get Rev. Bradford myself."

Not long after he left, Bradford came, and then the long watch began. Chris felt he would never forget that night. From time to time the three of them—Bradford, Patience, and himself—would notice that the dying man's eyes were open, and either Bradford or Patience would speak to Thomas softly. When Patience spoke, she quoted Scripture after Scripture. There was no light to see clearly in the darkness, and she had no Bible, but she quoted many Scriptures about the love of God.

Sometimes Bradford would urge the man, "Will you have Christ to come into your life, Thomas? Will you repent?" At such times as these Thomas grew restless, but the Scriptures seemed to calm him.

Finally, half an hour before dawn, Thomas opened his eyes and seemed to be himself. Bradford had gone to see to his wife, so that only Patience and Chris were left. "Are you awake? Do you know me, Jeff?"

His eyes turned to her. His lips were drawn back from his teeth and there was a rattle in his chest. "Yes," he said, "I knows you." His voice was hoarse, and Chris could hardly understand him.

Patience leaned forward, put her hand over those of the big sailor, and said, "Jeff, I've been reading to you from God's Word, and the Scripture says that the entrance of God's Word gives light." She reached up, touched his cheek, and said, "Christ is the Light of the World. Though we walk in darkness, he will bring light if we let him. Will you let Jesus come in and give you light?"

Thomas considered her, his eyes steady and his lips twitching. "I ain't—fit to come to God."

"No, none of us are fit to come to God. 'All have sinned and fall short of the glory of God.'" Patience spoke the words slowly. Then she said, "But listen, Jeff: 'as many as received Him, to them He gave the right to become children of God.'" She paused again and waited to let the words sink in.

Chris stood there as she spoke, always invoking the name of Jesus. Finally she whispered, "Jeff, you've got to trust in Jesus. You're going to meet him soon. Your only hope is in the blood of Jesus Christ. He died on the cross for you. Don't wait until you're fit. You'll *never* be fit. None of us will!"

"Wot—wot do you want me to do?"

Encouraged by the thin whisper, she said, "I'm going to pray for you, and as I pray you just say 'God be merciful to me, a sinner, and forgive me, in Jesus' name.' Will you do that?" Then, without waiting for an answer, she began to pray.

Chris stood there in the murky light, feeling the ship rocking from side to side, watching as the thin yellow light of the candle illuminated the face of the dying sailor. Patience had closed her eyes, he saw, but Thomas's eyes were fixed upon her, and as she prayed, Thomas's lips began to move. It was the sort of thing that Chris would have laughed or scoffed at once, but now, seeing the fear in Thomas's eyes, he felt only a somber awareness that something quite serious was taking place. *I'll be there myself one day. No better than him,* he thought. Then he heard the big man's voice.

"I'm a awful sinner, God, but save me for Jesus' sake."

The last words came in a gasp, and even as they were spoken, Patience said, "Trust him! Will you trust him, Jeff, to save you?"

Thomas nodded slowly. "Yes," he said. It was all he could manage, though he tried to speak. He closed his eyes wearily, and within moments it was over. Thomas spoke only once more, saying to Patience in a raspy, broken voice, "Thank you—thank God—!"

Finally, Thomas lay motionless, in that awful, eloquent stillness that the dead have, and Patience Livingston turned to put her fine blue eyes on Christopher Wakefield.

"He's gone, but I believe he went as a believer in Jesus Christ." There was hope in her eyes and in her voice. "You must do the same as he, Chris. You need God as much as Jeff Thomas ever did."

The words struck against Chris like a blow, and he could not stand to look into her eyes. Wheeling, he stalked away, leaving the lower deck and going as far away as he could from the dead man and the girl who sat beside him. Far up the prow he went and stared blindly out into the depths of the waters—but the blackness of the sea was no greater than the emptiness of his own soul, and he knew, time after time, he would hear those words, *"You need God as much as Jeff Thomas ever did."*

Five

"I'VE ALWAYS BEEN ALONE"

After Jeff Thomas's death, Chris made every attempt to keep as far away from Patience as possible. On a ship as small as the *Mayflower* chance meetings were inevitable, yet he successfully evaded her and spent long hours at the rail during the night watches. The sailor's death had marked him somehow and cast a gloomy spell over his mind. Time after time he went over the events of the thing, remembering most of all the agonizing fear in Thomas's eyes—and then the peace that had come after he had called on God. Try as he might, he couldn't rid himself of these thoughts. As the days passed, he grew more and more gloomy and despondent.

Surprisingly, he found himself going to visit Peter Maxwell, the young servant who had taken ill early on in the voyage. The first visit had been a bit of an accident, for Chris had gone to speak with one of the Saints who was supposedly caring for the boy. But when he entered the room, Peter was alone. Before Chris could leave, however, the boy opened his eyes, and the light that came into them upon spying his visitor had warmed Chris more than he cared to admit. Unable to disappoint the ailing servant, Chris sat for a brief while and talked with Maxwell, who proved to be unusually bright—and who held a surprisingly positive outlook despite his illness. Chris had gone to visit the boy on a fairly regular basis after that, and he had never heard the boy speak ill of anyone, even when they deserved it. Other passengers told Chris how, before Peter had fallen ill, he had gone out of his way to help others, no matter how menial the task. As a consequence Maxwell was a favorite of many on board the ship. And, with every visit together, the boy grew to be more of a favorite with Wakefield as well, and their visits became the one bright spot in Chris's increasingly gloomy life.

The ship continued to wallow through mountainous seas, sometimes pounded by gales, sometimes merely hounded by a typical North Atlantic winter. By now it had been weeks since anyone had been able to light a fire. The food, being brought up from the hold, was getting worse and worse. The biscuits had to be pounded to pieces with a chisel. The cheese was moldy, the butter rancid. Peas and grain had more and more creatures crawling in them. Endless slices of salt meat or fish had to be choked down with beer, which also was going sour.

The spirits of all on board seemed to droop—all but William Bradford. The pastor continually ministered to his little flock, saying over and over, "We have committed ourselves to the will of God, and we are resolved to proceed."

Somehow Bradford's words managed to cheer the weary people on. Despite being crowded with a hundred others into a space not much roomier in total square feet than a small house, despite being unable to change their clothes or wash for over thirteen weeks, despite the freezing water that sloshed and dripped around them—as damp and chilled as they were, most of the passengers were encouraged and uplifted, cheered on by the minister's calm assurances.

Other passengers, however, such as the minister's wife, continually bemoaned all that had been left behind. Dorothy Bradford talked constantly of the warm, neat houses in Leyden, where life had flowed past as placidly as a Dutch canal. She spoke of her childhood in the comfortable world of the Netherlands and was plagued over and over by the nagging, tormenting finger of doubt, which no amount of prayer seemed to dispel.

Late one afternoon a startling sound arose. Cries of pain came from the Great Cabin, and Chris, who had been furling the top royal, heard it even from high aloft. Startled, he looked down and saw Patience and Sam Fuller as they entered the forward hatchway.

"I wonder what's going on. Sounds like someone's hurt," he muttered, looking across the yard at Amos Prince, whose expression showed he had also caught the sound. Prince, who had become firm friends with Chris during the voyage, yelled against the wind that was still whistling through the shrouds and ratlines. "Reckon that's Mrs. Hopkins. I heard Dr. Fuller say her time was near."

When the two men descended Amos went his way, but Chris was approached by Captain Jones. "Go down to the galley. Have the cook give you some water."

"What's going on, Captain?"

"Mrs. Hopkins is having her baby." Jones had a pained look in his eyes and shrugged his compact shoulders. "Just what we need, isn't it, a baby being birthed in a gale like this. Go on, be about it now."

Hours passed, and for some reason Chris was fascinated. He knew practically nothing about the birthing of a baby; the whole affair frightened him. He was standing beside the rail, thinking about what a dangerous thing it was to have a baby, especially on board a tossing ship, when a voice spoke from behind him.

"Hello, Chris."

Whirling, he found Patience standing there. He nodded curtly, answering in a short tone, "Hello." He glanced toward the cabin. "How's Mrs. Hopkins?"

The young woman's clear eyes seemed clouded with worry. "Not having an easy time. Dr. Fuller is worried about her."

Startled, Chris blinked. "You mean—she might die?"

"There's always the chance of that."

"I hope not. She's a nice lady."

"I've been wanting to talk to you," Patience said abruptly, "but you seem to have been avoiding me."

"I've had work to do."

Patience shook her head, which sent one of the curls that had escaped the cap she wore to dancing. "No," she said calmly, "you've been avoiding me." She had an innate ability to contradict others without stirring them to anger. "I frightened you with my preaching, I'm afraid. I'm sorry for that."

Thinking of how she had nursed Thomas at the last, Chris felt ashamed of his attitude and mumbled, "Well, I'm past all that."

"No one is past the preaching of the gospel."

Patience watched as Chris shook his head stubbornly. The weeks of long exposure to the sun had tanned his face, and his bright blue eyes made a startling contrast to his darkened skin. His auburn hair blew in the breeze, its rich red tones echoed in the beard Chris had grown. Unlike many of the other sailors, Patience noted, he kept his beard clipped short.

He is a remarkably handsome man, she thought, though she doubted he was aware of that fact. His abrupt voice broke into her ruminations.

"My father and mother are fine Christians, Miss Livingston. If they couldn't do anything with me, I don't suppose anything can be done. So," he said with a grim smile, "don't waste your time on me." He shifted uncomfortably and glanced down at the deck, then lifted his head and shrugged his broad shoulders. "I'm sorry, that sounds unseemly. I appreciate what you did for Thomas. He was no friend of mine, but I'm glad you were with him at the last."

Patience realized that this was as close as Chris would come to commending her for her attempts to speak of God to the dying man. Regretfully, she considered him, then said, "I'm glad I was there to do what I could." Then she turned and walked across the deck, swaying gracefully to the rise and fall of the ship.

When she was gone, Chris had a momentary feeling of disapproval . . . of himself. "You act like a bear with a sore tail," he muttered and struck the rail with his hard fist. "What's wrong with you?"

Hours passed, and the sounds of the storm filled the ears of those who waited on deck or below deck. Childbirth was a hard thing in even the best of conditions. Childbirth in a damp, foul cabin with little heat or hot water was grim indeed. Finally, the cabin door opened and Patience came out. She saw Chris, who had been loitering nearby, and came to him at once. As she did, a lusty, yowling cry came from the cabin.

"It's a boy," she said, a gladness in her voice. Somehow her announcement relieved Chris. He could not understand why he was concerned about the woman except that she had been kind to everyone. Taking a deep breath and releasing it, he summoned a smile. "What's his name?"

"They call him Oceanus, Oceanus Hopkins." Patience allowed a smile to turn the corners of her broad lips up, and cheer came out of her eyes. "Oceanus Hopkins, named for Neptune, I suppose. Anyway, he's a fine boy, and he'll have a fine life in the new land."

For one moment the two stood there, then Amos Prince came by and said, "Miss Patience, I wish you would stop by and see Peter Maxwell. He's worse, I think."

"Thank you, Amos. I'll go right now."

"I'll go with you," Chris replied at once. The two of them went down the ladder into the dark crevice of the ship, and when they reached the tiny space allotted for Maxwell's bed, both of them saw at once that he was in serious condition.

"How is it with you, Peter?" Patience asked, kneeling beside him.

"Can't complain" was the feeble reply.

"You never do." Patience reached out, touched his head, and was alarmed at the heat of the brow. She turned and said, "Will you get some cool water, Chris? Maybe we can get the fever down."

"Right away."

The two of them worked together, applying cool compresses to the body that seemed fueled by some terrible, vitriolic fever. Finally, after what seemed to be a long time, the fever broke and the young man's restlessness abated. After a moment, he looked at the two sitting by his bedside and whispered, "I'm sorry to be so much trouble. I won't be much longer."

Alarmed, Chris said, "Now, don't talk like that, Peter. You'll be all right! We'll be at land soon, and there will be fresh water, maybe some fresh meat. I'll go out and shoot something myself and cook it just for you."

"Will you now? That'll be nice." Maxwell did his best to sound pleased, but his voice was thin—a high treble that was so frail Chris and Patience could hardly hear it. Still, he seemed to take comfort from their presence, and for a long time he lay there quietly, speaking now and then.

Finally Patience said, "Shall I give you some of the Word, Peter?"

"Yes, please."

"I'll go down and get my Bible." She left, but soon returned with the thick, black Bible she often read on deck when the weather had been good. Opening it, she began to read from the Twenty-third Psalm, "The Lord is my Shepherd; I shall not want." The sound of her voice was low but melodious, and Chris leaned back against the bulkhead, listening. The flickering yellow candle made an amber dot in the darkness, its feeble beams wandering over the sick sailor and highlighting the girl's face, making her smooth cheeks almost the color of old ivory. On and on she read, amidst the sound of the ship creaking and the low murmur of speech from those who were bedded down in the near vicinity.

Finally Maxwell went to sleep, and Chris and Patience arose and made their way down the passageway. Chris paused to look at Patience. "I've got to get up above and do my work. We'll be changing course soon, so I have to set the sails."

"Thank you for sitting with Peter. It means a lot to him."

Chris hesitated, then said, "Do you think he's going to die?"

"Yes."

The single word, which had been uttered with a total lack of doubt, seemed to strike Chris. Looking down with shock into her face, he said, "How can you be so sure?"

"The Lord has told me."

Again Chris felt a shock as the words fell from her lips, gently, yet firmly. "God . . . talks to you?" Chris said almost angrily. "He speaks down out of heaven and tells you what he's going to do?"

"Don't be angry," she said. There was strength in her face and compassion in her eyes as she looked up at him. "I've never heard the voice of God, not like I've heard your voice," she admitted, "but when I pray, things come to me. It says in the Bible, 'My sheep hear My voice.' Somehow the Lord has made me know that Peter will not live."

"I don't believe it!"

She did not argue with him, but merely said, "I can be wrong. I hope I am. I hope he lives to be an old man with his grandchildren around his feet. That's what I would like."

Chris narrowed his eyes. "That's not what you believe, though. You really think that God told you he's not going to live."

She held his gaze for a moment, then shook her head slightly. The wind had reddened her cheeks, but they were still smooth and somehow warm even in the gusty air. "God made us to have fellowship with him, Chris," she said simply. "It's always seemed strange to me that men and women can live their lives out and never show interest enough to listen to the one who made them."

Such talk, though he seldom heard it, always made Chris uncomfortable. And his feelings only increased when he saw the calm attitude and serene face of the young woman before him. Though he was sure she hadn't intended it as such, he felt that there was something about her calm assurance that was a rebuke to his own life. "I don't know about these things. I do know I want to see the boy live. I've grown very fond of him."

"So have I, but then, so have we all. He is the kind of person who makes you feel good just by talking with him."

Bitterness seemed to draw Wakefield's mouth into a thin line. "That's more than could ever be said about me," he said, then wrenched himself around angrily and marched away, leaving Patience to stare after him. She was not surprised by his intensity. She had long ago sensed within Chris a pent-up bitterness and harshness.

"Please, God, help him to realize that you love him," she prayed.

<hr />

"Can you come? I think Peter is dying."

Chris had been sitting near the galley, where the cook had actually managed to assemble enough firewood for a fire. The lively crackling and the yellow blaze had cheered him somewhat. He had been staring into the flickering flames, thinking of his home in England, when Patience had come up behind him and touched his shoulder. Startled, he whirled around and stood at once. The soberness in her face penetrated his awareness at the same time as her quietly spoken words. Lips drawn together tightly, he asked, "Are you sure?"

"Yes. Please, come quickly. He wants to see you!"

It was not what Chris wanted, and he went with lagging steps out of the galley, following the girl until they both came to stand beside the slight form of the young man. Sam Fuller and William Bradford were standing back, and Chris saw from their faces that they entertained no hope for the boy.

Kneeling down, Patience said, "Chris is here, Peter. Can you hear me?"

The eyelids fluttered and the thin lips moved as the young man whispered, "I wanted to say good-bye, Chris."

Chris moved forward numbly, hating every moment of this. He had seen enough of death. Thomas's death had been shocking, but he had not been close to the man. This young boy was a piece of living flesh, filled with dreams, hopes, aspirations. . . . A sharp bitterness filled Wakefield as he knelt beside the boy and reached out to take the limp, emaciated hand. "I'm here, Peter."

"We've been good friends, Chris," Maxwell said simply. His voice grew a little stronger and he managed to smile.

Chris felt his eyes smarting and blinked hard to keep the tears away. "I'm—I'm sorry it's come to this," he mumbled. "I'd hoped to see the New World with you."

"It's all right, Chris. I'll be seeing another world now, a better one than this . . . though I would like to have gone with you." His hand squeezed Chris's, and he whispered again, "We're good friends, aren't we?"

"Always good friends, Peter." The tears did come then, running down Chris's cheeks and into his beard. He fiercely wiped a sleeve across his eyes, clearing them. His throat was so thick he could hardly speak. "Always the best of friends, we were."

The words seemed to please Maxwell, and for a long time he lay there holding Chris's hand. Finally his breathing grew more shallow, and the doctor moved forward. He put his hand on the boy's head, then felt his heart and, without saying a word, shook his head and stepped back into the shadows.

Captain Jones said, "Nothing to do then, is there?"

"No, he's going out to meet God," Fuller answered simply.

Fifteen minutes later Maxwell opened his eyes. He looked around in the darkness at each face and tried to speak. When Chris leaned forward, all he could hear was "Praise the Lord," and then Peter's eyes closed and his chest stilled.

Chris rose, turned, and left without a word. He could not, for the life of him, contain the tears that flowed down his cheeks. He was not a crying man, but something about the fragility and the vulnerability of life had come to him as the young man had turned loose his hold on this earth and slipped out into that unknown void. Watching Peter's death had frightened Chris, even more than when Thomas had died. Not that he was worried about the boy's soul. If anything, he was more convinced of Peter Maxwell's arrival in heaven than he was of his own existence. No, it was more than that. It was his own soul that troubled him, and he knew that, sooner or later, he would have to face God.

They buried Peter Maxwell the next day. William Bradford preached a simple message, mostly containing Scripture. All on board lined up. Every crew member attended, except those needed to sail the ship, and all the passengers, Saints and Strangers alike. Then, after a brief remark, Peter Maxwell of Austerfield, almost three thousand miles from those green fields that he and William Bradford had called home, plunged into the gray depths.

"A fine boy he was," Captain Jones whispered to Chris, who was standing close by. "He's missed his chance at the New World, but then," he added, "he's found a better one."

❧

Morning came the next day, no different from the other mornings since they had come aboard. Above deck the crew plodded through their routines, and Captain Jones leaned over his poop deck watching the dawn grow on the glistening sea. Out of the West came a curious gull, dipping and weaving above the weary ship with astonished cries. Above, the sails flapped in the dying wind. Suddenly, an excited bellow came from aloft, "Land! Land ho! Land ho!"

Now the sun was making the ship's worn sails gleam as if they were made of gold. A breath of wind came on the spreading light as the crew and passengers rushed to the rail, all looking toward the horizon that lay before them. There, stretching out in all its glory, lay the New World.

Sleepy men and women stumbled from their bunks. Captain Jones barked commands, and all eyes followed him as he ordered the ship to set more sail. They were sixty-five days out from Plymouth, ninety-seven from Southampton. Shouts of joy and tears of relief mingled on the glad faces of those on the deck. Many people fell on their knees and thanked God with simple spontaneity. William Brewster, one of the passengers, led a song of praise that was raised heartily by the Saints.

All that day there was rejoicing—but it came to an abrupt halt when they discovered that they were not in the section of the grant that had been assigned to them. It had been a feat simply finding the New World, but now the passengers had discovered that they were in a territory that was south of latitude 41, which meant they were out of the limits set by their charter from the king.

However, the *Mayflower's* Pilgrims were men that believed in the personal guidance of God. They quickly gathered together, spent time in prayer, then decided it was the hand of God that had brought them here. Far into the night the leaders from Leyden and the leaders from London debated the situation until they finally decided that New England was where God had brought them. They communicated their decision to Captain Jones the next morning, and he promptly brought the *Mayflower* about, heading back up the coast to make a simple landfall.

No sooner had they done this than some of the Londoners, the

Strangers, decided that, since they were landing in a different location, the Saints, with their patent, no longer had the right to control them. This was a genuinely alarming development. Every able-bodied man was needed if the newly established colony was to get shelter up before snow began. The possibility of an armed revolt was by no means remote. All during the next day, November 10, the leaders of the little expedition met in the *Mayflower's* Great Cabin to discuss the problem. Instinctively, the Saints shied away from any use of force. Slowly, after much talk, they decided to become an independent body politic and abide by laws created for the good of the colony alone, laws that applied to Saints and Strangers alike.

While the *Mayflower* crept cautiously around the tip of Cape Cod, William Brewster, the university man, and Stephen Hopkins, also well educated, were given the assignment of drawing up a brief "compact." The two men went to work and soon had the words on paper. When all of the passengers were assembled, the leaders told them an agreement had been drawn up and that it must be signed. William Bradford stood up and read the Mayflower Compact:

> "We whose names are underwritten, the loyal subjects of our dread Sovereign Lord King James by the Grace of God of Great Britain, France, Ireland, King, Defender of the Faith, etc.
>
> "Having undertaken, for the Glory of God and advancement of the Christian Faith and Honour of our King and Country, a voyage to plant the First Colony in the Northern Parts of Virginia, do by these presents solemnly and mutually in the presence of God and one of another, covenant and Combine ourselves together into a Civil Body Politic, for our better ordering and preservation and furtherance of the ends aforesaid, and by virtue hereof to enact, constitute and

frame such just and equal laws, ordinances, Acts, Constitutions and Offices from time to time, as shall be thought most meet and convenient for the general good of the Colony, unto which we promise all due submission and obedience. In witness whereof we have hereunder subscribed our names at Cape Cod, the 11th of November, in the year of the reign of our Sovereign Lord King James of England, France and Ireland the eighteenth, and of Scotland the fifty-fourth. Anno Domini 1620."

As dawn broke on the eleventh of November, the ship came to the wide harbor. The leadsman chanted the fathoms, and the ship began the tricky business of entering. Below deck, the passengers were assembled and the signing of the Mayflower Compact took place.

First the leaders of the London group, including John Carver and William Bradford, were invited to sign. Then the goodmen, the next social rank, and twenty-seven did so. Finally all the signing was done and one piece of business remained: the election of a governor. John Carver was chosen to serve for one year. There was no opposition.

At ten o'clock, after searching the harbor and finding numerous sandbars, Captain Jones dropped anchor about a mile from shore. After two hard months at sea, his job was finally done. He walked along the rail, looking out at the land, and was joined by William Bradford. They both studied the passengers who were on deck, noting that an air of depression seemed to have fallen upon them.

Bradford said, "I cannot but be amazed at this poor people's present condition. We have come over a vast ocean and a sea of troubles before we even voyaged." He looked out over the land. "Now there are no friends to welcome us, no inn to entertain us, no houses, much less towns."

Captain Jones gave the minister a curious glance, "Has your faith fallen then, Pastor?"

"No." Bradford shook his head firmly. "Difficult times are before, but God—the Spirit of God and his grace—will sustain us."

Christopher Jones studied the minister's firm features and nodded slowly. "I believe you're right." Then he glanced at the land. "But it is a hostile place. It is not the Promised Land, flowing with milk and honey, and we've come at a bad time. Winter is upon us."

Bradford said simply, "But God knows our ways. When he has tried us, we shall be brought forth as gold."

Captain Jones nodded slightly. "Amen. Let it be so."

The first party ashore consisted of sixteen armed men who reconnoitered the area. With muskets primed and ready, the party marched inland several miles, far enough to know they were on a slender hook of land that reminded them of the sand dune country in parts of Holland. Only this was better, they reported when they came back bearing badly needed supplies of wood and water, for it had a topsoil of excellent black earth, and it was well wooded.

No work was done the following day, for it was the Sabbath. Instead, the day was spent on board in prayer and meditation. The next day, however, November 13, was New England's first Monday. The women were put ashore early under an armed guard to do the family wash—a chore for which they had great need. While they were beating and scrubbing and rinsing heaps of dirty clothes and bedding, the children ran wildly up and down the beach under the watchful eyes of Chris and the other sentries. The men, using the longboats stowed between the decks of the *Mayflower*, brought the great ship to shore and beached her for repairs. She had been badly battered and bruised by the storms at sea.

A gang went to work on the boat, and others prowled the beach in search of shellfish. Ravenous for fresh food, the group made a great feast on tender, soft-shelled clams and mussels. Unfortunately, this proved to be a grave error, and some of the group fell deathly sick.

Chris enjoyed the feel of earth under his feet again. He carried the musket issued to him by Miles Standish, keeping an eye out for hostile Indians, of which he saw none. All was open and quiet and peaceful. The wind was sharp, and he drew his coat closer about him as he made his way farther down the beach. He was still filled with thoughts of death, especially the death of young Peter Maxwell. Somehow the loneliness of the land brought a pang to Chris's heart as he thought of the young man now resting on the bottom of the sea.

He turned and would have returned to the others, but he saw Patience emerge from a group of spindly saplings. He waited till she drew close, then said, "You're not supposed to stray away from the others. There might be Indians."

"I know," she said, "but it's so good to be ashore. Look what I've found." She held up what seemed to be small flowers with tiny blue blossoms.

When she lifted them to her cheek, savoring the softness of the petals, Chris thought he'd seldom seen a prettier girl. "I'm surprised you found them this late in the year," he said. "Did you see anything else?"

"There seemed to be some berries." She opened the pocket of her apron and pulled out some, held them up, and said, "I'm afraid to eat them; they might be poisonous."

"Here, I'll be the taster for you." He put one in his mouth, bit down on it, and opened his eyes wide. "They're sharp, but good! Are there more of them?"

"Oh yes. I'll go back if you think they're good to eat."

"I'd better go with you. I don't think there are any natives here, but you never know."

The two of them walked back, and the next half hour passed pleasantly. The wind was cold, which freshened both their cheeks, but after the nauseating smells of the hold on the *Mayflower*, the fresh, salty air and the loamy smells of earth were like ambrosia to breathe.

"I'll be glad when spring comes," he said suddenly, then glanced around. "This land is quite different from my country."

"Where is your home?" she said.

He told her about Wakefield, describing the fields during spring that brought forth musky, strange odors, and the young blossoms that burst into buds. She kept her eyes fixed on him, enjoying the enthusiasm on his face and in his voice. Before long they had filled the pockets of her apron with the berries, and so they simply stood together, watching the clouds roll overhead.

He smiled down at her. "Where is your home?"

"I have none except here," Patience replied. Seeing the surprised look in his eyes, she shrugged. "My father died before I was born, and my mother died at my birth."

"Who raised you then?"

"A distant relative for a while, who soon grew too old. So I was farmed out as a servant."

Chris shook his head. "I'm sorry, that must have been hard," he said. "Were you unhappy?"

Patience pondered the question. Her eyes dropped after a while, and she studied the sand at her feet. Finally she bent over and picked up a small weather-bleached stick and began to draw patterns in the sand, almost as though she had not heard his question. But Chris kept his silence until, finally, she looked up, tremendously sober. "I was unhappy as a child. I was always alone," she said. "I've always been alone."

Something about her simple declaration touched Chris, and he said, "That's hard on a girl. How did you happen to come to the New World?"

"I prayed about it, and God directed me to come. I don't know why, though. I'm not fitted for this kind of a life, I don't suppose. I don't know anything about farming . . . but I can work, and if God brought me here, he has a purpose for me."

They stood there talking. Chris was fascinated by her simple faith. Finally she said, "It must be nice to have a family. Tell me about yours."

Chris paused, then began to speak of his parents. He was bluntly honest, not sparing himself. Patience watched, noting how he kept his eyes averted. A great sadness filled her when he confessed that his youth had been wasted and now his life had come to nothing. He looked at her finally and said, "Just a wastrel, that's all I am, I suppose. A prodigal son that hasn't gone home yet."

His words caught at her and she whispered softly, "A prodigal son . . . if you see yourself like that, there's hope for you. You know the ending of that story."

"What? The Prodigal Son?"

"Yes. When he had gotten to the very bottom, he said, 'I will arise and go to my father, and I will say to him, "Make me like one of your hired servants."' You remember that?"

"I suppose so, vaguely. He did go home, didn't he?"

"Oh yes." Her eyes gleamed and she smiled. "It's my favorite part of the Bible, I suppose. It shows us what God is. You remember what happened?"

"Tell me."

"When the young man was yet a great way off, his father saw him. He didn't wait for the son to come to him. No, he loved that boy so much he ran down the road and fell on him, and even when the boy tried to protest that he had done wrong, the father just seemed to ignore it. Oh, I *like* that story."

Chris was fascinated by the play of lights in her gray eyes, by the excited color in her cheeks, and the mobility of her lips. "That scoundrel didn't deserve it," he said. "If I remember the story, he'd wasted his inheritance, all his father had worked for to give him. He should have been whipped."

"That's what the elder brother thought." Patience smiled at him. "But the father said, 'Bring out the best robe and put it on him, and put a ring on his hand. And let us eat and be merry; for this my son was dead and is alive again.' Oh, that's the best picture of God that I know in the whole Bible. How he loves us! How he loves us!"

Chris was taken aback by her excitement. To see her usually calm face so filled with animation moved him in ways he did not understand. "You really believe that, don't you?"

"Oh yes!"

"I'm glad," he said simply, "and I hope you always do."

She put her hand on his arm and said quietly, "You'll believe it one day. I know you will."

They were very close together, and the pressure of her hand on his arm moved him deeply. He reached over with his free hand to cover hers where it rested. He could feel the strength in her fingers as he squeezed them. He saw surprise leap into her eyes at his action. They were very close, and he could see a line of freckles, very small, across the bridge of her nose, that he'd never noticed before. Her eyes grew wide and he felt drawn into them. Almost without thought, he reached out and put his hand behind her head. Pulling her forward gently, he kissed her, savoring her sweetness . . . until he suddenly realized what he was doing and broke away, stepping back.

"I'm sorry," he said abruptly, "I shouldn't have done that."

"No, you shouldn't," Patience said. For once her voice lacked the steady calm it usually carried. Though she tried to hide it, she had been taken aback by his caress. For one moment the two stood there staring at one another, until finally she shook her head. "It must never happen again."

"No, I don't think it will," Chris responded, angry with himself though he wasn't quite sure why. He had kissed girls before, but somehow this time it seemed like . . . like a violation of trust. He felt terrible, as though he had made a serious mistake. "Forgive me," he said again.

She considered the stricken look on his face, and a grin tugged at her lips. "Well, it's not all that bad," she said. "It was only a kiss."

Her grin was infectious, and he felt a flood of relief as he said, "I didn't think Saints did much kissing, but I've got a lot to find out about you people."

"I don't suppose you'll have much time. Now that we've arrived, Captain Jones will most likely sail the *Mayflower* back." She looked at him and said quietly, "I'll miss you, Chris."

Her remark took him off guard. The other women he'd known never would have confessed that. They would have waited for the man to make professions of emotion. But Patience was different. She had a simple honesty that flashed out at him, and he found himself saying, "I'll miss you, too, Patience. More than you know."

The two of them made their way back down the shoreline in silence, each occupied with his or her own thoughts. Later, when Chris went back aboard ship and lay in his narrow space, he thought about the softness of her lips and the look in her eyes when she said, *"I'll miss you, Chris."*

S i x

MR. BRADFORD'S
LOSS

Dorothy Bradford looked up at her husband, and her hands went out to cling to his lapels. "Please don't leave me, William, please," she begged. "I'll go mad if you leave me alone."

William Bradford carefully unwound her fingers, held her hands, and then leaned forward and kissed them. He was not an outwardly affectionate man, and now he wished he had been more so. Somehow he had become torn between his two responsibilities: one as a leader of the Saints, the other as the husband of this frail woman who stood before him. Now he felt he was being pulled in two. "I've got to go, Dorothy. We won't be gone long, and you'll have Patience here with you."

She trembled, as though a violent chill had suddenly assailed her. "The last time you went, I stayed awake all night. I expected news every day that all of you had been slaughtered by the Indians." Her voice was a mere whisper, and there was an irrational look in her gentle, mild eyes. "Let someone else do it, please."

Bradford, with some agitation, glanced down the beach, where a party of men were getting ready to depart. Earlier they had gone on an expedition and had seen some savages at a distance. They had made several discoveries and were searching desperately for a place to found their town in the New World. A wolf-keen winter was in the air.

"Dorothy," he said quietly, "it's not my choice to leave you. I wish I could stay here, but I can't. We must find a place to build before winter strikes. We have to have shelter. Why, it's been only the good heart of Captain Jones that has kept him here this long, letting us use the ship for quarters while we locate." He continued to speak, but he was aware that she was not listening, or, if she was, he was making no impact. *I never should have brought her into this place,* he thought. *God help us! How can we survive with frail women like this?* Then he put her hands aside, leaned forward, and kissed her cold cheek. "God will be with us, you'll see. I'll be back before you know it." He turned and left, pausing only when he saw Patience washing some clothes at the mouth of the fresh stream that flowed into the bay. He went to her quickly. "Patience," he said, "keep watch over Dorothy."

"Of course, Pastor." Patience nodded at once. "I would have done so in any case." She rose and glanced down the beach to where Dorothy was walking slowly back and forth, wringing her hands, looking down at the sand, the very picture of despair. "I'll go to her now. She'll need me for a while. How long do you think you'll be gone?"

"I'm not sure. This will be a longer trip than the last time." He shook his head. "One of the sailors who was here before has told us of a good place where we might found the town. We'll have to go look at it." He hesitated, then burst out with unaccustomed vehemence, "I *hate* to go. My place is here with her!"

Noting the distress that twisted his face, she said quickly, "You must go. I'll stay with Dorothy. Do your best; God will be with us." She turned and walked down the beach to Dorothy.

She reached out to gently touch the agitated woman's shoulder. "Dorothy, come along and I'll show you where there are some delicious berries. We'll pick some and we'll make a pie." She waited for Dorothy to respond, but when she finally looked at Patience her eyes held a vacuous expression. Patience felt a quick start of fear, for she had seen this blankness in Dorothy's expression before. *It's like she's not really there . . . as though she's gone out of herself,* she thought.

Further down the beach, with Coffin at the tiller, eighteen men pushed off in the small boat to have a look at Plymouth, as it had been named by Captain John Smith six years earlier. It was bitterly cold with a stiff breeze blowing, and the spray whipping across the open boat cut like a knife and froze their clothes. Many of the men were sick. Edward Tilly and the master gunner nearly fainted from the cold, but held to their course along the bay, making for a point to the north.

"Look!" Chris called out. He was sitting close to the front of the boat and had seen movement on the shore. "Natives! Over there!"

They all looked, and sure enough, ten or twelve Indians were standing on the beach. Smoke from a fire was seen just over the horizon, but Captain Standish said, "We can't stop now. It's going to take all we've got to find this place and get back again."

They journeyed until late afternoon, when at last they landed on the beach. Within a short time they found a small stream, where they began to throw up a barricade, brought in firewood, and finally settled down to eat a meager supper. Late that night, the cry came.

"Arm! Arm!"

Every man jumped to his musket. Unable to see in the darkness, Chris stood there holding his musket, ready to fire. "What is it, Captain Standish?" he whispered hoarsely.

"Indians, I fear." Even as he spoke, terrific screams and unintelligible words echoed terrifyingly from the surrounding woods.

Standish was cool as he commanded the men. Several recklessly dashed around, and he quickly cut them short until they had finished the barricade. "It's all right. I think they're just trying to frighten us," Standish said grimly. "Stand your ground, men, and they won't come in."

The night passed without further incident, though they all stood firm at their posts. When morning came at last, they discovered that the barricades were shot through and through with arrows.

In short order they loaded themselves into the boat and pushed off again for Plymouth. The weather was fair but it soon began to snow, and by midafternoon it was blowing a gale. In the rough sea it was as much as two men could do to steer the small craft with the oars. As night came on, the men ran up more sail to get in before dark, whereupon the mast broke into three pieces and went overboard. Fortunately, they managed to cut the mast and sail away before capsizing and made it safely to shore.

In the morning they learned that they were on an island in Plymouth harbor: Clark's Island, as they named it for the *Mayflower's* capable and kindly chief mate, who had first stepped foot on it and given them directions to locate it. Early on Monday, December 11, they sounded the harbor and discovered it could accommodate ships. Upon investigation of the area, they found plenteous cornfields and running brooks. By the late afternoon of the fourth day, after much exploration, they set sail. The mast had been repaired, and Chris said to William Bradford, "I'll be glad to get back to the ship. I know you will."

"Yes," Bradford said, nodding, "I'm worried about my wife. She's not at all suited for these circumstances."

Every day after the small boat left for the exploration, Patience found it more and more difficult to keep Dorothy calm. Concerned, Patience spoke of her difficulties to Samuel Fuller. The physician listened carefully as she explained the older woman's symptoms. "Dr. Fuller, I'm afraid she's losing her mind. She's in a terribly dark state and seems to have no faith at all in God."

Fuller shook his head doubtfully. "These conditions are bad enough for women who have known hard work all their lives, but Mrs. Bradford's life up to now has ill prepared her for dealing with the life she has known here." He bit his lip and added, "I wish Mr. Bradford had left her home until we had better quarters for her, something with a little comfort."

"When do you think they'll come back?" Patience inquired.

"Any day now. They simply had to find a place to build the town. Keep as close to her as you can, Patience. She trusts you and she needs you. It's a ministry I think only you can carry on right now."

Carefully Patience kept watch over her charge, but daily—indeed, almost hourly—she could see the condition of the woman worsening. What frightened her most was the way Dorothy would fall into long silences, sometimes for many hours. At first Patience tried to talk her out of these periods, but the woman appeared not even to hear when Patience spoke to her. Apprehensive, uncertain whom to speak with, she talked once to John Carver, the elderly governor of the colony. Carver was a strong man, hale and healthy for his age. But it was his kindness that drew Patience to him at this time.

"I commend you for what you have done for Sister Bradford," he said. "All of us must care for one another in this place. There's no salvation for us if we do not do that." He looked at her keenly. "I can see you're tired, Miss Livingston. You've not slept much lately. Why don't you go take a rest?"

"I'm afraid to leave Dorothy."

"Afraid? Well, she's not really ill, I take it?" Carver did not actually understand or grasp the gravity of Dorothy Bradford's condition, and so he insisted, "You can't go on like this, my dear. You go lie down. I will get one of the other women to sit with Mrs. Bradford."

Had he actually done so, things might have been fine. But after Patience reluctantly agreed to go rest for a time, someone came to ask Carver for help. He turned to this new task, all remembrance of his promise to Patience gone. And so Patience went into a restless sleep, exhausted after long hours of watching Dorothy, and no one entered the Bradfords' small cabin space.

After a long sleep of some eight hours, Patience awoke with a start. She had not slept soundly, but had been troubled with ill dreams. With a deep sigh she rose and got some fresh water, washed her face, then went at once to find Dorothy Bradford. When she arrived at Dorothy's cabin, however, she found the small room empty. A nagging fear seized Patience, and she at once wheeled and left the cabin. She made a search of the ship, and by the time she had looked in all the obvious places she was becoming desperate. She knew it was the wee hours of the morning and most of the people were asleep, but she hurried over to John Carver, reaching out to shake his shoulder.

"Mr. Carver, whom did you ask to watch Mrs. Bradford?"

Carver roused from his deep sleep and blinked groggily at Patience. "Why—why," he hesitated, then exclaimed, "I—forgot!" He looked through the darkness, illuminated by only one lantern hanging from a peg, and said, "What's wrong, my dear? Is Mrs. Bradford worse?"

"I can't find her," Patience said. "I've looked over the whole ship."

The alarm in her voice brought Carver fully awake, and he rose swiftly. "She must be somewhere. Come, we'll get help." He began to call out the names of some of the men, and Patience moved back and forth alerting some of the women. A thorough search was made of the ship, and an hour later a small group met on the deck. Daniel Clark, the first mate, looked at the grim faces about him and shook his head in answer to a question put by Carver. "There's been no small boat gone ashore, not since dusk, and none are missing. There's no way she could have gotten to shore."

A somber silence fell on the group. No one wanted to speak. The fear that fell over them seemed to have an almost physical form, and Patience felt her face growing tight and a tingling at the back of her neck. Finally she whispered, "If she's not on the ship and she didn't go ashore, that can only mean—" She broke off then, not wanting to finish the sentence. The thought that had leaped into her mind was too terrible to contemplate.

Clark shot her a startled glance, started to speak, then closed his mouth. Finally, his face settled into a grim expression. "I'll put the boat down, and we'll see what we can find."

For the next two hours there was great agitation among the Saints. They gathered together and prayed, begging God's mercy to be with Mrs. Bradford. Finally, the tension became unbearable as they heard the sound of a small boat approaching. It was an hour after dawn, and a thin gray light had broken in the east, casting its feeble gleams over the land.

"They've come back, Patience," John Carver said. His voice was hoarse with strain, and he peered through the mist that lay on the water as the boat touched the side. "I pray God they didn't find . . . anything."

But as soon as Daniel Clark stepped on board and Patience saw his face, she knew everything. The first mate came forward, looked at them, then dropped his eyes. "I have bad news," he muttered.

"She's dead, isn't she?" Patience whispered.

"Yes, we found her body washed up on shore. She must have fallen over the side of the ship and been washed in by the tide." Clark looked down at his hands, made fists out of them, then shook his head. "What shall we do, Governor?"

Carver was so shaken he could not respond. He could think of nothing to say. Patience saw his distress and turned to Clark.

"Bring her on board, Mr. Clark. We'll take care of her."

As the small boat approached the *Mayflower* on Wednesday, the sun shone brightly and the air was milder than it had been for days. A shout rang out, "There's the craft!" and a moment later the rail was lined with women looking for their husbands. They waved as the small craft came in, bending with the winds.

Nearer and nearer came the boat until the men could be identified. As the craft was made fast, the men started up the ladder. Patience moved toward it, dread in her heart. It had been decided she would be the one to tell William Bradford what had happened.

Bradford was one of the last to mount the ladder, and as the others were shouting and hugging their wives, Patience came toward the minister. The exploration group had been gone a full week, and many of the wives had given their husbands up for lost. Now they greeted their returned men with tears of gratitude.

As Patience drew near, she saw that Bradford was looking eagerly about him. *For Dorothy,* Patience thought with a pang. At last his eyes came to rest on Patience. He seemed to freeze in place when she went to him and then, as she stepped before him, he said, "It's Dorothy, isn't it?"

Patience put her hand out, and instinctively Bradford grasped it. She spoke quietly. "She's gone to be with Jesus, Mr. Bradford."

The minister's eyes seemed to roll back in his head for one moment, and he gasped for breath. Patience feared that he was going to faint, but then the harsh-featured man seemed to regain his strength. He stood there, staring at her, then without a word he turned and made his way below. She followed, wanting to speak to him, but he entered into the dark recesses of the deck, into the cabin where his wife's things were, and shut the door.

Patience turned and walked away, determined to be close by

when he came out. Hours passed, and still Bradford had not emerged from his cabin. Finally, at the behest of Captain Jones, Patience went to knock on the cabin door. To her surprise, Bradford opened it.

She met the older man's tortured gaze. "It is hard, Mr. Bradford, but everything you stand for calls for faith in God. You've lost the dearest thing in this world, in this life, and we grieve and weep with you. Dorothy's gone, but you must go on."

Bradford stood there, stock-still. Slowly he nodded. "Yes," he whispered at last. "We must go on."

He was a man filled with sorrow and grief, and impulsively Patience put a hand on his arm. "You mustn't blame yourself. It wasn't your fault."

He shook his head, torment on his face. "Aye, I fear it was! I shouldn't have brought her to this place."

"No, you mustn't say that. You mustn't think that!" Patience was almost aghast at her insistence. She was only a young woman and Bradford was the leader of the expedition, yet she felt the Spirit of the Lord rising within her. She began to speak words of comfort to him, and after a time his face began to soften and tears appeared in his eyes.

Finally, he nodded and said, "You are a comfort, Patience Livingston. God has sent you to give me peace over the loss of my dear one."

<hr />

Work on New Plymouth began in earnest on Monday, December 25. This was Christmas, but that made no difference to the Pilgrims—at least not to the Saints.

"Christmas is only a human invention," Mr. Bradford said with a snort. He had kept very quiet since the death of his wife, but now that the construction was actually started, he threw himself into building the town that would be their salvation when winter came. He had hounded all the able-bodied men looking fearfully at the sky as though winter lurked just over the horizon. Some men he put to felling timber, some to saw, some to carry. Not a man rested among all their number, and the women worked hard, too.

Though progress was slow, New Plymouth began to take shape. A short street was laid out along the high north bank of Town Brook. It was before long known merely as "the street." It climbed rather sharply from the beach and ran several hundred yards to the foot of a steep hill, which they called Fort Hill. Here Captain Standish built a wooden platform on which to mount his cannon. The lots for homes were staked out along the streets. They were very narrow, being only about eight feet wide and twenty feet deep. The company was reduced to nineteen household units by asking single men and widows to join a family of their choice for a time. A lot was assigned for every man and woman, but the assignments were for present use only and did not convey permanent title.

The Pilgrims could have done little if it had not been for Captain Jones, who inveigled the crew into helping throw up at least part of the structures. All worked from dawn till dark, and men and women alike became tired and hungry, chilled to the bone, and often lay down on the frozen ground to get some sleep.

"I don't see how this is going to be possible," Chris said one evening. He was sawing a board out of a log. At the other end of the saw, Captain John Smith huffed and puffed.

"What do you mean by that, lad?" Smith asked as he paused to wipe his face with a handkerchief. He had grown quite fond of Chris and smiled at him as he spoke.

"I mean, winter's almost here and we're not going to get houses built for these people, not even if Captain Jones keeps the ship here, which he's going to have trouble doing."

"The crew wants to return, I take it."

"There's even some talk of a mutiny." Chris stared across an open space, where Christopher Jones was working with a group that was hauling a fresh log in to be sawn into boards. "I'm surprised at the captain. He knows we've got to get back because we don't have enough supplies to last us the winter."

"He's a good man, Captain Jones," Smith said, "but that's not what worries me. We can work, and we can make the food last, but this sickness—" His face pinched up into a frown and he shook his head dolefully. "I don't know what it means."

Chris nodded grimly. He knew the Pilgrims' late departure from England meant that they could not prepare warm and adequate shelter. He felt fairly certain that this was the cause of what was now called the "general sickness." Every day, some member of the crew, of the Strangers, or of the Saints, seemed to fall ill. At first this was no real cause for concern. Until people began to die.

Chris had seen the notes that Captain Jones made in his journal when the two had talked about this. They seemed to come before his eyes now:

This day dies Solomon Martin, the sixth and last who dies this month, December 24

January 29 dies Rose, the wife of Captain Standish. This month, eight of our number die

February 21, die Mr. William White, Mr. William Mullens . . . the 25th dies Mary, the wife of Mr. Isaac Allerton. This month seventeen of our number die

March 24 dies Elizabeth, the wife of Mr. Edward Winslow. This month, thirteen of our number die, and in three months past dies half our company. Of a hundred persons, scarce fifty remain, the living hardly able to bury the dead.

As the two men stood there catching their breath, Chris said slowly, his voice thick with fatigue, "What do you make of it, Captain Smith?"

Smith had lost his own wife, Rose, and life had lost its savor, he'd loved her so dearly. Now he merely shook his head and said, "Let's get to sawing wood, Wakefield."

It was almost exactly twenty-four hours later, during the next afternoon, when Chris fell ill. He had been out in the woods hunting for game, only to return empty-handed. On his way back to the camp, a sudden weakness came upon him. His knees began to tremble and his breath grew short. *I'm just tired,* he told himself, but by the time he'd gotten back to the camp, he was scarcely able to walk.

The first person Chris encountered was Patience. She came to him and said, "No luck, Chris?" and then she saw his face, and at once something changed in her own expression. She stood before him, put her hand on his forehead, and then said quietly, "You must come and lie down right away."

"I'm all right," Chris protested. "I'm just tired."

Patience shook her head. "No, you have the sickness."

Her voice was quiet, but it sent a thrill of fear through Chris. He scowled. "I'm all right! I just need to rest a little bit."

Patience had helped dig the graves of those who had died. She had nursed many, young and old alike, and watched them slip away. She knew this sickness well and had no trouble recognizing the signs of it in the man who stood so resolutely before her. She spoke again, her voice quiet but firm. "No, you have the sickness. Come and lie down."

Chris stared at her numbly, unable to grasp what she was saying. How could this be? Those who had the sickness did not recover! If she was right, which, deep down, he knew she was, his life was over. The bitter thought filled his mind, *Now I'll never prove to Father what kind of man I could be.*

Patience took Chris's arm and led him inside, then put him to bed along with the others who were lying on the rude cots. She drew a blanket over him and, as he closed his eyes, stood looking down at him.

You've finally met an enemy you cannot defeat with your sword, she thought with mingled sadness and compassion—and with something more . . . for as she stood gazing down at the sick man, Patience was filled with a surge of fear. Before she could take the time to analyze her feelings, she turned her heart to prayer.

After a moment, she moved quietly back and forth among the sick, pausing often to murmur a word of consolation. Finally, when she came back and saw that Chris was asleep and he was breathing hoarsely, she put her hand on his hair and caressed it for a moment. Again, strange emotions surged through her and her heart cried out, *O God, save this man; let him do great works for you in the days to come. Don't let him die believing himself a failure. Don't let him die without knowing how much you love him!*

Seven

THE GENERAL SICKNESS

The sickness was like nothing any of the Pilgrims had ever seen. They had, of course, witnessed the plague that swept over villages, sometimes decimating men, women, and children. However, this disease that had come upon them was more terrible, more fierce than any they had ever encountered.

Day after day they underwent the melancholy sight of one of their number being sewed into a shroud and placed into one of the narrow graves on a low hill just above the shore. The cemetery was a forlorn place, the receptacle of grief and loss.

A cold wind was blowing across the graves as two men dug yet another hole in the bleak earth. A storm had come howling out of the north, and those who remained on shore shivered and crouched together, doing their best to endure the bitter cold of December.

"I don't know how much longer we can keep this up." Captain Christopher Jones looked down at the wet clay wearily and leaned on his shovel, then with a grunt hewed some of the mud loose beside the grave. His face was worn, drawn with fatigue, and thoughts of death haunted him. Now he looked across at Bradford and heaved a sigh. "There's just not enough of us to do the work," he said finally.

John Bradford leaned back against the sides of the grave and tried to wipe some of the red clay from his hands, but was unable to accomplish much. His face, also, bore the traces of the struggle that he had undergone. He was an aesthetic man, not accustomed to hard manual labor—but as the numbers had dwindled among the small group, he, along with the others, had thrown himself into the struggle for mere survival. His hands, he saw, were covered with blisters, and new ones were forming, but he ignored the pain and answered quietly, "God will see us through, Captain Jones."

Jones stared at his companion. "I don't know how you can believe that. Every day somebody dies." He looked out suddenly across the fields and added, "This is the last body we're going to put in this graveyard, Pastor Bradford."

"The last one? But—"

"Those Indians might not be able to read," Jones said grimly, "but they can certainly count! They know how many of us came ashore, and every time we bury somebody, they know there's one less of us. From now on, the graves will have to go inside the palisades, where they can't keep track of us."

"I suppose you're right."

"Not something I like to do," Jones added quickly. He knew that the idea of sacred ground ran strong in these people, and he himself had some ideas along that line. Still, he was a seaman, and as such was an imminently practical man. He had learned much from Bradford and others of this small crew of Saints. Still, as he gazed at the graves around them, he knew there were barely enough able-bodied men and women left to carry on the work that had to be done. He thought of the dwindling supplies on his ship and of the long voyage home again, and demons of doubt danced before his eyes as he considered the shrinking supplies. Mutiny was always a possibility, and he was well aware that his crew was not far from exactly that.

Bradford watched the play of emotion as it crossed the captain's weathered face. "It's been good of you to stay with us," he said quickly. "If you hadn't kept the *Mayflower* here and assigned the crew to help us, I don't think even one of us would have lived this long."

His words embarrassed the stoic captain. "I couldn't exactly leave you here to starve," he said shortly. "But we must be practical." He had been going over the situation in his mind and so said abruptly, "Have you considered changing your mind?"

"Changing my mind?"

"Yes, about going home again."

"Why, I've never thought of such a thing." Astonishment swept across Bradford's face and he shook his head firmly. "No, Captain Jones. God has brought us this far, and he will see us through."

"Not if you keep on dying," Jones argued, his firm jaw set and his lips drawn into a tight line. He swept his hand in a gesture toward the ragged palisades that represented all of their work. "It takes men to keep a work like this going, and you just don't have them."

"Well, I cannot argue that with you, Captain. But that doesn't change anything. We must stay." A thought came to the minister, and he looked eagerly at the captain. "Do you know, there's such a thing as God seeking a man. We call it *prevenient*—prevenient grace."

A puzzled look crossed Jones's face. "What does that mean?"

"It means that no man will ever seek God unless God has sought him first." He paused briefly and flexed his fingers, ignoring the pain and the broken blisters. "I cannot help but believe God has been seeking you, Captain. Now I would like to encourage you to seek him." He spoke for a few moments, encouraging what he thought was a conviction in the man that had done so much for them. Yet Bradford was wise enough not to push too far, so before long he said gently, "God has given me a great love for your soul, Captain, and I will pray that as God has sought you, you will seek him, for the Scripture promises us that those who seek will find."

Jones stared at the pastor's drawn face, then inclined his head. "It may be as you say, sir. I trust so. During this trip I have certainly learned that God must be in a man's life—and I have left him out." He hesitated, then added, "Thank you, Pastor. I'll think on what you've said." Then, as though anxious to change the conversation, he said, "You are worn out, Pastor. I'm relieving you from duty."

"Why, I can finish."

"Never argue with a captain." Jones smiled briefly. "That's the trouble with you and me—we're both accustomed to being obeyed! But in this case, I beg you to let me have my way. We're almost finished here. You go get ready for the funeral. I'll finish the grave. If I get too tired I'll get one of the men to help."

"Very well." Bradford looked up into the sky, which was lowering with a dark gray blanket of clouds coming in off the sea. "We would do well to have the funeral over before that rain gets here."

***

"How is he? He doesn't look very well to me, Miss Patience."

Christopher Jones had entered the room where rows of the sick were lying, some on roughly built cots. Patience was sitting beside Chris Wakefield on a small three-legged stool. She had been bathing his face with a wet cloth and looked up to give the captain a troubled look. "He isn't very well, I'm afraid, Captain Jones."

"That fever is a terrible thing." He examined her more carefully and said, "Have you realized you might catch this thing from some of those who are ill?"

"Never take counsel of your fears, Captain."

Jones grinned at once. He liked the spirit of this girl and took a seat on another stool across the bed. "I like that," he said. He studied her face, carefully noting the fine lines around her mouth that revealed her fatigue. She had struggled many hours—and even days—to keep the sick alive. In addition, she had assisted with burying the dead, cooking, washing, cleaning, even with the building. She had to be exhausted!

Still, she was a refreshing picture to the weary captain. The damp weather had only made her light brown hair more curly, forming a soft crown around her head, almost giving the impression of a corona. She had an oval face, and at the slightest hint of a smile, two dimples appeared, one on each cheek.

An attractive woman indeed, he thought to himself. *And totally wasted out here in this wilderness.* Aloud, he said, "Has he come out of the coma yet?"

"Not really. Sometimes he seems to wake up, but he doesn't know me, or anything."

Jones leaned forward suddenly, studying the man's face. Chris Wakefield's face was pallid and clammy with sweat. His eyes seemed to be sunken, as were his cheeks, giving his face a skull-like appearance. Jones had seen the look often, for any who fell under the destructive hand of the illness that was whittling away at their number soon took on this wasted appearance. He frowned suddenly.

"I thought he just tried to say something." He looked at Patience questioningly. "Does he speak at all?"

Patience nodded and thought for a moment. "He talks a little—but it's just babbling, most of it. He talks about his home a lot, about his childhood. I've made that much out."

Jones studied the young woman's face, noting the tenderness and concern in her expression as she regarded her patient, the gentleness in her voice as she spoke of him. His eyes widened slightly in startled understanding, and he looked down at the sick man and then up at the relatively healthy face of the young woman. "Have you any interest in this man, Miss Patience? What I mean is, have you ever thought of him as a man you might marry?"

Patience was carefully moving the cloth across Wakefield's pallid forehead. She completed the gesture, dipped the cloth into the pan of water, wrung it out, then bathed the drawn face—all without answering. Finally she looked up, a thoughtful expression in her gray eyes. "Perhaps I have, Captain." As tired as she was, he saw the quick quirk of humor in the girl's eyes. "When you are an old maid, such as I am, you think of every unmarried man as a possibility for a husband."

"Old maid! Why, you're no more than twenty!" Jones scoffed, eyeing her with admiration. He was interested, even fascinated, by her confession regarding Wakefield. "Not many young women will admit they are interested in a man," he observed thoughtfully. He leaned back, held one knee, and stretched tiredly, flexing his overworked muscles. His joints creaked, the result of the unaccustomed hard manual labor he had been performing, and he grimaced slightly. "I never thought I'd be digging graves on this journey," he said sadly. Then he resumed his inquiry. "What makes you think you'd be interested in our Mr. Wakefield? I'd think a man like John Alden would be more your style, fine, husky fellow that he is."

"Oh, indeed, he might be." The dimples peeked out again as she met the captain's interested gaze. "But John is so far in love with Patricia Mullens that he can't see straight. They'll be married soon, I daresay."

Jones's eyebrows shot up at this information, and he pondered it for a moment. "Well, then, one of the others." He shook his head regretfully. "Even if Wakefield gets well, which doesn't look too likely right now, he's not the sort of man I'd recommend to you."

At the slightly hard note in the captain's voice, Patience's eyes grew curious. "I had the impression you were fond of Chris, Captain Jones."

"And so I am, Miss. But I have no illusions about the man. I know him for the kind of man he is." He arched an eyebrow at her, his eyes reflecting a certain wry humor. "With your thoughts going in the direction they are, you must know about him as well, hmmm?"

Unruffled by the implied censure, Patience merely inclined her head. "No, indeed. I know little about him."

"Why, his own family cast him out. He's caused his parents—both of whom are good Christian people, mind you—nothing but grief and shame since he was a young man."

Patience nodded. "That much, Captain, I do know."

Again the seaman's eyebrows raised. "Well, I thought you Saints would want to marry other Saints."

Patience gave him a shrewd look. "You've become quite interested in the Saints—and God—haven't you, Captain?"

A flush touched the man's cheeks and he grinned almost guiltily. "A man can't help thinking about God around you people, Miss Patience. That's all you folks talk about! Perhaps I should start hanging around the Strangers a bit more. They are, after all, more my sort."

Patience shook her head, a surprisingly serious expression on her face. "No, I don't think so," she said. "I think you have a hunger for God. And a hunger such as that needs to be satisfied."

An astonished look leaped into the captain's face and he exclaimed, "That's what Pastor Bradford said! He told me that God's been after me, and now I need to be after him."

"Pastor Bradford is a very wise and discerning man. If I were you, I'd give heed to what he says." She looked down at Chris Wakefield's still face and was silent for a moment. From outside came the sound of an ax biting into a tree—a sound that had become so common no one paid it heed anymore, for anytime the people were awake they were chopping trees or logs, trying to build their houses.

Patience finally leaned forward slightly and gazed into the face of the sleeping man. "In truth, neither his past nor his present matter, Captain, for I couldn't marry a man who didn't know God, and Chris doesn't know God," she said simply.

Jones looked at her, aware he had touched on a sensitive element in the girl's makeup. "I suppose you do want to get married?"

"Of course, every woman wants that, doesn't she? To have a home and children? But I may never have it, and if that is what God wills, then I will ask him to help me be content."

Christopher Jones felt out of his depth. "Well," he said finally, getting to his feet, "I hope you get a husband, but not this one. At least, not until he's shown more judgment than he has in the past." He turned to go, and as he left the large room he thought, *That could be a bad situation. If Wakefield recovers, I'll have to keep an eye on it. That girl's too fine to waste herself on a scoundrel like him.*

⚜

Sometimes it seemed to Chris that he was falling down into a bleak, desolate hole in the earth. He wanted to cry out, to scream in terror, and he would brace himself for the terrible moment when he would strike the bottom. As he fell there was a roaring in his ears, and he felt stifled, as though he were wrapped in a massive, suffocating blanket.

At times, though, the dreams would fade away into a strange quietness. And then there was a bright light, rather soft and gentle, that bathed him in warmth until the bone-shattering chill that wracked him would at last go away.

Sometimes he dreamed he was on fire, that his body was burning with a searing heat that blistered him until his skin was parched and dry and crackled like old, old paper. Often, when that heat became unbearable, something unexplained would happen—something he learned to look for. A coolness would bathe his face, the touch of it so light that it was like a bird's wing whispering across his skin.

Cool moisture would then bathe his body, washing away the pain, and yet, there was little relief in this, for within minutes he felt he was drowning, trapped beneath a weight from which he could not free himself. Sometimes he seemed to draw close to the surface of the darkness around him, could even see movement and hear voices . . . yet he could not break through. When those times came, he would force a tortured whisper from his lips, desperate to make himself heard.

Finally, there came a time when he came very close to the surface. He felt his head throbbing, and his tongue seemed thick so that he was unable to speak, yet, when he opened his eyes, a face swam suddenly before him. It was not clear at first, as though it were hidden by a cloud. But after a moment he was able to focus his eyes and found himself looking into the steady gray eyes of a woman. He stared at her, licked his lips, and tried to think. The room swirled as he lay there, and he wondered if he was on board a ship. Then it steadied, and he realized he was in a room that he recognized.

He opened his lips, but they were so dry he could only make a rasping, coughing sound.

"Drink this." The woman held his head upright, and he felt the touch of a cup against his lips. He gulped thirstily. "Not so fast!" she said. "How do you feel?"

He drank all the water, then said, "Thirsty."

He watched the woman get the water from a jug on the table and come back, and recognition sparked in his eyes. "Patience—"

"You know me?" Patience stopped abruptly, her eyes wide. Then she leaned over him and touched his forehead. "Your fever—it's broken!" She smiled at him, and he vaguely noted the gladness in her tone and expression.

"How—how long have I been here?"

"Three days. You've been very sick."

He stared at her and tried to get his thoughts in order. "Can I have some more water?"

"Yes, of course." She sat beside the bed and tipped the cup to his lips slowly. He tried to sit up and was astonished to find he was so weak he could not do so.

"Let me help you," she said, slipping her arm around his shoulders and easing him to a sitting position. She gave him another few sips of water. "Not too much," she warned. "It might make you sick."

He stared at her, then looked around the room. "I don't remember coming here . . . or much of anything for the last few days. . . ."

"You're going to be all right," she said quickly, sure that this was true. As vicious as the sickness was, it was fairly predictable. When stricken, people always fell into delirium. From there the patients had followed one of two paths; either they never regained consciousness and so slipped away into death, or they came back from the delirium and, when they did so, almost always recovered fully. With this awareness, a glad light shone from Patience's eyes as she whispered, "You're going to be all right, Chris! I'm so glad."

Chris nodded weakly. "I don't believe I've ever been so sick before," he said, his words slow and somewhat labored. His bloodshot eyes met hers. "Makes a man feel like he's nothing, to have all his strength taken from him." A frown creased his forehead and he asked cautiously, "Did I say anything? Did I talk any?"

"A little."

"What did I say?"

Despite his weakness, he still managed to sound demanding. She recognized the apprehension in his eyes and realized he was somehow afraid he had said something he'd rather have kept to himself. She smiled reassuringly. "Oh, not much. You talked about your home at Wakefield, about the fields there, about hunting. You talked about things like that. And a lot about the sea and your voyages."

A flush came to his thin cheeks and he muttered, "I hope I didn't—shock you with my talk, Patience."

"No, nothing like that." She was glad that he was able to talk and that he was going to be well. She had not realized how afraid she was that he would not recover, and now she began to tremble. It was not a reaction common to her, for she was a girl who did not show fear. Now that the worst was over, she found that she was so weak she could hardly sit there without sagging.

Chris saw that her hands were trembling and that there was a tremor in her lips as well. "What's the matter?" he said. "You're not sick, are you?"

"No—no." She hesitated and put her hand on his and said, "I'm just so glad to see you well, Chris."

He did not know how to take this and said, after a long silence, "I've got the feeling I wouldn't be here at all if you hadn't taken care of me."

"We all cared for you," she said somewhat dismissively, wanting to break the mood that seemed to have settled over them both. "Now, do you think you can eat something?"

At her words, a ravenous hunger tore at him and he realized he was as hungry as he'd ever been in his life. "Yes, anything," he said.

She nodded, then left. As soon as she was gone across the room to where a fire was burning in the fireplace, he began to grow tired again. He forced himself to stay awake, half afraid to go back into that terrible sleep that had been something like death itself. He watched her as she prepared the food, and then the realization hit him: *She saved my life.* Almost at once, bitterness followed. *What for? I'm not worth anything.*

He sat there fighting sleep and depression, until she came back with some corn mush. "Can you feed yourself?"

"Yes."

He shoveled the mush down his throat so quickly she laughed quietly. "Don't choke yourself, Chris! And don't eat so much. You're going to make yourself sick."

She sat there beside him for a while after he handed the bowl back, and a strange silence fell between them. Patience was wondering at the relief that had swept over her when she knew Chris was going to live. Despite her words to Captain Jones, she had not known she was so caught up in this man. She had been interested, even fascinated, by him and, after having him tell her what he had of his story, longed more than ever for him to find God. But there was more than concern for his soul to the emotions that now churned in her breast. Inexperienced with men, still she could not help wondering, *Is this what a woman feels when she loves a man?*

After a while, he fell asleep. She left and went about her work, but after that first day, he was never again in danger. He grew well so quickly that those who observed were amazed. "He heals like an animal," Sam Fuller said to Patience. His small brown eyes considered her carefully, and he went on, "And a good thing, too. Now you can spare some time for the rest of the patients."

She flushed. "I didn't mean to ignore them. It was just that—"

"That's all right, Patience," Fuller said with a kindly smile. "Wakefield is an attractive fellow. Just be careful. From what I've seen of the man, I'd guess he's had far more experience with women than most. I'd hate to see you get caught up with someone like that."

Patience shook her head firmly. "You needn't worry, sir. There will be nothing like that between Mr. Wakefield and myself."

Chris had been such an active man that he had had little time for retrospect. Now, however, even though he grew well quickly, there were long hours he would have to lie still, often dropping off to sleep as his body renewed itself after the sickness. He found himself a poor patient, being a man of action who wanted to get up and move around, but Patience would not hear of it. Nor would Samuel Fuller. So Chris lay on his cot for long hours—but after only a day he rebelled and began to walk. The following day, he left the cabin, supporting himself by holding onto the walls. When he stepped outside, he drew deep breaths of the cold, biting air, feeling refreshed—or at least glad to get outside.

During these days, for the better part of a week, Chris did something he had never before done: reflect on his past. Until now, his life had left little time for such reflection. But now there was an enforced period of stillness and silence, and as he grew more and more able to walk, he found himself strolling around the settlement, immersed in thought. Scenes from his boyhood came flashing before his eyes, almost as real as they had been when they took place. He remembered things he had not thought of for years, such as his father taking him to fish for salmon. He remembered one scene in particular when he had hooked into a monstrous salmon and his father had stood beside, urging him on. Once he had almost given up and cried out, "Help me!"

He could still see the image of his father smiling at him and saying, "A man has to land his own fish, Chris. You can do it."

As the days went on, he thought of the kindness of his mother, of the friendship he had developed with the young Oliver Cromwell, and of other boyhood friends.

But over all of these pleasant memories was always a grim question that intruded on his thoughts: *What have you done with your life?* He had no answer to make except to grit his teeth and shake his head. Once, he said out loud, "Nothing! I've wasted it all!" It was a difficult thing for him to face up to. Though he'd had this awareness a few times before, he'd always been able to brush it off, or drown it in pleasure and drink. Now there was no escape.

As he pondered his life, his choices, he had to face, for the first time, perhaps, since becoming a full grown man, what he was.

Patience noticed him often, walking slowly about the compound, his face drawn and pained. Intuitively, she knew the struggle that was going on within him. Once she remarked to Captain Miles Standish, "Have you noticed Chris Wakefield? He's having a hard time."

Standish had been reassembling a musket he had taken apart to clean. He nodded. "Yes, but most of us have to have a hard time to pull us out of what we've become." He looked up to find Patience's attention fixed elsewhere. Following her intent gaze, he saw Wakefield standing a little ways off, leaning against one of the walls of the palisade and staring off into the distance. Standish's expression grew thoughtful, and he glanced again at Patience. He had his questions about the couple. He wanted to say something to Patience, though he was unsure whether he should warn her or perhaps encourage her. With a slight shake of his head, he turned his attention back to his musket. Being a simple soldier, wholly inexperienced in this sort of thing, he could not frame what he felt in his heart. Finally, he snapped the last piece of the musket together, sighted on it, then rose and said, "Marriage was the best thing in my life."

Shocked, Patience turned to him, her thoughts flying to Rose Standish. "You loved her very much," she said quietly.

"Better than I love the whole world."

"I think that's wonderful." Patience's face grew sober. "You see so many marriages that seem . . . empty, as though the man and the woman are tired of each other, or even dislike one another. I'd hate to find myself married to a man I couldn't like or respect." She fixed her gaze on Standish. "How did you and your wife keep your marriage strong? Did you ever stop feeling full of love for her?"

Standish ran his hand through his red hair. He was a man of few words—and most of those were violent words, the words of a rough soldier. He stood there, struggling to speak what was in his heart. "It was mostly her," he finally said. "I was never much of a man, not until I married Rose. Oh, I was a good soldier, but I had little sense." His eyes grew sad and thoughtful and he shook his head. "But she had enough sense for both of us, enough judgment, enough kindness for a whole world."

Patience moved beside him and put her hands on his arm. "I'm so sorry, Miles, I know you miss her."

Standish gave her a thoughtful look and touched his right arm. "More than I would miss this arm if it were severed from this body." He started to say something else, but emotion twisted his lips and he whirled and moved to the door. When he got there, however, he paused and turned to face her. "Be sure you get a man that is worth pouring yourself out for." He turned abruptly, marched through the door, and slammed it behind him.

Unaware he was the object of so much thought and discussion, Chris Wakefield went on, focusing on his recovery and pondering his life. As he grew stronger, he found himself more and more occupied with nursing those who were ill. There were so few who could care for those too sick to care for themselves. Once, when John Carver had an unfortunate accident as he lay in his bed, Chris went to him and began to clean him up. Though Carver was very ill, he tried to protest. "You don't have to do this for me, my boy."

Chris did not stop. He stripped the man's clothing, cleaned him carefully, put clean clothes on him, and then smiled. "Just get well, Mr. Carver."

An older man, Carver had been watching Wakefield's work among the ill carefully. Now he remarked, "You must have cared for many sick people. Your hands carry gentleness as well as strength."

Chris blinked in surprise. "No, I haven't cared for many

people," he said, and a sudden bitterness scored his face. A raw angle of light coming through the single window fell across his face, giving him a harsh look. "I've been too busy taking care of myself to care about anybody else, Mr. Carver."

"You mustn't talk like that," Carver protested. "All of us have noticed how you've helped here." He put his hand out and Chris took it. The old man's hand was as frail as the bones of a bird, but he squeezed the younger man's hand and smiled at him beatifically. "You've found something in this place," he said quietly. "I had the feeling that you didn't come here of your own will, that you didn't expect to find anything, but something has happened to you. I've seen it in you, my boy."

Holding the old man's hand, Chris paused. The truth of what he'd said struck him forcibly. Almost with amazement, Chris said, "You know, sir, I believe you're right. But . . . I don't know what it is. I've made such a wreck of my life, I can't even think straight."

Carver squeezed the strong hand again. "God has put his hand on you. I've seen it before. Don't turn him away when he comes."

Chris did not know how to answer this. He was aware that these people—Bradford, Patience, Carver, even the rough soldier Miles Standish—seemed to see something in him, something of worth that he could not identify. Not knowing how to reply, he said, "I'll go fix you something to eat, Mr. Carver."

Two days later, in the afternoon, Chris realized he was physically ready to go back to work. But something held him back, something troubling that clouded his mind, something he did not understand. He felt utterly miserable and said little to anyone. Others noticed it, though, and it was Bradford who whispered to Patience, "The boy's under conviction. God's hard on his trail. Pray hard, lass. Pray hard indeed!"

Later that same afternoon, the pressure Chris felt inside himself grew so great that he took a musket and grunted to Miles Standish, "I'll go see if I can bring down a deer."

Standish gave him a careful look. "All right, but don't wander too far away. The savages are still out there."

As Chris made his way into the brush, he felt so despondent he hardly cared whether the Indians were there or not. He tramped through the frozen woods, feeling worse with each step. Finally he came to the small creek that fed into the ocean. Seeing tracks of a deer there, he posted himself and waited. The cold seemed to grow more intense, but he did not even notice when his hands became numb. He had always prided himself on not being afraid of anything. Now some nameless, unknown fear had seized him. All he knew about it was that it had something to do with God.

"Am I afraid of dying and going to hell?" he asked himself, speaking aloud. The words seemed to hang in the frozen air so that he could almost hear the echo of them. They resounded within him, and he wished he had not given voice to the fear, for it would not be silenced.

A long time he stood there, moving only to find a new location when he grew so stiff he could no longer bear it. All afternoon, as the darkness came on, he moved silently, the internal pressure growing worse and worse. Finally he came into a small valley surrounded by trees that had been stripped bare by winter. As Chris looked about, the fanciful notion came to him that the trees were holding their leafless branches into the air like the arms of dead men. The sky itself was so bitter and cold that there seemed no mercy at all in it.

"O God! What am I going to do? I can't go on like this!" Chris was shocked to find that he had spoken these words aloud. And then, he began to hear in his own heart, in his mind, in his spirit, the words of Scripture: *"Unless you repent you will all likewise perish. . . . He that hath the Son hath life. . . . He who believes in the Son has everlasting life; and he who does not believe the Son shall not see life, but the wrath of God abides on him."*

The words of the last Scripture struck Chris with the force of a club. Fear overwhelmed him as he thought of the wrath of God, and his musket slipped from nerveless fingers as he fell to his knees on the hard, cold earth, bent over, and placed his face against the ground. A cry burst forth from the depths of his being, a cry such as he had never before uttered in all his life.

"O *God,* help me! Help me! Show me what to do!"

Patience looked up from the large blackened pot she stood over to find Chris Wakefield walking toward her. Looking at his face, she knew instantly that something had happened. She dropped the stick she'd been using to stir the clothes in the boiling, bubbling water and turned to him as he came to stand beside her.

"Chris! What is it? What's happened?"

For a few moments he did not speak. He was very pale, and there was a vulnerability in his firm lips that she had not seen before. His eyes were red-rimmed and swollen, and there was an unsteadiness in his hands.

Concern filled Patience. "Are you sick? Is that it?"

"No," he said at once. He shifted on one foot, then the other, and looked over to where two women were washing clothes in a pot suspended over another fire. His eyes came back to her face. "Will you come with me?" he said. "There's something I want to tell you."

"Why, of course." Patience called over and said, "Susanna, will you watch these clothes for me? I'll be back shortly."

She turned and walked with Chris along the edge of the palisades until finally they stepped outside. Still he had not spoken, and she was mystified, not knowing what was wrong with him. Yet something—a voice deep within—told her he had passed a crisis in his life.

When they came to the line of trees that led down to the sea, Chris looked at them silently, then said, "Let's walk down to the sea."

"All right."

When they reached the ocean, Patience looked at the *May-flower* bobbing up and down on the swells. She stood silent, waiting for Chris to speak. He seemed to be fascinated by the sight of the ship, and he watched for a long time. Then, finally, he turned and looked into her eyes.

"Patience, something has come to me." His voice was quiet, not at all like his usual tone, and there was something in his eyes and expression that she had not seen there before . . . yet she recognized it instantly.

"You've found God, haven't you, Chris?"

He nodded slowly. "I don't know how to talk about it." He shook his head, then pulled his hat off and ran his hand through his hair. "It's like—it's like nothing I've ever known."

Far overhead gulls were crying in their harsh, raucous voices, and he moved restlessly, looking up at them. Then he turned, took her arm, and said, "Let's walk along the shore. I'll try to tell you about it."

"All right, Chris."

The two walked along the rocky shore, Patience listening intently as Chris spoke hesitantly of his experience. There were times when he could not speak at all, when his voice would grow husky and his mouth would clamp shut, as though to forestall intense emotion. His entire manner held an odd uncertainty, something she had not seen in him before, but as he spoke of calling out, of crying to God, and how God had answered his prayer and brought peace to his heart, tears filled her eyes. She stopped abruptly, searching in her pocket for a handkerchief.

He turned as she found it and wiped her eyes, then he reached out and took her arms and held them. "I've never felt anything like this before," he said, his voice filled with wonder. "Such peace . . . I *know* God is with me."

"Yes, I can see that," Patience replied, smiling through her tears. "I'm so glad for you. I'm so glad."

"Will it last?" His voice was urgent, his eyes filled with sudden doubt. "I've been so . . . well, troubled, angry, I guess . . . all my life. Angry at myself mostly. Now I feel—just like I'm filled with peace."

"That's the peace that God gives," she said quietly, "the peace that passeth all understanding. And yes, it will last. Be faithful to God, Chris, and you'll see. It will last."

They had come two hundred yards down the beach. The wilderness was on their right, dark, trackless, mysterious. On their left, the gray sea stretched out, meeting the sky in such a thin line they could not tell where one ended and the other began. The waves were moaning, crashing against the shore. The air was cold, sharp, and cutting, but neither of those two who walked along seemed to notice it.

Suddenly Chris gave Patience a look and, without warning, reached out to put his arms around her and draw her close. "I know it's too soon for this," he said, "and I'm not asking you for anything, but I want to say something to you, if you'll let me."

Patience blinked with astonishment. The touch of his arms around her had sent strange emotions racing through her, and she could not answer for a moment. He held her loosely, and she did not resist him. "What is it, Chris?" she whispered.

"I've got a long way to go," he said softly. "I don't have anything. I've wasted my life. Even my own family couldn't put up with me." And then his tone changed and he said urgently, "But I know one thing. I love you, Patience. You may not believe it, but it is so."

Patience was filled with astonishment—mostly at herself that so few words could fill her with such joy. She knew suddenly as she stood there, held loosely by this tall man, that she loved him as she would never love another. Being the honest girl that she was, she could do no less than look up and say simply, "I love you, too, Chris, and I always will."

Joy came to his eyes, and he pulled her closer and lowered his head. Her lips were soft under his, and she gave herself to him in innocence. He held her, savoring the softness of her lips, the wonder of her response, but, most of all, the spirit that was in her—a spirit that he had long considered to be the finest he'd ever known.

Finally he drew back and said, "I've got to have you, Patience, for the rest of my life. I know I'm not much of a catch, that I come to you with nothing to offer but my heart. And yet, I know with a certainty that I will spend what is left of my life becoming a man you can respect. And I want you to marry me."

Patience didn't hesitate. "Yes."

He grinned suddenly. "Now if that isn't like you! Most girls would have a long, flowery response to give me. But you, my dear love, all you say is yes."

"When I say yes," she said, her eyes serious despite the smile that tipped her lips, "I'm giving you everything I am and have." She pulled his head down again with surprising strength and kissed him. Finally they drew apart, and he laughed suddenly.

"Well," he said, "I'm going to find out one thing, and, thanks be to God, you will find it out with me."

"What's that?"

Chris gazed out at the sea, straining his eyes as if he hoped to see England. Then he looked back at her and put one arm around her, holding her firmly. "I'm going to see if the story of the Prodigal Son will stand true. I'm going back to my father and ask him to forgive me, and I want you to come with me."

A gladness went through Patience. She squeezed his hand and nodded. "He'll forgive you, Chris. I'm sure of it. But even if he didn't, your heavenly Father has forgiven you, and that's all you could ever need." The two of them stood there, seeing the world in each other's eyes, then turned and walked slowly back down the rocky shore of the New World.

Eight

SIR ROBIN GETS
A SHOCK

Spring had come at last to the Plymouth Colony. Now every member of the colony, both Saints and Strangers, gathered together as the small boat from the *Mayflower* prepared to return to the ship with two passengers: Chris Wakefield and Patience Livingston, who bid their friends a fond farewell.

The harsh winter had been endured, and now, on this fifth day of April, 1621, a balmy breeze blew in from the sea, fragrant and gentle. Captain Miles Standish stood holding Patience's hand. He looked up momentarily, letting the breeze brush his raised face. "I wish we could have had that warm breeze a few months ago." He smiled at her and shook his head. "I do hate for you to be leaving, lass," he said regretfully. "This won't be the same place without you."

"I'll miss you, Miles, and I'll pray for you every day."

"Will you now? That will be kind of you." Standish turned to face Chris, who was standing beside Patience, a smile on his broad lips. "And, you, Wakefield," the soldier said with mock sternness, "you treat this girl right, or when I see you next, I'll pound you into the dirt."

Looking down fondly at Patience, Chris smiled and returned the soldier's glance. "I hope you'll do just that if I'm found lacking in my treatment of her," he said. Then he asked, "Why don't you come back with us, Miles? My father could find a place for a man like you, I'm sure of it."

"No, I can't leave this bunch of psalm singers in the lurch." Chris smiled, knowing that Miles often disguised his fondness for the group with harsh words. Standish glanced over at William Bradford, who had come to join the three of them. "Here, Pastor," he said loudly, "why don't you just join these two now in holy matrimony?" He grinned at them gleefully. "It's a long sea voyage ahead of them, and I don't know as I'd trust this young fellow with such a lovely girl."

"I'd be glad to," William Bradford said quickly. "As a matter of fact, I've tried to urge them to let me do just that."

"Nothing I'd like better," Chris answered quickly, "but it wouldn't be fair to Patience. I want her to meet my family, and I want them to get to know her and love her. It will give my mother a chance to have a big wedding. She loves things like that."

Bradford nodded, a genial smile on his face. He'd filled out during the spring, gaining weight, and now the wolf-lean months that had nearly destroyed him and the others seemed more like a bad dream than reality. If it were not for the sharp pang of loss so many felt as their gazes drifted to the cemetery, they could almost believe the hardships had never really happened. Almost.

Now Bradford put out his hand to Chris, and their handshake was firm. "God bless you, my boy," the pastor said, his heart full. "I can't tell you how happy I am to see you walking with God."

"I'll always remember you, Mr. Bradford, and when you return to England, I do hope you'll come to see us."

"It isn't likely I shall ever return, my boy, but thank you. And know my prayers go with you." Bradford turned to Patience, putting out his hand, which she took in both of hers, smiling up at him. He saw tears glistening in her bright eyes, and he cleared his throat, moved himself. "God bless you, my dear. You've found your way, and I rejoice with you."

"Thank you, Pastor." Patience held on to him for a moment. She had learned to love this man dearly, discovering, beneath his rather formal manner, a warm and generous heart. She smiled fondly. "I'll write you as often as I can, and you answer when you have time."

At this moment Captain Jones, who was standing up in the boat, cried out, "Are you two coming or not? We've got too many miles to go for you two to be lollygagging."

Quickly Chris and Patience shook hands, felt the hands on their shoulders of those who remained with the small company, and then turned and went to the boat. Two sailors held it firmly as Chris helped Patience inside. Captain Jones called out, "Perhaps I'll see you again soon, Pastor Bradford."

"I trust so, but if not in this world, in the next, eh, Captain?"

The words caught at Christopher Jones and he nodded soberly, saying, "Aye. That's the way of it, I'm thinking, and I have you to thank for turning me toward the Lord. Good bye, Pastor."

At the captain's command, the sailors shoved the small craft out into the frothy waters, leaped inside, and, with two others, began to row toward the ship.

When they were finally on board, Chris, Patience, and Captain Jones stood at the rail, waving good-bye. The group on shore looked small and vulnerable against the looming background of forest that lay behind them, extending for thousands of miles, trackless and dense. "By heaven, I hate to leave them here!" Chris exclaimed suddenly. "But we've got to go."

Patience took his hand and held it. "Yes, the Lord has things for you to do."

"One of which is to make myself into the best husband I can," he said. Then he grinned. "And to be a good father, too, I trust."

Patience blushed slightly. "We'll speak of that later," she said primly, then turned to wave again at those on the shore. The three of them stood there until the shoreline grew faint and dim, and then a sadness descended upon Patience. She excused herself and went off to be alone.

Chris heard his name and turned to see Captain Jones motioning to him. He immediately went to where the captain stood and said, "Aye, sir?"

"If you're through mooning around, you can come to the cabin with me. That is, if you intend to grace me with any work on this voyage."

"Ready for anything, Captain. Just give me the orders."

"The order, then, is to come below." He turned and stomped along the deck, going down the ladder with ease of familiarity. When they were in the captain's cabin, he went to the stern windows that rose high and covered almost the entire rear of the cabin. Outside, the gray sea was rolling in long, undulating swells. He watched the waves rise and fall, seeming to find them fascinating, then finally turned to Chris. "Well, what have you to say for yourself?"

"Say for myself?"

"Yes, man, don't stand there like a ninny." Jones slapped the desk with a hard hand and sat down in his chair. He pinned Chris with a hard look. "You're going home to marry this young woman. The last I heard, your family would have nothing to do with you. How do you propose to take care of her?"

Chris blinked, somewhat taken aback, though not intimidated, by the captain's intensity. "I guess I have to admit, Captain, that right now my prospects aren't good."

"I should think not. How old are you? Thirty-two is it? You own nothing but the clothes you stand there in."

"That's right, Captain. But I'm a good sailor, you know that. I'll get a berth and I'll prove to my father that I've changed."

"So you've changed, have you?"

"I have, sir, and I think you know it." Chris paused and looked at the captain. "As have you, Captain Jones."

The seaman gave him an affronted look, then laughed abruptly. "By heaven, I think you're right! We've both changed." He sobered then. "For the better, I trust. It does my heart good to be around men like William Bradford and know that God is still moving in our world." He reached down and toyed with a turkey quill that rested in an inkwell, then looked up again. "I never knew what it would be like to serve God. I always thought it would be a rather dreary, formal affair, but it's not like that."

"No, it's not." Chris thought for a moment, then smiled, saying, "I wish I'd known years ago what it was like to give yourself to God. I could have saved myself a lot of grief."

"Well, well, we can't undo the past." Jones stared steadily at the young man. "Now, I've something to say to you."

"Yes, sir?"

"I want to offer you a position as first officer on the *Mayflower* on subsequent voyages."

Chris was taken aback. He stared at Captain Jones, then asked, "What about Mr. Clark?"

"Leaving for another post," Jones said. "Does this make you think of something?"

"What do you mean, Captain?"

"I mean, I wouldn't offer you a job as first officer if I didn't have confidence in you, would I?"

"Well, I suppose not, sir."

Jones stared at Wakefield, almost with resentment. "Blast your eyes, have you gone completely loony over that girl? Don't you see what I'm saying?"

Chris stared at the captain with an air of bafflement, "Well, I appreciate the offer, sir, but—"

Jones grinned suddenly and leaned back. "You're moonstruck, that's what's the trouble with you. I've never seen it fail. A young man in love is not worth a dime. I'm talking about you and your father, Chris."

"My father?" Chris asked, raising one eyebrow. Then his mouth fell open in surprise. "Oh—!" he said rather foolishly.

"Yes, *oh,*" Captain Jones mocked him. He got up then and came around the desk to stand before the younger man. "I'm going to give your father the kind of report he's been hoping to hear. He asked me to tell him when you were a man that could be trusted. Well, the *Mayflower* is all I've got and I'm willing to trust you with her, so I think your father will believe me when I say you've changed."

Chris swallowed hard. "Indeed he will, sir. Indeed he will. He puts great stock in your judgment. I thank you."

Jones raised his hand. "No thanks to it. You've earned your berth. I've watched you carefully, and you know what caused me to make up my mind to tell your father you're ready to take up your life again?"

"No, sir."

"When I saw you caring for the ill, not even hesitating to wash those who had vomited all over themselves." Jones nodded firmly. "When I saw that I said to myself, now there's a young man who's ready to tackle anything. It was a fine thing you did, my boy, taking care of the sick."

"Well, they took care of me when I was sick."

"Some men wouldn't have seen it like that, but I'm glad you do. In any case, we're agreed, then?"

Chris hesitated, then said, "I can't agree yet, Captain Jones. I've got to go home and prove myself to my father. I know he'll take your word, but—" He hesitated, then shook his head. "I want to *do* something. You understand, Captain? I mean, I've given Father and Mother nothing but trouble. Now I want to find a way to make them proud of me, to show them there has been a change. And I want to be there when they meet Patience. You'll need another officer while I'm doing that."

"Well said, lad, well said. I hadn't thought of all that. We'll leave it at that, then. Still, I'll have that talk with your father."

"Thank you, Captain."

"Now, get out of here and get to work! Do you think I've got nothing to do but stand here and bandy words about with you all day? Get out of here, Wakefield! And stay away from that girl, you hear me?" Chris grinned and nodded with false humility. "Aye, sir, I'll do my best." His grin grew even broader. "But I can't make any promises."

"I can't tell what's going to happen. It looks like the whole country might go to war." Oliver Cromwell stood across from Sir Robin Wakefield, staring down at the large, fragrant roses that formed glorious red banks along the walkway of the garden. He reached out, snapped one of the flowers off, and sniffed it, his long, homely face showing pleasure. He looked over with a smile. "I'd like to forget it all and do nothing but take care of my farm, wouldn't you, Sir Robin?"

"Yes, that would be pleasant, but I suppose that isn't going to be our fate, is it?"

"Not as long as the king keeps agitating."

"The trouble with His Majesty," Robin said slowly, "is that he hasn't recognized the fact that, since Elizabeth's death, something new has come to England."

Oliver Cromwell shot a quick glance at his host. "By heaven, you're right!" he said. "Something *is* going on in this country. But how would you define it? What is happening? It feels as though the whole nation is fomenting, like water about to boil."

Robin reached out and touched one of the flaming red roses, enjoying the softness of the crimson petals. Then he turned and looked at Cromwell. "Somewhere," he said softly, "between the time that Queen Elizabeth drew her last breath as monarch of

England and James drew his first breath as the king of England, we English lost our taste for absolute monarchy."

Cromwell grinned suddenly. "You'll never make the king believe that," he declared firmly. He shrugged his shoulders restlessly. "If any man ever believed in the Divine Right of kings, it is James the First, our sovereign lord. He's convinced he's God's deputy on earth."

"Well, so were all of us of that mind at one time, perhaps more especially about Elizabeth. She kept us alive and free, as did all the Tudors, but these Stuarts don't seem to understand that. I fear the conflict won't be settled easily."

The two walked through the garden slowly, talking about politics until a voice caught at them. "Robin, come quickly!"

With a start, Wakefield glanced across the garden to see his wife, Allison, waving at him frantically. "Something's wrong!" he said with alarm. "Come along, Oliver!" The two men broke into a run. When he reached his wife, Robin demanded, "What's wrong? Someone hurt?"

Allison looked at him and her eyes filled with tears, alarming him tremendously. She was not a weepy woman. "For heaven's sake what's wrong, Allison? Is someone dead?"

She put her hand out and placed it on his chest, then whispered brokenly, "Robin . . . he's come home!"

Instantly Robin's eyes lit with understanding. "He's here?"

"Yes, he just came a few minutes ago. I've been talking with him."

Robin glanced across at Oliver, and his face settled into a frown. "It's Chris, but he's not supposed to be here. I told him not to come back until I had received a good report from Captain Jones."

"He has a letter from the captain," Allison said quickly. The tears were running down her cheeks now, and her lips were trembling. "Oh, Robin, it's not what you think! He's so changed!"

Robin stared at her, not sure he could believe that the thing they had hoped and prayed for had finally come to pass. "Changed? Changed how?"

Allison shook her head and took his arm. "He'll have to tell you himself. Come along."

Oliver watched the two, well understanding their situation. "I'll just go along—"

"Oh, no!" Allison reached out and took Oliver by the arm. Holding both men she said, "Both of you come. You're his friend, Oliver, and always have been."

The two men allowed themselves to be led into the hall. But when Robin entered and saw Chris standing erect, waiting for him, he swallowed hard. He caught one quick glimpse of a young woman standing by his son's side and he cleared his throat, saying, "Well, Son, you've come back!"

Chris didn't flinch at his father's tone. "I have a letter for you, sir, from Captain Jones." He crossed the room and handed it to his father, then went back to stand beside the girl. Robin noted the way his son reached out to hold the girl's arm with a proprietary air. A quick glance at Cromwell told the elder Wakefield his friend had noted the action as well.

"Well, let me see what the good captain says." Robin broke the seal on the letter, opened it, and drew out a single sheet. Cromwell and Allison watched his face carefully as he read, and Cromwell knew at once that it was good news, for relief washed across Sir Robin's face.

Folding the letter carefully, Robin slowly put it back into the envelope, then turned and placed it on the large mahogany table. After a moment he turned to look at his son and the young woman.

"Well—," he said, hesitating, unable to find the words to express his emotions.

Chris spoke into the emotional silence. "Sir, I havè come home to tell you that I've been wrong in the way I've lived, and to ask your pardon, yours and Mother's."

A sob escaped from Allison, and she ran to her son, throwing her arms around his neck. Robin stood motionless until Cromwell reached out and gave him a surreptitious, though forceful, shove. "Go to him, sir. Quickly!"

As though shaken from a daze, Robin moved at once across the room and put out his hand, which Chris took without pause, a glad light in his eyes. Again Sir Robin cleared his throat and said, "Your Captain Jones says very admirable things of you, my boy." And then he could not contain himself. He squeezed the hand with all his might and gave a great roar of a joyous laugh. "By George, I'm proud of you! Any man who has earned Christopher Jones's good opinion is a fine man indeed."

Chris felt the hard strength of his father's hand, and he wanted to put his arms around him, but he held back. Instead he said, his voice thick with emotion, "Thank you, sir." Then he released his father's hand and turned to indicate Patience, whose face was shining as she watched the glad reunion, and said, "Father, may I present Mistress Patience Livingston." He hesitated only one moment, then went on. "I have the glad honor of informing you that she will be your new daughter-in-law, sir."

Robin's jaw sagged, and he exchanged a startled glance with Allison. He saw at once that she had already had the news, and he straightened up and said rather brusquely, "Well! I'm glad you went through all the procedures before springing this on us."

But Oliver Cromwell came forward, saying in a hearty voice, "Congratulations, Chris! If I may meet the bride it would be my pleasure!"

Patience shook hands with Oliver, then turned to face her future in-laws. "I'm very happy to meet both of you," she said. "I know this comes as a terrible shock to you, but I hope that we will get to know each other better very soon."

Chris held her hand tightly. "I have one more thing to tell you." He hesitated, and Robin saw the young woman's hand tighten on his son's arm. "The thing is, I've become a Christian, sir. Something you and Mother always wanted, I know." He shook his head rather sadly. "It's taken me a long time and I have wasted years, but God has come into my life and I've yielded myself to him."

At this astounding news, Sir Robin Wakefield could withhold himself no more. With a glad cry he threw his arms around his son, and the two men held each other for a moment, both too moved for words.

Allison went to Patience and put her arms around her. As she held her she whispered, "I'm so glad you've come, my dear. I can see my son loves you very much."

"As I love him," Patience whispered.

Finally, Robin stepped back, a little embarrassed at his show of emotion. He laughed. "I didn't mean to blubber over you like a woman, my boy, but you can't know how happy I am—how happy we both are, your mother and I."

"Thank you, sir." Chris bit his lip, then said, "I ask only one thing of you. Will you give me a chance to show that I have had a change of heart? Captain Jones has asked me to serve with him as first officer on the *Mayflower*, but I begged his indulgence until I might serve you, in any way whatever. Give me something to do, Father, and I'll do my best to show you what kind of man I'm going to try to become."

"Well said! Well said, indeed!" Cromwell bulled his way forward, clapped Chris on the back, and said, "Bless your heart, my dear Chris! This is the best news I've had in a long time. I want you to know that you've cost me many an hour of prayer. Not as many as you cost your dear parents, of course, but more than you'll ever know."

"Thank you, Oliver," Chris said simply. "Somehow I always knew that you'd be good for me."

There was bustling and talk, and then Allison called the servants to lay out a meal for them all. Chris discussed eagerly with his father the estate and the possibility of serving on one of his father's ships. Oliver sat smiling at the happy event, and later, when Chris and Patience were alone for a moment, she said, "Well, the prodigal is home at last."

"Yes, I guess that story really does hold true, doesn't it?" Chris put his arms around her. "My parents love you, I could tell."

"They are so wonderful," Patience whispered. "I've never had parents of my own. It'll be so nice to have a mother and a father."

"And a husband!" Chris grinned. They were standing in one of the small rooms that looked out onto the garden. Night was coming on quickly; the sun was dipping in the west, leaving only a golden circle of light. They stood there watching, and Chris held her, saying, "I found a new Scripture last night that made me think of you."

"What was it?"

"It says, 'A prudent wife is from the Lord.'" He grew sober then, studying her hand as he held it and stroked it lightly. "I know the Lord has given you to me, and I will spend the rest of my life thanking him for it."

"Oh, Chris," she cried happily, then threw her arms around him. She kissed him firmly, holding to him, then drew back, her eyes glistening with happy tears. "God has given you to me, too. I don't have a Scripture for that."

Chris said, "I do." An impish look came into his eyes. "Isn't there some Scripture that says something like, 'I was a stranger and you took Me in'?"

"You silly fool!" she laughed, reaching up to give his hair a playful tug.

"Ow!" He grabbed her wrist and held it behind her back, pinioning her, then he kissed her thoroughly. He lifted his head for a moment, smiling at her. "Here I am, a Stranger, and you're taking me in."

"Yes," she whispered with her eyes glowing with love, "for the rest of our lives."

END OF PART ONE

Shadow on

1 6 2 4 | Part / TWO | 1 6 4 0

the Land

GATHERED TO HIS FATHERS

T he Thames River wound around, a serpentine form along the green grasses of the shore. A fish flopped, sending a series of circles that soon flattened out, leaving the surface smooth.

Oliver Cromwell watched as the oarsman dipped and pulled his oar in short, choppy strokes. Turning, he said to his companion, "Well, Chris, I suppose floating down a river is not much of an adventure for you, not after having crossed the sea." He looked up at the hard blue sky, admired the clouds that floated up overhead like fleecy sheep, and then made a grimace. "I've never been as fond of the sea as you are. Can't say I even like it much."

"I suppose that kind of love may be born in a man to some extent, Oliver." Christopher Wakefield studied the bend in the river, swaying to the patterns and rhythms of the waters as it moved the cockleshell of a boat down its broad bosom. "You know, this river flows two hundred crooked miles all the way to London. I've heard it's actually the longest river in England."

"I suppose that's so. Doesn't make me like this little slip of a boat any better though," Cromwell grumbled.

Chris studied his companion, noting the rather melancholy face, the heavy-lidded eyes, which he could never decide if they were green or gray, and he laughed shortly, belying the look of concern in his eyes. "Think of it like this: Almost every drop of rain that falls comes down this stream. The Thames swallows up all the other rivers, the freshets, all the streams and rills, every well of water in the region. Don't you feel important, now, to be carried on such a magnificent stream?"

"No," Cromwell said sourly. "I wish I were at home with Elizabeth."

"I know you do, for we're in the same condition. I don't know why these matters of business have to come up just when a man needs to stay at his home. Both your wife and mine are so near their times it hardly seems safe for us to leave."

"Well, thank God we've gotten this business over with and are on our way back home." Cromwell glanced up and pointed. "Look! There's Oxford!" He studied the institution that had produced the finest gentlemen and scholars of England. Cromwell found pleasure in the stately walls, the towers of the colleges.

Later, after beginning a taut loop, they made their way past Dorchester, then reached the spot where the Isis and the Thames joined together to form the main body of the river.

Chris and Oliver talked intermittently about their common interests and concerns, from farming to politics. Chris looked up after rounding a bend to say, "There's Windsor." The two men studied the gray freestone battlements of the castle, which made a lofty presence on one bank, and the school of Eaton on the other bank. "Windsor is a proper royal castle, don't you think, Oliver? And it has a splendid view. The king can see nearly everywhere, including the woods and the river and the field."

"I think the hunting's mostly ruined, though. Back during the days of King Harry it was a perfection, especially for red deer. He had sixty or more parks enclosed by gates, each opening into one another."

"I've heard that Arthur was supposed to have built the first fortress here. Some say he's coming back to England again when we fall upon hard times."

Cromwell gave his friend a sardonic look. "Well, he can come any time he pleases, for hard times are here."

"Oh, come now, it's not so bad as that!"

"Not so bad?" Cromwell's eyes glowered and he slapped at the water in an angry gesture, sending silver drops high to sparkle in the sun.

His action startled the boatman, who grunted, "Here now, sir! Be careful, else you'll tumble us right over."

Ignoring the boatman, Cromwell grunted. "We can't even take care of our own country, and King James decides to declare war on Spain. What idiocy!"

Chris glanced ahead at the boatman and whispered, "Take care, friend Oliver. Such statements might be considered treasonous."

"Let him hear!" Cromwell said, almost savagely. "Let everyone hear! Why do we want to go fight Spain? Don't we have enough trouble here in England?"

Wakefield did not answer, and Cromwell fell into a moody silence. Chris turned to stare at the river, deep in thought—though not about the state of the country. Indeed, his thoughts were of Patience. She had not been well, and although the doctor claimed she had been made for childbearing, there had been complications during her pregnancy that bothered him.

She had laughed at his fears, saying, "You're like all new fathers. But you wait. God's going to send us a fine son."

Even so, as the small boat made its way down the river toward London, Chris could not forestall his worries about her and their child. Turning suddenly to Oliver, he said, "You've gone through this business of your wife birthing a baby twice, Oliver." Worry scored his features. "I don't see how you did it. I'd rather face a storm at sea."

Cromwell's expression was a mixture of humor and compassion. "It's always that way with the first one, I suppose. I know when Robert was born I nearly drove everyone crazy. But then, when Oliver came two years later I was an old hand at it."

"You're not worried about Elizabeth and this new baby?"

Cromwell shrugged his muscular shoulders. He allowed a smile to touch his generous mouth and answered, "Well, to be truthful, my friend, I am a little concerned. Elizabeth hasn't had any problems, but this bringing a child into the world is dangerous for a woman." He put his hand suddenly on Wakefield's shoulder. "Still, we've prayed about it, haven't we? We've agreed together, and the Scripture says that where two are agreed, it will be done. We must have faith for this matter."

Something about Cromwell's manner assured Chris, and he relaxed a little. Glancing around, he saw that they were floating past a sparse island. "Look! There's Runnymede."

"Aye, where King John of England once bowed his head to the barons," Cromwell said, gazing at the small island with interest. "He managed to alienate everyone, but he changed the history of England forever."

Both men were silent for a moment, each thinking of the day—June 15, 1215—when King John of England had been forced by the nobility of England to sign the great charter, or the Magna Carta as it was called. This document granted Englishmen rights that they would never willingly surrender, such as the provision that no freeman could be arrested or imprisoned except by the lawful judgment of his equals or by law of the land.

Chris shook his head. "I fear this king of ours will fare poorly as well. The quarrel between him and the parliament is growing worse."

"Yes, it is." Cromwell said, then fell again into silence as they moved onward. The river snaked lazily along in the first warmth of spring, and soon the towns and villages pressed closer to each other: Egham, Staines, Walton, Hampton.

"Look, there," Chris said, "Hampton Court."

"Yes, Cardinal Wolsey's elephant of folly. It's a monstrous enough thing, a true monument to pride. The money could have well been spent elsewhere. Have you been inside?"

"No, never."

"Well, I must admit I was impressed. There are walls; two parks, one part for the deer, and the other for coursing hare; lots of residences and apartments; a magnificent chapel; and vaulted ceilings of Irish oak. Everyone who goes there is dazzled by the opulence of the whole thing—hangings, tapestries, paintings. I suppose it's no real surprise that, after Wolsey built it, King Henry never rested until he could take it from him."

Later on they passed Richmond, the favorite residence of Queen Elizabeth and the chief seat of her grandfather, Henry VII. "My father was here," Chris said, "many times when Queen Elizabeth was brought here."

"I wish those days were back again," Cromwell said. "The Tudors were the proper monarchs for us. These Stuarts, they'll ruin the country. You mark my words."

Down the river the little boat went, at times the wind causing it to bob up and down like a cork on a fisherman's line. Finally, beyond Richmond, they reached Lambeth Palace, seat of the archbishops of Canterbury. It was there, where the river ran deeper and clearer, that the waters of London were swallowed up. Both men caught the smell, for London dumped tons of waste into the river each year, yet the Thames still swarmed with trout, perch, smelt, shrimp, haddock, and many other sorts of sea life.

Finally the oarsman said, "There she be, good sirs—London Bridge." Across a slant of distance toward the city, rising above everything else, was the bulk of St. Paul's, which stood taller than all the other buildings. It had the shape of a sprawling giant, and Chris admired it. But then the London Bridge loomed ahead of them, and the noise of the water running through the arches was almost deafening. In addition, there was the dim clatter of traffic overhead.

As they drew near the bridge, Chris looked upward at the twenty-one stone piers holding up twenty arches. As they passed under in a swirling roar, Chris studied the houses built upon the bridge itself. Each domicile sent forth smoke out of the chimneys overhead.

Chris shook his head in amazement. "Magnificent thing, this old bridge. I can't imagine London without it."

Cromwell did not answer, but soon the boat pulled into shore and he said, "Look! There's those playhouses, the Rose and the Globe. Devil's work, that's what they are. We'll have them down one of these days."

"I don't find the works of Mr. Shakespeare completely objectionable," Chris said mildly.

"You don't? Well, I suppose I'm just a hard shell of a Puritan. I'd like to see every one of those houses closed."

For one moment there was a fanatical look in Oliver Cromwell's eyes, and it was a look Chris had seen before on rare occasions. He did not understand Cromwell during those times and made it a point not to argue with his friend when those moods hit. "Come along, Oliver, let's get out of here. I'm tired of the river myself."

The two men stepped out of the boat, paid their fares, and soon were in a coach headed for their home country. The carriage ride from London was rough. The spring rains had made muddy wallows out of the roads, and more than once the weary passengers had to get out while the coach was pushed out of the mud to drier ground. Finally, as they drew near to the village of Wakefield, Oliver said, "Your father isn't well, is he, Christopher?"

Worry drew a line across Chris's brow, and he rubbed his chin in a nervous gesture. "No, not at all, Oliver. I'm concerned about him."

"What does the doctor say?"

"Nothing, except to blame it on old age. But it can't be that. He's sixty-five, but he's led a healthy life. My mother's hale and hearty. Still, he is being badly affected by something. I believe it's his stomach. He doesn't complain, but I can tell that he's in pain most of the time."

"I'll be in prayer for him," Oliver said.

"Thank you. I knew you'd be doing that."

The coach stopped in the small village, and Christopher dismounted. He reached up his hand and Oliver shook it firmly. "Let me know when the baby comes, and I'll send word to you when we have ours."

"Yes, be sure you do. If you need any help, send word."

The coach rolled on, and Christopher turned and made his way to the stable. He was greeted many times as he made his way through the small village. As he walked, he thought, *They wouldn't have been so happy to see me a few years ago. Most of them, I suppose, made fun of me being a drunk and a wastrel.*

The blacksmith greeted him warmly. "That mare foaled two nights ago, Mr. Christopher, a likely looking foal."

"Fine," Chris said. He hesitated, then asked, "No word about—"

"About the baby? No, sir, not that I've heard this morning. I know you'll be in a hurry. I'll saddle up for you."

It was but a short time later that Chris rode through the gate in the walls that bounded the castle of Wakefield. The great house itself was enclosed by walls on three sides, and a small river bordered the fourth. A big gate stood by the tower, and over the gate, supported by cantilevers, was the Wakefield coat of arms, a falcon with widespread wings holding a sheaf of arrows in one claw. For one moment Chris stopped and looked at the coat of arms. He hesitated, then rode on inside. He glanced toward the north corner of the house, noting the tower pierced with machicolations for bows or guns. All sides of the house were protected by stockades and earthworks.

As he dismounted, he remembered asking his father about that, and Sir Robin had said, "We probably won't be attacked by anyone again. There hasn't been such activity for many years. This place is old, Son, seen many battles in its day. In fact, there was a time when we might have looked up and seen the Spaniards coming down that river across those fields. But we can know this: If they ever do come, we'll be ready for them."

Chris threw the reins of his horse to a tall, young serf, greeted him warmly, then went inside the house. He was met almost instantly by his mother, and he asked at once, "How is she?"

Allison Wakefield shook her head. She looked tired, and her lips were drawn together, revealing her fatigue. "She's having a bit of a hard time, but nothing yet. She'll be wanting to see you, Chris. You go along, and I'll fix you something to eat. You must be hungry."

Chris went at once to the bedroom, and as soon as he entered, Patience turned from where she was standing at a window, looking out. She smiled and said, "I saw you come in."

She held out her arms and he went to her, holding her gently, his hand caressing her back. She lifted her face, and he kissed her tenderly. He wanted to hold her with all of his might and said so. "I'd like to squeeze you, but that wouldn't be good for the baby."

"That time will come," she said. She leaned back in his arms and looked up, then touched his face with the palm of her hand, stroking his jaw. "You look tired, Chris. I'm glad you're back."

He led her to the bed and helped her sit down. She moved awkwardly—a sign that her time was very near. Chris looked at her, concern in his blue eyes. "I shouldn't have left you. I should have stayed."

"No, it was business that had to be done, but now you're back." She took his hand and held it against her cheek, and he marveled again at the smoothness of her skin. She whispered, "It will be soon. Don't worry."

She knew him so well, this man of hers! Although they had been married only three years, it seemed to her forever. Marriage, as she had hoped, had been a natural thing. She had given herself to her husband with a joyousness and spontaneity that had delighted him, as their marriage had been a delight to her. When they'd learned the child was to come, they only loved each other more. She held onto his hand tightly, stroked the back of it, and said, "Tell me the news."

He spoke to her about the details of his trip until his mother appeared at the door and said, "Come now, get something to eat." She led him down the stairs. While he ate hungrily, she said very little. Soon he paused, looked up at her, and said, "Is Father worse?"

Allison bit her lips. She was not a woman to worry or complain. There was a steadfastness about her that Chris had always admired and tried to emulate, but now, as she spoke, he saw that she was not at ease.

"He's not well. We had the doctor out three days ago. He left some stronger medicine. It makes Robin sleep so much that he won't take it—says he'd rather hurt a little bit and know what's going on."

"I'll go see him!" Chris started to rise, but his mother pushed him back down again.

"Eat your food, then you can go."

After he had eaten Chris went at once to his father's room. He found him sitting in a chair, staring out the window. He looked weak and drawn, and Chris thought, *He's worse every time I see him. There's only one end to that.* But he let none of that show in his eyes or his voice. "Well, I'm back," he said breezily as he went over to shake his father's hand. Grasping it in his own, he could not help but note how frail the once strong hand seemed. "I've made a mess out of it, I suppose. You should have been there. You'd have known exactly how to do it."

Robin smiled at this tall son of his. "Not a bit," he said. "You're a better businessman than I ever was. Though you'll never be the rider I was," he added with a smile.

It was not true, Chris knew, but he nodded. "You're right about that. I just don't have the touch. You tried hard enough to teach me."

Robin smiled, then laughed aloud. "You remember when that bay you tried to ride pitched you off on your head?"

Chris rubbed his neck, an embarrassed look creeping across his face. "Yes, I remember it. I wish you wouldn't, though. You bring it up every time we talk about horses."

"Well, if you'd done what I'd told you—" Robin broke off suddenly and his breath came shorter as he seemed to gasp. He shut his eyes momentarily, then drew his lips tightly together.

"Father—!"

"It's all right, it's all right." Robin gripped the arms of his chair for a moment and Chris had to watch helplessly as his father struggled against the pain. Finally he took a shaky breath and opened his eyes, tried to smile, and said, "I've got a bit of a bellyache. Bring me that brown bottle, will you, Son?"

Chris jumped up, ran across the room, and brought the bottle, saying, "I can't find a spoon."

"I'll take it like it is." Robin pulled the cork, took a swallow, shuddered, then took another, put the cork back in, and handed it back to Chris. "Horrible tasting stuff. Makes me sleepy, too. Sit down before I pop off, and you can tell me about your trip."

For fifteen minutes, Chris sat there recounting the details of his trip. He saw the drug was indeed powerful, for within five minutes his father was blinking sleepily. Finally he mumbled, "I'd better lie down, I think." Chris helped his father into bed, lifting his legs, and by the time his father was in bed, he had passed into a deep sleep. Chris stared down at him, shook his head, and left the room.

When he went back to the kitchen, he looked at his mother. "He's gotten much worse since I left."

"Yes, he has, but now that you're back you can spend more time with him."

For the next four days, Chris stayed very close to home. He'd taken over the affairs of Wakefield and was, in effect, the master of the place, but he was careful to spend all the waking hours he could with his father, going over the details of the estate. In the late afternoon of his fourth day home, the two men were sitting in the garden, talking. It was one of Robin's better days. He seemed almost hearty and very cheerful. Suddenly Chris looked up and said, "Look! There comes Cromwell."

"So it is!" Robin's face lighted and he said, "I've always admired that young man." Then he looked at the young man. "Get off that horse, you scoundrel. You ride like a serf."

Cromwell brought his horse up to the edge of the garden, stepped out of the saddle, and gave one of the serfs the bridle. He came over, put his hand out, shook the hands of both men, then said, "You've always been vain about your riding, Mr. Wakefield. Pride is a sin that has brought many a man down."

"Well, you might be right." Robin grinned. "Sit down."

"No, I don't think I can. I'm too excited!"

"The baby's come!" Robin exclaimed with a grin.

"Yes, it has! A little girl, no less. We named her Bridget, and she's hale and healthy." Then he demanded at once, "Now, what about your wife, Chris?"

"Any moment, my mother keeps saying, but she's been saying that two days now. Sit down while I get us some ale. Perhaps it will help calm me to do something. I'm nervous as a cat."

Cromwell took the seat across from Robin, and as Chris left he said, "He's pretty worried. I suppose that's natural with first-time fathers."

"I suppose so. It was with me. I'm glad your baby's come safely. Is Elizabeth all right?"

"Fine, fine." Cromwell did not inquire after Robin's health, since it was clear from the sickness that etched itself across the handsome features of his friend that all was not well. He leaned forward then and said, "I'm proud of our Christopher, sir, and you should be, too. I know you are."

Robin leaned back, folded his hands, and gazed at them for a moment, then looked up. "God has been good to me, Oliver. He's given my son back to me, and Chris has become a better man than I ever was down deep inside."

"No, never that," Oliver said firmly. "As good a man as you are—that'll be fine."

"Well, well, tell me the news. What's going on? You know every frog that croaks in this kingdom of ours. What's the king doing?"

"Dying, I suppose." Cromwell saw the alarm that leaped into Wakefield's eyes, and he held up his hand, protesting, "No, not literally, although he's not a well man. I apologize. I shouldn't joke about it like that."

"What about Prince Charles? Has he gotten over that Spanish princess yet?"

At the question Oliver made a small gesture of impatience. The subject seemed to be a rather sore one with him. The previous year, the Prince of Wales, the king's son, had been led by Buckingham to seek the hand of a Spanish princess. The prince had traveled all the way to Madrid to secure a betrothal to a young woman there, but it had been a total failure.

Cromwell snorted. "At least we can be grateful that alliance didn't work, but the news I have is almost as bad."

"What is it?"

"There's a new treaty to be made with the French. Charles is going to marry Henrietta Maria."

"Let's see, that's the daughter of Henry IV and Maria DeMedici, isn't it?"

"That's the one."

"You don't approve, I see."

"No, I don't. Why doesn't he marry an Englishwoman?"

"What's the matter with this girl?"

"She's Catholic! A papist to the bone! She'll make one out of Charles, too, you mark my words."

"Perhaps not. It could be that he'll make a good Anglican out of her."

"Charles? He hasn't got the backbone. No, if what I hear is true, he'll be swayed by this woman." He leaned back and said, "These kings have a way of being swayed by the wrong people. Look at James. He doesn't dare to cough unless George Villars, the duke of Buckingham, gives him permission."

"Now Buckingham is leeching on to Prince Charles, who will one day be king, is that it?"

"Exactly right. Buckingham's the most ineffective counselor a king ever had, and James and Charles listen to him as if he were God in heaven."

The two were deeply engrossed in discussing the politics of the country, when all of sudden there was a shout. Both looked around startled, and Oliver grinned. "Well! And it's about time! The baby must be here."

Chris burst from the door, running at full speed toward them, shouting, "He's here! He's here!" He drew up in front of the two men, pulled his father to his feet, and said, "Come on! See your new grandson!" Oliver moved at once to Robin's other side, and the two younger men supported the lord of Wakefield as they moved across the yard. When they went inside to the bedroom, Chris said, "There he is! The newest lord of Wakefield. Well, one day, perhaps."

Robin's eyes shone. "Let me see him."

Patience was lying in bed, her face drained of color, but a smile on her lips. She drew back the covers, and Allison went forward to take the child. She picked him up, held him out, and said, "Hold him, Robin. Your grandson."

Robin took the morsel of humanity and held him carefully. There was a strange beauty on the dying man's face as he beheld the child. He reached out one finger and touched the red cheek, which resulted in a cry of rage from the infant.

"Got quite a temper, hasn't he?" Robin said and looked proudly at his son. "Yes, the lord of Wakefield. After you, that is."

This was as close as Robin had ever come to mentioning the fact that he would not be living long. He at once passed the moment over by saying to Patience, "A handsome son, Daughter. I'm proud of you."

It was a glorious day for the Wakefields—and for the village, for Christopher had insisted on having a celebration for his firstborn.

"You'll have half the village attending," Cromwell remarked with a grin as Chris gave orders for ale to be poured in honor of his son.

"A man doesn't have his firstborn every day of the week. It happens but once in a lifetime," Chris retorted. He looked over at Oliver and said, "God has been good to us. A daughter for you, a son for me." A thought came to him and he smiled, saying, "Wouldn't it be strange if when these babies grew up, they'd fall in love and marry?"

"Nothing I'd like better than to see some good Wakefield blood mixed with the Cromwell line," Oliver agreed. "Come now, let's go admire that young gentleman again. What've you named him?"

"Gavin. 'Twill be a strong name for a strong man!"

***

Early in the year of 1625, King James I of England began to suffer from fever with convulsions while staying at his palace in Hertfordshire. His mother and the duke of Buckingham at once summoned all of the prominent physicians of the kingdom. They treated James with new medicines, with new so-called cures, but that simply made him worse. At one point, James found Buckingham kneeling beside his bed and accused someone of poisoning him. He said very little after that, and on March 27, surrounded by archbishops, bishops, and chaplains, without any pain or convulsions, King James I of England joined his forefathers in death.

Two days after the death of King James there was another death in England, this one in the castle at Wakefield. Robin Wakefield had grown steadily worse over the year. He had lived to see his grandson, Gavin, prosper, and one evening as the sun went down, the family was gathered about him. His daughter, Mary, and his son Cecil had warning enough to make the journey from their respective homes, and now, along with Chris and Allison, they surrounded the bed of Robin Wakefield.

Robin looked around and saw the sorrow on the faces of his children, then reached up and took his wife's hand, held it tightly, and said, "God has been good to me. All of my children are gathered in serving God, and I thank him for it." Seeing the tears running down Allison's face, he said, "Never weep for me, my dear. I will be with him whom I love more than I could ever say on this earth—with Christ Jesus, my Lord."

For all his illness, Robin Wakefield seemed at ease, as though the pain was gone. He asked that his grandson be brought in, and for a time he lay with the husky baby beside him on the bed, seeming to enjoy the tiny boy's kicking and thrashing. "He'll be a man of God in history," he said, his eyes shining. Then he looked up at Chris and said, "You've been a joy to me, my son. I thank God for the man you have become."

Chris's throat closed tightly and he shook his head, unable to speak. "I regret," he finally managed to say, "the wasted years."

"Nothing is wasted," Robin whispered, "not in God's economy. The years you were gone from me, God was doing something in you. Then he brought you to this woman." He reached up and took Patience's hand, squeezed it, and said, "You two share a marvelous love, the same as your mother and I have had for so many years."

Then, one by one, he went around and blessed his children. At last they withdrew from the bedside, and Allison came, bent over, and kissed her husband tenderly. The others were in the shadow of the room, and they listened with a hushed respect as the two told their love to one another for the last time. Finally, Robin reached up and touched her cheek and said, "My dear, your love has been—all to me."

Then his hand fell back and he ceased to be.

Allison leaned over to kiss him for the final time. Then she folded his hands and turned to say, "And so this mighty man of God is gathered to his fathers! How well he endured his going forth!"

T e n

GAVIN MEETS A ROYALIST

1 6 3 6

As Gavin Wakefield threaded his way through the tall oak trees, the leaves crunched noisily under his feet. Impatiently, he frowned and tried to avoid making any more noise than he had to. Ahead, he knew, lay a favorite watering spot for the deer that roamed around the river, and he crouched over, his eyes searching the thick woods as he advanced. Overhead the September sky was a leaden gray and threatened rain. The trees, giants that had been lifting their arms for a hundred years in this spot, were stripped and now made bony blackened skeletons etched against the heavens.

Gavin had tried for the last two years to creep up on one of the fleet-footed deer, starting when he was only ten. His father had taken him to the woods often and had taught him some of the skills of a hunter, but he had never brought down anything larger than a rabbit. Even that, he knew, had been almost a lucky shot.

He'd left the house early that morning, and instead of taking his small bow that had been made for him by the carpenter, he had appropriated the tall longbow that his father used. It had taken all the strength he had to string the bow, and now as he advanced through the woods he suddenly stopped, planted his feet, and raised the weapon. Carefully, he pulled an arrow and notched it on the string, then slowly pulled the string back to full draw. He eased up, though he kept the arrow in place, and, with a little more confidence, advanced through the woods.

The vines tugged at him, and once a thorn ripped across his cheek. He opened his mouth to make a small cry and at once was disgusted with himself. "Hunters don't cry," he said in disgust. He wiped the blood off fiercely and continued his stalk.

As he approached the river he became even more cautious, looking down to place his feet on the moss-covered sections of the earth rather than on the crispy sere leaves that carpeted the ground. He recalled that it was here, at this watering spot, that his father had shot and killed the animal whose antlers now decorated the study at Wakefield. That had been a moment he had never forgotten, and he had purposed in his heart that he would one day do the same. His father had applauded his ambition, but cautioned, "Wait until you are a little older. Your arm will be stronger, your eye steadier. Then you'll bring a buck in that will make this one look like a baby."

Gavin, however, was not the kind of young man to wait. Impetuous in all things, at the ripe old age of twelve it seemed to him that he would never grow old enough or strong enough. Every day passed with a leaden slowness. Now, as he pressed through the woods, he determined to get his deer, and so please his father.

Finally he reached a massive yew tree, situated himself behind it, and held the bow with his left hand, his fingers on the notched arrow. He froze there, having learned that deer are among the most alert of all creatures. The slightest unexpected movement, the boy knew, would send the fleet animals bounding out of sight in a twinkling. He knew that wild creatures protect themselves by quick movement and so had learned to stand motionless, not allowing so much as a blink of an eye. He had so mastered this that he had enticed a fox up to within a few feet of where he sat, still and silent.

Hunting was a serious game to the boy, and within ten minutes the birds had returned and one crow lit no more than five feet over his head, cawing with a harsh, inquiring voice. Still the lad did not move.

A slight movement caught his eye. He watched breathlessly and was delighted when a doe stepped out from a thicket down the river and went to drink. It was too long a shot, he knew, so he sat there waiting, praying that she would come closer. But she turned to go away, and in desperation, he stepped out from behind the tree, using one smooth motion to pull the arrow back as far as he could and let it fly. The arrow whistled through the air, but the doe leaped quickly away and it passed harmlessly over her head.

As the graceful creature disappeared almost magically in the brush, Gavin threw his father's bow to the ground, harshly uttering a word that his father had thrashed him once for using.

Suddenly, from nowhere, a loud laugh rang out. Gavin whirled, fright running over him for an instant. A man stood there, and Gavin supposed he must have stepped out from behind a tall, thick tree. Hot shame washed over the boy, not only for missing his deer, but for cursing. Angrily he said, "What are you doing here spying on me?"

The man's eyebrows raised. "Spying on you? No, lad, I was admiring your skill as a hunter." The man was of no more than middle height, but his build was solid and strong. He had the blackest hair Gavin had ever seen, with heavy eyebrows to match. His face was tanned, and he peered out of a pair of sharp, dark brown eyes. He had a short, neatly trimmed mustache and beard and wore clothes that were much the worse for wear. He carried a staff in his hand and wore a knife in a sheath at his waist. When he spoke again, Gavin struggled unsuccessfully to pinpoint the man's strange accent. "Well, devil fly off," he said cheerfully and gave his head a woeful shake. "That's the way it is with a thing like this. No help for it, now, is there?"

He advanced somewhat closer, and Gavin, in confusion, leaned over and picked up the bow. "I've got to get that arrow," he mumbled. "It's too good an arrow to lose."

"Right, I'll go with you." The man stepped alongside the boy, and as they moved across the opening, he said, "That was a good stalk you made, sir. You'll be a fine hunter. Your arm's not quite strong enough for that bow, but it will be one day."

Gavin was mollified by the man's approving tone. "It's my father's bow," he explained as he reached down, picked up the arrow, and looked at it anxiously to see if it was damaged. With relief, he saw it was no worse for its use. He held it in his hand loosely and said, "I've never seen you before, have I?"

"No, lad, I'm new to these parts. Just passing through, as it were."

Gavin's eyes fell. "I—didn't mean to curse," he said, "but it makes me so mad when I miss like that!"

"Why, we all miss a shot now and then, lad, but you'll make up for it the next time."

"I've been in these woods since I was ten, and that's the first time I ever got close enough to a deer to actually hit one."

"Is that the truth, now? So then, what's your name, lad?"

"Gavin Wakefield."

"Will Morgan, you can call me." The man stood with an almost athletic ease, and there was a wild air about him. He noted how the boy studied him cautiously. "You're not quite sure about me, are you, lad?"

"No, I'm not."

Morgan smiled briefly at the blunt response. He narrowed his eyes. "Good for a boy to be cautious. I've heard there were evil men that would steal children and sell them. I might be one of those, now, mightn't I? What would you do if that were so?"

With a quick motion, Gavin notched the arrow, stepped back, and drew down—not pointing at the man, but ready. "I'd shoot you with this arrow," he said simply. He was somewhat frightened of the man, for there was a dark air of competence about him. Despite his calm response, he knew he would have no chance if the man decided to overpower him.

Morgan threw his head back and laughed. Then he said, slapping his thigh, "I *like* a lad with spirit! You remind me of myself when I was twelve." A thought came to him and he said, "Would you really like to take a deer home?"

Gavin's eyes lit with passion. "More than anything in the world."

"Come along, then. I think we can arrange that. If, that is, you'll let me have a shot with your bow."

Gavin hesitated, then nodded. "It won't be quite the same as doing it myself, but I want to learn." He followed the man, who made his way through the woods with practiced ease, until they finally came to a spot Gavin had never seen before.

"The deer tracks are thick here," Morgan said. "We'll wait a bit, and you'll see a deer, I doubt not. Be still now."

It only took thirty minutes, then, surely enough, a buck stepped out of the woods and came down to the water. Despite the thrill of excitement that danced along his senses at the sight of the magnificent beast, Gavin knew it was a long shot and was sure Morgan would not make it. But, with speed and polished action, the man drew the bow and loosed the arrow, which sang silently through the air and struck the deer behind the left shoulder, driving straight into the heart.

"You got him! You got him!" Gavin shouted, dancing around. He jumped and ran to where the deer lay, but before he could reach the fallen animal, Morgan grabbed him and held him back. "Careful there, lad! True enough, the mighty beast looks dead, but I've seen a dying hart rip a hunter to shreds with those sharp hooves of his. Let's wait just a moment."

Gavin stilled instantly, watching Morgan for a sign that it was safe to move in. After a few moments, the man nodded, and they moved to kneel beside the animal. As Morgan sliced the deer's throat and bled him, Gavin said, "Can we take him to my house? I want to show him to my father."

"I don't see why not. It'd be kind of a load, but we could make it. How far do you live?"

"It's nearly four miles."

"Well, let's go to it then."

The two made their way back to Wakefield, and when they came into the grounds, Gavin said, "Put the deer there. I'll go get my father." He raced upstairs and found his father in his study. "Father! Come and see the deer we killed!"

Chris Wakefield looked up, surprised. "Deer? What deer are you talking about?" He got up and came over to the boy, studying him carefully. "Have you been out in the woods again?"

"Come and see it, Father!"

The two made their way down the stairs, the boy tugging at the elder man's arm. Chris smiled at the boy's eagerness. He had no idea what Gavin had been up to, but was more than willing to indulge the lad. Then, when he got outside and saw the carcass and the poorly dressed dark-haired man standing to one side, he stopped. After a moment, he nodded. "Well, you do have a deer."

Gavin said at once, "I shot at one, but I couldn't pull the bow far enough to hit the deer, Father. Then Will came along and he took me to a new spot. You should have seen the shot he made; it must have been a hundred yards!"

"Not *that* far, lad." Morgan smiled, then looked over at the tall man and nodded. "'Tis a fine hunter you have here, sir. He'll be bringing his own deer in before too long, I'm thinking."

Sir Christopher could not restrain a smile. "I'm glad that he had a good teacher. That's a fine buck," he said, considering the man carefully and seeing the signs of travel and the weariness around the dark eyes. He added in a mild tone, "There's a law against poachers, you understand."

The dark-eyed stranger merely smiled. "Aye, sir, I well know that, but—" he grinned at Gavin—"I'm thinking that this lad be no poacher if he's the son of Sir Christopher Wakefield, as he claims to be."

Chris laughed and said, "Well, if you'll dress that deer, we'll let the cook have her hand at it. Then we'll have a supper, just you and this boy of mine and me."

"Right, sir, I'll do that."

Gavin stayed and watched the man as he expertly dressed the deer, cutting it up into parts, explaining each cut as he did so. Finally, after one of the quarters had been delivered to the mercies of the cook—a tall horse-faced woman named Jane—Chris joined them, and the three of them sat in an alcove, the two men drinking ale and Gavin enjoying apple juice. Sir Christopher, being an expert at drawing men out, soon discovered that his guest was widely traveled. "You come from Wales, I take it?" he asked when they finally sat down to the perfectly cooked, still-smoking joints of meat. Then he hesitated and said, "We'll ask the blessing, if you don't mind."

"Not at all, Sir Christopher." Morgan bowed his head and after the brief blessing said, "You have a good ear, Sir Christopher. True enough, I'm from Wales, although I've been gone from there many a year."

Christopher sliced off a helping of the meat with his knife and passed the platter down. When they all were served, he placed a sliver of the meat in his mouth, chewed carefully, and nodded. "Nothing like fresh meat, is there?" Then he studied Morgan and added, "My people came from Wales, part of them anyway."

"Do tell? What might their name be?"

"The same as yours, Morgan, but it's a common enough name. Still . . ." A thought crossed his mind and he smiled. "You and I might be distant cousins, I suppose."

"Perhaps, but as you said, there are as many Morgans in Wales as there are fleas on a dog. I don't know much about my family past my own father." He looked over at the boy and said, "Well, Master Gavin, not a bad supper, eh?"

"It's good!" Gavin tore into the meat, grinning with pleasure. "Tell some more stories like you told while you were cutting up the deer."

Morgan protested, but he was an excellent storyteller, and the two Wakefields were thoroughly entertained by him. Finally, when the meal was over, he nodded. "Sir Christopher, it's been good of you to allow me to sup at your table."

"Well, you furnished the meal," Chris said. He hesitated, then asked, "Are you bound for any certain place, Morgan?"

"No, sir, just wandering. I guess I've got a wandering foot, just like my father before me."

"Do you know much about farming?"

"I know I don't want to do much of it, not potato farming, anyway. I've dug enough potatoes to do me for a lifetime."

Christopher hesitated again, then said, "I could use a little help here. If you have any skills besides shooting deer, I could put you in the way of it."

"Well . . ." Morgan shrugged. "I've done my share of black-smithing. There's those that say I'm not bad at it. I'm good with dogs, too. Truth be told, sometimes I think I can teach a dog to be smarter than I am."

"Stay on awhile," Chris urged. "We need help in the smithy, and I've got dogs now that don't know a deer from a fox. Winter's coming on, and you can teach this young fellow more about hunting. I'd like to do it myself, but I'm afraid I'll be gone quite a bit. From what I've seen, you'd be a fine teacher."

Gavin held his breath. He desperately wanted Morgan to stay, and when the man finally agreed, he was delighted.

For the next two weeks, Gavin followed Will almost constantly. The Welshman had an inexhaustible fund of stories. Though

Gavin was never quite sure how many of them were true, Morgan told them so well and with such humor that the boy loved to hear them. He would perch on a stool nearby as the new blacksmith worked and ask him to tell his tales again and again. In addition, he found that Morgan truly did know all there was to know about dogs. This only thrilled Gavin the more, for the boy loved dogs, and so he soaked up the knowledge the Welshman poured into him.

It was only three weeks later, when Gavin and his father were speaking of their new servant, that Gavin posed a question that had been in his mind. "Did you know that Will is a Catholic, Father?"

"No, but it comes as no surprise, since most Welshmen are Catholic, I think."

"I was surprised," Gavin confessed.

"How did you find out? Was he sharing his teachings with you?"

"Oh no, I just said something about him coming to church with us. He said he would go to his own church, if he went. I asked him what his church was and he said he was a Catholic, or at least he said his parents were. I don't think he goes anywhere himself, to any kind of church."

"There are many Catholics like that, just as there are members of the Church of England who give nothing but a lip service for the things of the Lord." Wakefield looked over at the boy and wondered what was going on in that neat head. He admired his son's strong, attractive features, for he saw echoes of Patience in the lad. Gavin had his mother's ash-blond hair and his grand-father's blue-gray eyes. He had a long face, with high cheekbones, and was very tall and slender.

He'll be as tall as his grandfather was, Chris thought, and the memories of Robin Wakefield came flooding into his mind. He often saw his father in the boy, in the way Gavin tilted his head slightly to one side when he asked a question and the way his hair grew down into a widow's peak over the broad, pale forehead. He thought, *It's odd, how blood will tell. There he sits, and I see myself and Patience and my father, my mother. Probably if I had known those who came before, I would see them, too. There's power in the blood.* He reached over and slapped the boy on the back and said, "We'll be going on a journey soon, did you know?"

"No, sir. Are we going to London?"

"Not this time. We are going up to the north of London to visit a family called the Woodvilles. I've done some business with them, and they've invited us for a visit. We'll stay there for as much as a week."

"Is Mother going, too?"

"Oh yes, I wouldn't go without her. And I doubt if she'd leave you here to your own mischief."

"Is there a boy my age there?"

"I don't think so," Chris said. "There's a small child, a girl, but there'll be plenty to see. Sir Vernon is one of the wealthiest men in England. He has a huge estate. I expect there'll be some time for you and me to sneak off and perhaps do some angling or hunt one of his deer."

"Oh, I'd like that. Can Will go with us?"

A momentary pang of jealousy touched Chris, but he put it aside. The boy's devotion to the servant was only reasonable, for, as Chris had requested of him, Morgan spent a good deal of time with Gavin. Chris regretted his own busy life and purposed to spend more time with his boy.

"I suppose that would be a good idea. He can drive the carriage. But you and I will have more time together. I'd like that."

Gavin looked up. "So would I, Father," he said. "Let's go get a deer, shall we?"

The ancestral home of Sir Vernon Woodville reminded Gavin of the castles he had seen near London, particularly the castle of Windsor. He looked up as the turrets rose out of the mist and was shocked at the size of the establishment. "It's big, isn't it?" he exclaimed.

Patience leaned over, looked out the window of the carriage, then drew back, saying, "Yes, it's one of the biggest, most ornate castles in England."

"A bit too ornate, if you ask me," Chris grunted. "A man can only live in one room at a time. Why does he need a castle with a hundred bedrooms?" He grinned rashly and stroked his short, neatly clipped beard. "Lord, think how it'd be to have a hundred overnight visitors come piling in on you! I think I'd lose my mind, and so would the cooks and the maids."

"Will there be a hundred people here while we're visiting?" Gavin inquired.

"I don't think so," Patience said. "It's just a small group, isn't it, dear?"

"Yes, perhaps two or three other families." Chris fell silent, and Patience grew curious.

"Why do you suppose they asked us? Do you know Sir Vernon that well?"

"We've done some business together," Chris admitted. He stared out the window as they approached the huge gates, manned by servants in livery, and said, "To tell the truth, I think we're being courted."

"Courted?"

"Yes, Sir Vernon is one of the staunchest supporters of King Charles. I suspect he's invited us here to demonstrate the loyalty that he has and to draw us a little closer into his circle."

"Oh." Patience thought about this for a moment, then asked, "Is Sir Vernon very close to the king?"

"Oh yes. Ever since Charles lost Buckingham, his chief adviser, he has listened to Vernon more than anyone else." A slight frown crossed Chris's face. "Unfortunately, that could be trouble."

"Trouble?" Patience frowned. "How so?"

"Well, you know the Catholic leanings of the queen, and the Woodvilles are staunch Catholics." He glanced down at Gavin, who was staring out the window in awe at the magnificent building that stretched along the open space inside the wall, and shook his head. He did not want to get the boy embroiled in the war that was going on between the parliament and the king, although he suspected Gavin knew more about it than he let on. "Perhaps I'm wrong," he said. "In any case, it'll be a good outing for us. You'll get to see some beautiful gardens, my dear, although there's probably not a great deal left of them now, with winter coming on. I'll have to bring you back sometime, for it's been rumored that Lady Woodville's garden is the finest in England."

The carriage drew to a stop, and when the coachman leaped to the ground and opened the door, Chris got out and helped Patience down. A servant approached, a tall man with an icily formal face, who said, "My lord and my lady would appreciate your coming at once so they can greet you in the library, Sir Wakefield."

"Yes, of course." Chris turned, taking Patience's arm, and the three of them followed the tall servant into the house. All about them was an ornate, palatial decor beyond anything any of them had seen. The enormous foyer was fully twenty feet from floor to ceiling. The walls were lined with large portraits of the Woodville family. Ornaments of gold gleamed richly from the polished mahogany tables that lined the walls, and as the Wakefields passed by the windows, richly embroidered drapes were drawn back to allow the sun to pass through the stained-glass windows.

"Looks like a blasted cathedral," Chris muttered. "Man couldn't spit around this place."

"Do you want to spit, Father?" Gavin grinned.

"No, but if I wanted to, there'd be no place to do it, would there, Son?"

They followed the servant down a long hall and around several turns, then finally arrived before a massive set of double doors, each ornately carved out of burled walnut. The servant rapped gently, and when a voice spoke, he entered, announcing, "Sir Christopher Wakefield and Lady Wakefield."

Gavin edged in beside his parents, eyeing the couple who had risen from their seats. The apartment was enormous, much larger than many full-sized houses of manor farmers. It was like being in an auditorium of some kind. Everywhere he looked there were statues, paintings, carved cabinets of every sort, and tapestries. Gold and silver glinted as the pale October sun sent feeble gleams through the high-arched, mullioned windows.

"Well, Sir Christopher!" A tall, handsome man in his forties advanced and put his hand out to shake that of Christopher Wakefield. "By George, it's good to see you again, sir. And this is your lady, I take it?"

"Yes, my wife, Patience. May I present Sir Vernon Woodville and his wife, Lady Woodville."

Lady Woodville was fully as handsome as her husband. She had a heart-shaped face and enormous brown eyes. Her hair was fixed in some sort of ornate fashion that Gavin had never seen before— nor had Patience, for that matter. Lady Woodville's dress was composed of pale green silk, cut rather low in the front. As she came forward, she smiled and raised her hand, allowing Christopher to kiss it, then said in a languid voice, "We're so happy. We've looked forward so long to having you, Christopher, and you, too, Lady Wakefield."

Lord Woodville smiled indulgently. "Well well, sit down now and tell us what you've been doing? Oh, who is—this is your son, I take it?"

"Yes, this is Gavin. Gavin, Sir Vernon Woodville and Lady Woodville."

Gavin felt himself being examined by the eyes of the two and said, "I'm glad to know you."

Lady Woodville's red lips pursed and she said, "What a handsome boy you are!" She lifted those liquid eyes to Chris. "Like your father in many ways."

Patience watched this interaction carefully. There was something feline about the woman, and although Patience was hardly a woman given to instant likes and dislikes, there was something about the charming, beautiful Lady Woodville that she found disturbing. She did her best to keep her voice calm as she remarked, "Yes, he is like his father. And even more like his grandfather."

"Ah yes, Sir Robin." Sir Vernon shook his head sadly. "What a loss we had, eh, when he went to be with his fathers. He was faithful to the ground, wasn't he? Served the queen all his life."

"Yes, he was very fond of Queen Elizabeth, and she of him, I understand."

Sir Vernon gave Chris a careful look, almost calculating, and studied him as if trying to read his mind. Carefully he pulled a snuffbox from his pocket, popped the lid open, and scattered a few grains on his wrist. Closing the box, he sniffed at the grains, then let his eyes fall almost half shut. "Well, Christopher, these are times when our sovereign king needs the loyalty of all good men. Will you say amen to that?"

"Amen," Chris said at once. He had been fairly sure this was why they were there, but it surprised him that it had come so quickly. "Have you seen the king lately, Sir Vernon?"

"Oh yes, I just came back from the palace. He's quite disturbed, you know, quite disturbed."

"Oh, about what?"

"Oh, this fellow—what's his name? Cromwell! I believe you know him."

"Indeed I do, if you mean Oliver Cromwell."

"Yes, that's the name. What a scurrilous fellow he is, indeed. Always stirring up seditions against the king."

"Oh, I think Mr. Cromwell is not guilty of any such thing as that. He disagrees, of course, with some royal policies, but even the most faithful subject seldom agrees with everything the king does."

The two men continued to talk, and finally it was Lady Woodville who said, "Oh, Vernon, that's enough talk about politics. We have all week for you and Sir Christopher to talk about the king and the parliament and all of that. Come along, sir, let me show you around the place. I'm sure you'll like your quarters."

Later on, Gavin was at last set free from further duties when he begged to go exploring.

"All right," Patience said, "but you'd better put on your old clothes. I know you, you'll be rolling in the dirt or falling in the river, or some such trick." Since it was late afternoon, she reminded Gavin that time was limited. "Now, we're having dinner with the Woodvilles and you'll be expected to be there, so come home early enough so that I can clean you up. Off with you now."

Gavin emerged from the house—if it could be called such, for it was an imposing three-story building with a hundred rooms and fifteen or twenty chimneys piercing the air—and went unerringly to the stables. He loved horses and longed to ride some of the fine stock he saw, but when he timidly inquired of the chief hostler, the man said, "Oh, we'd have to have Sir Vernon's permission for that. Why don't you ask him? I'm sure he wouldn't mind, but I couldn't let you ride a horse without his permission."

Gavin was in no hurry to encounter the lord of the manor again, so he asked, "Can you tell me the way to the woods? Is there a river close to here?"

The hostler, a short, stocky man with a round, red face and a pair of bright eyes, said, "Why, of course I can, young sir. Is it a bit of angling you would like to do, perhaps?"

Gavin's eyes lit up. "Is there a good place to fish? Where I might catch a big one?"

"Well, I'm a bit in that way myself. Come along, I'll show you the way and you can use some of my tackle."

"Oh, that's fine of you! I appreciate it."

Gavin followed the chunky hostler and was soon not only equipped with a pole and line and various gear, but taken down to a spot where the hostler pointed and said, "See that line of trees? Just beyond you'll find one of the nicest little streams a lad ever caught a fish out of. Now, it's deep and swift, so be careful you don't fall in and drown yourself."

"I won't." Gavin could hardly wait to get to the river. Twenty minutes later he plunged into the water up to his belt, casting for the trout he was sure lay there waiting for his hook.

He fished for an hour, catching several small ones. Then deciding to rest a bit, he started up the bank. His feet hit a patch of slippery mud, flew out from under him, and he rolled down the muddy bank. He got to his feet and looked down at himself in disgust. His clothes were coated with rich, black mud, and even his hair was caked with it. He looked up at the sky and realized his time was fast passing. He'd have to get back and clean up. Gathering up the hostler's tackle, he set the few fish loose that he'd caught, then hurried back to the house. He was almost halfway there when, from a side path, he heard voices. When he'd gone twenty feet farther, from behind a privet hedge that was carefully trimmed to form a lane, a young girl of no more than nine or ten and a boy about three or four years older than Gavin stepped out. They halted abruptly and the girl laughed, "Look at that dirty boy!"

The young man with her was large-boned and tall and had a

mop of blond hair. He also had a pair of pale blue eyes that somehow looked cold even when he laughed. "He *is* a filthy rascal, isn't he?" He stepped closer. "My, he stinks!" His eyes seemed to pin Gavin to the ground with disdain. "What a dirty creature you are!"

Gavin stared at the two, then clamped his lips together and would have passed in silence, but the boy caught his arm. "Now wait a minute, boy! Who are you, anyhow? You look like a beggar. Don't you know you're not allowed to fish in the river? This is Sir Vernon Woodville's property. I'd better take you in and see that you're soundly caned for invading private property."

"I'm not a beggar," Gavin snapped, trying to pull his arm away. But the boy's large hand held it firmly. "Let me go," he said.

"I'll let you go when I'm good and ready. Now, come along! I'm going to see that you get what's coming!"

It was then that Gavin lost his temper, something he seldom did—but when his anger was roused it was a fearsome thing to behold. His father had said, "You'll have to learn to hold that fury down, my lad, otherwise you'll wind up on the gallows. It's fine for a young boy to have spirit, but you've got to learn how to control yourself."

Control was the last thing on Gavin's mind as he jerked his arm away fiercely. The boy reached out and cuffed him across the mouth, sending him staggering backward. When Gavin tasted blood on his mouth, a blind fury seized him. Dropping the fishing gear, he threw himself forward, ramming his head into the boy's middle. The hit sounded like someone struck a drum, and the larger boy uttered a *"wuff"* and staggered back. Gasping for breath, he looked down and saw mud on his fine clothing, but before he could react Gavin was pounding at him with both fists.

"Why, you impudent—!" The large boy, obviously more skilled at the art of fighting, simply stood off Gavin's rush, then deftly began to pound him in the face and in the body. Gavin was too blind with anger to even feel the pain. He ignored the strikes until they finally drove him to the ground. At once the boy straddled him and his pale face glowed red with anger and his blue eyes gleamed with malevolent light. "Now!" he panted, "I'll teach you a thing." He began to drive his fist into Gavin's helpless face, grunting with the exertion of each blow.

"Stop it, Henry! That's enough!" The girl came and tried to pull him away, her eyes wide with fright. "You'll hurt him!"

"I *mean* to hurt him. He won't have any teeth left when I get through with him." Henry continued to pummel Gavin, who struggled fiercely but could not free himself.

Suddenly a voice barked out, "Now, that'll be about enough!" and a large, strong hand closed firmly on the back of Henry's neck. He felt himself plucked up and shoved rudely backward. Staggering, the lad found a servant, dressed in brown, with a pair of dark brown eyes, regarding him. "You're a bit large for this lad," the black-haired man said. "Be on your way now, before I take a cane to you."

"How dare you speak to me like that! I'll have you whipped!"

"We'll see who gets the whipping, if you don't be on your way." Will Morgan took one step and half lifted his hand, and the boy scampered back defensively. "On your way, and I mean *now,* or I'll put you flat on your back!"

The boy's face went pale with rage, and his voice was low with frustrated fury. "You'll see about this!" He turned and walked away, saying, "Come on, Susanne, we'll have the dogs on these fellows."

Will ignored them and went at once to where Gavin was struggling to lift his head and get to his feet. "Here now, that was a bit too much." Morgan lifted Gavin into a sitting position, took out a bit of cloth that he used for a handkerchief, and began mopping at the bloody face. "Let me see now—well, you got a bit of a beating. No matter."

"No matter?" Gavin sputtered in anger. "He'd have killed me if you hadn't come along."

"Oh, not so bad as that! Come along now. We'll have to go get you cleaned up. Lady Wakefield will have a fit if she sees you in a condition like this. She sent me to get you."

Gavin struggled to his feet, assisted by Will, then shrugged off the helping hand and started toward the house angrily. "I'll get him for this," he muttered. "You see if I don't. He may be too big for me to fight, but he's not bigger than a knife or a stick."

"Here now, lad, enough of that!" Morgan's voice was rough as he reached out and caught Gavin's arm, jerking him to a stop. "You'll not be talking like that or thinking like that. Part of being a man," he said evenly, "is learning to take a licking. You just took one, and now you'll act like a man about it."

"But he's bigger than I am! It wasn't fair."

"Fair? Well, if you're looking for a world where everything's fair, you'd better go to meet the good Lord in heaven. That's the only place where everything's fair."

Gavin's face was still mutinous. "Would *you* let somebody beat you like that?"

"I've been beaten in my time, more than once," Morgan said, and a fierce light suddenly glowed in his eyes. "Listen, Gavin, I'm not saying I like it, but I am telling you that a man has to learn how to suffer, to take his lumps. You hear me now?"

"Yes, I hear you, Will, but . . . well, I don't like it."

"You don't have to like it. I didn't like it myself. I'd like to take the scoundrel and throw him into the river or take a stick to him, but we'll have to leave things like that to God. Come along now. You'll be taking quite a few beatings before you lie down in the earth. Learn to make the most of it."

As Gavin approached the door that led to the Great Hall, he felt severely chastised. His father had not beaten him, as he had threatened to do at first when he'd seen his condition, for his mother had been too concerned about the damage to her boy's face. After Will had explained what had happened, Christopher softened some.

"Well, it wasn't entirely your fault, it appears. Get him cleaned up and made presentable, Patience. We can't have a rioter on our hands, not while we're visitors."

As they entered the Great Hall and saw the long table occupied by at least twenty guests, Gavin stopped dead, for his eyes had fallen upon a young girl—the same one he had encountered earlier. Quickly shifting his eyes, he saw the large young man, Henry, sitting across the table from her.

"Look! It's him! The dirty boy you had the fight with, Henry!"

The girl, who had recognized Gavin at first glance, spoke so loudly that all the guests heard. Faces turned to look at Gavin, who longed to turn and run from the room, but his father's hand was strong on his arm.

"That's him," Henry said. "That's the vermin that was sneaking around the grounds."

"Why, no, this is the son of Sir Christopher and Lady Wakefield," Sir Vernon said quickly. "What sort of story is this?"

Sir Thomas Darrow, Henry's father, said, "Oh, there was some sort of mix-up. Henry here didn't recognize your guest. I think he was in rather a disreputable state, if I understand correctly."

"He was filthy as a pig!" Henry said, "and he needs to be whipped for laying hands on me!"

"From the looks of his face," Lady Woodville said demurely, "it seems you got the better of the exchange." She smiled and said, "Come in and sit down. You three must all be friends. Susanne, after dinner you and Henry must entertain our guests."

That was all that was said, but from the cold look of bitter anger that Gavin received from Henry Darrow, he knew that he had made an enemy.

The incident seemed to be forgotten, and the talk that ran

around the table was mostly political so that Gavin did not understand most of it. The name of Cromwell he heard often. He knew that his father and Oliver Cromwell were great friends, and he was alert enough to understand that some of those at the table feared Cromwell and wished to warn his father of the dangers of knowing such a man. Gavin was aware of the politics of the day only slightly. He knew that Oliver Cromwell and his father were what was called Parliamentarians. Somehow the king was angry with them because they would not do what he asked. But as the dinner went on, his mind wandered. He found himself looking more often at the young girl, who was very pretty. She had blonde hair and expressive eyes, a very pretty heart-shaped face, but somehow her chin seemed a little bit too determined for a girl.

They endured the dinner, and finally Sir Darrow said, "This Cromwell is a dangerous man, one of those ranting Puritans that despises the throne and all authority. He'll break out, you'll see!" Then he lifted his cup and said, "A toast to our sovereign lord, King Charles I." Everyone rose and repeated the toast. All eyes seemed to be fixed on Christopher Wakefield, and when he repeated the toast it was Lady Frances Woodville who turned her smooth cheeks toward him, her eyes going over him in a curious way. "You see, my dear," she said, "he is loyal to the king." She whispered this so that no one heard it, and her husband said, "We'll see. It would be well for him if he did give his loyalty to the king and shuffle that fellow Cromwell off."

The next morning, Susanne Woodville rose early. She had stayed up as late as her parents would let her and had gone to sleep thinking of the young boy who had had the fight with Henry. Quickly she dressed and went down to breakfast. The adults were still asleep and she went outside, heading for the stables to visit her pony. As she approached she saw Gavin Wakefield and at once said, "Hello, Gavin."

Stopping abruptly, Gavin gave her a look and said grudgingly, "Hello," and then turned to leave.

"Where are you going?" Susanne said. She saw the pole in his hand and said, "Are you going fishing?"

"What else would I be carrying a fishing pole for?"

"Let me go with you."

"No. I don't want you." Gavin saw the youthful face suddenly show hurt, and he realized he had spoken in an ungentle fashion. *After all,* he thought, *she wasn't the one who punched my face.* Aloud, he said, "I don't think your mother would like it. You can't fish without getting dirty."

"Oh, it doesn't matter. I'm wearing my old clothes." Her old clothes really consisted of a rather ornate dress, but perhaps for one of her standing, Gavin thought, this was old clothes.

"All right, come along, but stay out of the way."

The two made their way back down to the river, and soon Gavin found himself teaching the girl how to fish. "Haven't you ever fished before?" he asked.

"No." Her eyes were very dark blue, and there was a liveliness about her that Gavin found very likable. He taught her how to fish, and when she caught a fair-sized trout and squealed with excitement, Gavin said, as he put it on a forked stick, "We'll take it home and you can eat it for supper, if you can get the cook to cook it."

"Oh, they'll do what I say."

Gavin stared at her and a grin touched his broad lips. "They always do what you say?"

"Yes, why wouldn't they?"

"Well, some might say, because you're a little girl and they're grown."

"Oh, but they're servants!" Susanne said.

The idea of someone not obeying her never occurred to her, and Gavin studied her carefully. "Well, you'll find out someday that you can't always have your own way."

He hesitated, then said, "Who is Henry Darrow, a good friend of yours?"

"Oh, the Darrows live on the land next to ours. They have a big home, and we go to visit them often." She hesitated, then said, "I'm sorry about what happened. Henry has a bad temper."

Gavin shrugged and said, "So do I, but I wasn't big enough to do much about it."

"I tried to get him to be friends, but he won't. He's like that, you know. If he likes you, he'll do anything for you, but once he gets mad at someone, he never forgives them."

The two went up and down the river, and finally it was time to go back. When they reached the house, they went at once to the cook, who admired the fish. "Oh, these will be fine for supper. Not enough for the whole house, but enough for you, Miss Susanne."

"And enough for Gavin, too?"

"Yes, I would think so."

That night at supper, when the rest had other dishes, a maid brought two dishes in with the smoking trout and whispered, "Here you are. You ordered these, I believe."

Susanne looked up at her mother and said, "Look, Mother! I caught this fish myself. Gavin showed me how."

The adults smiled, all except Henry Darrow, and Patience said, "Well, that was very sweet of you, Gavin."

Gavin flushed and said, "Oh, it wasn't much—even girls need to know how to fish."

A laugh went around the table and the meal went on.

From that day on, Gavin and Susanne were inseparable. The girl followed him everywhere. He felt like an older brother. He said as much to his mother. "Susanne's a nice child, isn't she? A little bit pesky sometimes, but not bad for a girl."

When it came time to leave, he received one embarrassing moment. Susanne had come out to the carriage along with her parents, and just as the good-byes were being said, she rushed over and threw her arms around Gavin's waist. Gavin looked helplessly over her head and caught the amused light in the eyes of the adults.

Susanne lifted her head and said, "We'll always be friends, won't we, Gavin." Then she pulled his head down and kissed him firmly and smiled at him.

Gavin flushed red as a beet as the adults laughed and hurriedly got into the carriage. "Good bye," he mumbled and on the way back, as soon as they were out of sight of the estate, Patience took his hand. "She's a sweet child, so don't be embarrassed. I think she has a hard life."

Gavin was surprised. "Why would you think that? She has everything a girl could want."

"Except a loving mother."

Chris had been listening to this, and he gave Patience a sharp glance. "You saw that, did you? Well, it's too bad. They don't have much time for the child—she's lonely."

Patience nodded. "Yes, that's why she took to Gavin. The servants say she doesn't have anyone to play with. A rich girl who has no friends."

Gavin rode silently for a while, then he looked up and said, "Mother?"

"Yes, Son?"

"I'll be Susanne's friend." His face was so trusting and appealing Patience leaned over and kissed him.

"Good. Always be kind to those who need you, Son. That's what life is about."

Eleven

LOVE AT FIRST SIGHT

Charles I, the sovereign king of England, was a startling contrast to his father, King James I. Though king of England, James had been an informal man, scruffy and always out of fashion, yet infinitely approachable. Charles was more aptly described as withdrawn, shifty, glacial, almost impossible to know. In physical form, Charles was quite small, a weakling brought up in the shadow of a very accomplished elder brother—until that brother died of smallpox at the age of twelve. What was worse, Charles was a stammerer and a man who could not make up his mind—yet once he did so, right or wrong, he could seldom be swayed. He was one of those politicians so certain of his own purity and confident of his own actions that he saw no need to explain himself to anyone.

By 1630 the parliament and the king had repeatedly locked horns in a series of stormy confrontations over every policy imaginable. The conflict reached such a peak that Charles decided he would rule without a parliament, hoping that the generations of hotheads and malcontents would die off, at which time the once-harmonious relationship between king and parliament would be restored. Unfortunately, this was a simplistic and totally erroneous notion.

In the summer of 1637 Charles's lack of understanding of the

Puritans became glaringly evident. Three Puritan writers, William Prynne, Dr. John Bastwicke, and a clergyman named Henry Burton, were tried and convicted of sedition for production of a pamphlet that strongly criticized the Crown—and Charles. All three defendants received the same sentence: Their ears would be cropped. Prynne suffered an additional refinement of cruelty with the letters *SL* branded on his cheek. The letters stood for "Seditious Libeller."

This was a rather mild punishment when compared to the hundreds of unfortunates who were burned at the stake by Bloody Mary and by her father, Henry VIII. Still, it had been several years since the people had seen such treatment of England's subjects. During the reign of Queen Elizabeth, England had known a more compassionate ruler, and so the mutilation of the three men had a profound effect on the spectators. Far from discouraging anyone from following the men's lead, many determined that Charles was in the wrong and deserved to be spoken against.

As Prynne's ears were snipped from his head, he cried out, "The more I am beat down, the more am I lifted up."

A woman from the crowd answered, "There are many hundreds, which by God's assistance, would willingly suffer for the cause for which you suffered."

In that same year, while the populace was complaining against the treatment of these three men, Charles, desperate for money since he had to rule without parliament, hit upon what he thought was a simple method for raising funds. It involved the levy of a tax known as ship money. In theory ship money was not inflammatory. It provided for the naval defense of the coastal towns and had been levied for many years. But when Charles proclaimed that all of England benefited by this defense and insisted that the interior counties pay their share as well, a minor revolution began. Oliver Cromwell's cousin, John Hampden, refused to pay the twenty shillings he was assessed. A test case was brought against him, the judges found for the king, and Hampden went to prison for a short time.

Yet another serious mistake that would haunt Charles for the rest of his life occurred in 1637. Charles had neither understood nor liked Scotland. He was alienated from that part of his kingdom, and he certainly did not understand the staunch conservatism of the Scottish Church. When he laid a heavy tax upon the Scots, then spent most of the money for lavish church buildings and appointed Archbishop Laud, the Scots replied at once. In a document dripping with anger, Scottish minister George Gillespie wrote, "The rotten dregs of popery which were never purged away from England and Ireland and having once been spewed out with detestation, are with us again in England. Her comely countenance is miscolored. The luster of the Mother of Harlots is with us. Her lovely locks are frizzled with the crispins of Antichrist fashions. Her chaste ears made to listen to the friends of the Great Whore."

Despite the bold resistance, Charles was determined to have his own way and so began a war within his own nation. This military action began what was called the First War—a cause that was far from popular with the people of England. The war cost the Crown a great deal of money, which Charles did not have, and accomplished nothing.

As the year 1640 approached, the feeling in England was one of gloom. Because of the money wasted in the Scottish war, the king was compelled to summon parliament once more. This assembly was known as the Short Parliament, and it was into this parliament that Oliver Cromwell came once more. His family had changed somewhat in the years since parliament last met. His wife had borne two babies, both of whom had died at birth, and, in 1639, Robert, his eldest son, had died of a fever. The memory of his fierce grief at the death of his beloved child remained with Cromwell to the end of his life.

Short Parliament was marked by the leadership of the great Puritan John Pym. A lion of a man, a veteran of fifty-five, he set forth the philosophy of the Puritans clearly in his beginning speech. "The powers of the parliament are to the body politic as the rational faculty is to the soul of man."

Charles reacted to this typically by dismissing the parliament in a high-handed fashion. However, unable to patch up his differences with the Scots, Charles engaged once more in military action, which was called the Second Bishop's War. Once again, to find money to carry on this struggle, Charles summoned a new parliament.

On November 3, this crucial gathering, which was known as the Long Parliament, met for the first time. The date was significant, for it was the anniversary of the parliament of Henry VIII, the parliament in which Wolsey fell. Some members of the Long Parliament tried to persuade Archbishop Laud that the date should be altered in view of circumstances, but Laud refused.

At the time, of course, no one recognized the significance of what was happening, for seated in that parliament were the men who would eventually bring the monarchy down and cause the head of Charles I to be severed from his body.

***

"That's it—the large white house. Do you like it, Susanne?"

Susanne Woodville had been watching the boats that plied the Thames, but at her mother's question she turned to look out the window. She saw a long building of two stories that stretched along the banks and said, "Oh yes, it's very pretty, Mother. Is that where we'll be staying?"

Lady Woodville shook her head. "No, that's the banqueting hall, really. It was built by a very great designer called Inigo Jones."

"But will the royal family be there?" Susanne asked eagerly.

"Oh yes, we'll be joining them, along with others." She leaned back in the cushioned seat and smiled at her daughter. "You're really getting to be very pretty," she remarked. "But you make me look like an old woman."

"Oh no, Mother," Susanne said quickly. She had learned that this was a real issue with her mother, who always tried to look her best and to preserve her beauty. "You'll never be old."

A frown creased Frances Woodville's smooth brow. "We all come to that," she murmured. Then she fell into a silence that Susanne had learned not to disturb.

This was the first time she and her mother had ventured to London together. Her father was ill and unable to come, but he had said, "You two go on. Have a good time. I don't want to spoil your pleasure."

Now, as the boat drew into a wharf, the two women rose and were handed ashore by the servants. Lady Woodville paid the fare, saying, "Have our baggage sent to the royal palace."

"Yes, Mum!" Properly impressed, the servant began busily unloading the bags that the two had brought. They had come, apparently, for a long stay, for there were a number of bags, some of them quite large.

"Come along, we'll go at once to the palace." The two made their way to Whitehall and were greeted by a majordomo, who, upon discovering their names, said, "Ah yes, Lady Woodville, and this is your daughter? Sir Vernon will not be with you?"

"No, he's not feeling well."

"Ah, too bad. Well, come along, I'll show you to your rooms. I hope you'll find them suitable."

The palace was a good deal more than suitable. It actually glittered, and the bed in Susanne's room was unlike anything she'd seen before. The carved bedposts had fantastic figures, all covered with gold leaf so that when the sun came down through the high windows, the very bed seemed to glow with a life of its own. Throwing herself on the thick mattress, she said to the maid who had been assigned to her, "Oh, I've never seen a bed like this!"

"Queen Elizabeth slept in that bed. It came here from None-such Palace."

"Queen Elizabeth! Think of that!"

For some time, Susanne moved around the room, touching the ornaments and staring at the pictures that adorned the wall. Some of them were rather stuffy. There were portraits of old men with long beards and stern-looking eyes. She had no idea who they were, but she didn't care much for them. Some of the other pictures, however, were of scenes in the country: a pond surrounded by tall trees reflected in the greenish water, a flock of sheep grazing out in the distance. "It looks like home," she murmured. Then, growing restless, she decided to explore the palace.

Leaving her room, she made her way down the wide corridors, which also were lined with portraits of stern-faced men. Even the women looked imposing, though Susanne thought they probably were very beautiful in their time. It disturbed her somewhat to think that all these people were dead now. *All that's left is their portraits on the wall. I wonder if a painting of me will be on the walls of a palace one day.* With a shrug, she continued exploring.

Finally she made her way into a large room filled with furniture. Obviously this was some sort of drawing room, much as they had at home but considerably larger.

"Hello! Who are you?"

Susanne turned to see a boy who was dressed in dark blue velvet and watching her carefully. "I haven't seen you before," he remarked, rising from the chair where he'd been sitting to come over and look at her more closely. "What's your name?"

"Susanne Woodville. What's your name?"

The boy laughed, his eyes sparkling. "You don't know who I am? I'm the Prince of Wales."

Susanne gasped, mortified. "Oh, Your Majesty, I'm sorry!"

Charles, the Prince of Wales, the eldest son of Charles I, stared at her out of large brown eyes. He had a rather ugly mouth, large and sensuous, but it twisted upward in a grin. "You don't have to call me that. Not until Father dies, then I'll be 'Your Majesty.' I thought everyone knew that. You must not have learned much from your tutors."

Susanne flushed, but then laughed aloud, "I suppose you're right. What do I call you, then?"

"Oh, just call me Charles until I get—until I get to be king. Then you'll have to call me 'Your Majesty' or I'll have your head cut off."

"I wouldn't like that," Susanne said. He was a rather attractive boy, especially his hair, which was long and black and hung down over his shoulders in thick curls. His eyes were his most notable feature, however, for they were large, luminous, and deep-set. He had very pale skin and delicate hands and seemed, for all his position and responsibility, to be rather cheerful.

"I've never met any royalty before," Susanne said. "I live in the country. My father is Sir Vernon Woodville. My mother and I are here for a visit."

"Can you play cards?" Charles asked abruptly.

"A little."

"Come along. I can teach you some new games. The emissary from France taught them to me." Susanne followed him to another room, where they soon were seated at a heavy mahogany table. Charles dealt the cards with a flourish, and Susanne learned the game quickly, but had judgment enough to lose several times.

"I'm a very good cardplayer," Charles said. "If you are going to be here very long, perhaps you'll get better."

"Are there other children for you to play with?"

"Oh, my brother, James, but he's only six and no fun at all." Charles studied her for a moment, then said, "Come along, let's go get something to eat. I'm hungry."

Susanne followed the self-assured young man straight into the kitchen, where all the cooks at once went into a frenzy of bowing. One woman produced a plate of cakes, which Charles took without so much as a thank you.

"Come on, we'll go sit outside," he said. When they had left the kitchen he led her to a low wall that enclosed an orchard full of fruit trees of all sorts—apple, pear, and cherry. Sitting down, he said, "Here, these are good. They make them especially for me."

Susanne took one of the cakes, nibbled it, and found it to be delicious. "It must be nice to be the Prince of Wales," she said with a wistful smile. "Everyone has to do exactly what you want."

Charles stared at her for a moment then shook his head soberly. "I suppose so, but it gets a little lonely sometimes. How old are you?" he demanded.

"Thirteen."

"Is that all? You look older. I would have thought you were at least sixteen or seventeen. You're very pretty." He reached out suddenly and held a strand of her blonde hair in his hand. "I don't like ugly people."

"That's too bad for them." Susanne smiled, amused by his frankness. "They can't help it, I suppose."

"No, but I don't have to like them." He continued to caress the hair and said, "You have such fine hair. I wish I had blond hair. Mine's black and coarse."

"No, I think you look very nice."

Charles released the hair and picked up another cake. He stuffed it into his mouth, chewed it for a moment, then said, "Did you have lots of friends where you grew up? Friends your own age, I mean?"

"Not too many. I don't have any brothers or sisters, either."

"Well, perhaps you get lonely like I do sometimes, but when I get older I'll be able to have my own friends, and that'll be different." He stared at her and said, "Are you for the parliament or for the Crown?"

Startled, Susanne said, "Why, for the Crown, of course. My father's loyal to the king, and so is my mother. What a strange thing to ask."

"Not really." Charles stuffed another piece of cake into his mouth and swallowed it whole. He seemed to eat without even tasting anything, for no pleasure showed on his face at the delicacies he was devouring. "The parliament doesn't like my father. He has to fight them all the time. They don't understand that he's the king and that God put him to rule over England. He's God's deputy on earth, and anyone who strikes at him is striking at God."

Susanne listened with interest, noting the way the prince repeated the words, much as she had repeated the school lessons that had been drummed into her: without any real emotion or conviction. "Of course we must all serve the king."

This simple assurance seemed to please him, and he said, "There'll be a party tonight. Will you be going?"

"If my mother says so."

"Good! I'll be there, too. We'll have something to eat there. They always have lots of food at these things." He jumped up and ran off without another word.

Susanne watched him go and finally rose and went back toward her room, saying slowly, "Well, I haven't met a king yet, but I've met someone who *will* be king one day."

<hr />

The banqueting house in Whitehall was like nothing Susanne had ever seen before. The huge room had ceilings thirty feet high and, halfway up, a balcony in gleaming white and gold that encircled the room. Chandeliers that seemed to be made of pure gold hung suspended, and as the young girl looked up at them she gasped. "Look at that, Mother!" she said, pointing at the ceiling.

Lady Woodville looked upward and smiled; she had been to Whitehall before. "Yes, beautiful, isn't it." The ceiling was composed of massive paintings surrounded by filigree of finely wrought carvings, which also were painted white and gold. "Those were done by a man called Rubens, a very famous painter from the Netherlands."

Suddenly Susanne looked down and saw a small group enter from the massive doors at the north end of the room. "Look, Mother! Is that the king?"

"Yes, try not to stare too hard. It might embarrass the royal family." She smiled and took the girl's arm. "Look, he's going to greet some of the guests. Come along."

She led Susanne to the line of waiting guests, and soon the king and the queen paused in front of them. "Ah, Lady Woodville," the king said.

"Your Majesty."

Susanne barely heard her mother's response. Her eyes widened at the sight of the queen, for Henrietta Maria was a striking woman. Her dark royal blue dress was made of silk, the puffed sleeves adorned with fine embroidery. A double row of pearls fell across the queen's shoulders and over her breast, and a golden tiara studded with diamonds was fixed atop her regal head. She was approximately the same height as the king, who was a very short man, Susanne saw with surprise. She had thought all kings were large and tall and strong.

The king noted her fascination with his wife and smiled. "Ah yes, and this young lady? W-Who is she?"

"My daughter, Your Majesty," Lady Woodville murmured. She curtsied deeply and Susanne imitated her.

The king wore a doublet of dark green with knee breeches to match. A white lace collar rode high under his chin, accentuating the pointed beard. His legs gleamed with white hose, and his feet were adorned with a pair of scarlet velvet slippers. He wore a large green stone ring on his right hand, but no other jewelry.

At that moment, a voice said, "I—I know her, Papa." The Prince of Wales had suddenly come to stand beside his father. "Her name is Susanne. We're friends, although she can't play cards very well."

Charles had a pair of moody, dark brown eyes, and he turned them now on Susanne. "Well, I'm glad that you've e-entertained the prince. He grows lonely up here." The royal family stood there, speaking for a moment, then moved on down the line.

The banquet that followed was not ornate, insofar as food was concerned, as Susanne had expected. She was sitting there eating her food, when a young woman across from her, who had been regarding her, said, "Not very satisfying for a hungry young girl."

Susanne looked up startled and met the gaze of a young woman of perhaps eighteen or nineteen. She wore a brilliantly colored emerald gown, which was cut low in the front and showed off an attractive figure. Her jet-black hair fell over her shoulder in long ringlets, and there was something about her eyes and lips that caught Susanne's attention. She smiled. "I'm Francine Fourier. We haven't met yet."

"I'm Susanne Woodville." Susanne looked at the young woman and said, "I've never been at court before, but we have better food than this at our house sometimes."

Francine smiled and said, "But you don't have the king and queen and all these handsome young courtiers at home, do you?"

The two young women sat there talking across the table, then they rose and began to walk around the room. Francine Fourier spoke to everyone, seeming to know most of the people there. Finally she turned and studied Susanne carefully. She smiled almost covertly and said, "This is the place to find a husband."

"A husband! Oh, I'm not looking for that, not for a long time."

"You're thirteen? Well, that is a little young, I suppose. Perhaps next year, though, you'll be a little bit more anxious."

Susanne lifted her chin. "I won't be anxious." Then she blurted out, "Are you looking for a husband?"

Francine threw her head back and laughed. She reached out and took the girl by the hand and shook it playfully. "No young woman will admit to that, but that's what we all do."

"Not I!" Susanne said adamantly. "If I ever get married, some man will have to come hunt me."

A rather playful light shone in Francine's eyes and she said, "I trust it shall be that way. The trouble is," she added thoughtfully, "the handsome ones that come are not always the ones you need or want."

"What do you mean?"

"I mean, handsome is fine, charming is very nice—but money is the essential ingredient."

Susanne stared at her new friend in amazement. "You mean you wouldn't marry a man who wasn't rich?"

"Certainly not! I like nice things too much for that." She saw the shock in Susanne's eyes and smiled at her again. "Don't pay any attention to me. I don't want to offend you, but I suppose every young woman here wants to find a rich, charming, hand-some husband. Look! Let me point out the candidates. See over there? That's Marcus Stovall, the eldest son of Lord Stovall, who happens to be rich as Croesus. He could have any woman in the kingdom he wanted."

Susanne looked across and saw a rather ill-favored young man with a beaky nose, a dissatisfied air, and a spindly body. He looked wholly unappealing. Her eyes widened in disbelief as she turned back to her companion. "You wouldn't marry *him,* would you, Francine?"

"Whyever not?"

"He's so . . . homely."

"I'm not marrying someone to look at them," Francine shot back. "Despite what you say, in a few years you'll be thinking about the kind of man you will marry. I suspect your mother already is doing so. Now, let me point out some of the other prospects." She went around the room, indicating several other young men. Finally she said, "Look! Now, there is a youngster you might be interested in. A bit young, not over sixteen, I'd say, but a handsome lad. I don't know him."

Susanne looked through the crowd and suddenly exclaimed in astonishment, "Why, I know him!"

"What's his name?"

"Gavin Wakefield. We're good friends. Come along, I'll introduce you. I didn't know he was coming."

Francine allowed herself to be towed along through the ballroom, and as soon as they were in front of the young man, Susanne said at once, "Gavin! I didn't know you were coming here!"

Gavin blinked in astonishment. "Why—why, I didn't know you were here, either. I just came with my uncle, Cecil Wakefield." He turned and introduced the tall young man standing beside him. "You know Susanne Woodville, I believe, Cecil?"

Gavin's young uncle bowed and said, "Certainly, but she was only a baby the last time I saw her. Is your family here?"

"My mother is, but Father isn't well." Susanne turned and said, "This is Miss Francine Fourier."

Francine extended her hand, and the elder Wakefield took it and kissed it gallantly. Then she extended it to Gavin, who shot an agonized look at Susanne, then awkwardly performed the same action.

"You didn't tell me you had such a handsome friend, Susanne," Francine said with a smile.

Cecil laughed aloud. "I assume you refer to my nephew. There, you see—" he slapped Gavin on the back—"I told you the ladies at court would find you attractive."

Gavin shuffled his feet nervously and tried to think of something to say, but nothing came. He was, in all truth, awed by the court and had said not half a dozen words since they had entered Whitehall. Finally he said, "You didn't come back for me to take you fishing again, Susanne."

"I wanted to, but Mother wanted me to stay at home." Susanne was staring at Gavin. She had only seen him in workaday clothes and was unprepared for how tall he had grown in the year that had passed since she'd last seen him. At only fifteen he was almost as tall as his uncle, and his slight form had filled out quite nicely so that he was lean, but muscular. "You look very nice," she said.

"So do you," Gavin mumbled, and at that moment music began.

Francine said, "Time for a dance." She reached out at once and said, "I choose you, Mr. Gavin Wakefield."

Gavin lifted horrified eyes to her face. "Oh no, I couldn't!"

"Of course you can. You've taught him how to dance, I trust, Susanne?"

"Not really."

"Well, I shall then. Come along."

For the next twenty minutes, Gavin found himself occupied by Francine—and before long he was transfixed. Though this beautiful young woman was older than he by at least three years, she did not make him feel so. He did know the steps of the dance despite his Puritan upbringing, for his uncle Cecil, who was not quite so strict a Puritan, had taught him some of the more formal dance steps. As he sailed about the room, Francine smiling at him, he felt intoxicated by her perfume and dazzled by her beauty. More than once as they danced she squeezed his hand, and by the end of the dance, Gavin was completely filled with admiration for the young woman.

Later, as the evening wore on, Susanne grew impatient. "Is he going to stay with her all the time?" she asked Cecil with irritation.

He looked across the room where his tall nephew and the shapely young woman were speaking together with great animation. A speculative light came into his eyes and he said, "Do you know that young woman well, Susanne?"

"I just met her tonight."

"I suspect she is in the market for a husband." He saw the startled look Susanne gave him, and he laughed. "Did she tell you that? I've seen the type before. A beautiful thing, isn't she? I suspect she comes from a poor family and is in the market for an older son of some Lord—someone such as our young Mr. Gavin."

"Why, she's so much older than he is."

Cecil looked over and shook his head. "That doesn't seem to matter, does it? Look at him! I think the poor lad's fallen in love. I've heard of that all my life, the old 'love at first sight,'" he said and took a swallow of his drink. "Never saw it, though. I'll have to get him out of here as soon as the meal is over—and before he asks her to marry him."

The evening wore on, and later Francine and Gavin found themselves seated at a smaller table with Cecil and Susanne. Susanne, who was not having a very good time, suddenly smiled. "There's Henry!" she exclaimed, pleasure on her face.

Gavin looked up instantly and frowned. Francine noted it and said, "Henry? Who is he?"

"Henry Darrow," Susanne said.

"The son of Lord Darrow?"

"Yes." Susanne stood up and waved, catching the attention of the tall man who had come in.

He came to them at once and smiled. "Ah, Susanne. I was looking for you."

She returned his smile, then presented him to those seated at the table. "You know these gentlemen, but I don't think you've met this lady."

Darrow had changed as well. He was eighteen now, tall and

already a self-assured young man. When his eyes fell upon Francine they at once lit up, and when they were introduced he said, "Charmed. You're new at the court, I take it, Miss Fourier."

"Yes, I'm here on a visit. Won't you join us, Mr. Darrow?"

Darrow looked over at Gavin and Cecil, and a smile tugged at the corners of his lips, "If these gentlemen do not object." He did not wait to see if they did, but seated himself.

Time passed and Darrow dominated the conversation. Before long the music began to play and he at once rose, saying, "I claim the honor of this dance, Miss Fourier."

"Certainly." Francine rose and the two moved away.

Cecil glanced at the scowl on his nephew's face and said, "Don't frown, my boy, he'll bring her back again." His brow furrowed in thought. "Darrow . . . Darrow . . . ah yes, I recall the fellow." He slanted a look at Gavin. "You two never have gotten along, have you? Why is that?"

"Oh, they had a fight several years ago," Susanne said. "They should have gotten over it by now. It's silly!"

Gavin looked at the couple dancing and said, "He's arrogant. I've never liked him."

Susanne studied Gavin's face and thought, *Why, he's jealous of Darrow. He's just met Francine, and already he acts as though she should only spend time with him.* She looked across the room and studied Francine Fourier. As young as she was, she had seen enough to know what the woman was. *She's a huntress,* she thought. *She as much as said so.* Then she said quickly, "They look charming together. I believe Francine would be a good wife for Henry, wouldn't she?"

"I don't know why you say that," Gavin said with a sullen anger. He got to his feet and said, "Come on, Cecil, let's go home. I've had enough of this foolishness."

"Sit down, boy!" Cecil knew his nephew very well. "We have things to do, people to meet." He looked around the room.

"These are the people the king trusts, and, since he invited us here, we'll behave like gentlemen."

Gavin slumped down in his chair. "All right—but it seems like a waste of time."

It certainly does! Susanne echoed with feeling as she watched Gavin follow every move Darrow and Francine made.

⚜

The next morning Susanne met Gavin for breakfast. She had insisted on it. As they ate, she said, "You were upset last night. Henry always makes you angry."

"I suppose I've got to learn to get over that."

"I know what it was." Susanne put down her spoon and looked across the table. "You were jealous over Francine, weren't you."

Gavin looked at her and suddenly summoned up a superior smile. "When you grow up, you'll understand more about these things."

Even as he spoke, Susanne's chin went up in the air. "Grow up! I *am* grown up! I'm thirteen years old! That's a woman—almost."

Gavin grinned broadly at her. "I'll throw you in the river next time we're home like I did last year, the last time we went fishing. As long as I can do that, you're a little girl."

Susanne grew angry. "You're no gentleman, Gavin, and don't you ever throw me in any river again! I won't go with you anymore!"

Gavin saw that he had hurt her feelings. He rose and went over to her. "Don't be angry," he said. "I'm just in a bad mood. We're friends, right? Always?" He squeezed her shoulder and said, "Do you remember that time at your house, when you told me that? Come now, do you remember?"

Susanne felt his hands on her shoulders and she rose to face him. "Yes," she said quietly, "I remember. I've never forgotten."

"Do you remember what you did?"

"No!"

"I'll bet you do," Gavin teased. "You said, 'We'll always be friends, won't we, Gavin,' then you reached up and kissed me, right on the cheek." He smiled fondly at her. "It embarrassed me to death then."

"I don't remember that," Susanne lied, for she remembered it well. She remembered every meeting she'd ever had with Gavin.

"You were a little girl then, but I see you're not one any longer. Are you sure you don't want to give me one more kiss before you become a completely grown-up young woman?"

Susanne studied him for a moment, then glanced around quickly to be certain they were alone. For a moment she did feel like a young girl again, but something told her those days were gone, that she and Gavin would never wander through the fields again, that she would never shriek with delight as she pulled a wriggling trout in. A sadness came on her as she realized she was losing something precious.

Now looking up at Gavin, so tall and earnest, his eyes smiling down at her, she said good-bye to her childhood. Reaching up, she tenderly placed her hands on his face and said, "We'll always be friends." Then she kissed his cheek and held him for one moment. Finally, she stepped back. "That's the last kiss you'll get from me," she said firmly. "You'll have to find another little girl to play with."

Gavin looked at her, surprised at the seriousness in her voice. He took in the sweet, oval face, the well-formed figure, the blonde hair and the dark-blue eyes, and he too felt some strange loss. He said quietly, "It's a shame things have to change. We can't ever be what we were before." A thought came to him and he shook his head. "Your family and mine don't agree on politics." He looked anxious and said, "But we mustn't let that ever come between us, Susanne."

She shook her head, fighting the urge to give in to the tears that stung at her eyes. She forced a smile. "No," she said, "never that, Gavin. Friends always! That's what we'll be."

Twelve

A LIFE FOR A LIFE

Winter had come suddenly, almost as though it passed autumn with a single step, and the bitter cold that shrouded the entire countryside brought a shudder to Christopher Wakefield as he marched up the steps to the house. He stomped his feet, moved his stiff lips in a wooden gesture, and muttered, "Lord, but it's cold out here!" then entered the house. Slamming the door behind him, he moved down the Great Hall, then paused thoughtfully and turned and made his way to one of the rooms that lay at a right angle to the main part of the house. Knocking on the door, he called out, "Mother, are you there?" Hearing a response, he entered and walked across to where Allison Wakefield sat beside a cheerful fire. Spreading his hands to its warmth, he flexed his fingers and shook his head.

"We could lose stock if it keeps on getting colder, Mother."

Allison rose and moved to the large table that held several pewter vessels. Choosing a cup, she poured it full of a pale amber liquid, then moved to the fireplace, picking up the poker that was resting in the blaze and inserting it into the liquid. It hissed and an aromatic smoke began to rise. She held the cup out to her son. "Here, have some of this, Chris. It'll warm your insides."

Chris took the warm drink and he sipped it, blinked at the heat, then carefully took a swallow. "Ah, that's good," he said. He sat down and leaned back, watching his mother as she resumed her seat and sat there looking at him. "It's almost Christmas," he said idly. He was examining her carefully, thinking that, even at the age of seventy-five, she was still alert and healthy. In a time when many died in their middle thirties, he was grateful every day for the survival of his mother. She had filled up the void that his father's death had left years ago, and he treasured her greatly.

"What's troubling you, Son?" Allison inquired abruptly. Her eyes were still dark blue, almost violet, and formed a startling contrast to the corona of silver hair that framed her face. Her once-smooth skin now bore fine lines, but her lips were still firm, as were her cheeks, and she smiled at his blink of surprise. "You never could hide anything from me, could you, Chris?"

"No, I couldn't." Chris leaned back, took another sip of the cider, and said, "It's Gavin. I'm worried about him. What do you make of him? He acts like he's drunk or gone daft." A gust of wind entered through the long narrow window, keening shrilly for one moment, then falling silent.

"Why, he's lovesick. I'd think you'd know that. You were troubled with it often enough when you were his age."

Giving her a half-embarrassed smile, Chris shook his head. "I thought it might be as much. I'm worried about it. Do you suppose it's one of the maids around here?"

"No, nothing like that, although I suppose he's chased them enough, just as you did."

"Do you have to keep bringing that up, Mother? That was all a long time ago."

Allison folded her hands and touched her chin with them in a familiar gesture, and her eyes grew dreamy as she thought back over the long years of her life. "I remember," she said softly, "when the Spanish Armada appeared. I stood on the shore and watched it, knowing somehow that Robin could be there and could be killed, as his uncle, Thomas, was killed. I remember the death of Queen Elizabeth and the funeral. I remember so many things." Her voice had grown quiet and a silence fell on the room, broken only by the soft murmurings of the wind outside and the crackling of the fire. She looked over at her son, affection in her face, and said, "And I remember you, the many years I prayed for you, that we prayed for you, Robin and I. Now, don't drop your head, Chris. That's all over. You've been a fine son to us after God did a work in your heart." She straightened up and said, "The boy's got a sweetheart. That's all there is to it. He's almost sixteen, what do you expect? Be patient with him. Hopefully he'll outgrow and survive it, along with the other pains of growing up."

They sat there and talked for a long time. It brought peace and comfort to Chris's heart and mind to talk with his mother. She was an island of stability in a world that seemed to be rocking. Finally he rose and went over to kiss her fondly. "You're good for me," he said. "I don't know what I'd have done without you all these years. I suppose you're right about Gavin. At his age you can't tell a youngster much, so I won't try." He left the room then and went to his own.

He found Patience inside sewing and grinned at her. "Are you ever going to get that blasted thing finished?" he said. "You've got enough baby clothes there for a battalion."

Patience looked up at him. She was swollen with the child that was soon to come. Her face had a pale cast, almost ashen, and the smile, when it came, was not as easy as he was accustomed to. He knew she was in pain, although she never complained.

She answered him serenely. "You can never have too many baby clothes."

He went over, sat down beside her, and kissed her soft lips. "I'm worried about you," he said. "You haven't been well."

"I'm an old woman," she said, stroking his cheek. "Thirty-seven is too old for most women to have a child." She saw the worry in his eyes and said, "But I will be fine. Don't worry, dear, it will be all right, you'll see. Now, tell me where you've been."

She listened to his talk, enjoying simply being with him. Their marriage had been a union of heart and spirit, for they had been, from the time they gave their vows, not only lovers but the best of friends. There had been a few stormy, turbulent times of course, times that threatened to rock their marriage, but there had never been a thought on either one's part that the marriage would not last. "We may quarrel," he had said, "but when it's over, we don't have any choice. God has joined us, and we are together forever."

She had always liked that attitude, and now she sat there enduring the discomfort of her advanced pregnancy and enjoying the sound of his voice. At the age of fifty, Christopher Wakefield was as handsome as he had been the first time she had seen him. His chin was still strong and pugnacious, his auburn hair still thick, though it now had silver threads. He was ever lean and trim, far more so than most men half his age. He was, she knew, a man among men. And he was hers.

When he spoke of Gavin, she smiled. "He came in a moment ago. He wants to go to visit at the Woodvilles."

"The Woodvilles? What for?"

"He's always liked Susanne, you know. They've been like brother and sister." She picked up the sewing, fingered the fine stitches for a moment, then put it down. "I suspect he wants to talk to someone about this sweetheart that's so mysterious. He can't talk to you or me—I guess we must seem as ancient as the pyramids. But he and Susanne, young as she is, have always been great friends."

"Shall we let him go?"

"I think so, just for a short visit. He'd be back in time for Christmas."

Later that afternoon, Chris decided to give Gavin an opportunity to talk. Hoping that he would say something about what was troubling him, he went to the boy's room, knocked, and when no one answered, he stepped inside, half expecting to find him asleep. The room, however, was empty. He turned to go, but paused when he saw a sheet of paper on the floor. Bending over, he picked it up and saw a fragment of poetry written on it. Chris noted as he read that the handwriting was not Gavin's. The title was provocative, and he read it aloud: "'To the Virgins to Make Much of Time.'" He stirred his shoulders restlessly and stood there reading the poem silently:

Gather ye rosebuds while ye may,
Old Time is still a-flying;
And this same flower that smiles today,
Tomorrow will be dying.

The glorious lamp of heaven, the sun,
The higher he's a-getting,
The sooner will his race be run,
And nearer he's to setting.

That age is best which is the first,
When youth and blood are warmer;
But being spent, the worse and worst
Times still succeed the former.

Then be not coy, but use your time,
And while ye may, go marry;
For, having lost but once your prime,
You may forever tarry.

"Father—"

Chris twisted his head with surprise and saw Gavin standing there. Guiltily, he said, "Oh, I came in looking for you—and found this on the floor."

Gavin took one look at the paper and his face turned red. "Yes, a friend of mine sent it to me. I don't suppose you're much interested in poetry."

"I'm interested in this," Chris said. He looked at the paper again and shook his head. "I don't know much about poetry, but I know I don't agree with what this poem says."

"Why not? I thought it was well written."

"Well, if I read it correctly, it is telling us to have all the fun we can because we'll soon be dead."

Gavin's lips drew together in a tight line. "I wouldn't put it exactly like that."

"How would you put it, then? Look what it says. 'Use your time and while ye may, go marry, for having lost but once your prime, you may forever tarry.'" He lifted his eyes and met his son's gaze. "I don't mean to be prying, Gavin. Here." As the boy took the paper and held it, standing there looking awkward, Chris felt a pang of guilt. "There's nothing worse than prying into another fellow's secrets," he said quietly. "I read much worse than this when I was your age."

"It was written by a man called Harrick. John Winters sent it to me. He writes once in a while." Gavin looked down at the lines and said, "I suppose you're right. That's pretty much what it says, all right."

"Not a very good philosophy, Son," Chris said. "I ought to know, for it was mine for many years. Until I met your mother—and God. 'Have all the fun you can,' that was my battle cry. If I'd gone on like that I don't know what would have become of me. The world always makes that sound like such a grand idea, though." He stood there helplessly, wondering how to bridge the gap between himself and the young man. Gavin might be only fifteen years old, but at this point of life, the lad was far from him. "Your mother tells me you want to go to the Woodvilles for a visit," he said.

"If it'd be all right with you, sir."

"I don't see why not, except your mother's not well, you know. The child could come very soon. I'd hate for anything to happen—"

A worried look crossed Gavin's face. "Do you think she'll be all right?"

"I hope so. I pray God she will, but one never knows about these things." He tried to put a cheerful note in his voice. "Tell you what, go ahead, ride over to the Woodvilles, but don't stay more than a few days. I'd rather have you here. You're a comfort to me, Son."

His words seemed to cheer Gavin. He smiled at his father. "Yes, sir, I'll be back within two days."

"Be sure you talk to your mother before you go. She'd like that."

Gavin made his plans at once, and early the next morning he was in his mother's room. His father had already left. They'd had an early breakfast, and he came to give his mother a farewell. "I won't go if you don't want me to," he said. "I know you don't feel very well."

"I'll be all right," Patience said. "Now give me a kiss." She kissed him firmly and said, "Go, have a good time with Susanne. You two are such great friends."

A pang smote Gavin and he started to speak, stumbling over the words, "Well—Mother—it's not exactly—"

"What is it, Gavin?"

Gavin looked down and bit his lip. "I'm not going because of Susanne. Not really. There's a young woman—I didn't tell you about her, but I met her at the palace. Her name is Francine Fourier."

"I see." Patience studied the boy carefully. "And you like her very much, don't you?"

"She's the most beautiful thing I've ever seen, Mother."

"I see. A girl about your age, I take it?"

"A little older. But that doesn't matter." He stumbled over his words, telling her, with his eyes bright, how much the girl had come to mean to him. When he was finished, he said, "I know I'm young, but I've never met anyone like her."

Patience Wakefield had too much wisdom to tell the boy the complete truth. She had listened to his tale carefully and sorted out even from his fragmented story what was truly at work. *The girl is older than he, and yet she fawns over him. There is usually only one reason for such attention from an older woman, and that is that she is from an impoverished family and out to find a wealthy husband. But I can't say any of that to Gavin.*

She touched her son's shoulder. "Go ahead, Gavin, have a good time, but promise me this, that you'll spend some time with Susanne. It would be easy for you to forget her, you're so taken with this other girl. But she is your friend, so that wouldn't be right."

"I promise, Mother." He hesitated, then said, "I hate to go with you so close to your time, but I'll be back and we'll have a great Christmas, won't we? I'll bring you something pretty, you'll see." He kissed her again and then was gone.

Patience sat there for a moment, then rose to go to the window. She was almost dizzy with pain. She held on tightly to the window, biting her lips, standing there long enough to watch him dash out of the house and spring into the stirrup of a horse that Morgan held for him. She began to pray, "God, don't let him fall into the snare of a strange woman." She watched as he disappeared, the horse sending a flying storm of fresh snow as he sailed down the road. Then she turned and went to the bed and lay down carefully.

⚜

"Be careful now, don't fall through the ice."

"Hold on to me! I'm afraid, Gavin." Susanne and Gavin stood

in the fresh fall of snow that came up to her knees. It was a light snow, the flakes being laid down in a feathery blanket, and one kick sent the tiny showers of sparkling fragments glittering in the sun. The two had walked down to the river and now stepped out on the frozen surface. Gavin had arrived early that afternoon and at once had made his peace with Susanne. It had not been easy for the young girl, but she was sweet-tempered and unable to hold a grudge.

"I bet there are some big fish down there," Gavin said, stomping his foot on the hard ice. "Maybe we could break a hole later and see what we could catch." He looked over and said, "We'd probably better get back to the house. You're almost frozen." He reached over and thumped her ear, and she yelped. He grinned at her playfully. "You ought to wear some kind of a wrap around your head. Your lips are blue."

"So are yours," Susanne snapped back. She reached up and pinched his nose, and when he yelped, she said, "There! That'll teach you to keep your hands to yourself."

"Let's go down to the wide spot and see if we can see any deer tracks," he said. "I bet I could get one now, if your father would let me use his bows."

The two of them followed the serpentine tracings of the river and arrived at the wide spot in the river. They looked carefully for tracks and found none, but it didn't seem to matter. The sun was a dim, pale yellow globe in the sky and a silence reigned over all the earth.

"It's so quiet," Susanne whispered. She looked around at the woods, which were transformed into a fairyland of glistening white, and said, "There's no birds singing, no sound at all. Just us, Gavin."

He smiled down at her fondly. "I'm glad to be here," he said. "Maybe we can't go fishing, but it's fun all the same."

"Can you stay over for Christmas?"

"No, I'm afraid not. Mother's expecting a baby, you know. I'll have to be back for that." He hesitated, then said, "Francine's here, isn't she?"

Susanne gave him a quick glance. "Yes, she came a week ago. How did you know?"

Her question seemed to embarrass Gavin. "Oh, she wrote me a letter," he said. "Let's go back. I'm freezing to death out here and hungry, too."

As they trudged back through the snow, Susanne seemed strangely quiet. She had spent a great deal of time with Francine, and the older girl's views on marriage and womanhood disturbed her. She glanced over at Gavin, admiring the brightness of his eyes. He had odd-colored eyes, as much gray as blue, and even now she could not tell which they were. He had a long face, with high cheekbones, and his straight nose had been broken the year before, giving him a rather tough appearance. He towered over her, and she knew he was two inches over six feet. As much as she hated to admit it, Gavin occupied her thoughts a great deal. Now she asked cautiously, "Did you come to see me, Gavin . . . or Francine?"

"Why, I came to see all of you," Gavin said quickly, apparently bothered by the question. "I don't get to see many people, always stuck at home. My father's gone to the parliament most of the time, so I've done more and more of the overseeing since he's been gone. With Morgan, of course." They were silent for a moment, until he looked at her suddenly and said, "I dreamed about you last week."

"You did? About me? What was it?"

"Oh, it wasn't much, really. I dreamed I was walking down a road. It was dark and night was closing in, and I heard all kinds of frightening noises out in the woods." He thought of the dream and shook his head. Gavin had long realized he had a mystic streak. Morgan told him it was from his Welsh ancestry. He dreamed often and asked his mother what the dreams meant. Her common response was, "They mean you're Welsh. Don't make too much out of them."

"What was the rest of the dream?" Susanne asked.

"Why, I felt like I was getting lost and the road seemed to be disappearing and the bushes were scratching me in the face. You know how it is when you get lost in the woods. I began to get afraid and I called out and then I looked up and saw a little light, far off. I began to run to it and the closer I got, the brighter it got, and you know what I found when I got there?"

"What?"

"Why, it was you. You were holding a candle in your hand, and when I came up close you held it high and said, 'There, you found me. I'll always have a candle for you when you get lost.'"

Susanne smiled. "I think that's a nice dream. I'm going to write it down so I won't forget it, and you do the same thing."

He laughed at her. "You do a lot of writing down in that journal of yours, don't you? I'd like to read it sometime."

Susanne's face flushed. "You can read some of it, I suppose."

"You don't have any secrets from me, do you? I thought we were friends."

"Even friends have secrets," she said primly.

The two of them arrived back at the house. After they changed clothes, it was time for supper. There was a fine meal that night. The Yule log had already been laid across the hearth. It was expected to burn for four days, but Gavin had no eyes for logs, for Francine came toward him, holding out her hands. "Gavin!" she said, her eyes glowing with pleasure. "I'm so glad to see you again!" She looked at him and said, "My, you're so tall. I keep forgetting. Or maybe you've grown."

Gavin flushed and shrugged his shoulders. "I'm glad to see you. I got your letter. I came as soon as I could."

"Well—" Francine shrugged her shoulders—"it was dull in

London, and when the Woodvilles asked me to come, I knew I'd get to see you. So, now, we're going to have a wonderful Christmas, aren't we?"

Gavin dropped his head, his face going glum. "I can't stay," he mumbled. He explained his mother's condition and said, "I wish I could, but I need to be there."

"Of course you do," Francine said. "Naturally you'd want to be with your mother at such a time." She took his arm, then led him in toward supper, where they ate the wonderful food, including a pigeon pie, a boar's head, mincemeat pie, plum porridge, and saddles of mutton. Gavin ate heartily but hardly tasted a bit of it, so caught up he was with Francine's eyes and red lips.

After supper they sang madrigals and carols, and it was Lady Frances Woodville who came to him and said, "I'm glad you came, Gavin. Susanne gets lonely." She looked over to where Francine was talking to her husband and said, "Miss Fourier is very beautiful, isn't she?"

"Yes, she is."

"All the young men are after her. I don't know which one she'll choose. I rather think it could be Henry Darrow." She watched the light die out of his eyes and somehow seemed pleased by it. "He's got plenty of money, and he'll have the title." She hesitated, then said, "Of course, you'll have a title, too, one day, won't you?"

"Not for a long time, I hope, Lady Woodville. My father's lord of Wakefield and will be for many years."

"Well, you are a bit young for her. Henry's just about right, I think." She tapped her rich lips with one forefinger and nodded. "Yes, I think that would do well." She smiled as though pleased with herself and their conversation—and Gavin's discomfort. In truth, she had seen the boy's adolescent love and found a perverse pleasure in probing at him without seeming to do so.

Perhaps all would have been well if Henry Darrow had not made his appearance, but two days later he did come. He arrived in the middle of a masque that was being given by a traveling group of players that had stopped for refuge at the Woodville household. It was not a particularly well-done masque, but at least Gavin was enjoying sitting beside Francine.

Then Darrow entered, and at once the attention seemed to fall upon him. Gavin fought against the irritation that seized him and managed to smile and speak cheerfully to young Darrow. "Good afternoon, sir. I trust you had a safe journey through all this snow."

Darrow shrugged. "It was a hard journey, but the horses were good. How are you, Wakefield?"

"Very well."

It was a short conversation and the end of ease for Gavin. Throughout the masque he sat in silence. Afterward, when there was a gathering in the large library, he sat silently while Darrow told stories of his encounters in London, mostly involving the rich and famous.

Susanne watched carefully, painfully aware of Gavin's jealousy of Darrow. She watched as Francine played the two men against each other, carefully and deliberately provoking the ill feelings they harbored.

The next afternoon, trouble broke out. The entire group was gathered in the great hall, snacking after an outing in the snow, when Francine looked up on the wall and said, "Are those your swords, Sir Vernon?"

"Family heirlooms, Miss Fourier," Woodville said. He reached up and picked one off the wall. "They're called foils by the French, I believe."

A calculating look crossed Darrow's face. He said lightly, "Perhaps you and I could have a try at it? Just a little contest, sir?"

"Oh, I'm too full of dinner for that," Woodville protested.

Lady Frances Woodville said abruptly, "Weren't you telling me that your father had been giving you instructions in fencing, Gavin?"

"Oh yes, father's very good, too."

"Why then, you could give Henry a bout, couldn't you?"

There was nothing much that Gavin desired less than to engage in any kind of activity with Henry Darrow. He opened his mouth to refuse, but Francine said, "Yes, by all means. Let's have a bout."

"Oh, I hardly think it would be fair," Darrow said. "After all, the boy hasn't had the advantage of a good instructor."

A start of anger at the implied insult ran through Gavin. "My father's as good as any Frenchman," he snapped. "I'll be glad to have a bout with you, sir."

The idea caught on at once, and Sir Vernon immediately took over. "I will be the judge," he said. "Here, we must put tips on the ends of these foils. We wouldn't want anyone to get hurt." He picked another foil off the wall, then adjusted the leather tips that covered the points. Finally, he took a third foil down for himself. "Now, are you ready?" When Darrow said, "Oh yes, quite," and Gavin nodded, his face a little pale, Woodville said, "Very well, we'll have three goes at it. The winner will be the best at two out of three. Now, begin."

Gavin turned his body to one side, bent his knees, and extended the thin-bladed rapier to touch the blade of Henry Darrow. He liked fencing very much indeed, and his father had been a good teacher. He kept his guard well up, and the two men circled the room, casting shadows on the walls. They swayed back and forth, their feet making swishing noises as the ring of steel sounded in the stillness of the air.

The expressions on the faces of the spectators were varied. Vernon Woodville liked nothing better than fencing, and he circled the two, constantly watching for a foul. Lady Woodville's lips curved upward in a strange smile, her face somewhat reminiscent of a cat watching a bird it was about to devour.

Susanne, clearly, was frightened. She knew fencing was a dangerous sport, made even more so by the bad blood between the two opponents. She glanced over at Francine, anger in her eyes and dislike flowing through her as she saw the young woman watching with a strange, hungry expression on her face.

The feet of the fencers slid across the stone floor, and the steel of their blades pinged and clashed repeatedly. Soon, however, Darrow's experience and greater strength won out, and his blade touched Gavin on the chest.

"A touch! I do confess, a touch!" Gavin cried out.

"That's enough, isn't it?" Susanne spoke up nervously.

"Oh no, that's just the first touch," Francine protested. She smiled at Gavin and said, "I'm sure Gavin will do much better next time."

Her words inspired him, and when the two fencers squared off again, Gavin took a chance and slid past the quivering blade of Henry Darrow to touch the breast of the larger man. Anger ran across Darrow's face, and he would have plunged on, but Sir Vernon stepped up and thrust his sword between the two. "One each. Now, this time will tell the master."

Something in Darrow's face warned Gavin that the next session would be fierce. True enough, as soon as Sir Vernon stepped back, he was suddenly besieged by a furious rush from Henry as the young man pressed him backward. It was all Gavin could do to keep the flashing sword at bay, and he backed up steadily.

Suddenly Susanne saw something fly through the air and roll to her feet. She cried out, "The button has come off of the foil!"

Gavin had seen the small black cushion slide off Darrow's blade and expected the man to stop, but Darrow did not. He pressed forward, coldly determined. *Why, he's going to kill me!* The thought sent a shock through Gavin as he met the cold, pale eyes of his opponent and saw death written there. But he had no more time to think.

Sir Vernon was calling out for a halt, but Darrow seemed not to hear. Suddenly Gavin backed into the wall and a fleeting slash by Darrow's blade caught him against the right cheek. A sharp pain ran down his face and a scream rang out, though Gavin never knew from whom. Darrow drew back his blade to make a final plunge, and in desperation, Gavin broke every rule his father had taught him. He leaped forward, toward the blade, and gave a fierce shout that so startled Darrow that he lowered his blade for one moment. Seizing that opportunity, Gavin reached out with his left hand and struck at Darrow's wrist. The hit was so forceful that the foil in Darrow's hand fell to the ground, and at once, Gavin extended his blade to touch his opponent's throat.

Darrow's eyes went blank, his mouth fell open, and Gavin could see his enemy realize himself to be a dead man. For one moment, Wakefield felt a fierce, unreasoning desire to plunge the blade into Darrow's throat—and then a cry rang out.

"Enough! Enough!" Sir Vernon's voice was stern and almost angry, and at once Gavin stepped back and began to tremble.

It was Susanne who ran to him then. "Your poor face," she moaned. "Someone help us!"

Gavin felt the blood dripping down, and Darrow said in a tense voice, "Sorry, I didn't know the button had come off."

Gavin knew that was a lie, and at once he lifted his eyes and saw the hatred in the face of the other man.

Francine said quickly, "Come, we'll have to do something with that wound."

"Yes," Sir Vernon said. "That's a bad cut. It's going to leave a scar."

Gavin did not argue, but as they treated the cut, cleansing it with warm water, he watched Susanne, who was weeping. "Don't cry," he said, "it's not all that bad."

She clung to his hand, saying, "It was awful. I thought he was going to kill you."

Gavin looked across the room, where Darrow was talking with Francine. "He meant to, I think."

"Stay away from him," Susanne said. "You don't know what he's like. He's got an awful temper. He beat a horse to death last year, just because the horse failed to make a jump. Stay away from him, Gavin."

Gavin stared at Darrow, then shook his head. "I don't think that will be too hard," he said, his voice bleak. "I will be at Wakefield. And he . . ." Gavin took in Francine's expression as she talked with Darrow. "He will be in a more enviable place."

⚜

Gavin lay in bed, unable to sleep, thanks to the throbbing pain in his cheek. Finally he threw back the covers, dressed, and went to the study. Lighting a candle, he went to the liquor cabinet and pulled out a bottle of brandy. Perhaps the amber liquid would dull his pain and enable him to get some rest.

A soft step sounded behind him, and he turned, startled.

Francine stood before him, her face filled with concern. "I didn't mean to surprise you," she said in a low tone. "But I couldn't sleep. I was so worried about you!"

Gavin merely started at her, uncertain what to say. She moved across the floor, coming to lift her soft hand to his face. "I'm so sorry you were hurt," she whispered. "I fear it was all my fault."

Gavin's throat grew thick. He could smell the musk-like perfume of the young woman and he said huskily, "It's all right. No harm done."

The candle was burning over on one table, guttering quietly, as Francine gently stroked his face. "I feel very bad," she whispered. "Will you ever forgive me?" Without waiting for an answer, she reached up and pressed her lips to his.

A sudden fire blazed through Gavin's veins. His arms went around her, and he held her tightly.

Francine murmured softly to him, running her hand through his hair, stroking his neck. She whispered, "You're so brave, Gavin,

211

so confident. You're the kind of man a woman can trust to care for her forever."

His senses swam with the heady feeling of holding her close, and he touched her face, then went to kiss her again. But she suddenly pulled away, whispering, "Oh, I can't permit this." She tried to draw back but he fiercely drew her closer, ignoring her feeble, half-hearted struggles.

"I love you, Francine," he gasped and sought her lips again.

She let him kiss her, then put her hands against his chest and pushed away. "I must go," she said. "This isn't right." He caught at her wrist and would have held her, but she drew back with a strength that surprised him. "Later," she whispered, "later." She touched his cheek, the uninjured one, and whispered in a husky voice, "You're such a sweet young man. I can't trust myself with you any longer."

Then she turned and left the room. The door closed and Gavin stood there, transported. *She must love me,* he thought, *or she wouldn't care so much about my being hurt!*

The next morning at breakfast, Susanne seemed withdrawn. Whenever he tried to talk with her, she barely acknowledged him. Gavin grew more and more concerned, for he could find no reason for her offhanded behavior.

What he did not know, indeed, could not have known, for she would never have told him, was that Susanne had seen Gavin leave his room. She had been restless last night, unable to sleep because of her concern for Gavin. When she heard soft, cautious footfalls in the hallway, she had thought someone might be in need of help or direction. She had opened her door just in time to see Gavin going down the stairs. As she stood debating whether or not to follow him, she heard another door open and saw Francine slip out of her room to follow Gavin. Saddened, angry, and humiliated by the sight of what she assumed was an assignation, she had closed her door at once and slipped back into her bed, telling herself that her tears were out of disappointment in her friend and nothing more. Now her anger burned hot against Gavin.

Later, he tried to talk to her again, but she answered only in monosyllables. "What's wrong?" he finally asked. "Why are you angry with me?"

For a moment he thought she would just walk away from him again, but she looked up at him, and he saw her eyes were bright with some deep emotion. When she spoke, her voice was cold and distant.

"I saw Francine go to meet you last night," she said.

Nonplussed, Gavin felt his face begin to redden. "Why, that was nothing," he said quickly. "She just came to tell me she was sorry that I was hurt." He looked at her and saw that her face was pale and her lips were drawn tightly together. Impatient at feeling so bad for having done nothing wrong, he drew himself up and spoke with a condescending tone. "You'll understand these things when you get older, Susanne. You mustn't be angry with me."

Deep hurt sprang into her eyes at his words, and suddenly he was filled with the certainty that this argument was not like any they had had before. Somehow, this was much worse. And yet, he didn't know what to say or do to make things better. "I'm sorry," he said finally, "but I love her and that's all there is to it."

"She doesn't love you," Susanne said stubbornly.

"Why—what makes you say that?"

Susanne wanted to tell him what she knew. That she had heard from Francine's own lips that she was out for a husband with money, but even at her youthful age she knew that a man would never believe a thing like that about one he thought he loved. "I just know, that's all." She turned and walked away—and somehow Gavin felt he had lost something very precious.

It was two hours later, when Gavin was out for a ride, that he saw a horseman coming down the road. For a moment he thought it was simply a traveler, then something familiar attracted his attention. He strained his eyes, then straightened his back. He touched the horse with his spurs and galloped forward.

"Morgan!" he said when he reached the other man's side. "What's wrong?"

Morgan's face was pale with the cold, and his lips were blue. The horse was heaving great sighs and seemed to be almost ready to collapse. "It's your mother," he said shortly. "We've got to get back at once!"

"Is she dead?" Fear shot through Gavin. "She's not dead! Tell me she's not!"

"Not yet, but she's bad. We'll have to have fresh horses."

Gavin went at once to Sir Vernon and explained the situation.

"Of course, my boy. Have the stableman give you the best horses we've got. You can return them later. I hope all goes well with your mother. Pass my good wishes along to your dear father."

As Gavin left the room, he encountered Francine. She smiled at him and said, "Well, you're looking—" And then she halted, seeing his troubled expression. "What's wrong?"

"It's my mother. She's very sick. I've got to go."

Francine came to him at once. "I'm sorry," she said, concern in her eyes and voice. She leaned against him, and as the scent of her musk surrounded him, he longed to bury his head in her fragrant hair and let her soothe his fears. There was something in this woman, something powerful that drew him. She leaned forward, kissed him, and said, "Let us know how things go and if I can do anything to help you or your family."

Gavin held her for a moment, then left the house with quick strides. As he and Morgan went to their horses, he saw Susanne, who was returning to the house from a walk. He looked at her and said, "I have to go. My mother's very sick."

Susanne blinked and all of her anger seemed to leave. "I'm sorry, Gavin. I wish I could go with you. I hope she'll be all right."

She put her hand out to him and he took it and held it in both of his and said finally, "Always friends, aren't we, Susanne?"

Tears came to her eyes and she nodded. "Always friends."

Emotion filled him, though he did not stop long enough to analyze it. Without thought, he leaned forward to kiss her hand, and her face flushed red. He mounted his horse and, with a last glance at Susanne, whirled the animal and galloped toward home, Morgan beside him.

Susanne stood there, watching the two men pound off across the hard, packed snow. Then she turned and went back into the house.

Gavin had little recollection of the trip back to Wakefield. Morgan drove his horse fiercely, and Gavin followed suit so that by the time the two had arrived at the house, both animals were almost dead. "Go to your mother, Gavin," Morgan said huskily, as the two dismounted. "I'll care for the mounts." Gavin turned at once and ran up the steps.

Even before he got to the front door, it opened. His father stood before him, and one look at his face told the boy everything.

"She's gone, Son," Chris said. He reached out, pulled the boy in through the door, and then held him by the shoulders. "She died with your name on her lips."

Gavin felt as though the heavens had fallen. He could not think, could not speak. More than anything in the world, he wanted to weep, but he could not. He stood there stunned, a roaring in his head and a grief blacker and more bitter than anything he had ever experienced rising up in him.

"Come along, Son. She's gone, but you can say good-bye."

Chris turned the young man around and noted that he was like a man who had been shot—his eyes were blank and his expression fixed on his face. Gently, the father led the son to the room where a still form lay.

Gavin did not even notice that his grandmother sat across the room close to a fire, holding a bundle on her lap. He moved stiff-legged and looked down on the face of his mother. He studied the still features and tears rose in him, but he fought them back. Finally, after what seemed like a long time, he felt his father's hand on his arm.

"Come over here, Gavin."

He turned and followed his father to where his grandmother sat.

"This is your brother, Amos," his father said.

Gavin watched as his grandmother moved the cloth back, and he looked down at the infant's face. For the life of him, he could not say a word, and he turned and walked out of the room silently.

"I wish he'd been here," Allison Wakefield said. "He's going to blame himself. Go to him, Chris."

"Yes, Mother."

Allison held the baby in her arms, chortling to him and laughing at his attempt to reach her. He had his mother's eyes, but everything else was like Christopher. At the age of three months, Amos had grown strong and well. Allison held him up and kissed one fat cheek, then handed him to his nurse, a stocky woman named Martha Simms. "I think he needs changing, Martha."

"Yes, Lady Wakefield." Martha picked the baby up and tossed him in the air. "Aren't you a big, fine boy, though." She was as proud of Amos as if he were her own and said, "Isn't he a beautiful child! I never saw one prettier. Too pretty for a boy—should have been a girl."

Allison smiled, but there was a sadness in her. She rose slowly.

Arthritis ravaged her knees, and she moved slowly with the use of a cane. As she left the room she thought, *Yes, he's a beautiful child—and his father and brother don't even know it.*

Chris looked up as he heard the sound of his mother's cane out in the hall. He rose and opened the door for her. "Come in, Mother," he said, waiting till she had crossed the room to ask, "Is everything all right?"

He expected her to sit down, but Allison turned to face him. "No, it is not!"

Chris frowned in concern. "Why? You're not ill, are you?"

"Ill? Yes, I am ill, with disappointment—in you."

Christopher Wakefield blinked with surprise. "With me? What have I done?"

"You have a baby son, a delightful child named Amos, yet you seem to have completely forgotten him."

Chris bit his lip, his eyes clouding over with emotion. "I know I've been remiss, but I'm so lonesome, Mother! I miss her so much, and every time I look at the baby, I think of Patience."

Allison stared at her son. When she spoke at last, there was an uncharacteristic sharpness in her voice. "Son, you're bitter at losing Patience, aren't you?"

"I—I suppose I am. It's so hard."

"A life for a life," Allison said. "Sometimes that's the way it is. God, for his own reason, allowed Patience to be taken from us. But Christopher, he left part of her here. Patience lives in the babe, even as she lives in Gavin." Her old eyes glowed then, and she put her withered hand out and touched her son's arm. "God has spoken to me. He said the very spirit of Patience will be in this boy, but he needs you."

Chris put his lips together in a firm line, shut his eyes for a moment, then shook his head. "I know, I know, you're right."

"You are father *and* mother to him, Son. He needs you very much."

Christopher Wakefield made a resolve that struck deep in his heart. "I've been selfish, Mother," he admitted, "but it will be different now. God's been speaking to me about this thing. Come! Let's go see my son."

"That's my good son," Allison said, and the two walked slowly down the hall, the strong man helping the frail woman. When they reached the room where the child was, the nurse looked up with surprise. She was even more surprised when the master of Wakefield took the child from her and held him close, saying quietly, "There, Son, you and I are going to get to know each other better."

The nurse threw a quick glance at her mistress, who merely smiled through the tears glimmering in her eyes.

<hr>

Gavin had watched in silence as his father spent more and more time with his baby brother. The months since his mother's death had not eased the guilt that ate at him, and he was sleeping badly. His dreams were dark and ominous, and he spoke to no one about them.

Then one day Morgan came to him and said, "You're taking this wrong, lad. Losing your mother, I mean."

"What do you know about it?" Gavin snapped at him.

"Why, I lost a mother of my own, didn't I? Do you think I don't know what it is? Devil fly off, boy! You're not the first to lose a loved one and you certainly won't be the last. We each must eat his peck of dirt."

"It's none of your business," Gavin retorted angrily, walking away. He spent the rest of the day alone, sinking deeper into self-pity. When he roused himself enough to stop for a visit with his grandmother, he was shocked by her greeting: "You're filled with guilt, Gavin. What have you done?"

Gavin stared at her. She had always been able to see things that others couldn't, and now, suddenly, he felt she knew all about him. That was impossible, of course. "Nothing," he said.

"What have I done that you would lie to me?" Her voice was calm, but Allison's old eyes were wise. "You think I don't know guilt when I see it? What did you do? Is it just that you were not here when your mother died?"

"No!"

"Well, what then?" Allison watched the struggle on the young man's face and said gently, "Tell it, boy! If you bottle things up they go sour, and sooner or later, you die of it. But if you tell it, the burden becomes easier. You think I'll love you the less because of something you've done? The more fool you!"

"Grandmother, you don't understand. . . ." And then Gavin blurted out the whole truth, confessing to her what he believed was his horrible sin. He told about his love for Francine and ended by saying, "All the time my mother lay dying, I was caught up in pursuing some silly woman."

When he was finished, Allison rose from her chair. He was standing in front of her, tall as a tree, it seemed. She put her arms out, and he grabbed her, feeling her frail bones. She held him, and when his body began to tremble, she said, "Weep, my lad. A strong man must know when to weep. If he doesn't, he'll die of his own strength."

Gavin Wakefield did weep. The two sat down on the couch, and he put his face in his hands and wept like any schoolboy. Finally, he lifted his tearstained face and said, "I was wrong. I should have stayed here. I was wrong to leave."

Allison began to speak. For a long time she spoke of love and what it was like, and finally she said, "Do you think your mother wouldn't understand? Why, she loved you more than she loved life. Her last words, almost, were of you. She told me how much she loved you and how proud she was of you."

"But I should have been there, I shouldn't have—"

She cut him off with a nod. "You did wrong, but Christ died for our wrongs, you know that. Now, don't let this shame become a bitterness that poisons you." She removed a handkerchief from her pocket and wiped his tears away. "Terrible things lie ahead for our nation. I am sure of it. I will not be here to see it, Gavin. I must go to be with my Lord soon." She met his eyes. "But your brother will be here. He'll be trapped in the middle of these times that are going to try all the Wakefields, all of England. Help him, Gavin."

"What can I do?" he said in confusion.

"Love him, take care of him. If you want to make up for anything you may have done to your mother, pour your love into this child."

Gavin stared at her, then nodded slowly. "That's what you talked to Father about, isn't it?"

"Yes, the two of you are all Amos has. Will you do it, Grandson? Will you trade your guilt for love?"

Gavin nodded. "Yes, I promise. I will love Amos and be a friend and a brother to him."

The two sat there for a long time, and as the shadows grew long, Allison said in her heart, *Thank you, God, for giving this lad a hope.*

END OF PART TWO

Shadow

1 6 4 1 **Part** / **THREE** 1 6 4 5

of War

DEATH BE NOT PROUD

A ragged line of high-flying blackbirds moved across the iron gray sky. Oliver Cromwell looked up at them, squinted his eyes against the pale sunlight, then lowered his head and considered the mound of earth, still raw and broken. At the head of the mound a slab of white marble rose. He read the words silently: *Allison Wakefield, beloved wife of Sir Robin Wakefield. 1564—1641: Thou God seest me.*

The enigmatic words struck Cromwell, and he asked, "What is that, Christopher? 'Thou God seest me'?"

The gusty wintry wind blew a lock of Chris Wakefield's auburn hair over his brow. Brushing it back, he looked at his friend and said, "It was a Scripture that my mother loved. My father said she lived her life by it."

"I don't recall it. The Old Testament?"

"The book of Genesis, the sixteenth chapter."

The two men were standing in an ancient graveyard that flanked the Wakefield parish church. Some of those who slept beneath the green-moldered stones had come to England from foreign shores, and time had almost obliterated the names and dates that once were deeply etched in the stones. One stone, however, was still sharply new and unstained; it bore the name of Allison Wakefield. The mound was rounded by rains, and sharp emerald tongues of green had pierced the earth and had grown thick with the passage of months. Now the grasses had been turned sere and gray by the winter's iron breath.

"I'm afraid I'm being terribly dense, my friend, but what does it mean?"

Chris, his eyes fixed on the stone, was silent for a moment. His mother's death had left a void in his life, and when he answered Cromwell's inquiring glance, his voice was soft. "It's the name that Hagar gave to God."

"Ah yes, I remember now!" The long face of Oliver Cromwell grew thoughtful. He knew his Bible very well indeed and mused, "When she ran away from Abraham and Sarah and was lost in the wilderness." He drew his brows together in a knotty expression, then asked, "But it's a strange Scripture for an epitaph. There are others more victorious, I would think."

"Mother said she desired to live her life under the eye of God." A smile came to Chris's lips as an old memory came to him. "Once she caught me doing something I shouldn't, and I said it didn't matter, that no one had seen me. She quoted that Scripture, and I never forgot what she said. 'Christopher Wakefield—I live every second of my life under the eye of God. He is watching all of us, and we had best give thought to what we're about.'" The crows overhead uttered raucous cries, and Chris looked up, then shook his head. "She lived like that, Oliver. Under the eye of God."

"She was a handmaiden of the Lord. I've never known any woman more saintly."

"Aye, she was that."

Cromwell gave a compassionate look at Chris, then said, "They leave us, don't they, good friend?"

Chris nodded, then said heavily, "Come along. I know you have to get back to your home."

The two walked slowly across the frozen ground, and when

they were inside the house, Cromwell said abruptly, "I have something for you. Let me get it."

Somewhat surprised, Chris waited, using the poker to prod the fire until it sent up myriad yellow and red sparks. He sat down, thinking of his mother. *How empty the house is without her! You wouldn't think one small, frail woman could leave such a hole in a house—or in a man's heart!*

Cromwell's voice brought him out of his reverie. "Here it is. I wasn't certain I'd brought it." Cromwell entered the room, holding a single sheet of paper. He came over to stand beside the fire, then turned and faced Chris. "Do you know of Rev. John Donne?"

"Why, certainly, Oliver. Dean of St. Paul's, wasn't he?"

"Yes, and a fine preacher, despite his high-church views. Do you know his story? No? Well, he was a young prodigal, a worldly sort of chap indeed. But he found God and became a great preacher, who, strangely enough, was a poet as well."

"What's strange about that?"

"Why, ministers have better things to do than make rhymes, I think!" Cromwell saw the smile on Wakefield's lips and looked embarrassed. "I do read a little poetry, but only *good* poetry," he said. Holding up the paper he nodded firmly. "Like *this* poem. It's really a sermon, and I thought of you when I read it. It's from one of his Holy Sonnets. Shall I read it for you?"

"Of course!"

Cromwell was a rough enough sort of man, caring little for dress or fineness of manners, but he had a wonderful voice and a flair for the dramatic. Throwing his head back, he began to read:

> *Death be not proud, though some have called thee*
> *Mighty and dreadful, for thou are not so,*
> *For those whom thou think'st thou dost overthrow,*
> *Die not, poor Death, nor yet canst thou kill me.*

From rest and sleep, which but thy pictures be,
Much pleasure, then from thee, much more must flow,
And soonest our best men with thee do go,
Rest of their bones, and soul's delivery.
Thou art slave to fate, chance, kings, and desperate men,
And dost with poison, war, and sickness dwell,
And poppy, or charms can make us sleep as well,
And better than thy stroke; why swell'st thou then?
One short sleep past, we wake eternally,
And death shall be no more; Death, thou shalt die.

Cromwell's voice fell silent, and he said gently, "I love those lines, 'One short sleep past, we wake eternally, and death shall be no more.' He hesitated, bit his lower lip, then said regretfully, "Perhaps such as this is out of order in your grief, Chris."

"Not at all! Not in the least, Oliver!" Chris nodded emphatically and reached out for the paper. "May I keep this?"

Relief washed across the man's homely face, and he said, "I'm happy if it gives you comfort. I'm just a rough fellow, you know, and it's a—a *delicate* thing, speaking to one about loss of a loved one."

"You have a loving spirit, Oliver. I, of all men, should know that. One of my finest memories is of the time when you came to stand beside me and said you were my friend. You were just a child. Do you remember that?"

"Very well! Very well, indeed!" A smile creased Cromwell's lips, then disappeared. "I'm such a moody fellow, and there were times when I suffered such terrible doubt."

"Yes, I know. But that's all in the past, isn't it?" Chris was well aware that Oliver Cromwell had been diagnosed by one doctor as being *melancholicus,* which meant simply that as a young man Cromwell had been moody and unhappy. Robin had told Chris that what the young man was going through was known as "the dark night of the soul," which meant he felt God had forsaken him. "You don't still have those awful struggles with doubt, I trust?"

"No, thank God!" Cromwell's voice was fervent and he slapped his hands together. He walked back and forth, seeming to put his thoughts in order, then said, "Do you know, Christopher, I think that struggle was part of what God had to do in me to convert me. . . ." He spoke rapidly, his face intent and his eyes almost burning as he related how God had finally run him down. "It was a time of great joy for me, and I thank God for his mercy to a poor sinner!"

"No man loves God more than you, Oliver." A thought came to Chris, and he rose and moved to the oak desk that had belonged to his great-grandfather, Sir Myles Wakefield. Opening a drawer, he shuffled through some papers, then said, "Ah, here it is—" Turning to Cromwell, he smiled, saying, "You wrote this letter back in 1638. I've never read it without thinking of what God has done for you."

Cromwell lifted an eyebrow, took the letter, and began to read:

I am willing to honour my God by declaring what He hath done for my soul. Truly no poor creature hath more cause to put forth himself in the cause of his God than I. The Lord accept me in His Son, and give me to walk in the light, and give us to walk in the light, as He is in the light. He it is that enlighteneth our blackness, our darkness. I dare not say, He hideth His face from me. He giveth me to see light in His light. One beam in a dark place hath exceeding much refreshment in it. Blessed be His name for shining upon so dark a heart as mine! Oh, I have lived in and loved darkness and hated the light. I was a chief, the chief of sinners. This is true; I hated godliness, yet God had mercy on me. O the riches of his mercy! Praise Him for me, that He hath begun a good work should perfect it to the day of Christ.

Cromwell's eyes were wet with tears as he lowered the sheet of paper. "I had forgotten this. It brings back that glorious time when I first found the Lord Jesus!"

The two men talked for over an hour, and Cromwell finally said, "I must go, Christopher!" As he put on his cloak and fur hat, he said, "You will be at Westminster when parliament meets? John Pym made it a point that you should come."

"What is the urgency?"

"He distrusts the king."

"Do you, Oliver?"

"Why, I honor the king, but I fear he has designs to reestablish popery and destroy Puritanism." Cromwell shrugged, his craggy features turning heavy. "The king feels that since he is God's anointed deputy on earth, that *whatever* he does must be of God. I do not think such is the case."

"What is the king doing now?"

"He's gone to Scotland, making up to the leaders. After fighting a war with them, he's now seeking their aid. And if he gets hurt, we'll have to fight Scotland!"

Chris walked with Cromwell to the door, clapped him on the shoulder, and said fondly, "You've been a comfort to me, Oliver—and I know that's why you came. Not to talk politics."

Cromwell was known as a hard, slashing fighter to his enemies. He could be ruthless when he chose, but to his friends and family, there was a no more loving and caring man. He smiled, and a gleam of humor touched his greenish eyes. "That son of yours, he behaving himself?"

"Better than I did at his age!"

"That's not saying a lot, is it?" Cromwell shot back, but he touched the arm of his friend with a sudden gesture of affection. "I hear good things of him—and that he's interested in some young woman."

"Puppy love, at least I think so. I'll keep an eye on him.

Good-bye, Oliver, and thank you for coming." When Cromwell was gone, Chris turned back to his study, thinking of the man.

Strange how he can be so compassionate and caring at times, and yet, given the right circumstances and people, he can be hard as a diamond. Nobody knows what to expect of Oliver Cromwell. Not even he himself!

***

"Sir Christopher—could I have a word with you, sir?"

Wakefield, who was examining the foreleg of a tall stallion, glanced up to find Will Morgan standing to one side. Releasing the hoof, he straightened and stepped back. "Certainly, Will. What is it?"

Morgan bit his lip, then said, "It's time for me to leave you, sir."

"What's that?" Chris said in surprise. He had come to depend on Morgan for many things and knew that the Welshman had been a very good influence on Gavin. "Why, I'd hate to think so, Will," he said at once. "Is it a matter of wages? Because if it is—"

"No, sir, it's not that. Ye've been more than generous with me."

Wakefield was disturbed. "I can't spare you, Will—I really can't." The clanging of the blacksmith's hammer rang from across the yard, and one of the maids walked by the open door of the stable, calling out to someone, "I tell yer, it won't do—!"

Morgan stood there silently, his dark eyes fixed on the master of Wakefield. He had learned to trust Sir Christopher Wakefield— no, it was more than that. He had learned to *like* the man a great deal. Being an independent fellow, he did not give his loyalty easily, but in all the time he'd known the master of Wakefield, he'd never seen a dishonest or cruel act in him.

"Have you been mistreated?"

Morgan shook his head. "No, sir, not likely. I like it fine here—better than anyplace I've ever been. But—" He hesitated, then noting the encouraging look on the face of Sir Christopher, he blurted out, "Well, sir, it's family trouble."

"You're not married, Will?"

"Oh no, sir, it's my father, back in Wales, and my sister, Angharad." Morgan clenched his fist nervously, then spread his hands out in a helpless gesture. "You see, it's hard times in Wales, Sir Christopher. The farm was never much. That's why I left and came to England. But my oldest brother died last year. He was the only one of us younger men left, excepting me—so now there's no one to run the farm."

Christopher nodded slowly. "I've heard that there's famine in Ireland, and I suppose that means Wales, as well."

"Yes, sir. It's very bad."

"But can you make the farm pay?"

"I can try."

The answer troubled Wakefield. He shook his head, saying, "I know you'd do it, Will, if it could be done. But from what you say, it sounds like a hopeless situation."

Morgan shook his head stubbornly. "You're probably right, sir, but I have to go. My father is sickly, and my sister needs someone to watch over her."

A thought came to Wakefield and he demanded, "Would they leave Wales, do you think?"

"Leave Wales? For where, sir?"

"Why, they could come here! Plenty of work for two more people."

Morgan twisted his hat out of shape, then shook his head. "It's kind of you, Sir Christopher, but it wouldn't do. I got a letter from Angharad, and she says our father is too weak to work."

"Well, blast it all, Will, bring him anyway!" Wakefield was a man of quick impulses, and the notion that had popped into his head seemed more and more logical. "Your sister, she's old enough to work, to be a maid or something?"

"Oh yes, Sir Christopher! She's thirty now, and a good hard worker. But my father—he's not able to do anything. I don't know how much longer he will be with us."

"Well, you can go get them, Will. I'll pay for the trip. You can take one of the carriages or a wagon. When would you think to start?"

Morgan swallowed and twisted the hat into a contorted form. "I'd start today, sir, God willing." He hesitated, then said in a voice that was a little unsteady, "Sir, it's a fine thing for you to do. I'll work hard to make it up to you."

"I know you'll do that, Will," Wakefield said. He hated being thanked and added gruffly, "Now, get on with you. Come to the house and I'll give you enough money to make the trip."

Will Morgan was an emotional man and for the life of him could not control the sudden rush of tears to his eyes. He wiped them quickly as Sir Christopher walked away, and muttered hoarsely, "And what other man would do such a thing?" Then he suddenly threw his hat at the stallion, and when it struck the animal on the nose, the beast rattled the boards of his stall with a vicious kick. Will struck his hands together with a meaty sound and began to sing lustily.

⚬

"Ah, my d-dear, you look very well."

Susanne had never been comfortable in the presence of King Charles, but she had learned that his formal manner covered a warm spirit. "Thank you, Your Majesty," she answered, making a curtsy. "The queen helps me a great deal with my dress."

Charles smiled at Henrietta Maria. "Your taste is always good, my dear," he said. Lifting his hand, he ran it over his neat mustache in a manner that was almost effeminate. Yet Susanne did not believe there was that kind of thing in the man's nature. He was an excellent horseman and hunter, able to keep pace with most of the more virile members of his court. Susanne had decided that the thing that worked against the king, detracting from his more masculine qualities, was his lack of size and his almost fanatical devotion to fine clothes.

Susanne glanced at the queen, who was wearing a fine silk dress ornamented by Dutch lace at the neck and wrists. "If you were not a queen, you would be a fine dressmaker, Your Highness," she said.

Both the king and the queen gave her a startled glance, then the king laughed aloud. "What a thought!" he said. "M-my Henrietta not a queen but a *dressmaker!* You h-have the m-most curious mind, Susanne!"

The queen smiled as well, for she had grown fond of the young woman. "You are right, Husband," she agreed. Handing her latest baby to a ready attendant, she moved over to give the girl an affectionate hug. "But we are entertained by your wit, Susanne." She moved away to stand beside the king, adding, "We need a little joy with such dark times around us."

Charles took her hand and kissed it gently. "We will see better times. God will not forsake us."

Susanne had carefully noted the affection between the two for some time. As a young woman of fifteen, she was most interested in love—and the couple she now watched intrigued her. She knew that Charles had married Henrietta when she was also sixteen, but he had not been in love with her. He had been under the almost total domination of George Villers, the duke of Buckingham. When the duke had been assassinated in 1628, Charles had been distraught. It had been, Susanne had learned, the tact and understanding of his youthful bride that had comforted him over his loss.

"When the duke died," Henrietta had once said in an unguarded moment, *"we were free to fall in love."*

Now the two were inseparable and gave themselves to their brood of children and to each other with full devotion. Perhaps it was the fact that the two were cut off from others because of their position that they clung together. Susanne was sure it was this isolation that caused Henrietta to bring her into their small circle.

What Susanne did not realize was that the queen was charmed by her beauty, and by her cheerful wit. Her comments so delighted the royal couple that they did not hesitate to include Susanne a little farther into their lives.

"I *would* make a good dressmaker," the queen remarked playfully, smiling at her husband. "And it would be easier than being queen of England."

"T-true, my dear." Charles nodded. "But we must serve where G-God sets us." There was something almost pompous in the manner in which he said this—but Susanne had learned that he meant every word of it. "God sets the dressmakers in the kingdom as firmly as he sets those who rule."

"And does he set men like John Pym and Oliver Cromwell in place?" Henrietta said, her tone growing bitter. "I think the devil must have something to do with that!" This daughter of the French king, Henry IV, was a gentle woman, except where the king and his position were concerned. Then she could become a tigress!

Charles gave her a warning in a most gentle fashion. He was never angry with her, but he was sometimes disturbed by her militant spirit. "We must not l-let ourselves think such thoughts," he said quickly. But then he himself seemed to grow quite disturbed. "We tried ruling without parliament, b-but such a thing is impossible."

"I don't understand, Your Majesty," Susanne spoke up. "Queen Elizabeth didn't have to put up with a parliament."

"No, and she ruled England well," Charles said instantly. "How I would l-like to see those days back again!"

"You will not, I'm afraid," Henrietta said dolefully. "Not with men like Oliver Cromwell sitting in parliament! I can't abide the man!"

Charles sighed, then shrugged his thin shoulders. "We must abide him, unless—" He broke off sharply, throwing a glance at Susanne. Whatever he intended to say, he decided that it would be better said for the queen's ears alone. "I must m-meet with the council," he said. He kissed the queen, spoke in a friendly fashion to Susanne, then left the room.

"He's distraught," Henrietta said, taking a seat on the silk-covered couch. "His subjects never know how many sleepless nights my dear husband must bear over their welfare."

Susanne stood beside the window that looked down on the court. The snow covered the ground, and the air was brisk and cold. She loved changes in the seasons and would have hated to live in a place where there were none.

The queen studied her, noting the well-shaped figure, the thick mane of blonde hair, and the clean-cut features. *She's a beauty—but she's not proud as many would be,* the queen thought. Aloud she said, "Have you seen young Wakefield of late?"

"Why—yes, Your Majesty." Susanne turned to face the queen, her face suddenly alert. "He came to our home last month."

"You two are very close," Henrietta observed.

"He's much closer to Francine Fourier."

"The young French girl?"

"Yes, my queen. Gavin is in love with her."

"She has no position or family, has she?"

Susanne Woodville's dark blue eyes grew moody. "That doesn't seem to matter to him."

The queen, an astute observer of character, had sensed long before that this girl was unhappy. Carefully she said, "He would not be suitable for you, Susanne. Perhaps it is fortunate that he has turned his attention to this young woman."

"Not suitable for me?" Susanne stared at the queen with dismay. "Why not, Your Majesty?"

Henrietta Maria rose and came to stand beside the girl. She was a small woman and had to look up into the dark eyes that watched her. "Because the Wakefields are not our friends, my dear. You must know that."

Susanne, as a matter of fact, was well aware of the gap that grew wider each day between the Puritans and the Crown. She had been lectured on it by her parents, who had warned her that sooner or later there would be a rift between the two groups.

"I can't think of Gavin as an enemy, Your Majesty!"

Compassion touched the dark eyes of the queen, and she felt a rush of affection for the young woman. *When I was her age—I was given to Charles. And there was no one I could tell my fears—*

"You must not throw your life away, Susanne," she said gently. "We women cannot always go where we wish. There is a dark and troubled time coming to England. God will give his appointed rulers the victory. Those such as Cromwell and Wakefield, who are set on going against God's will for our country, will not be blessed."

"Sir Christopher is a good man," Susanne insisted. "He's a man of great faith, and he's so kind . . . and his son is the same."

"No doubt, but he is wrong, my dear." Queen Henrietta Maria shook her head, and a portent of tragedy touched her dark eyes. "God has set my husband as king, and those who do not bow to the Lord's will must suffer for it!"

Fourteen

"I SEE THAT THE BIRDS ARE FLOWN!"

W ell, it is hard to look on it for the last time."
Will Morgan turned to his father, drawing the horses
to a stop. The faded blue eyes of Owen Morgan were
turned to gaze down at the valley beneath the road, which led
upward to a steep crest. Will allowed himself to slump in the seat,
weary to the bone. The trip to Wales had been hard. Now he
thought of how difficult it must be for his father to leave the only
life and land he'd ever known.

"You'll like it in England," Will said comfortingly. "It's a pretty
land."

"I'd thought to rest my bones in that valley, Will." Owen
Morgan's sixty-eight years had worn him thin, and there was a
fragility in his hands and face that spoke of impending death. He
had grubbed at the rocky land, scratching a living out of the soil,
but never gained more than that. He had buried his wife, his two
sisters, and four children in the valley—and now looked as if he'd
rather join them in their narrow graves than leave the hills of
Wales.

The woman who sat behind him leaned forward and gave his
shoulders a quick shake. "Well, now, I'll have none of that! You'll
do well in England—and it's time someone kept an eye on Will!"

Angharad Morgan was a tall woman of thirty, with the blackest possible hair and warm brown eyes. The worn coat she drew about her revealed a well-developed, though somewhat under-nourished, figure. There was a vibrant quality in her expression that drew the gazes of men. She had passed over many offers of marriage, saying, "When God sends a man, I'll have him—but not before!"

Owen turned his face to her, smiled slightly, then nodded. "When did I last take a stick to you, girl? Too long, by far."

Angharad laughed and drew the ancient wool blanket around her father, patting his shoulder affectionately. "Now, see how daft you've grown, wanting to cane your beautiful, well-behaved daughter?" Wanting to take his mind off the hard parting, she said, "Will, how long will it take to get to this place . . . this Wake-field?"

Will understood what she was doing. They had always been close, these two, though he was more than ten years her senior. He spoke to the horses, and when they moved out, he said, "A week, I suppose. We've got plenty of food in the wagon, and if we take a notion, we'll just stop at an inn." He reached out and squeezed his father's thin arm. "Maybe we'll have a drop or two of that brandy you insisted on bringing, eh?"

"Never you mind about that! You're not going to take to strong drink while I'm alive to see to it!"

The wagon jolted over the bony rocks that pierced the thin soil, and, as the morning mists were blown away, a pale sun rose. When it was directly overhead, Will drew to a stop and they had a cold lunch, then forged ahead. Angharad made a bed for her father in the wagon, wrapping him in so many blankets that he protested he would suffocate, but he drifted off to sleep at once. They moved through the forests and fields, the horses laboring at times to climb the steep, narrow roads leading out of the deep-gouged valleys. Other times, though, they moved along at a fast trot.

Finally when the shadows lengthened, Angharad said, "Look,

there's a nice stream, Will." He nodded and pulled the wagon in under a group of tall trees, then they made a camp. Angharad made her father stay in the wagon until Will had a rousing fire going, then said, "Now, get out and warm your toes while I cook us a little bite." Will watched as she helped Owen down and seated him on a padded blanket. "Now, sit you and watch," she said, smiling.

Will cared for the horses, gathered up a large stock of firewood, then sat down and stared drowsily at the fire. The smell of cooking beef roused his appetite, and when Angharad put the plates before him and his father, he said, "Smells good—I'm starved." He almost took a bite, but saw his father watching him. Quickly he said, "Why don't you ask God to bless the food, Father? It's been a long time."

As the fire cracked and the green wood seemed to sigh, the three bowed their heads. Owen Morgan spoke to God in an intimate fashion, much as he would speak to Will or Angharad. "O Lord, thank you so much for this food. It is always your gift when something good comes. Remember us as we travel—and let us not offend you in any way. In the name of Jesus I ask it."

Angharad had cooked juicy steaks and roasted potatoes. When Will cut his blackened potato open, it expelled a steamy breath, and he sniffed it eagerly. The white meat crumbled and he ate it rapidly, burning his hands and his lips in his haste.

"You've not improved your table manners," Angharad said, a smile on her broad lips. "I'll have you for it if you eat like a wolf at my table!" She cut a small portion of her meat, chewing it thoughtfully. "We've had little of this lately, haven't we, Father? Oh, it's so good!"

They ate until they were filled, and then Angharad made a strong tea out of roots she'd dug herself. As the pungent odor of the drink came to Will, he exclaimed, "I've missed your cooking! It will be good to have food that sticks to the stomach!"

They sat quietly, speaking little. Owen was filled with thoughts of the land he was leaving, but expressed no regrets. He had learned that complaining was useless, and he was, in truth, happy to be with his son again. He'd been worried over the fate of Angharad, and now as he looked across the fire and studied the pair who were laughing, he thought, *God has been good—he's sent Will to take care of his sister.* Actually, Owen was surprised to be alive, but he was thankful for this turn his life had taken. It would have been pleasant to have passed on in his homeland, but he was a man who believed in the purpose of God, so he prayed, *God, I would have chosen to come and be with you—but here I am, ready to obey.*

Soon afterward he grew sleepy, and Angharad helped him to bed. She came back and sat beside Will. "He will not see another winter, I think."

Will was not surprised at her statement. He had been somewhat surprised by his sister's gaunt appearance when he'd seen her, but his father's poor condition had truly shocked him. He remembered thinking to himself that his father could not last much longer. Picking up a stick, he poked the fire, then watched as the dancing sparks swirled upward, rising high into the air, seeming almost to intermingle with the glittering points of light far overhead. "I should have come home sooner," he muttered.

When her brother fell silent, Angharad understood that he was grieving over his long absence. Leaning over, she stared into his eyes, then laid her hand on his knee. "You came home in time, Brother. Who knows but that it was God who set you to wandering? I dreamed of that once—and how you came back for us."

Smiling, Will put his hand over hers and squeezed it hard. "You and your dreams! But this time, I think you may have dreamed aright. We will be together, and Father will die with his children beside him."

"This man you work for, he asked you to come for us?"

"Yes. He's the best man I've ever known, Angharad. You will think so when you get to know him."

"Tell me about him, and about Wakefield." Angharad hugged her knees and turned to watch Will's face as he spoke quietly of Wakefield. She was a deeply thoughtful young woman, mystic in nature. Her face was round, and there was a classic look to her features that gave her a typical Welsh grace. She had worked hard all her life, but there was no dullness in her face, nor any stoop in her shoulders. Her lips were molded into a soft curve as she tilted her head to one side, and finally Will saw that she was half nodding.

"To bed, girl, we've got a long journey ahead of us."

They traveled steadily for a week, and once the shock of leaving his home had eased, Owen Morgan seemed to improve. He sat up for long periods on the seat of the wagon, sometimes singing the old songs of Wales, sometimes telling ancient Welsh legends. Will sat beside him, idly lounging and listening carefully. He especially loved the tales of the Morgan clan—and his father was the repository of a host of those.

"Strange that he can't remember what he did with his spoon," he observed once to Angharad. "But he knows the history of every Morgan in our family back for a hundred years."

"Those things are more important to him than spoons." Angharad shrugged. "A spoon is only a piece of tin, but blood is what makes us what we are."

Will had agreed with her and had drawn out more tales from his father. At night the cold drew them to the fire, but by day the sun seemed to smile on them. The bitter cold of December was muted into a milder weather, so that by the time they reached the shire and Will began pointing out landmarks, the temperature had risen steadily.

Finally Will drew the team to a halt and gestured toward the small village that lay in the circling grasp of low-lying hills. "Wakefield," he said. "Your home now."

Owen and Angharad stared at the cluster of houses, marked by rising spirals of wispy smoke from a hundred chimneys. They were on a ridge looking down, and when Angharad had gazed for a moment, she said, "Look, there's a river, just like the one back home."

"More fish in this one," Will said with satisfaction. Turning to his father he asked anxiously, "Does it please you?"

The eyes of the older man were fixed on the scene, and he nodded slowly. "Not as pretty as our valley, but not bad for England."

Will winked at Angharad, for they both were thinking that their father had never before seen a single inch of England, but he said, "You'll like it in the spring. We'll walk some woods together, you and I."

By the time the wagon pulled into the village, the sun, an orange-yellow ball, was half buried behind the low hills to the west. Will drove straight to the castle, and Angharad gasped as she saw the big house. "He must be a king, Lord Wakefield!" A young man on a tall bay horse saw them and came toward them at once. "Is that Sir Christopher?" she asked.

"No, he's the son of the house." Will pulled the horses to a stop and lifted his hand in greeting. "Mr. Gavin, my father, Owen—and my sister, Angharad."

Gavin was wearing a blue doublet and a short scarlet coat made of wool. His rich ash-blond hair escaped from a dark fur cap, and he wore knee-high leather boots. "Welcome home, Will—and welcome to your family."

"Is your father at home?"

"No, he's gone to meet with parliament. But he's given me orders to see that your father and sister are provided for." His horse cavorted and reared, and he struggled to bring him to a halt, saying, "Hold still, Caesar!" When he had the animal under control, he said, "Come along, I have a surprise for you."

As Will slapped the team with the lines and they lunged

forward, he said, "Fine lad! I've had the raising of him, you see. He's lost his mother and grandmother, and his father's gone on politics pretty often."

"How did he get his nose broken?" Angharad inquired.

Will laughed at her. "What a thing to ask! Most women don't mind his broken nose!"

Gavin led the way to a small cottage that lay about five hundred yards from Wakefield manor. Swinging down from his horse, he turned to the wagon and, to Angharad's surprise, put his hand out to her. She colored slightly and murmured as she took it and allowed him to help her down, "Thank you, sir." Then she turned to help Will get her father to the ground.

"Well, here's your surprise, Will," Gavin said proudly. "How do you like it?"

Morgan stared at the cottage in confusion. "But—this isn't for us?" Will stammered. "It's the widow Marlow's house."

"She moved north to be with her daughter. Father and I fought off several others who wanted the place," Gavin said with a grin. "We both thought it would be good for your family."

Angharad stared at the house—a timber-and-wattle structure with a good thatch roof. She took hold of Will's arm and squeezed it. "It's fair beautiful, sir," she whispered, and her eyes glowed at Gavin.

Gavin gave the woman a thoughtful look, then shrugged his shoulders. "Father thinks so much of your brother, he'd have given him the house we live in to keep him here. Now, come inside and see what we've done."

When the three stepped inside, Will gasped, "Why—it's a palace you've made of it, Gavin!" He stared around at the fresh paint and the sturdy furniture, and then said, "It's a home such as I never dreamed of. Do you like it, Father?"

Owen Morgan peered around, his eyes adjusting to the light that filtered through the small window, then nodded. "A haven of rest for a tired old man, sir. I thank you, and will be obliged to see your father and give him thanks as well."

"He'll be gone for a time, but you can be sure he took great pleasure in having the house ready for you." Turning to Angharad, he said, "My father and I are two lonely men in a big house. Would you like to come and help Agnes—that's our house-keeper—make life a little more pleasant for us?"

"I thought I'd be called on to work in the fields," Angharad said. "I'm not used to fine ways, only to simple things."

Gavin liked her attitude. He found her very pretty, and he smiled as he answered, "Those are the best, and you'll find us very simple people." He turned to leave, but stopped at the door and added, "Welcome to Wakefield. It will be your home now."

"I didn't know English lords were so thoughtful," Owen said, cocking his head to one side. "You'd have thought we were important people, the way he and his father have made this place ready."

"I think Sir Christopher and his son think people *are* impor-tant," Will said, nodding. Then he said, "Well well, let's get settled in. I'll bring your things inside, and you can cook your first meal at Wakefield, Angharad."

"God has brought us to this place, my son," Owen said. He smiled warmly on Will, adding, "Like Joseph, who was sent to find a place of safety for his family during the famine, God sent you here before us. I'm afraid I'll have to tell you what a good son you are, Will!"

And Will Morgan dropped his eyes, unwilling to let his father and his sister see the tears that had come to them. "To God be the glory—and none to me," he whispered, then wheeled and left the room.

⸻

In a powder house it takes only one small spark to set off an explosion. Likewise with history, for great events are often triggered by an event so insignificant that only in retrospect can the link between the small event and the cataclysmic result be traced.

The reign of Charles I was highly charged, to a fault, with what might be called "political gunpowder." In 1637 Charles stood at the height of his power, but he made almost every wrong choice a man could have made. That very year he blundered into civil war with the Scots. In 1639 and again in 1640 he planned to invade Scotland, but on both occasions the Scots mobilized more quickly than anyone had dreamed possible. Instead, the Scots invaded England, occupying Newcastle and refusing to go home until the king made a treaty with them—and even forced him to pay their expenses!

Charles had ruled without a parliament, but he was forced to call one, and one that could not be dismissed! This group was led by John Pym, a man determined to uproot the evils of the monarchy. It was Pym, called "King Pym" who had the political steel and genius that pushed the nation into civil war.

Another keg of gunpowder that exploded in Charles's face was the Catholic violence against the Ulster Protestants. The Catholics claimed to be acting on the king's orders, and the Puritans rose up as one man to condemn the king for the deaths of their fellow religionists.

The actions of Archbishop Laud, his efforts to bring about "high church" policy to England, created another explosive matter, and the same spark that began the civil war touched off a religious war between various groups in the country.

But the single spark that ignited the civil war was a document called the Grand Remonstrance.

John Pym was the author of the Grand Remonstrance, which was an enormous, wide-ranging attack on the position of the monarchy as a whole. On the very day that the news came of the massacre of the Ulster Protestants, Pym introduced the document to the Commons.

The Grand Remonstrance was passed by the Commons on November 22, 1641, and was a truly amazing document. Cromwell joined his friends in fighting for the passage of the bill, which only barely squeaked through. Cromwell said to one of his friends, "If the Remonstrance had been rejected, I would have sold all I had the next morning and never have seen England anymore!"

***

"But if we let this pass, my husband, they will next pull the crown from your head!"

Charles stood before the queen, a nervous tic in his right eye—a certain sign that he was in one of his emotional turmoils. When he spoke, his stammer was more pronounced than usual. "B–but we c–cannot arrest the m–men, my dear—!"

Henrietta Maria stood stiffly, her eyes bright with anger. She had been urging Charles to arrest the five members of the House who led the opposition to the Crown.

Charles was more cautious. "My dear, I h–have promised reform in the ch–church. This will b–be sufficient for Pym and his f–followers."

"Why do you think so?" Henrietta demanded. Her well-shaped face, which was usually pale, now flushed with anger. "We know that Cromwell has been urging the parliament to raise an army. What will we do if that happens?"

Charles stared at his wife, struck by her words. There was no standing army or organized police force in the realm. Even the guards' regiments, which protected the king and performed ceremonial functions, were more ornamental than a real fighting force.

Relentlessly the queen went on, taunting Charles with cowardice. "If you do not meet this challenge, you prove that your love for me and the children is a vain, weak thing!"

"It is not so!"

"It *is* so! Those who are plotting against us will not spare me or the children. If you are not a coward, you will cast these rebels into the Tower!"

Pressed on all sides, stressed to the limit, King Charles I made a fatal error. Drawing himself up firmly, he said, "I will arrest them m-myself!"

He summoned three hundred swords, called Cavaliers, and they left the palace at once. As they rode to the House of Commons, Charles revealed his plan of action to his nephew, Walter Fitzhugh.

"But—you cannot enter the House, Your Majesty! Such a thing has never happened."

Fitzhugh was quite correct. No king had ever set foot in those chambers. But Charles was determined. "I will arrest Pym, H-Hampten, Haselrig, Holles and S-S-Strode," he said grandly. "See to it, Nephew!"

The armed force was observed by several sharp eyes, and a message from a lady of the queen's bedchamber sent Pym a timely warning that the king was on his way.

Cromwell was seated next to Christopher Wakefield, listening to a speech, when a note came to the House. John Pym read it, then said in a strong tone, "The king is coming to arrest five members of this house." He and the other four members left at once.

"He'll never dare to do it, will he, Oliver?" Wakefield demanded.

"I think he will." Cromwell said nothing more, but thirty minutes later the doors opened, and the king of England entered the room, accompanied by his nephew.

The members of the House stared at each other in shock. All rose at once, their eyes fixed on the king. The speaker went to the king and knelt before him.

"Mr. Speaker, where are the other members of this body?"

Speaker Lenthall said slowly, his tone a mixture of reverence and defiance, "May it pleasure Your Majesty, I have neither eyes to see nor tongue to speak in this place but as the House is pleased to direct me."

King Charles licked his lips. It had just dawned on him what a terrible step he had taken. In an attempt to make some sort of light matter out of the thing, he muttered, "I s-see that the b-birds are flown." Then he wheeled and left the House.

Cromwell whispered, "The thing is done! There will be no peace in England as long as that man sits on the throne!"

He was an accurate prophet, for London went mad when the news reached the city. Infuriated mobs gathered outside the palace, screaming out threats against the king and queen. Charles and Henrietta escaped from the capital to Hampton Court.

King Charles I, the sovereign lord of England, never saw London again—except when he came to suffer trial and death.

Fifteen

LET SLIP THE DOGS
OF WAR

B ut, Oliver, are you so certain that war will come?" Christopher Wakefield's face was perplexed, and when he received only a stern glance from Oliver Cromwell, he added hastily, "I know it's serious, but surely the king will see the folly of such a thing."

"He sees one thing, Christopher," Cromwell shot back. "He sees the crown of England, and he will sacrifice every man in this nation to keep his station!"

The two men were standing outside the front gate of the Cromwell home, waiting for their horses to be brought from the stable. Sir Christopher Wakefield had arrived shortly after dawn, and the two men had spent two hours in Cromwell's study talking about the problems of state that confronted them. Since the king had invaded the House, Cromwell had been feverishly making preparations for the war he felt certain was coming. He had served on innumerable committees, and when the king had refused to give up control of the militia, the Tower of London, and the forts, Cromwell was among those who offered to finance raising a force to withstand the king.

To counter this, Queen Henrietta Maria departed for the continent with the royal jewels, hoping to raise support for the king.

The country swarmed with rumors of war. Many preachers of

the Parliamentarian view delivered vitriolic sermons urging war. One such sermon, Rev. Stephen Marshall's call for war, was preached up and down the country. Chris Wakefield had heard the original speech, which was built on a verse in the book of Judges: " 'Curse Meroz,' said the angel of the Lord, 'Curse its inhabitants bitterly, because they did not come to the help of the Lord, to the help of the Lord against the mighty.' " Marshall equated the crime of the people of Meroz—which was the failure to join in a battle—with the refusal to support the Parliamentarian forces in the struggle against the Crown.

Now, as the grooms brought Cromwell's and Wakefield's horses forward, Oliver asked suddenly, "What's the date, Christopher?"

"Why, August 14."

Cromwell swung into the saddle. "Come along. We've got work to do." He spurred his horse, and the two men rode side by side down the dusty road.

"What's the work, Oliver?" Chris asked, seeing that Cromwell was so occupied with his thoughts he seemed to have forgotten him. Wakefield had grown accustomed to this behavior from Cromwell, where the man seemed to become lost in his thoughts.

Chris's question jolted Cromwell back to the present, and he looked at his friend and responded, "Do you remember our talk about the king's plan to take the silver plate from Cambridge and Oxford?"

"Yes, to finance his army."

"Well, word has come that he's doing just that." A grim frown pulled Cromwell's face into a knot, forming the fierce expression that had intimidated many who opposed him. He shrugged his shoulders, adding, "We'll put a stop to that, eh?"

"We've got the men for it, I trust. You've done a fine job, Oliver. Your troops are the finest in the land."

Cromwell spurred his horse forward, riding like a centaur, his strong body moving to the motion of the horse. He had raised a small cavalry, and they had proven to be excellent soldiers. But he frowned and called to Christopher, "We are few, and I've heard that Prince Rupert has joined the king. Do you know of him?"

"No, never heard of him."

"He's a Cavalier, well enough! He's the nephew of King Charles—German-born and one of the most able cavalry commanders in Europe, it's said. I'm glad we're not going to meet *him* this morning!"

"Where *are* we going?"

"Why, the king has sent one of his troops under a Captain James Dowcra to lift the treasures from the universities. But we'll see to that!" Spurring his horse, he galloped ahead, and soon the two men drew up in front of a troop of armed horsemen. He greeted the officers and held a short council.

"We know that Dowcra will be coming along the Huntington Road. We'll strike from two sides." He had pinned a paper to a tree, and now he quickly gestured as he spoke. "I'll come from the east with half our force. Sir Christopher, you will come from the west." Excitement was in his gray eyes as he spoke. "We'll be the nutcracker, and we'll crush them like a walnut!" The officers laughed, and when Oliver had made certain that the orders were clear, he pulled his hat off and began to pray. He did this naturally, without ceremony. Every man there knew that Oliver Cromwell felt himself to be the servant of God in what was to come. When the prayer was over, he said simply, "We have committed ourselves to God, now let us do our duty!"

Wakefield assumed command of half of the force and followed Cromwell as he led the column down the quiet lane of Anglia. The birds were trilling loudly and the fields were loaded with a fine harvest. When they reached a turn in the road, the two groups separated, taking cover behind the huge yew trees that bordered the road.

Chris at once commanded his men to dismount. "We'll rest

the horses for now. And prepare yourselves, men, so that when we hit, you will give them all you have!"

The action took place in less than an hour. Cromwell's spies had been accurate in every detail. An outpost had come galloping in, his face red with excitement, shouting, "They're coming!"

Chris called out, "In the saddle, men! And remember, wait until Colonel Cromwell strikes!"

It worked like an exercise in a military tactics textbook. As the unsuspecting captain led his horsemen down the road, he sat tall and confident in the saddle, sure no one would dare strike the king's army. When Cromwell's men burst forth with full force from out of the trees, the king's men were thrown into total confusion. Many of them never drew their swords, and those with muskets had no time to unload the cumbersome weapons.

Chris saw Cromwell's men strike the column and yelled, "Now! Charge the enemy!"

It was Wakefield's first battle, and it was over so quickly that he was a little shocked. In less than ten minutes from the time his men struck the bewildered forces of Captain Dowcra, it was over. Five of the Royalist troops lay dead in the thick dust of the road, while many others bore minor wounds. Chris had lost one man and had taken a nasty cut on his right forearm. When Cromwell saw it, he was concerned. "See that you take care, Christopher," he urged. "When a wound like that goes bad, sometimes the arm goes with it."

Captain Dowcra was downcast with shame. He had fought valiantly himself, but there had been no chance. "You attack the king's force, Colonel Cromwell?" he demanded angrily. "You will suffer for it."

"Be content, Captain," Cromwell said, all the wild light of battle gone now that the action was over. "You will not die in this war that is to come. You'll be in prison, but that is preferable to death."

"I think not!" Dowcra said, shaking his head. He was a proud man, and the defeat had humiliated him. But he still had spirit enough to say, "Wait until you try this rabble against the trained troops of Prince Rupert! Then you will have a taste of defeat!"

Afterward, when the prisoners had been sent to confinement under a lieutenant, Cromwell and Chris spoke of the battle.

"It was scarcely a battle," Cromwell admitted. "More of a skirmish."

"The men fought well, Oliver."

"Very well indeed; still, I doubt that Prince Rupert will allow himself to be so easily taken." He shook his head, thoughtful and grave. "The Cavaliers have the advantage of us, Christopher. They are from the aristocratic class and, like yourself, have been riders and hunters all their lives. Our men will come from the lower classes. They know a plow better than a sword." Then his eyes glowed and he struck Chris a blow on the shoulder, exclaiming, "But God will make them good soldiers, will he not?"

"Indeed he will!" Chris agreed. Then he said, "If you have no immediate need of me, Oliver, I must return to Wakefield." He ran his hand over his jaw in a nervous gesture. "I'm worried about my son, Amos. It's hard to raise a young child and fight a war at the same time!"

"Find a good nurse for the boy, and see to that arm," Cromwell counseled. "I fear you will be gone from your home much in the days and months to come. You're a bonny fighter, Christopher, and I need all of your like I can find. Go now, and God give you wisdom with young Amos!"

***

Owen Morgan had settled into the cottage at Wakefield with an ease that surprised both Will and Angharad. At the breakfast table, over their porridge, Will mentioned it. Taking a steaming spoonful of the dish, he chewed carefully. "You've settled in, Father. It was easier for you to leave Wales than I thought."

Owen tasted his porridge, added a little cream, and ate noisily.

"A place is a place." He shrugged. "It was good of the Father God to give us a home."

"I'll say amen to that!" Angharad poured a cup of milk for herself, then sat down to eat. She had picked up a bit of needed weight in the months they had been in the cottage and was looking better than Owen had ever seen her. "I'm worried about Sir Christopher," she announced. "It's a battle he went to, you say, Will?"

"I don't know that for certain, but when Cromwell sends for a man to join the troop, fighting is likely."

Owen said suddenly, "He's fine, Sir Christopher. I saw him last night."

"You *saw* him? But he's with the troop—!" Will broke off suddenly, remembering how it was with his father. Many times the elder Morgan had "seen" someone in dreams and visions. More than once, Will remembered, his father had calmly announced that he had seen one of the relatives who lived far away. One time Owen had had a vision of a man at three in the morning—and they had learned later that the man had died at exactly that hour!

Angharad was more accustomed to her father's visions and asked with a sudden intensity, "What did you see, Father?"

"I saw soldiers fighting," Owen said, lowering his spoon and half closing his eyes as memories came to him. "Some were bloody and dead, but Sir Christopher was well. He had a wound, but it was not serious."

Angharad leaned forward, her brown eyes fixed on her father. "That's a blessing," she said. "It's hard enough on Amos, losing a mother. He needs his father."

"The child is healthy?" Will asked.

"Oh yes, I should be so healthy!" Angharad laughed at the thought of the sturdy three-year-old who had taken her heart so quickly. Her maternal instincts had always been strong, and Amos

Wakefield had played a large part in her life since she had joined the servants at Sir Christopher's house. "But he's a handful, that child."

"I expect his father was the same at that age—hard to handle." Will ate with enjoyment, then rose and said, "I've got to go to work. Father, you and I can go fishing later. Should be a good afternoon for it."

"Aye, so it will."

Owen sat in his chair, watching as Angharad cleared the table, washed the dishes, then took off her apron. "Off to the manor?" He smiled. Then a thought came to him, and he spoke it slowly. "You love the boy so . . . you should have had a husband and children of your own, Daughter."

He had not said anything like that lately to her, and Angharad looked at him with surprise. Then she came and put her hands on his shoulders, noting how thin the once sturdy frame had become. "I'll have a husband when God sends one," she said quietly. "As for children, I've got you and Will!" She laughed, then bent over and kissed him. "You and Will catch lots of fish. We'll have them for supper."

The walk to Wakefield Manor was pleasant for Angharad. She knew every single servant and field hand there and spoke to them with pleasure. There was a happy air about the place that she had learned to treasure, and she thought of how different things were now with her and her father. Times had been so hard in Wales, and now they were so easy! Plenty of food, a warm, snug little house, no backbreaking work! She was not a woman given to worry, but there had been many times back in Wales when they were down to their last crust of bread that she'd almost fallen into despair. Only her strong faith in God had kept her going.

Now as she turned down the lane that led to the front of the house, she offered up a little song, praising God. Even in the hardest times, she'd done this, having discovered that praising God did something to her. Her father had said once, "Praising God makes a man or woman attractive." To prove his point he'd quoted the Scripture, "Praise from the upright is beautiful." Angharad had laughed at him, yet she felt there was something to his theory. People who cut God off, she noticed, looked fearful and miserable. But people like her father, who loved God and said so, had a look of peace that she found among no other people.

Entering the house by the side door, she went at once to find Amos. He was usually playing in the large room next to his father's, but that room proved to be empty. A thought came to her, and she turned to the door of Sir Christopher's room. Amos had been forbidden to enter it, but he had stubbornly insisted on doing so in the last few weeks.

Opening the door, Angharad saw the child sitting in the middle of the floor. He was so engrossed in what he was playing with that he didn't hear her enter. Moving closer, she saw he had taken one of his father's pistols and had taken parts of it off. Still, it was dangerous, for sometimes they were charged.

"Amos! There's a bad boy you are!" Angharad cried and ran across the room. She knelt beside him, and even as she spoke strictly to him, she could not help but admire the childish beauty of the boy. He had dark red hair, curly and thick, and a pair of large eyes, so darkly blue that they looked almost black. Any woman in the world would have given her treasure for a skin as clear and smooth as this boy had!

"Pistol—Papa's pistol!" Amos exclaimed proudly, holding it up and pointing it right at Angharad's face.

"Amos, put that down!" Angharad snatched the flintlock, which brought a wail of anger from Amos. "You're not supposed to be in here. I'll have to switch you for it!"

"Papa brought me in here!"

Angharad opened her mouth to scold him, but suddenly a voice said, "I'm afraid that's right." Startled, Angharad whirled and found Sir Christopher lying on the bed watching, a wan smile on his face. "I didn't know you'd forbidden him to come in here."

"Sir Christopher!" Angharad felt awkward kneeling beside Amos. She rose with confusion in her face. "I—I didn't know you were home, sir!" She had forgotten the pistol in her hand. Now, as she moved her hands nervously, the muzzle of the gun came to bear on Chris's heart.

"Don't shoot!" Chris grinned. "It's not that bad."

"Oh—!" Angharad looked down at the pistol as if she'd never seen it, then flushed. The rich color made her more attractive than she knew as she said lamely, "Amos loves your guns, sir, but I'm afraid he'll hurt himself."

"Right! That one's not loaded, but he could get hurt."

Angharad stared at the master of Wakefield, then frowned. He looked strange . . . his cheeks were flushed and his eyes were dull. "Are you all right, Sir Christopher?"

"Well, I've felt better a few times in my life." He lifted his left arm, which was swathed with bandages that were stiff with dried blood. He had developed a fever on the way home from the battle and felt terrible. "I took a little cut, and it's not doing too well. . . ."

Angharad came closer and saw that he had lain down in his clothes, which were dusty and bloody. His face was drawn, and the unhealthy flush rose high on his cheeks. "Why, you've got to get out of those dirty clothes!" she exclaimed. "I'll take Amos down to Mary. I'll see that arm of yours, too. Now, come along, Amos." She ignored the boy's clamorous pleas to stay with his father and hauled him out of the room unceremoniously.

Chris looked down at his filthy clothes, then slowly got up and removed them. He found a clean nightshirt and pulled it on with some difficulty. Then he collapsed onto the bed and managed to pull the sheet over himself.

His tongue felt thick, and he felt as though he were burning up. He fell into a fitful sleep, but awakened when he heard the door open. Angharad entered with a pitcher of hot water, a towel, and a small sack. She came to him at once, saying, "Let me see . . . ," then peeled off the blood-stiffened bandages. She stared down at the wound for a long moment, then shook her head. "It's not good, sir. I'll clean it for you, then I'll make you something that will help with the pain."

"Oh, it's just a cut—!"

She cut him off with an impatient gesture. "Sir Christopher, I would expect such carelessness from Amos. After all, the babe is only three. But there's a fool you are, sir. You're a bit older than the lad and should have more judgment!" Angharad was deeply concerned, for she'd seen wounds like this fester until they became deadly. So engrossed was she in determining the best way to care for the master that she forgot to speak like a servant. Firmly she said, "We'll have the doctor, but until he comes, you'll have me for a nurse! Now, be still—this will hurt . . . !"

Christopher watched the face of the woman as she cleaned the wound. What she was doing *did* hurt, but not enough to draw his attention away from the smooth planes of her face. Her raven-black hair was braided and made a coil of some sort, and there was a firmness in her strong neck and arms. He was struck by her beauty, even as he felt a growing admiration for her strength of character. She had come to his house quietly, but from the day she arrived, Chris had been surprised to note how smoothly things ran. He'd been around enough to see that Amos loved the woman. It didn't seem to matter that she was strict with the tyke, for he wanted her constantly.

As she leaned over to rinse out the cloth she was using, he wondered why she had never married. She continued to carefully clean the wound, and he was tempted to ask her, but held his tongue. If he had learned anything about women, it was that they didn't like to feel a man was meddling in areas where he had no right.

When Angharad had cleaned the wound and applied some sort of cooling salve, she bandaged the arm carefully, then said, "Now, we'll change that twice a day."

"Thank you, Angharad—"

"Oh, I'm not finished," she cut him off calmly. She looked at his face, then said in a matter-of-fact tone, "Pull your shirt off, Sir Christopher."

"My—shirt!"

"Your nightshirt, sir. You're filthy!" She saw the shock on his face and laughed aloud. "I've nursed my brother and my father for years. Do you think to shock me with a bare chest? Come now, off with it!"

Feeling rather foolish, Chris managed to get his nightshirt off, keeping the sheet well up over his lower body. "Now then, we'll have a wash," Angharad announced calmly. Taking a clean cloth, she poured cool water into a basin and proceeded to wash Chris's face, then his chest and back. "There, that's better," she said, then helped him pull the shirt on. "Now, a bit of tea. . . ."

Despite his initial embarrassment, Chris realized he was feeling much better. He watched as she poured some sort of powder from a small bag into the teapot. Taking the pitcher of water, which was still fairly hot, she poured it into the pot, and the room was filled with a strong aromatic fragrance. "Take a cup of this," Angharad commanded. "There, drink it all down." When he had finished it, she took the cup and smiled down at him. "Now, that's all I'll make you do for now, Sir Christopher."

As Angharad started to pick up his dirty clothes, Chris said meekly, "Now, Angharad, I've done everything you say, so let me be the master of Wakefield for a moment. I have one order for you."

"Yes, sir?"

"Sit down and talk to me."

"Talk to you, sir?"

"Yes. Tell me about Amos. What's he been doing?" Chris

nodded at her, saying, "Sit down, please. Surely you can give a sick man some company."

Angharad dropped the clothes, sat down, and began to speak of Amos. The sun fell in yellow bars across her face, smoothing her skin and giving it an ivory cast. "Well, Sir Christopher, yesterday we went for a boat ride—"

Chris lay there, growing drowsy, enjoying the sound of Angharad's low voice. When she grew silent, he found himself beginning to talk almost dreamily—something he would never have done if not for the mellowing effects of the medicine he'd taken.

"I—miss Patience so much," he whispered, in that state that comes just before sleep. "She was such a joy to me. . . ."

Angharad listened carefully, her heart moved by the man's whispered admission. *He must have loved her greatly,* she thought. *I wonder what it would feel like—to have a strong man like Sir Christopher love you.*

Finally, his eyelids fell, and he begged in a slurred voice, "Don't send for the doctor—not yet. You—can take care—of me—"

Angharad looked down on the face of the man as he dropped off to sleep. He looked tired and weak, not strong and healthy as he usually did. There was something of a child in him for all his fifty-two years. He was, she realized, one of those rare men who keep a childlike faith all their lives. Perhaps it was this—along with her maternal instinct—that caused Angharad Morgan to put out her hand and stroke the auburn hair. A tender smile came to her lips and she whispered, "Sleep well, sir." Then she sat down and kept her gaze on his face as he slept.

❧

On August 22, 1642, King Charles raised his standard at Nottingham. He was surrounded by a company of noble families—including Sir Vernon Woodville. It was Vernon who said to the king, "Your Majesty, perhaps it would be better if we waited a few days."

Charles, filled with enthusiasm for what he saw as the beginning of a movement that would wipe out all his enemies, stared at the man. "Why should w-we do that, Sir Vernon?"

"Well, sire, after all, this *is* the anniversary of the day when Henry VII won the crown at Bosworth field—and that was the beginning of the Tudor dynasty." Woodville hesitated, then added quickly, "After all, this is the *Stuart* line of monarchs, not the Tudors."

"Nonsense, Woodville!"

A handsome man in his late twenties, who had been standing by the king, lifted his cup. This was Prince Rupert of Continental fame. He had a fine head of black hair that flowed down his back, a pair of large dark eyes, and was as handsome as a man can safely be. Ignoring Woodville, Rupert said, "I drink to the leader of England, King Charles I. God save King Charles, and hang the Roundheads!"

The toast was loudly repeated by the host of men, who wore brilliantly colored clothing. "Roundheads!" Charles frowned. "That's what you call C-Cromwell and his men?"

"I call them much worse than that, Your Majesty," Rupert laughed. He was filled with life, this young soldier, anxious to prove his genius on English soil as he had abroad. He looked proudly around at the young men, all aristocrats from noble families, then cried out, "Your Majesty, can you not see that with these men of honor, we cannot lose?"

Charles nodded eagerly. "When will we fight them?"

"As soon as I can run them to earth," Rupert said, and a cry of agreement went up. He smiled at the king. "Just let us cross swords with these men who have no sense of honor or loyalty for their king, and we shall see them run like rabbits!"

"God b-be with us!" the king said, and all around the room the young men in fine clothing lifted their swords, crying aloud, "God be with us! Death to Cromwell and the Roundheads!"

Sixteen

A SUITOR FOR SUSANNE

Marry you, Henry? Why—I never thought of such a thing!"
Lord Henry Darrow's long lips curved upward
at the startled expression that his proposal had
brought to Susanne. The two of them had been sitting
beside each other in the ornate drawing room at the Woodville manor house. Darrow had been away for weeks, fighting with Prince Rupert, and Susanne had been surprised to
see him come riding in that morning. They had spent the
day together, and she had invited him to see some new
sketches by Van Dyke of the royal family. Darrow had
admired them properly—then had given her a sardonic look
and said, "I want you to marry me, Susanne."

Susanne had been so startled that she had blurted out the first
thing that came into her mind—and now she laughed in a forced
manner, saying, "You can never be serious for long, can you,
Henry?"

"Indeed, I am quite serious about this." Darrow was wearing a
fine doublet of green silk, gray knee-breeches, and a pair of soft
leather slippers. His blond hair fell over his shoulders in ringlets,
in the fashion made popular by Prince Rupert, and his pale blue
eyes and fair skin made him a handsome young man.

He watched Susanne for a few moments, then reached out to

put his arms around her and—before she could protest—drew her close and kissed her.

It was a rough, demanding kiss. Susanne had been kissed before—at the age of sixteen, she had many suitors—but she always had been in control of the flirtation. Darrow's caresses were demanding in a manner she'd never experienced before.

Pulling away from him, Susanne wiped her hand across her bruised mouth. Her eyes snapped angrily and she said indignantly, "You've never even *looked* at me, Henry. What's this all about?"

Far from offended by her tart question, Henry grinned. "You're not the little girl I grew up with, Susanne. You've become a fine-looking woman—and women should be used, not set on some forgotten shelf and wasted."

Susanne was well aware that Henry Darrow had been a greedy, demanding child, and as a man he had only become even more so. She had always known that when he wanted something, he would find a way to get it—no matter whom it hurt. Now she cocked her head to one side, saying, "You can have all the women you want, Henry. Everyone knows that."

Her comment brought a reddish tinge to Darrow's fair cheeks. He was not one to blush, but her reference to his reputation as womanizer dampened him a bit. Shaking his head, he said, "Why, Susanne, a man has to study women, to learn their ways so he might learn how to please and care for them." He smiled at her in a way that other women had found irresistible.

She was unimpressed. "I'm not about to be one of your 'studies,' Henry!"

"Why, I didn't mean—!"

"You would make the world's worst husband, anyway."

"Why do you say that?"

"You'd have a dozen affairs with women!"

"But they would never be vulgar, my dear!" Darrow understood himself very well, and looking at the young woman, he was impressed at how well she had turned out. Susanne Woodville was beautiful enough to grace his house, and he said so. "You've become a very beautiful woman, Susanne. I believe we would serve quite well together. I'd very much like you to marry me."

Susanne stared at the young man's handsome face, a shrewd expression on her face. "I know what you're up to. You want the Woodville property."

Again, the unaccustomed flush came to Darrow's cheeks. However, he managed a smile and reached out to take her hand. Kissing it, he said, "Why, it would be a good match for both our houses, Susanne. My father is gone, and some day you must lose your parents. A woman is at the mercy of unscrupulous men," he added rather piously, "but if I were your husband, I could protect your interests."

"A matter of business, is it, Henry?" Susanne shook her head firmly. "No. I think not. Thank you all the same, but I still have the idea that men and women should marry for love."

"Love comes and goes, but estates like ours, why, they remain forever!"

"No, they don't." Susanne looked at him almost pityingly. "They go to dust. There is only one thing that lasts forever, and that is love."

Darrow shook his head in disapproval. "You've got a romantic streak in you, Susanne. Eternal love is a fine notion for poetry, such as my friend Lovelace writes." He halted, studied her face carefully, then said, "Make up your mind to it, Susanne, we *will* marry. Your parents have agreed to it."

Susanne blinked with astonishment. "No! They can't have agreed!"

"You're just nervous, which is fitting for an innocent young woman." Darrow's tone was condescending. He was in charge of the situation now and was certain that he would win this girl as he had others. As for after marriage, well, a man had to have his diversions! "I will teach you the ways of love," he murmured and came closer to her. A smile curled his lips up into a sardonic twist. "It's one of the advantages you will have from my—experience!"

⁂

Francine Fourier leaned back and stared at Darrow, cynicism in her eyes. "You're going to *marry* her? I don't believe it!"

Darrow let his fingers trace the smoothness of the young woman's neck. "Just a business matter, my dear. It will change nothing between us."

"Don't be a fool! Of course it will change things." Francine was more beautiful than ever, but now anger twisted her lips into an ugly form. She'd held little hope of marrying Henry Darrow, though she had tried hard to bring him to that. Oh, she had received offers enough, but none that would have brought her the wealth she yearned for. Now she pulled away from Darrow and walked across the room to stare out the window.

Henry shrugged, for he had known what Francine's reaction would be. He had enjoyed his affair with her more than any he'd ever had, but never had he considered marriage. Still, he hated for something so pleasurable to end. He came to stand behind her, putting his arms around her and whispering, "No, it will never change! I feel something for you I've never felt for any other woman, Francine. And I can't lose you!"

Francine knew that part of this was true. *He doesn't want to lose anything,* she thought as she turned to face him. *He's the most possessive man in the world!* Then she slipped her arms around his neck and whispered, "No, we'll never lose each other. . . ." She kissed him, holding him close, and when he was stirred, she drew her head back, saying, "But I must marry someone."

Darrow smiled. "We'll find you a nice rich old man, preferably one who is sick and has no heirs," Darrow answered. "Love isn't enough, is it?" he asked suddenly, thinking of what Susanne had said.

"Of course not. Only fools think that."

"I'm glad you're a practical woman, Francine," Darrow whispered, drawing her closer. "A *beautiful* practical woman."

But Darrow little knew how very practical this lovely woman was. Even as she returned his kiss, she was thinking of her future. *If Cromwell and his Roundheads win, Henry will be penniless, along with all the Cavaliers. But Gavin won't be! I'll write him tomorrow. He'll come as he always does.*

———

Owen Morgan looked up as Angharad and Sir Christopher came across the field and headed toward the cottage. Angharad carried a basket and was laughing at something the man had said. The manner of the two stirred memories in the elderly man, and his brows raised as he realized the pair reminded him of the days he had walked in the fields with his wife, Ceridwen.

She would be seventy-one next month, he thought, and the past rested on him with a sweetness that made him close his eyes. Not a single day had passed since Ceridwen's death that he hadn't thought of her.

"Well now, napping are you, Father?" Angharad put her basket down and came over to push the snow-white locks back from Owen's brow. She was wearing a simple green dress, and her face was alive with pleasure. "You'll sleep your life away," she said fondly.

"Not sleeping," Owen denied. "Just thinking of your mother."

Angharad's eyes grew wide and she said quietly, "She's never far from you, is she?"

"I know a little about that, Owen," Chris said. "A good woman doesn't leave a man, not even when she's gone to be with the Lord."

"Aye, that's the way of it." Owen nodded. He gave the younger man a quick glance, then said, "Will you have a bite, sir? Angharad's an awful cook, but no matter."

"I know better than that, you old rascal." Chris smiled. "I come this way so I can be a guest at your table."

This was true enough. The months since he had recovered from his wound had been more and more punctuated by visits with the Morgans. Wakefield knew some might consider theirs a strange sort of relationship between master and servants—but he had learned to soak up the peace of the small cottage. Amos came with him often, and the two of them would sit for hours listening to Owen as he told the old tales of Wales.

And Chris was painfully aware that, whenever he returned from fighting with Cromwell, his thoughts were filled more and more with Angharad—often causing him to spur his horse to a dead run as he came closer to home.

For her part, Angharad had never presumed on him. She had done wonders with Amos, yet was always careful to remind the boy of his mother and how he should honor her memory. Still, it was inevitable that Sir Christopher would want news of how his son was doing, so the two of them would spend time as Angharad would report on Amos's progress.

Now Angharad insisted, "Sit down, Sir Christopher. Will butchered a sheep yesterday, and it is wonderful good! You talk with Father while I stir the pot."

And so Chris sat and talked with Owen. When the old man asked after Gavin, he said, "He's off on some sort of journey. I expect it's a young woman, though he didn't say."

Later Will came in and the four of them sat down and ate together. It was a fine meal, and afterward they all sat down outside, enjoying the sunset.

Owen told stories as usual, a mixture of tales of ancient Welsh heroes along with stories of the Morgan family.

"How one man can keep so much history in his head, I'll never know," Chris said when Owen finally ended one of his sagas.

Owen hesitated, then said, "Sir Christopher, I've got one tale for you, but I'm not sure you'll like it."

Surprised by the statement, Chris gave Owen a strange look. "Won't like it? Why, I like all your tales."

Owen's face was set in a strange manner, and Angharad and Will exchanged glances. "Why do you say that, Father?" Angharad asked quietly. The setting sun, a rosy disk settling behind the low-lying hills, tinted her skin a delicate pink, and Chris thought he'd rarely seen anything more lovely.

From far away a dog barked, and Owen Morgan let the sound die away before he spoke. "It's a tale that could touch you very close," he said almost in a whisper. "I'll not tell it, sir, unless you say for me to."

Mystified, Chris looked up at Angharad, then nodded. "Tell it, Owen," he said.

"Right, then," Owen said. "This is about the Morgan family. My father's name was Kelwin. He married Arwain Ellis, and I was the oldest of their children. My grandfather, my father's father, was Gwilym. He married Beth Rhys—"

Chris sat there listening carefully, but there was nothing in the story to move him. It was not a stirring adventure— merely a history of the Morgan family. He relaxed and tried to follow the twistings of the Morgan line, but did so only with difficulty.

"Now John Morgan, who was the son of Evan, married a girl named Eileen Harris." Owen related some of the history of John Morgan, and then he lifted his dark blue eyes and placed them on Chris, saying, "John had a sister, Sir Christopher. Her name was Margred."

An alarm seemed to go off in Chris's brain. Staring at the old man, he licked his lips, then asked, "Margred, you say?"

"Not an unusual name among us, sir," Owen said, his eyes fixed on the face of the master of Wakefield. "Shall I go on?"

"Yes."

"Very well, then. Margred was a fine girl for a time, but she brought shame to her family. She got with child, and would not say who the father was."

When he did not go on, Angharad asked, "Well, don't leave us hanging, Father, what happened to her?"

Sir Christopher Wakefield's voice was strained as he said abruptly, "She had a baby boy, Angharad—she came to England." When Will and Angharad stared at him, he nodded slowly. "The father of the child was my ancestor, Robert Wakefield, the first to hold the Wakefield title."

"The boy's name was Myles, so the old story goes," Owen said thoughtfully, his eyes on Christopher. "There was a letter from Margred—I saw it once—she said that the father of her child was of noble blood, but that she would never name the man."

Quietness settled on the small group. Finally it was broken by Angharad, who was watching Chris carefully. "But, Sir Christopher—how do you know this?"

"I've heard my father, Sir Robin Wakefield, tell it many times," Chris said. "He heard it from my grandfather, Myles, who was Margred's son. Myles remembered Wales and the trip that he made with his mother to get to England."

"Did your ancestor marry her?" Will asked.

"No, she never saw him again until she was dying. Then she sent the boy to get him. When he came, she told him Myles was his son—he hadn't known there was a child until that time. Sir Robert loved Margred, my father said, but she was not of noble blood, and so he could not marry her. But he always loved her, so my father said Myles told him. And he took Myles as his son and gave him his name. When Sir Robert died, Myles received the title."

The three from Wales watched Sir Christopher carefully, saying nothing. There was a look of shock in his eyes, but finally he put his hand out to Owen, who took it. "I'm proud of my Welsh blood, Owen," he said simply. Then he gave Angharad a peculiar look, one she never forgot. "We are of one blood, you and I," he said to her, then put out his hand. When she took it, something passed between the two.

"And you, Will, you had no notion of this?" Chris asked.

"Not a bit of it!"

"How very strange!" Chris murmured. "Out of all the houses in England, that you would come to this place!"

"God is in it," Owen said with a half smile. "He is in all things."

Chris nodded slowly. "I believe that," he said simply. Then he turned and left, saying, "I must think on this."

When he was gone, Will asked at once, "Father, did you know any of this when I came to Wales to bring you here?"

"Not at first, but I have been thinking of the old stories, and James, the steward, spoke one day of Sir Robert Wakefield. He mentioned that he'd found a lost son—a Welsh son. It seemed likely that the mother might be our lost Margred." He closed his eyes and after a moment's silence said, "It is much like the story of Joseph. He was sent to Egypt so that his family would not starve."

"And if it had not been for Sir Christopher," Angharad whispered, "we would all be starving in Wales." Her eyes followed the man's sturdy figure as he moved across the field. "He's had a hard bump, I'll wager, to find out he's got peasant blood."

"Every man has that, for we are all of the stock of Adam," Owen remarked. His eyes rested on his daughter's face. She was watching Wakefield with an expression that made him pause, but he kept his thoughts to himself, leaning back and saying, "He's a man, all in all. And no man is worse for a touch of Wales in 'im!"

If an urgent message had not arrived from Cromwell, Chris might have had more time to talk with Owen about his roots. But a message from the colonel came, and he had time only for a brief word with Angharad.

He sent for her, asking her to come to his library. When she arrived, he said, "I've got to go join the troop, Angharad." As he spoke, he saw that she was disturbed. "What is it?"

"I don't like for you to be in a battle," she said simply. Then she colored and added quickly, "For Amos's sake, of course."

Chris held her eyes, a slight smile tilting his fine lips. "For Amos, eh? I'd hoped that you'd miss me a little yourself, especially now that we're practically related."

Angharad lifted her head, taking in his dark blue eyes and erect figure. "I always miss you, sir," she said simply. "I think you must know that."

Chris thought for a moment that this woman's spirit was reminiscent of the spirit he had seen so often in Patience. *How many times did Patience look at me just like this when I was leaving?* he thought. For one moment he had a flash of guilt for the feelings he had come to hold for Angharad. Before the Welsh woman's arrival, Chris had not even considered looking at another woman, but now he knew that he was not too old for stirrings of the heart. Clearing his throat, he said, "Well, I shall miss you, too. When I'm away, I always think of you and Amos." He reached out and took her hand.

She looked at him in astonishment. He had never touched her, but now he held her firm, strong hand and said, "You've become a mother to my son. He loves you dearly."

Angharad was acutely conscious of the feel of Chris's hand, of the way it gently held hers. She dropped her eyes, trying to ignore the rush of emotion that flooded her. She had never known or loved a man, but now she caught her breath and wondered, *What is this? What's happening to me?* Finally she whispered, "It's a joy, sir . . . to care for your son."

Chris had a sudden strong desire to reach out, to lift her chin . . . and he did so. "Never bow your head to me, or to any man, Angharad," he said. He held her chin, tenderness in his touch, and looked deep into her eyes. What he read there moved him, and he leaned forward and kissed her lips. They were smooth and soft under his, and for a moment intense emotions swept over him. He longed to draw her close, to savor the feel and scent of her—but he drew back, saying, "I mean no disrespect, my dear, but you have come to mean a great deal to me." He studied her, then asked anxiously, "I haven't offended you, I hope?"

"No, never that," Angharad said quietly. Her expression was sober and she gave him a long look that he could not read. "You had better go, sir. I'll take care of Amos—and pray for your safety."

Chris nodded and left the room. As soon as she was alone, Angharad took a few quick, nervous paces, then hugged herself. Thoughts were running riotously through her head, and she could feel the pounding of her heart.

What is it with you, girl? she demanded. *You can't be thinking such thoughts!*

"Oh, but I am," she whispered, a strange joy running through her. "I am, indeed. And what wondrous thoughts they are!" Then, a smile on her face and a glad light in her eyes, she took a deep breath and moved to the window to watch Sir Christopher Wakefield leave the manor.

❦

Colonel Cromwell's regiment was made up of five troops, and as he waved his hand toward the ranks, he said proudly, "Fine men, eh, Sir Christopher?"

Chris looked at the horsemen and noted that the chaplain had a pistol in one hand and a Bible in the other. He smiled. "Yes, sir, a fine force."

"Now then, we have no time to talk. Do you understand the movements?"

"Yes, sir."

"Then let us move ahead!"

The battle at Grantham was not one of the larger battles of the English Civil War, but Chris always remembered it more clearly than any of the others. The purpose was to attack the prominent Royalist stronghold of Newark, and as Cromwell's forces moved forward, they faced twenty-one troops of horse and three or four of dragoons—mounted infantry, armed with musket and short swords.

When the two forces met, for a time all Chris knew was the sound of battle. The enemy was screaming and cursing, but the Roundheads went into battle singing psalms! Chris kept his troop at an even pace until they met the enemy and, after a hard fight, found himself cut off from the rest of the army. He turned his horse and started to make his escape, but a line of Cavaliers suddenly drew up in front of him, the leader pointing a musket directly into his face and shouting, "Surrender or you're a dead man!"

Chris ignored him, wheeled his horse around, and was thundering away when something struck him in the back. He felt himself falling—but he never felt the impact as he struck the ground.

***

It was early evening when a servant interrupted Gavin as he was working in the study.

"A messenger, sir. He insists on seeing you."

Quick concern washed over Gavin, but he pushed it away as he rose and went to where the messenger waited. He took the envelope, but stared at the rider who had brought it. The courier was a Cavalier.

"Who did you say sent this?" Gavin demanded.

"Sir Henry Darrow," the man replied, staring down at Gavin proudly. "Do you wish to send an answer, sir?"

Gavin broke the seal, took a single sheet of paper from the envelope, and scanned it quickly. Though he did not allow it to show on his face, alarm filled him as he read:

> Mr. Wakefield, I must inform you that your father was taken prisoner this afternoon in a battle at Grantham. He was wounded and is not expected to live. Some thought to have him sent to your home, but I persuaded them to refrain. When one lifts his hand against the king of England, he must bear the consequences. There will be no exchange for your father. If he dies, I will allow his body to be shipped home. I trust that this grievous matter will cause you to reflect on your traitorous behavior. I would urge you to leave the traitors you are aligned with, but I know your pride too well to believe that you would listen to sound counsel.

Gavin's face hardened, but he said firmly, "There is no answer."

"Very well!"

As the rider drove his horse out toward the road, Gavin turned to find Angharad and Amos waiting. "Is it bad news, sir?" the woman asked.

He glanced at his small brother, but decided it would not help to hide the truth. "My father is a prisoner of the king." He saw the grief rise in Angharad's eyes and added, "And he's been seriously wounded."

"My papa won't die!" Amos cried out, but there were tears in his eyes as he turned to Angharad, who held him tightly.

Angharad and Gavin exchanged a long glance, then she said, "God will not let him die!" and somehow she made Gavin believe her.

Seventeen

WHAT'S IN A DREAM?

The turning point of the English Civil War occurred on July 2, 1644, on a ridge near Marston Moor. It was the biggest battle ever fought on English soil, and it created the largest communal burial ground in England.

At the beginning of that year, the king had most of the country behind him. Military victory lay within his grasp, so it seemed. Prince Rupert had fought his way into Lancashire, striking the Parliamentarian forces heavily. Lathom House was freed, Stockport was crushed, and Bolton taken. On June 1, the prince was joined by Lord Goring, with five thousand mounted troops. They stormed Liverpool and saved York from the Roundheads.

The Royalists were exuberant at what appeared to be certain victory for the crown—but they reckoned without Oliver Cromwell. Though he had not yet been given the highest rank, his regiment had a discipline that was formidable, and he had never been beaten in battle. He ignored the advice of those who wished him to place high-ranking gentlemen in command, saying, "I had rather have a plain, russet-coated captain that knows what he fights for, and loves what he knows, than that which you call a gentleman and is nothing else. I honor a gentleman that is so indeed."

Now, at last, the war had come to a duel between two men:

Prince Rupert and Lieutenant General Cromwell. The contrast between the two was great. At forty-five, Cromwell was twenty years older than Rupert, and the prince was a true Cavalier in his dress, while Cromwell was rather slovenly. But more important, Rupert was in the prime of his fame as a military genius. Cromwell was unbeaten as a cavalry leader, but had fought only in relatively minor engagements. Still, he had shown greatness, and among his followers his victories seemed a mark of divine favor.

"It was observed God was with him," wrote Joshua Aprigge, "and he began to be renowned."

Now, on the first day of July, as the two forces approached Marston Moor, Prince Rupert asked a scout eagerly, "Is Cromwell there?"

"Yes, sire!"

"Good! We shall settle this matter this day."

Cromwell, being told that he would face Prince Rupert with his splendid cavalry the next day, replied, "By God's grace we shall have fighting enough!"

And so they came together—the Roundheads of parliament and the Cavaliers of King Charles I. Following the old manner, the foot soldiers were placed in the center, flanked by cavalry on both wings. Manchester commanded the foot soldiers of the Parliamentary force, with Sir Thomas Fairfax on the right flank, Oliver Cromwell on the left. The entire force numbered twenty thousand on foot and seven thousand on horseback.

Across the ridge, Rupert led eleven thousand on foot and seven thousand on horseback—and the prince was anxious for the battle to begin.

"I think we will be struck by Rupert first." Cromwell was speaking to his commanders. "He has been boasting of how he will defeat Ironsides." Cromwell allowed a rare smile at the nickname he and his soldiers had been given. "But by the help of God, we will see victory this day. Now, see to your men!"

Riding up and down his lines, Cromwell stopped to encourage the men. Gavin caught his eye, and he pulled up long enough to say, "Well, sir, and how is it with you?"

"I am confident, General Cromwell," Gavin said at once. He had, in fact, been tremendously worried about his father, who he was told still lived. "I wish my father were here to help you, sir."

"So do I, my boy." Cromwell nodded, and even with the greatest test of his life before him, he said, "Let us pray for him now, that he will be delivered from the snare of the fowler."

Soldiers snatched off their helmets and the chaplain beside Cromwell said "Amen!" as the great commander bowed his head and prayed a fervent prayer for Sir Christopher Wakefield.

Then Cromwell rode on, and Gavin blinked back the tears that had sprung to his eyes. He sat on his horse, waiting for the battle to begin, and he thought of Francine. He had answered her summons of more than a year ago, but she had teased him the entire time, promising much, yet yielding nothing. At last she had drawn back, saying, "If we were married, Gavin, we could love freely."

He had almost proposed. Almost. But something kept him back. Finally he had told her, "After the war, we will see. Things are too much disturbed now."

Displeased by his response, or what she considered to be his lack of response, she had sent him away. When he returned home only to discover that his father had been captured and was likely to die, he raged at himself for being away. "If I had been with him, I might have been able to save him!" Angharad had seen the guilt eating at him and had tried to reason with him, but nothing had helped.

Now he faced those who had captured and wounded his father, and he grimly determined to make them pay!

But Prince Rupert did not attack. In his view there would be no battle until the following day. So the senior commander, along with Cromwell and Sir Thomas Fairfax, had a council of war.

"We will attack," Cromwell said as he came back to his troops from the council. A thrill ran over Gavin, and the sky, which had already turned dark with an impending storm, split open with a drenching rain that hailed down on both armies.

But Cromwell's blood was up. He lifted himself in the saddle, calling, "By the help of God, charge!" Then began the type of charge that he had trained his Ironsides to make—rapid, controlled, riding short-reined and short-stirruped, close in together. Cromwell had explained to Gavin wherein the prince's cavalry charges were weak: "They are furious, but there is only one chance. He has no control of his men, for they have gone wild with looting, so there is no chance for a second blow. We will control our men, so that they will not scatter wildly."

Prince Rupert was sitting down eating when the sounds of battle reached him. Startled, he ran to his horse, calling his men to action—and so the Cavaliers rode to meet the charge of Cromwell.

Gavin was in the front rank of the charging Ironsides and was shaken at first when he saw the enemy flying right into his face. Rupert's men were excellent horsemen, and when the two forces met, it was with a clash that smote Gavin's ears. A pistol went off, almost in his face, but he struck out with his sword and it sliced into the neck of the trooper who had fired it. When the man fell to the ground, blood spurting like a crimson fountain, Gavin's stomach lurched and he fought against the bile rising in his throat—but there was no time for giving in to reaction. The battle was raging, and over all he heard the loud psalms sung by the Ironsides.

He fought until his arm was weary, and when he thought he could not go on, he saw Oliver Cromwell engaged with a powerful horseman whose long, flowing locks were soaked in the rain. Gavin tried to spur his weary horse to the general's side, but the beast collapsed. Gavin fell to the ground with a grunt, then looked up to see a Cavalier riding at him full tilt, his pistol aimed right at him!

I'll never see Susanne again, he thought with startling clarity, then straightened up to face his death—and in the brief moment he had left, the thought came to him: *Strange that I would think of Susanne instead of Francine.*

The horseman was no more than ten feet away, and his finger was on the trigger, but Gavin did not blink. He kept his eyes wide open, ready for his fate—but the Cavalier suddenly disappeared, swept off his horse by a force that was so abrupt Gavin could not believe it!

"Be you all right, sir?"

Gavin turned to gape at a tall, heavy young man who held a bloody pike in his hands. He had a round face and a pair of bright blue eyes, and he asked again, "Not hurt, are you, sir?"

"No—," Gavin managed to say. He swallowed and glanced at the enemy who lay on his back, his chest leaking blood. The long pike had caught him just as he was about to pull the trigger, and Gavin turned to say, "You saved my life, soldier!"

"Well, glad I was here to help." The soldier looked around at the still-raging battle and said, "I think we better find you another horse."

Gavin was experiencing a belated reaction, and he could only watch as the tall man ran across the field to grab the reins of a gray battle horse whose rider had fallen. Bringing the animal back, he said, "Get astride, sir."

Gavin swung into the saddle, and when he took the lines, he asked, "What's your name, soldier?"

"Bunyan, sir—John Bunyan."

"Well, John Bunyan, I'll find you after the battle to thank you properly."

"Ah, sir, we're all soldiers together!" Bunyan flashed a grin, then turned and ran toward the battle line, disappearing into the ranks.

Gavin saw his troop forming for another charge and rode to take his place in line. "You all right, Gavin?" Lieutenant Spines demanded. "I saw you go down and thought you was lost."

"An angel saved me," Gavin said with a grin, and when the lieutenant stared at him, he nodded. "An angel named John Bunyan," he added.

"Peculiar name for an angel," the lieutenant said, grinning back. "Look out, here we go—!"

The two armies wavered back and forth, and finally Rupert was winning over the parliamentary right wing commanded by Lord Leven. Oliver Cromwell and his Ironsides came to render aid. On they came, in ordered ranks, and when they smote the Cavalier army, it was with a devastating force.

The Cavaliers had met their match, and soon they fell in defeat.

Cromwell spoke of it later, saying, "We drove the entire cavalry of the prince off the field. God made them as stubble to our swords."

And so the battle ended, and Rupert's defeat proved to be a disaster for the king. His northern army was shattered, and the whole of the north was lost. The battle opened the door for the Puritans to win the war—and it was the sword of Oliver Cromwell that had won the victory.

***

"Gavin, you've got to stop blaming yourself!"

"I can't help it, Angharad!"

Angharad stared at the young man's pale face, then said in exasperation, "Well, devil fly off! What good will it do your good father if you put yourself into an early grave worrying over him?"

The two were standing in the garden, watching Amos as he chased a huge monarch butterfly, yelling like a banshee. Angharad had tried to make conversation, but when Gavin had answered her with glum monosyllables, she lost patience with him.

At her harsh tone, he turned tortured eyes to her. "But—what if he *dies* in that prison? I thought . . . I hoped he would be free by now. It's been so long . . . more than a year! And with every passing day I grow more afraid that he . . . he will never come home."

Angharad started to scold him, but at that moment Gavin, for all his nineteen years, seemed as childlike and vulnerable as Amos. She moved to stand beside him, putting her hand on his arm and saying compassionately, "Is it so terrible with you, boy?"

"Yes!" Gavin cried. "I can't stand it, Angharad!"

"I know, Gavin . . . I know it well." Something in her tone drew his eyes to her face as she went on. "And you're slow indeed, young sir, not to see that—I'm hurting, too."

Gavin had grown very fond of Angharad, admiring her stately bearing and the keen wit that she often revealed. She had made life easier for all of them—but especially for his father. Now Gavin looked at her, startled by her admission. The sound of bees made a humming in the air as they looked at each other, and it was Gavin who said quietly, "I see that now, Angharad. You and father, you've gotten very close."

"I'm only his housekeeper, Gavin."

"No," he said, shaking his head slowly. He remembered then how his father had been very happy when she was around—happier than Gavin could remember him being since Patience's death. "You've been good for my father. He's been so lonely since mother died."

Angharad lifted her eyes to the young man, who looked so much like his father, and said, "I never met a man like him. Blessed are you to have such a father—"

Where the conversation might have gone, Gavin never knew, for a voice came from the door, calling his name. He turned and brightened as he saw Susanne come toward him.

"Susanne!" he cried and ran to meet her. She put out her hands and he took them. "I'm glad to see you!"

Susanne was flushed with the heat of the summer sun, but her face was bright as she said, "Hello, Gavin. It's good to see you, too."

Gavin held her hands for a moment, then remembered Angharad—and Amos, who had come to stare at the visitor. "This is Angharad Morgan, our housekeeper. Angharad, this is Miss Susanne Woodville, a very dear friend of mine."

Angharad nodded slightly, but Susanne stepped forward and put her hands out—an unusual gesture for one of her class to make to a servant. "I've heard about you," she said, examining the woman carefully.

"About me?" Angharad blinked with surprise. "Where would you be hearing about me?"

"From Sir Christopher."

"You've seen Father?" Gavin demanded. "Where—when did you see him? How—"

Susanne interrupted, "I went to see him two days ago." She gave a warning look toward Amos, then bent to say, "Your father loves you, Amos. He told me to give you a kiss for him. Is that all right?"

"I guess so." Amos endured the kiss with the stoicism of a four-year-old, then demanded, "When is my papa coming home?"

Susanne hesitated, then said, "Soon, I hope. He's very anxious to see you."

Seeing that Susanne didn't want to talk in front of the child, Angharad said, "Amos, let's you and me go see the funny old cow down in the pasture."

Gavin waited until the two were out of hearing, then said, "Now—tell me."

Susanne's face sobered and she spoke with hesitation. "It's not good news, Gavin. I went to the prison to take him some food, and he's not well."

"The wound is still giving him trouble?"

"It's never healed properly. They give him just enough care to keep him alive, but not to clear up the infection! Not entirely. He no sooner gains ground than they cease any care, and the cycle begins again. And the prison is foul! No air nor sun, and so filthy! I tried to get the commander to give him better care, but he refused. I—think he's had orders to that effect."

"Sir Henry Darrow's orders!"

"I can't say, but we've got to do *something*, Gavin! He'll die in that place!"

Gavin's face twisted in impotent fury. "I've tried to get an exchange, but the crown won't hear of it. I've driven myself crazy thinking about it!" He stood there dejectedly, his eyes filled with despair, but he seemed to recover himself enough to smile at her gratefully. "Thank you for going to see him—and for coming here. Nothing but kindness in you—there never was!"

His compliment brought color to her cheeks, and she made a deprecating gesture. "It was nothing—but I wept to see him, Gavin! He's always been so strong, and now he's sick and alone!"

The two stood there, and finally he led the way into the house. When Angharad brought them to the table where they ate, Susanne studied the Welsh woman covertly. When it was time for bed, Angharad led her to a room, but when she turned to leave, Susanne said, "Sir Christopher talked about you a great deal, Angharad."

"Did he, indeed?" Angharad turned at once, her eyes huge in the yellow lamplight. "My heart cries out to God for him!"

"He said to tell you that it was the thought of you caring for Amos that gave him the most comfort." Susanne had listened to Chris Wakefield speak of this woman, and now she added, "Do you know he loves you?"

"No—!" Angharad protested, her lips growing tense. "I'm only a servant to him!"

"I don't think so. When he spoke of you, he changed. His voice grew tender when he spoke your name—and I know him well enough to understand him. He was deeply in love with Gavin's mother, but she is gone and Sir Christopher is a man who needs love in his life. A woman's love."

Angharad stood very still, her face turned downward. She was rejoicing in the thing she was hearing, but when she lifted her eyes, she said, "It can never be more than it is, Miss Woodville. He's a lord—and I'm a poor woman."

Susanne said quietly, "When a man loves a woman, if he's a good man—he doesn't ask what her station is. He follows his heart."

"That's—a strange way of looking at things, Miss Woodville," Angharad whispered. "But say nothing of this to Gavin, please. Or to anyone else."

"Of course not. I simply thought you ought to know."

The next day Susanne spent all day with Gavin. They walked through the woods, remembering childhood days, and once he stopped and said, "In the battle at Marston Moor, I was almost killed. . . ." He told her the story, and then said, "When I thought I was going to die, I thought of you, Susanne."

She looked at him in surprise. "Me? Not Francine?"

Gavin looked embarrassed. "I don't know why I didn't think of her . . . it seems I've loved her for so long." He reached out and touched her cheek gently, then smiled. "But we've been friends for as long as I can remember. You've been my best friend, Susanne."

"That's sweet, Gavin!" Susanne was acutely conscious of his hand on her cheek. "It's nice to have a friend. And I've always . . . liked you. Even when you were horrid to me!"

"Like when I threw you in the river?" He laughed at her, then the two of them moved along the path. Their time together was a brief respite for Gavin from the heavy burdens he bore, and when they got back to the house, he said, "I'm glad you're here." He frowned and asked, "Are you going to marry Henry?"

"My parents say I must."

"But you don't love him?"

Susanne shook her head and moved away without answering him. She had been pressured by both her father and mother to marry Darrow, but somehow she had resisted them. But she was well aware that they would have their way, for young girls of her class had little choice in these things.

❦

Susanne stayed for two more days, and during that time she found herself drawn close to the Morgans and the inhabitants of Wakefield. Amos stole her heart, but as Angharad told her, "He's a charmer! Wait until he gets his growth—what he'll do to the girls I hate to think!"

Gavin was busy with the many duties of the estate, and Susanne was surprised to see how competent he was. She told him so one morning when she'd gone with him to buy new horses, and he looked at her, then shrugged. "My father brought me up to do it. He thinks the lord of the manor should know as much as the serfs."

"I think that's wonderful. No one else I know among the nobility knows anything much about how to actually *do* the work."

The sun was rising, shouldering white clouds aside. The crops were in, so there was little work to do until harvest. A few laborers were working in the fields, the sound of their laughter drifting across to the pair. "I like it here, Gavin," Susanne said as they moved toward a pasture where sheep made black-and-white-dotted bundles. "And I like the Morgans so much."

"They're fine, aren't they? Will practically raised me—and what we'd do with Amos without Angharad is past me." They came to a fence, and he helped her through the gate. Picking up a woolly white lamb, he put it in her arms, and she held it awkwardly.

"He's so soft!"

"You wouldn't want a hard, tough lamb, would you?" he jibed. The wind was blowing slightly, and Gavin admired the picture before him—the snow-white lamb cradled in the arms of the beautiful girl. Susanne was wearing a blue dress that was molded to her firm figure by the wind. Her eyes were so dark blue that they seemed almost black, and the small mole on her left cheek merely accented the smoothness of her skin.

Her skin looks soft as satin, Gavin mused. He let his eyes rest on her heart-shaped face for a moment—and suddenly she lifted her head and their eyes met. Taken off guard, he stammered, "Well— it's going to be a good day—"

"Yes, I suppose it is." Susanne felt the same awkwardness that she'd seen in Gavin, and she put the lamb down carefully. It gamboled away on unsteady legs to its mother, and she said, "Let's go see Owen. I love to hear his stories."

They made their way to the Morgans' cottage and found that Angharad had brought Amos to play. The husky boy was digging a hole in the earth beside the wall that enclosed the cottage, and as the two of them sat down, Angharad said, "He's so serious about that hole. He works on it every time I bring him here."

Owen watched the boy fondly, then turned to Gavin. "I dreamed about you last night."

"About me?"

"Yes, and about your father."

Angharad put her cup of tea down, and there was a serious light in her fine eyes. "Was it from God, this dream?"

"I think so, Daughter." Turning to the two young people, he

explained, "We've been asking God to show us a way to help your father."

Gavin and Susanne exchanged glances, and Angharad caught it. "Don't be forgetting that God spoke to many of his people in dreams."

Gavin asked curiously, "Tell us the dream, Owen."

"It was very short, just a single picture really." Owen half closed his eyes, his lips drawn close together as he let the thing take shape in his mind. "I saw you and Will driving a wagon down a road. You were both in rough clothes—not like you usually wear. There were some armed men in a building, king's men, I'm guessing. And then I saw your father—"

"My father?" Gavin shot at Owen. "What was he doing?"

"I couldn't see that he was doing anything. He seemed to be in the back of the wagon. You turned and said something to him that I didn't get, and then he lay down in the wagon and Will pulled covers of some sort over him." Owen opened his eyes, and Gavin saw that they were as bright and shiny as he'd ever seen them. "It was clear as a picture, lad! And I think it's God's message to us."

"Message? What kind of message?" Gavin asked. And then it came to him like a flash. "Oh—you mean that Will and I are to get my father out of prison?"

"It may be." Owen nodded. "I can't say for sure. Many don't put stock in dreams, but Angharad and me, we've seen God do things with them, haven't we, Daughter?"

"Yes," she agreed softly. She was staring at her father, her eyes intent on his face. Finally she said, "I believe this is from God. We will pray about it, and God will confirm it if it's his direction to us."

All of this was too much for Gavin and Susanne. They had never heard of a dream having meaning, and when they left the cottage, Susanne said, "I don't see how Owen's dream could be from God."

"I wish it were, but I'm just not sure about it."

Later that day, at dusk, Will came to the house seeking Gavin. When Gavin came to him, he said promptly, "Well, we'll be helping your father, will we?"

"What do you mean?"

"The dream, boy! My father's dream!"

"Oh, Will, we can't go charging off on some mission with no more than a dream to go on!"

Will Morgan's eyes narrowed. "You don't believe God speaks to his people?"

"Through the Bible, yes, but in dreams? I'm not sure." Gavin bit his lip nervously. "You know I'd give *anything* to save my father, but Owen dreams a lot. Surely not all of them are from God. What was it Angharad said—about confirmation of some kind?"

"Indeed, we did pray about it," Will said. His teeth suddenly shone very white against his tanned skin. "And the good Lord has given us the sign. So get yourself ready, boy, for we're going to obey God!"

"A sign? What sort of a sign, Will?"

"Why, last night I had a dream myself," Will said. He grew very serious then as he said slowly, "And it was the exact same dream my father had, Gavin—down to the least detail!"

Gavin Wakefield was not an expert on God, but as he heard this, a feeling grew inside of him. He stood there and the feeling grew stronger, and finally he smiled.

"All right, Will, we'll leave at dawn. Come now, we'll have a council of war."

Long into the night, Gavin, Susanne, Owen, Will, and Angharad talked and prayed. Gavin discovered that the Morgans believed in *fervent* prayer—and as he listened to them, he felt he had never really prayed. The three bombarded heaven, and when the meeting finally broke up, all plans were made.

"I've been missing something, Susanne," Gavin said to her

when they left the cottage and moved toward the house. "I don't know anything about prayer—not like those three!"

Susanne had been a faithful Catholic, but she had never had her heart touched as it had been for the past hours. "I feel so strange," she whispered as they came to the door. Turning she said, "They *know* God, don't they, Gavin? And I—I only know *about* God."

The next morning Gavin and Will, dressed in the rough clothing of farmers, drove a wagon loaded with vegetables out of the gates of Wakefield and headed for Oxford. The sun was a feeble, pale disk that cast only a yellowish glow in the sky, and when Gavin looked back he saw Angharad holding Amos, and Susanne waving. He lifted his arm, waved, then said grimly, "Will, I feel like we're headed for a rough time. It's a little bit like being blind. We don't know where we're going or what we'll do when we get there."

But Will laughed in his throat. "It's an adventure, boy, an adventure with God leading us! Now all we have to do is whatever he says! He's never lost a battle yet!"

The wagon bumped over the rocky road, and the closer they got to the enemy, the more Gavin was conscious of God. "I've been in church all my life, Will," he said finally, "but I feel God more in this old farm wagon than I ever felt him in a cathedral!"

A LESSON IN
HUMILITY

L ook at you, holding your head up like you were a king!"
Will was scoffing at Gavin, who glared at him indignantly.
The older man reached out and pulled the battered hat
the boy wore down over his eyes.

"Devil throw smoke!" he exclaimed loudly. "It takes more than
wearing old clothes to fool people. Now get your head down. I
know it's a stretch for you, lad, but be humble!"

The two were standing beside a fire where the carcasses of two
naked rabbits sizzled on a spit. They had stopped long enough to
cook the pair, and Will had said, "Now, while supper's cooking,
let's give you a few lessons in how to be a peasant."

Gavin's erect figure would be a dead giveaway, Will knew, so he
began by getting the young man to stoop. But no matter how
hard Gavin tried, he could not seem to please Morgan. "Proud!
That's what you are, Gavin Wakefield." He nodded. "Get rid of it,
I tell you. And while we're at it, did you wash your face this
morning?"

Gavin looked at him indignantly. "Of course I did."

"Well, there you are! Do you think us common folks do
nothing but wash?" Will stepped over, scooped up a handful of
dirt, and, before Gavin could move, clapped it on the young man's
face.

"Ow! Watch out, Will!" Angered, Gavin rubbed at the dirt that marred his forehead and glared at Morgan. "Don't maul me like that!"

"And what will you do if some officer or nobleman gives you a lick across the face?" Will laughed roughly, "Give it back to him? That's all we need—to lift our hands against the nobility. Then we'll be in jail just like your father." Will leaned over and touched one of the rabbits, then stuck his finger in his mouth. "Well, let's eat, then we can get on with your schooling."

The two sat down and devoured the rabbits, which were flavored by a bit of salt. They washed the meal down with creek water, then Will said, "What will you do if we get caught, lad?"

"Fight!" Gavin slapped the sword he wore, and his gesture drew another sad look from Will. "Oh—I'm not supposed to wear a sword, am I?"

"How many serfs do you see wearin' a blade?" Morgan stood up. "Keep the blade, but be sure it's hidden." A light touched his dark eyes, and he asked, "Can you use that weapon?"

"Will, you know I'm good with the foils!"

"Are you now? Well, see if you can stand against me."

Glad to be able to excel at something, Gavin stood up and, as Will picked his own sword out of the wagon, assumed the classic duelist position, his right leg advanced and left bent behind. He kept his left hand behind his back and, as he advanced with his blade pointing, said, "I don't want to hurt you, Will—"

"Is that all you can do?" Morgan grinned at the young man, adding, "There is a fool you are!" He suddenly bent down and came up with a handful of dirt, then, before Gavin could move, threw it in his face!

Blinded and in pain, Gavin clawed at his eyes with his left hand, and as he lowered his blade, he felt the touch of steel at his breast. "That—wasn't fair!" he shouted, and finally cleaned his eyes enough to peer through them. He saw Morgan laughing at him and was filled with rage. Dropping his sword, he threw himself onto the older man and caught him off guard. The two of them rolled in the dirt, giving and receiving a few blows, until Morgan cried out, "Ho—enough, boy!"

Gavin came to himself, jumped to his feet, and stood glaring at Morgan, who was rubbing his left cheek. "Now, was *that* low enough for you?" he demanded.

Will gave a shout of laughter. "You've got a spot of Welsh blood in you, lad! This will be no gentleman's duel, I'm thinking. Now, go and scratch!" But he nodded with approval at the rough appearance of Gavin. "You look less like a lord and more like one of us common ones," he commented. "Now, let's get to sleep. We'll be in Oxford tomorrow, and how we'll get your father out of that prison is more than I know!"

"I wish you'd dreamed *that* part of all this," Gavin grunted. He rolled into his blanket and soon was fast asleep.

That's the way of the young, Will thought as he lay there looking up at the stars. *They can sleep in the shadow of the gallows. . . .*

The day was half gone when Will drew the team to a halt, waved his hand toward the city that lay down the busy road, then said casually, "Well, there's Oxford."

Gavin stared at the buildings that made up the city, then said, "Now all we have to do is find the prison, get inside it, get my father out, avoid all pursuit, and make our way through enemy territory until we're free."

"And if we slip up one time, we'll get our necks stretched!" Will snapped the reins, and soon the two were in the busy street that ran through the heart of town. The street teemed with horsemen, wagons, carts, children at play, dogs, pigs, and even cows.

"We'll find a stable for the wagon, then we'll look the place over. We'll have to know it well to get out when we've got your good father."

Two hours later the men had found their stable, and Will had located the prison by simply asking the stable owner, "Which be the prison for the Roundheads, I wonder?"

They had gone at once to the prison, and when they stood outside, Gavin shook his head doubtfully. "It's right in the middle of town, Will. I was hoping it'd be out by itself somewhere. Look at the soldiers swarming around it!"

"Shoosh, lad! you're always looking at the dark side." Will shoved his hat back, considered the two-story stone building carefully, then said, "Let's take a turn around the place."

By nightfall they had not only studied the outer limits of the prison, but had wandered the streets leading from it to the outskirts of the city. Finally Will said, "We've got to find out what it's like inside. Did that girl Susanne tell you what she saw when she was inside visiting your father?"

"No, not any details." Gavin shook his head regretfully. "I should have thought to ask her." He studied the building, his lips pulled together tightly. There was a stubborn streak in the boy, Will had noted, and now it surfaced. "Look, I'll go inside to visit Father."

"Why, you can get in, but I'm not sure you can get out," Will said with surprise. "Why would they let a scruffy fellow like you inside?"

"Because I've got some fresh vegetables for Sir Christopher Wakefield from Miss Susanne Woodville," Gavin said, his blue-gray eyes glowing with excitement. "And because I'll give the jailer this—" He held up a silver coin he'd fished from his pocket. "They won't dare deny the daughter of Sir Vernon Woodville!"

"Well, look for me on the floor!" Will Morgan exclaimed. "You should be a lawyer, Gavin Wakefield! You've got all the craft of one of that tribe!" He slapped Gavin on the back so hard the young man coughed, then said, "Well now, let's get the food the nice young lady sent. . . ."

Thirty minutes later, Gavin approached the entrance to the prison, his heart beating fast. This was as dangerous as battle, and he knew his only hope lay in convincing the guards he was only a simple farm boy.

"Don't talk more than need be," Will had cautioned him, *"and keep stooped over."*

"Wot's this, fellow?"

Gavin swallowed hard as a short, thickset guard barred his way. "Why, oi've got sumpthin' fer one of the prisoners, sir," he said in a rough voice.

"No visitors without a pass from the commandant!"

Gavin had expected this, and stood there, his head down for a long moment, then said, "Please, master, I don't know no commandant. But I got to give this 'ere sack to some'un named Wickfield."

"Wickfield? We ain't got no prisoner named Wickfield!" the guard snorted. "Be off with you!"

"But the lady said to give you this," Gavin said quickly, holding up the silver coin.

The guard's eyes grew smaller, and he snatched at the coin. "Wot's this? A bribe?"

"Oi don't know, sir, wot a bripe is. But Lady Woodville, she tole me—"

"Lady Woodville?" The guard grew more careful. "Wife of Sir Vernon Woodville, is that her?"

"No, your honor, it be his daughter." Gavin nodded eagerly. "She came to visit Wickfield, and she told me—"

"She did come here . . . but she visited Wakefield. Is that who you want?"

"Ah—I don't know, sir, but she said I had to give 'im this here food, and that the two coins wuz for the man who'd let me in—and she said I had to give it to 'im myself."

"Two coins? Where's the other one?"

"Well she said—Lady Woodville, that is—to give one when I went in, and one when I comes out, yer see?"

Greed scored the guard's face, and he thought hard. "All right, but I got to be with you. And lemme see that sack—" He took the sack, sorted through it roughly, then shoved it back to Gavin. "Yer got only three minutes."

"Oh, that be fine, yer honor!"

The guard led Gavin inside, then said to another armed guard, "Got a visitor for Wakefield."

"He ain't suppose to see no visitors."

"I know that, but this is a *special* visitor from Lord Woodville. Besides, I'll be right with him." Casting a glance at Gavin, who was drooling slightly and looking around with a slack-jawed expression, he winked. "This un ain't got enough sense to do nothing!"

Gavin nodded and gave a blank smile, then when the two men laughed, he joined them. He followed the guard down a hall and up one flight of steps. He kept his head down, but saw that there was no guard except the one at the front door. *One inside and one outside,* he noted, but when they got to the second floor, another guard rose to challenge them. He gave way at the name of Woodville, picked up a lantern, and led the way. Gavin squinted in the darkness of the corridor as he was guided down.

The guard stopped to throw a dead bolt. *No locks—just bolts on the outside,* Gavin thought.

Then the guard called out, "Wakefield!" and Gavin stepped inside the cell. As he stood there, blinking in the darkness, the guard held the lantern high, casting an amber glow over the cell.

Gavin's heart squeezed as he saw his father lying on a cot, his eyes shut against the light. He had not shaved since his capture, and his beard was streaked with white.

"What is it?" Chris asked in a thin voice.

"Visitor from Lady Woodville."

Christopher had been in a near comalike sleep when the sound of the bolt sliding had awakened him. He slowly sat up, pain shooting through his back. The ball had hit him high on the back of his right shoulder, and the recurring infection was once again raging. He was now racked with the fever that comes with such a wound. Slowly, as though it cost him greatly, he looked up—and caught his breath, for it was Gavin looking back at him! But he said nothing, noting Gavin's warning look. "From Lady Woodville?" he asked groggily.

"Yes, sir," Gavin said. "She says to tell yer she 'opes you enjoy these 'ere things to eat." Gavin extended the bag, then risked saying, "She 'opes yer feeling better, and Mr. Gavin, 'e said the same."

Chris nodded slowly, his eyes fixed on Gavin's face. "Tell them both I thank them."

"I'll do that, sir, and I 'opes to see yer soon in better 'ealth."

"All right, that's enough!" The guard pulled Gavin out of the cell and slammed the door, ramming the bolt home. "Let's have that other piece of money!" he demanded.

"Yes, yer honor, 'ere it is."

Gavin said nothing more. He shuffled along as he was unceremoniously escorted outside. He walked away from the jail and was joined at once by Will.

"I was that worried, boy! Did you get a look at the place?"

"Yes, and I think we can do it, Will. There's one guard outside, and another on the second floor."

"Just two guards, and there's two of us," Will said.

"I think we can handle them—but when we're outside, that's when it'll get difficult."

"When shall we try? In two or three nights?"

Gavin stopped and stared at his friend. His mind had been working rapidly, and now he smiled. "Tonight, Will."

Morgan blinked and his voice was high as he said, "Tonight! Why, lad, we can't do that!"

"Tell me why we can't." Gavin listened as Will brought forth arguments, but then he shook his head stubbornly. "The horses are fresh, and the longer we stay here, the more chance of someone recognizing us—or they might add more guards. No, tonight at midnight we march into that prison and we come out with my father."

Will Morgan was a bold man, but the audacity of Gavin's plan took away his speech—but only for a moment. Then his lips parted and he exclaimed, "Well, devil throw smoke! We'll do it, boy!" He threw his arms around the young man and whispered, "It's a man you are, Gavin Wakefield! Sir Christopher has a son to be proud of!"

<hr />

The moon was a sliver of yellow in the black sky. "It looks like a piece of cheese the rats have been at," Will whispered, glancing upward. He turned to his companion, squinted to catch a glimpse of his face, then said, "Are you ready?"

"Let's go." Gavin was tense, but the two of them had been over the quickly made plan so many times that he'd finally said, "It's in God's hands, Will. We'll do all we can, and leave the rest to him."

"Amen!" Morgan had intoned, and the two of them had brought the wagon to a side street close to the prison. They had crept along the streets, dodging the night guard, and now as they stood looking at the dark bulk of the prison, Gavin felt a spurt of fear. Not for himself, but for what would happen if they were captured. *God, this has to be in your hands!* he prayed, then he whispered, "All right, Will, here we go!"

The two men stepped out and when they reached the door, Will moved to one side where he could not be seen by the guard. Gavin lifted his fist, took a deep breath, then knocked on the door. Almost at once was a hoarse call, "Who's there?"

"I've got a message for the captain of the guard, from the king's council."

A long silence lay over the scene, and for one desperate moment Gavin thought they had failed. Then with a scraping sound the door opened a few inches, and a guard wearing a steel helmet and holding a sword peered out. "What's that you say? A message from the council?"

"Yes. I'm to give it to the captain of the guard."

"Give it to me, an' I'll see he gets it."

"All right." Gavin held out an envelope, and when the guard reached out to take it, Gavin grabbed the man's wrist and threw himself backward with all his might. There was a faint cry of shock, then a solid clunking sound as the man's forehead battered the edge of the door. At once Gavin yanked the door open, and Will was beside him.

The guard was only stunned and began to rise to his feet. He opened his mouth to cry out, but Will quickly lifted the man's helmet and gave him a hard rap on the skull with a short, heavy stick. The cry was cut off at once, and Will whispered, "Quick, Gavin—inside with him!"

The two dragged the man inside, and quickly Will tied and gagged him. "Now, let's take the one upstairs."

"Right!"

The two moved to the stairs, Will going first. When they came to the top of the stairs, the guard saw them. "Who the blazes—!" He came to his feet and swept a pistol up from a table. Will lunged at him, but the explosion rocked the silence. Gavin saw Will stumble, then he leaped at the guard and caught him in the mouth with a terrific blow. The man was tough, however, and after staggering back against the wall, threw a blow that caught Gavin in the temple. Bright light exploded inside his skull, and he could barely see the guard coming at him. Fortunately, when he slumped to the floor, his hand fell on Will's heavy stick. He managed to bring it up with a wild swing and catch the guard in the throat. The guard staggered back, gagging and choking, and Gavin rose and hit him a blow in the head that put him down like a felled steer.

"Good lad!" Will had regained his feet and managed a smile. "Now—which cell is Sir Christopher in?"

"Will, are you all right? He shot right at you!"

"Just a graze, no more," Will said. "Quick, lad! Everybody in Oxford must have heard that pistol shot!"

Gavin raced down the hall, found the cell, and yanked the bolt back. When he had opened the door, he found his father standing in the center of the cell. He looked pale, but there was a thin smile on his lips. "Well, Son, I've been expecting you," he said quietly.

"Father!" Gavin leaped forward and the two embraced. Then Gavin said urgently, "Come now, we haven't got much time. Can you walk?"

"Yes, to get out of here." But Gavin found that he had to half carry his father down the stairs. He noted that Will was moving slowly, and asked, "Are you hurt badly?"

"No. Let's get out of here." Will was moving stiffly, but he got to the door first. Opening it cautiously, he peered into the darkness. "Come on! I don't see anyone."

Five minutes later Chris was lying in a wagon bed, covered by a canvas, which in turn was covered by loose hay. Gavin took the lines and forced himself to drive slowly. The moments seemed to drag and time felt frozen, but eventually he straightened up and looked back at the city.

"I think we're all right now." Then he felt Will slump against him and wheeled to catch him as he fell. "Will!" he cried out.

Stopping the wagon, he pulled Will's clothing back and found a raw, bleeding wound in the unconscious man's right side. Quickly he stripped off Will's coat and shirt and cleaned the wound. Ripping up one of his own shirts, he made a bandage and fastened it as best he could.

He had just finished when Will's eyes opened. He looked around, then struggled to sit up, ignoring Gavin's protests. "I'm not hurt bad," he muttered. He glanced back toward Chris's hiding place and then smiled at Gavin.

"Well, boy, I've got to sit on the seat with you, because that's the way the dream was. We've got to be true to our dreams, we Welshmen!"

Gavin nodded and whipped the reins. As the animals moved forward, he thought of what Will had said. After a few moments he nodded at Will and smiled. "Yes, a man has to be true to his dream, or he's not a man at all!"

The sound of the horses' hooves made a rhythmic pattern, and soon Will dropped off to sleep, leaning against Gavin. Beneath his cover of canvas and hay, Sir Christopher Wakefield smiled, thinking of how few sons would have been able to do what his son had done. And Gavin Wakefield sat on the seat of the swaying wagon, his eyes darting back toward the city whence he expected pursuit to come at any second. But it did not come, and by the time dawn had reddened the eastern skies, Will awakened and looked around. He licked his lips then smiled at his driver.

"Well, lad, you've done it! God was with us, wasn't he?"

"Yes, he was, Will." They were miles from home, in hostile territory, but Gavin Wakefield felt hope burning in his heart. He said quietly, "God never fails, Will, does he now?"

Nineteen

"GOD IS WITH US!"

Susanne learned of the escape of Sir Christopher Wakefield from a very angry Sir Henry Darrow. She had just returned from a ride on her favorite mare. No sooner had she swung down from the saddle and handed the reins to a servant, than her maid came running to the stable yard. "Oh, Miss Susanne, your mother wants you at once!" she cried in agitation.

"Is something wrong, Sarah?"

The little maid rolled her eyes. "She ain't happy, Miss, and that's a fact! And Mr. Darrow is with her and your father in the library." Sarah was fiercely curious concerning the Woodvilles and whispered, "What have you done now, Miss Susanne, to get 'em all stirred up?"

"I haven't the foggiest idea."

Susanne walked rapidly to the house, then went at once to the library. All the while she was thinking, *It must be they've decided to make me marry Henry—they're all so set on it.* But when she entered the library, she was greeted by an angry question from her father that confused her utterly.

"Susanne, what do you have to do with the escape of Christopher Wakefield?"

"Why—!" Susanne hesitated, her mind working furiously. *Gavin and Will—they must have succeeded! Just like in the dream*

Owen had! But she said only, "I hadn't heard about any escape."

"Now don't deny that you're mixed up in it," Darrow broke in. "We know you've had a hand in it." He was covered with dust from the road, and anger glinted in his eyes. "I knew you had a senseless weakness for the son, but I didn't think you'd go this far!"

Susanne pinned him with her eyes and said evenly, "I don't know anything about this." She met their accusing eyes. "When did he escape?"

"Now don't act innocent! We have evidence that you were a part of this thing." Vernon Woodville had been ill, and his hands trembled as he spoke. "If you have any sense at all, girl, you'll turn the man in! After all, he is the enemy of the king!"

"Father, I didn't know Sir Christopher had escaped until I stepped into this room." Susanne had regained her composure and turned to Darrow, asking, "What is this 'evidence' you have, Henry?"

"You visited him in his cell, for one thing. I've talked to the commandant, and he says you were there two weeks ago. The fool! I had the hide off him for allowing you to see Wakefield."

"Yes, I saw Sir Christopher and I'm not ashamed of it. He's an old friend and he's suffering from a wound."

"He's gotten what he deserves!" Lady Woodville had decided that Susanne's best marital venture would be Sir Henry Darrow, and she saw that her prospective son-in-law was very angry. She had always dominated her daughter and snapped, "Now, out with it! We know from the guards that you're involved. Where is he hiding?"

Susanne thought with a rush of satisfaction, *They've not been caught, or they wouldn't be questioning me like this.* She was heartily glad, for the sight of Christopher Wakefield in such a terrible condition had angered her. "I visited him, but I know nothing of his escape."

"You're happy about it, though, aren't you?" Darrow snapped.

"Yes, I am." Susanne lifted her chin and faced the tall man squarely. "I hold it a fault that you treated him so shabbily. He would not have done so to you!"

That statement precipitated a fierce argument, Susanne facing off with the other three. Finally her father said, "Go to your room, Susanne. You'll have to learn obedience and loyalty, so you can stay at home until you do!"

When Susanne left, she found Francine outside waiting. The young woman had come for one of her visits, and she said quickly, "I saw Henry ride in. He looked terribly angry."

"He is. He thinks I helped Sir Christopher escape from prison."

Francine's eyes opened wide, and she drew the story of the angry confrontation out of Susanne. When she was satisfied she had it all, she shook her head. "You made a mistake going to visit Wakefield. Henry hates that family, especially Gavin."

Susanne was shaken by the scene and made her escape from Francine as soon as possible. She enjoyed the young woman's company—at times. But she had no real friendship with Francine, for their ways and points of view were far apart. Francine was self-centered to a fault, and Susanne suspected that the older girl was in love with Henry Darrow. Once she had asked her, but Francine had merely smiled, saying, "He's wealthy and handsome, Susanne. I could be in love with any man with those qualities."

Susanne kept to her quarters all that day, going down only for lunch at noon at her mother's bidding. Henry was still angry with her and spent most of the day talking with Francine. Afterward, when she returned to her room to rest, her mother entered and said angrily, "A fine mess you've made of things!"

"Mother, I had nothing to do with that escape."

"I don't mean that! I mean you're a fool for treating Henry as you do." Lady Woodville was an expert in men, for she had practiced on many of them. She was still an attractive woman, but there was a hardness in her features that no cosmetics could disguise. Her eyes were cold as she stood over Susanne. "Do you think fortunes like his are to be picked off the trees? Don't you see how he attracts women? Why, if Francine had a title or money, he'd marry her in a flash."

"I see that," Susanne said, but added with spirit, "But do you think he's not doing exactly what you are, Mother? He's after *our* lands, just as you and father are after his!" Suddenly the whole charade disgusted her and she said wearily, "I get so tired of it all, the eternal chasing after money and titles and lands, parents swapping their daughters off like brood mares to add a few acres to an estate."

Frances Woodville's god was money—and her daughter's words brought a rush of rage through her. "You're a fool, Susanne!" she whispered, her face pale. "There's only one way to treat a fool, and that is to control her. I shall see to it that you marry Henry—and very soon!" She whirled and left the room, and Susanne could only try to contain the tears of frustration that rose in her eyes.

Though her room seemed oppressive, she stayed in it until dusk, then left and went for a walk through the park. It was a secluded place, with tall hedges that had been planted to form complicated walkways. One who didn't know them could get lost, but rarely did anyone come except visitors and the gardeners. There was a solitude about the place, and as Susanne walked slowly through the maze, she tried to think how she could stand against her parents. She had come to understand that not only did she *not* love Henry Darrow, she disliked him intensely. The idea of being married to him was abhorrent, but how to avoid it she could not think.

The sun had dropped low, and darkness covered the walkways. She had reached the end of a tall hedge, and just as she turned, a movement caught her eye. She thought at first it was Firth, the gardener, but before she could speak, a man in ragged clothes had grabbed her! She opened her mouth to scream, but a hand clamped over it, and she was held in strong arms.

"Susanne, don't be afraid. It's me, Gavin!"

The hand moved from her mouth, and Susanne stared up, whispering, "Gavin—what are you doing here?" The fear left her, and she at once knew the answer. "You helped your father escape! Oh, I'm so glad!"

"Yes, but we've gone as far as we can." Gavin's eyes, Susanne saw, were red-rimmed with fatigue. Under the ragged hat, his dirty face little resembled the one she knew. His lips were drawn tightly together, and she saw that he was running on nerve alone.

Susanne took his arm and looked around. "Henry is here," she whispered. "He thinks I helped with the escape!"

Gavin was so tired he could barely stand up. Will had been hurt worse than he had admitted and had collapsed from loss of blood. Gavin had driven the team far off the main road and for three days had scarcely closed his eyes. He'd had to care for both men while keeping a constant vigil for those who sought them. He'd talked to one farmer, risking a visit to get food, and discovered that search parties of militia were combing the countryside for the fugitives. He'd had to be even more alert, and now as he stood beside Susanne, he was trembling with fatigue.

"Your father, is he all right?"

"He's not well, and Will Morgan took a wound, so he's weak, too." Gavin drew a hand that was not steady across his face, then let it fall. "I shouldn't have come here, Susanne, but I couldn't think of anything else to do."

At once Susanne knew what she had to do. A courage she had not known she possessed rose up in her breast. Firmly she said, "I'll help you, Gavin."

"You shouldn't."

Susanne smiled at him and, reaching up, tucked a lock of his blond hair inside his cap. "Good friends, aren't we, Gavin? Always good friends?"

The words and the smile on her face brought a needed touch of cheer to Gavin. He took her hand and held it briefly. "Always good friends," he whispered. They stood there in the twilight, and he drew strength from her calm demeanor.

"Now, where are your father and Will?"

"In a grove over by the lake."

"They can't stay there." Susanne shook her head. "I know where you can go. Do you remember the old barn, the one where we took the dogs to kill rats when we were small?"

"Yes, down by the bluff on the river."

"It's still there, more or less. Nobody ever goes there, Gavin. It's dark now, so you go take the wagon there. I'll come as soon as I can with food and medicine."

Gavin nodded, then whispered, "You're my good angel, Susanne!" Then he was gone, slipping down the darkened aisles of the maze.

Susanne at once returned to the house. She crept in through a side door, and as she passed down the long hall she saw Henry and Francine in the library. They were looking at a book, and Francine was laughing softly at something he had said. Susanne hurried to her room, and Sarah prepared her for bed. "I don't feel too well, Sarah. I'll sleep late in the morning. Tell my parents that I won't join them for breakfast."

"Oh, they went to visit the Sanders family late this afternoon, Miss," Sarah answered. "They won't be back until Tuesday."

Relief at this news swept over her, though Susanne didn't let it show. As soon as the house grew still, Susanne rose and put on her riding dress. She opened the door to her room, peered out, then moved down the hall. As soon as she had gathered food and bandages, she hurried to the stable, grateful she'd learned to saddle her own mare. When she had the saddle on, she grasped the sack, mounted, then guided the horse out of the stable. The night was still, but her nerves were tense until she was a good distance from the house. Then she said, "Come on, Lady!" and the startled mare broke into a brisk gallop.

Three days later, a fine drizzle of rain fell across the field, lending it a gray texture. It softened the ground and muffled the hooves of the mare that came into the clearing. Will Morgan's quick ears, however, caught the faint sound, and he came to his feet at once. Snatching up his sword, he moved to the door of the dilapidated barn, stared out, then tossed it down as he recognized the rider. "It's Miss Susanne," he said and flung the door back. Catching the sack she tossed down to him, he grabbed the mare's reins as she slipped to the ground.

"Hello, Will." Susanne smiled at him. "How's your side?"

"Fit as a Welshman." Will nodded. "These days of good nursing did the trick. Go on in. I'll take care of the mare."

Susanne entered the barn and was met at once by Sir Christopher. "Well now, it's early for you to be out. And dangerous."

"No, I think the patrols have about given up. And everyone's used to my rides." She took his hand and smiled. "You're looking better than when I saw you last, sir. There's more color in your cheeks and your eyes are clearer."

"Thanks to you. Good food, good nursing, that's what's bringing me back." He held her hand for a moment. "I think I shall have to tell you what a fine young woman you are, Susanne Woodville!" He smiled as color flooded her cheeks, then released her hand. "I know you don't like to be thanked, but I must say it."

Gavin entered from the back door. He noted the two and said, "I saw you riding in, Susanne."

He came to stand beside his father, and Susanne looked at them for a moment, then remarked, "You two resemble each other so much!"

"I think all the Wakefield men look pretty much alike," Chris said. "Amos looks very much like Gavin did at his age." He sobered then and shook his head. "I never expected to see Amos again. God is so good!"

"I think it's safe enough to leave now," Gavin said. "Do you feel up to making a dash for it tonight?"

"Try me!"

Will entered in time to hear this exchange. "Right you are! I've had enough hiding. We go at dusk."

That was a fine day for Susanne. She and Gavin had a grand time fishing in the stream. Then, when she caught an eel, she threw her pole down and slipped, trying to get away. Gavin picked up the eel and pretended he was going to let it bite her.

"No! Please Gavin, I hate those things!"

"They make a pretty tasty dish." He grinned, holding the wiggling creature high. "I think you should clean it and cook it for us."

Susanne shuddered and made a face. "I'd as soon eat a *snake!* Please, Gavin, don't tease me!"

Gavin looked at her, then threw the eel back into the water. "I'm sorry, Susanne," he said and came to put his hand on her shoulder. "I always did like to devil you, didn't I?"

Susanne was conscious of how tall Gavin was—and of the firm pressure of his hand on her shoulder. "You always did," she said quietly, savoring the moment. She was wearing a fitted brown riding dress and fine black boots. Her eyes were wide and there was a softness and a vulnerability in her lips that marked her youth. She smiled, saying, "I could never let you alone, could I? Always tagging along with you."

"I guess you were like a little sister to me." He looked down at her, admiration in his blue eyes. "But you're more a big sister now."

"No, I am not your sister!"

Her tone was so sharp that Gavin blinked. "Well, not *really* my sister, of course." His hand left her shoulder and he touched her cheek, marveling at its smoothness. "Friends always, aren't we?"

"Yes."

Gavin saw something in Susanne's eyes that he couldn't understand, and removed his hand quickly. Each time he was with her, he grew more aware of her loveliness and her character—and of other emotions that he couldn't sort out. "Well, we'll be gone tomorrow," he said quickly. "What will you do when you don't have a pack of fugitives and invalids to take care of? Be glad to be rid of us, eh?"

"No, I won't." Susanne turned and moved to the bank. Finding a grassy spot, she sat down, and Gavin came to join her. She was so quiet that Gavin thought she was upset with him for touching her. "Don't be angry," he said. "I meant nothing by touching you."

She gave him a quick glance, then shook her head. "I'm just thinking of how lonesome I will be when you're gone." She tried to smile but it was a futile effort. "It's been so good to help you and your father and Will. I do so little that amounts to anything."

"Why, that's not so!"

"Yes it is, Gavin. I-I've been dreading what's ahead. My parents are going to make me marry Henry—and I don't love him!"

Suddenly the bleakness of her future rose up before her, and Susanne began to weep, her shoulders shaking. She had not done so before, but the three days of helping her friends had somehow changed her world. Always before she could put the idea of marriage off into some vague future, but now it was confronting her with all its grim reality.

Gavin was shocked at the grief that racked the girl's shoulders.

He had not known how unhappy she was. *I've been so taken up with my own problems, I haven't thought of her! What a swine I am!*

Compassion filled him, and he put his arm around her and drew her close. He said nothing as she turned to him and let the tears flow, feeling safe within the circle of the strong arms that held her. Finally she drew back and looked up at him. They were so close he could see the tiny gold flakes in the pupils of her eyes and smell the faint scent that always reminded him of lilacs. Her lips trembled and she whispered, "I'm sorry to be so—"

But she didn't finish, for Gavin lowered his head and put his lips on hers. It was a gentle, tender kiss, and his arms pressed her close. Susanne was startled, but there was nothing demanding in his caress—and she could not help but think how different it was from Henry Darrow's unwelcome embraces. She leaned against him, conscious of his strength, and then she put her hands behind his head and drew him closer.

It was a moment of complete tenderness for both Gavin and Susanne. Gavin was filled with gratitude for what Susanne had done for him, but he knew there was a great deal more to what he was feeling than mere gratitude. As the firm curves of her body pressed against him, he knew that never could he think of his childhood friend in the same way again, for she met his kiss as a woman. There was a sweetness and wildness in her lips that he had never known, and when she drew back, he said huskily, "Susanne!"

But she put her fingers on his lips, saying, "Hush! This is what it is, Gavin! Don't make more out of it!"

Gavin rose and helped Susanne to her feet. He was shaken by the kiss and knew that he would be affected by it for days. Somehow something had changed between them—but he could not say what it was. Before, she had been Susanne, the friend of his boyhood, but now as he looked at her, he knew with a sense of strangeness that she had become something different . . . something he could not yet define.

"Susanne, you're so beautiful," he said unevenly, "and the sweetest girl I've ever known."

Susanne gave him an odd look, sure that he was thinking of someone else. But she forced a smile and said, "I must get home." Somehow the words were difficult to say and she found herself wanting to weep again. "I don't expect we'll be meeting again, so I'll say good-bye now."

Gavin took her hand and tried to think, but he was confused. "I'll write—"

"No, my parents would see the letter and never allow me to have it," she said. Pain was slicing at her like a razor, and she could not bear it. "I'll say good-bye to Will and your father—"

Ten minutes later the three men stood watching as the young woman rode her mare over the ridge. When she was out of sight, Chris sighed heavily, "We can never repay that young woman, can we, Gavin?"

"No sir."

The bleakness of his tone drew the attention of both men. They exchanged knowing glances, but neither of them spoke. They loaded the wagon, and when dusk fell they made their way down the dusty road. Gavin was silent all the way.

Once, as they were camped and he was gone for firewood, Chris said, "Gavin is changed, isn't he, Will?"

"Aye, sir, that he is."

Chris looked at the compact Welshman and remarked, "I think he's a little mixed up about himself."

"Weren't you at his age? I couldn't tell my head from my feet when I was nineteen."

They said no more, but gave their attention to getting safely back home. For three days they traveled at night, and then at dawn on Tuesday they came to Wakefield.

"I never thought to see it again, Son," Christopher said quietly. Gavin nodded. The experience had strengthened him—and brought a new soberness to his spirit. "It's good to be home, sir," he said simply. And then he snapped the reins and they entered the gates of Wakefield.

Christopher Wakefield stood beside Amos, a hand on the boy's shoulder. The skies were red and gold, colored by the sinking sun. The two of them had been for a long walk, and looking down, Chris thought, *How much he's like Gavin!* The thought pleased him, and he let his eyes rest on the four-year-old's sturdy body and the dark auburn hair.

"Papa, can Angharad go with us to the village tomorrow?"

"If she wants to."

"She'll want to," Amos said. "She always likes to go every place with us."

"Does she? Well, I expect she will then. Now, go wash your hands."

"But I didn't fall down!"

"No, but you picked up the toad in the garden." Chris smiled at Amos's protest, thinking of how much the child hated washing. He used all his wiles to get out of baths, but Angharad would say, "There's an old pig you are! Now, into it!"

As Christopher wandered along the path that led by the rose garden, he thought of how he'd enjoyed the last two weeks. He'd come home sick in body, but Angharad had taken him into her strong hands at once. She'd stuffed him with delicious food, seen to it that he rested for long hours—including a nap, which he took with Amos—and had dosed him with potions that tasted horrible, but had evidently given him new strength.

"Where is Amos?"

Chris turned to Angharad, who had come to stand beside the large clump of red roses. She was wearing a pale green dress, and her hair fell down her back in black waves. Chris said, "He's getting cleaned up, then I believe he wants to invite you to go with us to town tomorrow." Chris grinned. "The boy tells me you want to go everywhere the two of us go."

Angharad flushed at his words, but rapped out, "Did you give him a paddling, then?"

"No."

"I should have been here!" She turned to go, but stopped when he called her name. "Yes, sir? Is there something you wanted?" Angharad let her large eyes dwell on the master of Wakefield. She knew that something was troubling him, for he had been silent for the past few days. She thought of the long hours they'd spent together while he was recuperating, how he'd talked of his youth and she had been drawn out enough to speak of her own life. But lately he had watched her, she noted, with a strange expression, and she racked her mind trying to think of how she had offended him. *Now is a good time to find out,* she thought, and said, "Sir Christopher, have I displeased you in some way?"

He looked at her, surprised. "Why do you ask that?"

"You're so quiet lately. Not at all like you were when—"

Chris studied her as she broke off, then came to stand close to her. The tang of fall was in the air, with all its richness, and overhead a flock of nightingales uttered their melodious language.

To Angharad's total surprise, Christopher reached out and took her hand. She stared at him blankly, her lips parted. "Why—sir—!" she gasped, but she did not pull away.

"Angharad, I'm an old man and you're a lovely young woman."

"You are not old! And I'm certainly no babe."

"I'm fifty-five and you're thirty-three." Regret lay in Chris's voice, but his hand tightened on hers. "But I'm a lonely man, Angharad, and for my own selfish reasons, I'm asking you to marry me."

Angharad stared at Christopher, shock running through her.

She loved this man, she well knew, but never once had the thought of marrying him come to her. Though he was older, she loved the lean look of him, the wedge-shaped face, the wide mouth, and the pugnacious chin. But she said haltingly, "You— can't mean it—I'm only a servant—"

Christopher took her in his arms and, when she would have drawn back, held her firmly. "You're the woman I love, Angharad. Don't you remember your family history? Margred Morgan was of peasant stock, but Sir Robert Wakefield loved her—as I love you."

At his words, pure joy swept over Angharad. Words escaped her, but when he bent his head, she raised her lips to his. He held her as if she were a precious thing, and she knew then that this was to be her life. When he raised his head, she looked at him with tears glittering in her dark eyes.

"I've always said when God sent a husband, I'd have him." She lifted her hand and stroked his cheek. "You are the one God has sent, so I will be your wife—and a mother to Amos. With all my heart, I will serve you and our children!"

He kissed her again, then said in a voice that was both unsteady and strong and clear, "He who finds wife finds a good thing, and obtains favor from the Lord."

They walked in the garden for a long time, speaking little, filled with a joy that seemed to grow as the moon rose. They watched the huge silver disk as it sent pale waves of light to wash the earth, and then they turned to each other and made their vows of love.

END OF PART THREE

A Royal

1 6 4 5   **Part**
─────
FOUR   1 6 4 9

Death

Twenty

THE SWORD OF OLIVER CROMWELL

R-Rupert—what is this n-new army that Cromwell has designed?"

King Charles had called his two chief military advisers into a war council, and the three of them stood looking down at a large map spread out on a low table. Charles was much thinner in this spring of 1645 than he had been earlier in the war, and his stammer was more pronounced. The defeat at Marston Moor had unnerved him, but the war had not slackened. The Cavaliers, undiscouraged by their dwindling territory and strength, fought in pitched battles with a continued ferocity.

Prince Rupert stroked his long black curls in a feline gesture. He had the affected mannerisms of a dandy, but he was a tough, hard soldier despite his foppish appearance. "Oh, it's called the New Model Army, sire." He shrugged. "Cromwell is the architect, but it's a foolish notion."

"H-how so?"

"Why, Cromwell has made a *church* out of it!" Rupert slapped the sword at his side in disgust. "Our informants tell me that a soldier is whipped for swearing! The chaplains have prayers ten times a day. Foolishness! Blasted foolishness!"

Sir Henry Darrow glanced at Rupert. Darrow had risen to the king's confidence by his political powers rather than his soldierly qualities. True, he did ride with the king to the battles, but both kept well back from the hard fighting. Now he considered Rupert with doubt. "Yes, but religion isn't all there is to this New Model Army. I've been watching Cromwell's work, and it's a formidable army." He overrode Rupert's protest, insisting, "It's large, for one thing. Ten regiments of horse with six hundred men each, twelve foot-regiments of twelve hundred men each, and a regiment of one thousand dragoons."

"Wh-why, that's over twenty thousand men!" Charles exclaimed.

"Numbers don't matter, Your Majesty," Rupert insisted. "These psalm singers, we'll run them into the sea! And the sooner we strike the better!"

Charles stared at the flamboyant cavalry commander, his eyes narrowed. "But d-do we have the force for such a th-thing?"

"We're as strong as we'll ever be," Rupert stated. "And Cromwell and his Roundheads get stronger every month. I say it's now or never!"

"I fear the prince is right, sire," Darrow agreed. "It's a risk, but if we hit hard and unexpectedly, we can gain a victory that will bring many back to your support."

Charles was in an agony of indecision. The defeats of the previous year had reduced his holdings, and he burned to regain them. "Very w-well—" he nodded finally as the two men waited—"where shall we bring the enemy to ground?"

"I would like to strike at Naseby, Your Majesty." Rupert had already made a master plan, and he sketched it out on the map. He was full of confidence, this German-born prince, and his ability to wheel and whirl cavalry troops around the countryside at a striking pace had become legendary. He had an iron confidence in his Cavaliers, scorning the lowly commoners who made up the New Model Army—and scoffed at Cromwell's insistence on passing over noble-born men for his officers, choosing instead the man best fitted even if he'd been born a serf.

Charles and Darrow listened, both of them slightly in awe of Rupert's military genius, and when the Cavalier was finished, Charles nodded eagerly. "Splendid! Wh-when can we be ready to move?"

"It's the fifth of June. We can strike the enemy next week, sire."

King Charles was a devious man in many ways, but he had longed for victory for so long that now he grasped eagerly at the hope held out by Rupert. "I sh-shall ride at the head of the army, Prince," he said, and there was a bright glimmer of confidence in his dark eyes.

After the council of war, Henry Darrow left the royal chambers, his mind full of politics and battle. He spent the day attending to the multitude of details that the new campaign demanded, for this was something he did better than Rupert or the king, and he took pride in it. When he finally made his way to his apartment, an ornate room the king had insisted on his using while at Oxford, he found Francine in a bad frame of mind.

"I've been waiting for you all day, Henry," she said with irritation marring the smoothness of her features. She was wearing a scarlet gown with pearls sewn into arabesque patterns on the low-cut bodice, and two large diamond earrings glittered at her lobes, catching the reflection of the chandelier overhead. "A troop of actors arrived here today and we missed their performance."

"Sorry, Francine," Darrow said briefly. He tossed his hat on the floor and walked to the couch that rested under a magnificent painting, done by a man named Rembrandt. It was a strange picture, featuring a group of surgeons observing as a teacher dissected a corpse. Francine hated it, and Darrow grinned at her, asking, "Been admiring the fellow's insides?"

Francine uttered a short ugly word, then came to sit down

beside Henry. She leaned against him and pulled his head down, and he kissed her. She had come to Oxford under the guise of being a member of the queen's group of young women, but she and Darrow had carried on a torrid affair, enjoying the spice of keeping the thing hidden from the eyes of the royal couple.

Francine knew that she would never find a husband in Henry Darrow, but to her surprise she found herself in love with him. The only greater surprise was that Henry had found himself somewhat in the same condition. He said so now. "Too bad you don't have a fortune, sweet. What a shame!"

The next morning as Francine was carefully arranging her hair, Darrow said suddenly, "You had better make some arrangement, Francine." He was lying in bed, regarding her. When she turned to him, he added, "I don't have as much confidence in Rupert as he has in himself."

"You think we might lose the war?"

"Very possible." Darrow rose and came over to put his hands on her shoulders. "Cromwell is a fool, but he's never been beaten in battle. At Marston Moor he whipped Rupert badly. If we lose this next battle . . ."

When Darrow paused, Francine rose and came to his arms. "What would happen, Henry?"

"What would happen to Cromwell and his Roundheads if we defeated them?" A cynical smile curled his lips, and he put the matter bluntly. "We'd grind them into the dust. I expect something like that would happen to us if we lose."

A shiver ran through Francine, the specter of a penniless future giving her a quick spurt of fear. "You're probably right," she said slowly. "But perhaps it won't happen."

"Don't wait to find out," Darrow said, his handsome face suddenly turned serious. "I hope to win, but I'm making plans in case we don't—and that's what I'm telling you to do, Francine." He kissed her tenderly, then said almost sadly, "I'd miss you, more than I ever thought I'd miss a woman. But we must look to ourselves in this world."

Francine left Darrow's room, carefully avoiding the guards' eyes. When she got to her room, she paced back and forth for a long time, her mind busy with what Henry had told her. She had accepted the fact that Henry would not marry her, but she knew that she had to do *something.* The sun rose as she stood at the window and watched the crimson globe fire the tops of the tall trees that flanked the palace. She was not only a beautiful woman, but an astute one as well. Where her own safety and comfort were concerned, she was very able indeed!

Finally an idea came to her, not all at once, but in fragments. All day long she nurtured it, and by late afternoon, she had formulated a plan. *Gavin—it has to be Gavin,* she thought. *He'll be safe if the Roundheads win.* She felt somehow that a great burden had lifted, and as she moved among the flowers, one thought rose in her: *I can't have Henry, but I can manage Gavin. He's a fool about love!*

⸻

Sir Thomas Fairfax was the overall commander of the parliamentary forces approaching the area northwest of the small village of Naseby. Having discovered that the king was set between two ridges, he called his captains together. "The battle is upon us. Skippon, you will hold the center with your foot soldiers. Ireton, put our cavalry on the left wing, and Cromwell, you will hold the right flank."

When the order came to form ranks, at ten o'clock on the morning of June 14, 1645, Gavin was visiting an old friend. He had left his station under Cromwell and gone to search the ranks for John Bunyan. After some difficulty, he found the soldier in the second rank of the musketeers. "Hello, John," he said warmly, dismounting and shaking the tall young man's hand. "Ready for the battle, are you?"

Bunyan's complexion was reddened by the bright sun, but he seemed cheerful. "Why, the battle is the Lord's, sir!" He grinned broadly, adding, "I'll try to keep an eye on you. You must try not to let those long-haired Cavaliers get the best of you this time!"

"I'll do my best, John. Now, tell me about yourself. What have you been doing?"

The two men stood there talking, and Gavin examined the portly young fellow with affection. After the battle of Marston Moor, he had found Bunyan and thanked him heartily for saving his life. The two had formed a friendship, and during the months that had passed, had encountered each other twice. Bunyan was a cheerful young man, given to sports and frolic. But there was a sober side to him, and he exhibited it now as the two spoke.

"At times like this, sir, when a man faces death, he wishes he'd lived a different sort of life."

"Why, you've not been a bad man, John!"

"I've done my share of cursing, and I've not followed after God," Bunyan said simply. He turned abruptly and demanded, "Do you believe in hell, Lieutenant Wakefield?"

The question caught Gavin off guard, but he answered at once. "Certainly! It's not a pleasant thing, but it's plainly taught in the Scripture." He hesitated then said, "You're worried about your soul, I take it!"

Bunyan shrugged his heavy shoulders and glanced across the way where the king's forces were lining up, obviously ready to give battle. "I might be tossed into eternity in half an hour. What would I say to God when he asks me why I ignored him?"

"Well, there's time to seek him now, John."

"No sir, I don't like the idea of ignoring God when I'm hale and hearty, then running to him when things get hard. That's no part of a man!"

"Better get rid of that idea," Gavin said soberly. "My father's the best Christian I know, and he says that it's only God's grace that saves any of us."

"Well enough, but what part does a man play? Is he to just let God do it all?"

"That's what my father says. He quotes a Scripture all the time: 'By grace you have been saved through faith, and that not of yourselves; it is the gift of God, not of works, lest anyone should boast.'"

Bunyan seemed uncomfortable with the idea. "Don't seem right to me, sir. A man's a man and ought to do all he can to make his way right with God, keeping the commandments and so on."

Gavin had been over this ground himself and longed to help the soldier. "John, if a man could save himself, why did God send Jesus to die on the cross? Why, it would have been wicked of God to send his Son to suffer if it wasn't necessary!"

The idea caught at Bunyan, and his large, expressive eyes grew bright. "I never thought of that, sir," he confessed. "But it's hard for a man like me to grasp such things. I'm no theologian, just a plain, simple tinker." He peered at Wakefield carefully, asking, "You're not afraid of death, then?"

Gavin had thought this all out long ago. "I suppose any man is afraid a little of a new experience, and death is the one thing we can't 'practice,' can we, John? This flesh trembles when I think of getting a sword in my guts, but I'm not afraid of what comes after death." He thought hard then said, "I'm not afraid of what happens *after* I die; it's the *getting there* that's a bit frightening."

The two men stood there watching the forces form lines of battle, talking of God and death and salvation, and when the trumpet sounded, Gavin took the strong hand of Bunyan, saying, "Time for me to go, John. I'll pray that God will spare your life. You're seeking God, and I don't want you going off until you've settled this thing."

"Why, God bless you, Mr. Wakefield!" Bunyan nodded. "I need

your prayers, and for whatever a rough soldier's prayers are worth, you'll have mine, sir!"

The two parted, and Gavin had no sooner gotten back to his place than Cromwell called him to his side. The face of the commander was alive with joy, and his mood was close to glee. He greeted Gavin, saying, "I wish your dear father were able to be here and share in this battle."

"He would choose that himself." Gavin nodded. Glancing over to the ranks of the enemy, he asked, "Are you certain of victory, General?"

"I can but smile out to God in praises," Cromwell cried out, loudly enough for those in the vicinity to hear him, "in assurance of victory, for God brings into being things that are not! This day we will see the hand of God, Lieutenant Wakefield!"

The king's battle line advanced, the center held by the footmen under Astley, the right wing of cavalry led by Rupert, and the left by General Langdale. Thus it was that Cromwell and his New Model Army were met by Langdale rather than Rupert.

Suddenly Rupert saw a weakness in the enemy line and did what he did best: led a slashing cavalry charge. The Royalists cried out "Queen Mary," a tribute to Henrietta Maria, and the soldiers of the New Model Army shouted at the tops of their lungs, "God and our strength!"

The charge of Rupert's men swept Ireton's cavalry back, and soon the left side of the New Model Army was in difficulty. Ireton was wounded and ultimately taken prisoner. The entire left wing of the New Model Army was in fearful disarray, and the foot soldiers of Skippon—himself wounded and his deputy killed— were giving way.

All seemed lost, but on the right, Oliver Cromwell had drawn up his regiments into three lines. When the two forces clashed, the iron discipline that Cromwell had instilled into his men kept them holding firm. In that moment, when the forces of Langdale faltered, Cromwell showed his military genius. He launched his men like a thunderbolt, and the raging Ironsides hit the line with a devastating effect.

Gavin was in the thick of it, slashing with his sword after he'd fired his pistol. He felt a musket ball pull at his hair, but took no notice. In the hottest part of the battle, he looked across to see the king of England at the head of a force of Cavaliers. "Look—!" He yelled to his colonel. "There's the king!"

Charles had led a part of the army in a countercharge, but even as Gavin watched, his supporters gathered around him and pulled him back out of the heat of battle.

Ten minutes later Cromwell passed, his face alight with joy. "We've beaten them, Gavin!" he shouted.

"What about Rupert, sir?"

"He did what he always did, let his men get out of control. They cut their way through our lines, but then instead of stopping to fight, they rode on to the baggage train. We caught them there and cut them to pieces!" Cromwell's eyes glowed, and he pulled off his helmet and looked up to the heavens, saying, "I thank thee, O God of battles, for the victory we have from thy mighty hand!"

And so the battle of Naseby ended. It was the final defeat for King Charles I and his forces. There would be other battles and sieges, but the final military decision of the English Civil War had been made.

Charles escaped and in April made his way to Scotland. He hoped to raise an army there and recapture his throne, but on June 24 of 1646, Oxford surrendered and the war was over once and for all. The Scots handed the king over to Cromwell, now head of the nation for all practical purposes. Charles returned to England, not as king, but as a prisoner.

And a prisoner in dire straits. Charles's papers were found among the baggage of the royal forces after Naseby. In them was clear evidence that Charles had planned to bring an Irish Catholic army to England with the promise of making the nation Catholic! When these papers were read aloud in the House of Commons, then printed and distributed, Christopher Wakefield said to his wife, "Angharad, the king is a dead man! He has done what Mary Queen of Scots did, and he will meet her fate—death under the ax of the executioner!"

Twenty-one

THE WAY OF A WOMAN

B y the spring of 1646 the Puritans had beaten down all military opposition, but the hostility of the populace made the fruits of victory hard to harvest. To win the war, parliament had been forced to tax every group heavily and, even more disturbing to some, had promised the Scots that the Elizabethan Church would be dismantled and reassembled "according to the word of God."

On paper this was done. Cathedrals, church courts, the Book of Common Prayer, and the church calendar (including the celebration of Christmas and Easter) were abolished. Those who were set as leaders in the new structure were empowered to impose moral duties on the nation. But many Independents refused to accept the new church, and many people hated it. They had come to love the Prayer Book and the celebration of Christmas.

So it was that even while the king was held a prisoner, many spoke of restoring him to the throne. But to Oliver Cromwell and others of his camp, it would be a betrayal of God to do so. Nevertheless, efforts went on constantly in parliament to find terms of reinstatement to which the king could agree.

As for King Charles, since his military defeat he had simply kept talking, watching for another chance to overcome. The king was far from disheartened. He had been brought to Holdenby Hall, a fantastic structure with fantastic embellishments that had been built by a favorite of Queen Elizabeth's, Christopher Hatton.

While Charles was at Holdenby, Cromwell became quite ill. He suffered from an infected swelling, or abscess, in his head, and there were some who whispered that the sickness was partly emotional. The high ideals for which he had fought had fallen away into cantankerous bickering between the leaders in parliament, and the peace of England for which Cromwell had longed had not come. He said of his sickness, "And I do most willingly acknowledge that the Lord (in this visitation) exercised the bowels of a Father toward me. I received in myself the sentence of death, that I might learn to trust in him that raiseth the dead, and have no confidence in the flesh."

During this period of time, a peace settled on Wakefield, though as Christopher said one fine June morning, "Someday the pot in this country will boil over, but not today." He was still not completely recovered from his captivity, but there was color in his cheeks, and the long rides he took daily had brought him back to reasonable health.

Angharad was sitting beside him, and she lifted one eyebrow at her husband's words. "What 'pot' do you speak of?" she asked. "The war is over, isn't it?"

"No, and it never will be, not as long as Charles and the parliament carry on their interminable debate."

"I thought Charles had agreed to most of the terms laid down for him," Gavin said in surprise. He was very tanned and fit, having spent all spring in the fields. Lifting a glass of fresh grape juice to his lips, he continued, "People expect things to be back to normal."

Chris shook his head, picked up Angharad's hand, and stroked it. He had found a surprising vigor in his love for this woman, and she had returned his passion fully. They were like young lovers, and the sight of them pleased Gavin. He had accepted Angharad freely, happy that his father had a companion who brought such joy to his life. Now the younger Wakefield said, "Are you two going to moon around like starstruck lovers until you're ninety? It's really embarrassing!"

Chris laughed aloud, kissed Angharad's hand, and turned his fond gaze on Gavin. "Just pray that you get a wife who'll take care of you the way this one takes care of me."

"You're spoiled to the bone!" Angharad sniffed. She was looking better than ever, for her skin glowed with health, and the rich clothing Chris insisted on her wearing set off her figure well. "What's happening, Chris? I thought the war would be over when the king was beaten at Naseby."

"It's not so simple, I'm afraid." Chris stood up and stared out over the fields. The grass was almost green enough to hurt the eyes, and he let his gaze linger on the cattle that dotted the rising meadows before he turned and said, "It's the New Model Army. It's gotten completely out of hand. We had to have the army to win the war, but now that that's been done there's no longer need of it."

"Why aren't the soldiers just sent home?" Angharad asked.

"For the simple reason that they haven't been paid," Chris answered, "and they refuse to go until they are."

"How much is owed them?" Gavin inquired.

"Over three hundred thousand pounds, and parliament doesn't have a shilling! I spoke with Oliver about it, and he said he was sick of the bickering between parliament and the army, but he has no answers. He has confidence in his army, but he has problems that could bring on another war, this time the army against parliament itself!"

※

As the months dragged on, Cromwell's problems—and those of the entire nation—seemed to grow. The king and parliament could not agree, and the movement to put Charles back on the throne grew stronger.

The army became the most potent force in England, and all sorts of new figures sprang up, proclaiming things such as, "The poorest he that is in England hath a life to live as the greatest he," and "A man is not bound to a system of government in which he hath not had any hand in setting over him!"

Cromwell heard all this and said once to Christopher, "Such claims would lead to anarchy! We must not have it!"

Then, to complicate matters, the king, hearing that he was about to be murdered by the army, escaped and made his way to Charisbrooke Castle, on the Isle of Wight. Here he dwelt for months—and here he made his fatal mistake.

In desperation King Charles signed a secret treaty with the Scots, which brought on a second civil war!

There had never been anything like this second war, not in all English history, but it was a short, simple affair. Everyone—the king, Lords and Commons, landlords, the city and the country-side, the Scottish army, the Welsh people, and the English fleet—*all* turned against the New Model Army.

And the army beat them all! With Cromwell at their head, the army marched and fought. They invaded Wales, they took Scotland, they conquered the fleet!

By the time it was over, Oliver Cromwell was the most powerful man in England. The Royalists were crushed, and Cromwell used parliament as a tool. The Scots were conquered, as were the Welsh—and by the end of 1648 there was no one left on the Island to challenge Oliver Cromwell!

Wakefield had prospered during the past months, and as Christopher and Gavin went over the improvements that had been made, Angharad interrupted long enough to say, "I've got to go see to Father."

"Where's Amos?"

"Susan is watching him."

"Owen's not doing well?"

Angharad shook her head, a troubled light in her eye. "Not well at all. He can't shake off the cough that put him down last winter. I'm worried about him."

"Better have Dr. Wheeler in to see him," Chris suggested. He got to his feet. "Take some of that fresh venison we had today."

When Angharad left the room, Chris shook his head. "I fear Owen is not going to live much longer."

"I've thought the same," Gavin admitted. The two sat there silently for a time, and Gavin said, "I'll miss him, Father. He's a fine man, a real man of God."

"None finer, and he's given me a fine wife." He looked suddenly at Gavin, an odd expression on his face. "I've got something to tell you, and I don't know how you'll take it."

"Why—what is it?"

Chris shifted in his chair uncomfortably, then blurted out, "Angharad is going to have a baby!" He laughed suddenly at the expression on Gavin's face. "Go on and say it—it's ridiculous!"

But Gavin broke into a broad grin. He sprang up and came to his father, pounding his shoulders and exclaiming, "Why, I think it's wonderful!"

"You do?" Christopher stared at him with amazement. "I've been feeling . . . well, like a fool ever since she told me. After all, I'm an old man—"

"At fifty-nine? You're better than most men half your age!"

"Well, I'm glad you see it like that, Son." Chris seemed relieved, and for a long time he sat there, speaking of the child to come. "I'll not live to see him or her grow up," he said once. "But you will, and the child will be a blessing for Angharad." Gavin saw that there was a peace in his father and was glad for him.

Finally Gavin rose and went to his duties. He had discovered that he had a gift for farming, or at least for administrating the various activities that a large establishment like Wakefield required. All the rest of that afternoon he moved among the workers, saying a word to the steward about the affairs of the house, going over the needs of the blacksmith, visiting a sick worker—nothing vastly important, but all tasks that he enjoyed thoroughly.

Gavin stopped by the Morgan cottage, and when Angharad came to the door, he grinned at her, saying, "Hello, little mother!"

Angharad flushed, her smooth cheeks turning red. "Go and scratch!" she said shortly, but Gavin grabbed her, lifted her off the floor, and swung her around. Mimicking her speech, he cried out, "There is proud I am of the old woman!"

"Put me down, you fool!" When Gavin set her down she looked up at him, and he saw that there were tears in her eyes. "God is good to me," she said simply.

"And to my father, to give him a wife like you." Gavin cocked his head to one side and asked, "And when will my little brother make his appearance?"

"Not a brother, but a little sister for Amos."

"Sure of that, are you?"

"Yes." Her tone was firm and she smiled at his expression. "Her name will be Hope, for that's what the good Lord told me to name her."

Gavin visited with Owen, noting that he had grown much weaker, and when he left he felt a sense of loss. *I've let that old man get into my heart,* he thought.

As he rode into the courtyard, he was filled with a gladness that he had a place such as Wakefield. *Not many men have such a heritage,* he thought. He finished his work, then rode home. Dismounting, he tossed the reins of his horse to the stableman.

"Ah, sir, the young lady just came an hour ago."

"Young lady? Which young lady?"

"The black-haired one, sir. I disremember her name."

Quickly Gavin made his way into the house, where he was met by Francine. She came to him at once, her hands outstretched and a smile on her lips. "Gavin—!" she whispered, and there was an urgency in her manner that disturbed him.

"What is it, Francine?" he asked, holding her hands. He wanted to kiss her, but one of the maids was cleaning windows and had her eye on them. "Is something wrong?"

Francine hesitated, then shook her head. "Oh, I just wanted to see you."

"That's rather different," Gavin remarked, not quite believing her. "Usually I'm the one who hunts you down." He was puzzled over her appearance. Always before she had sent for him rather than coming to Wakefield. "Come along," he said. "We'll go have something to eat."

"Oh, I'm not hungry," Francine said. "Could we go for a walk? You can show me what you've been doing with Wakefield."

Gavin was willing enough, for he was proud of what he'd done with the estate. For the next hour he took her on a guided tour, pointing out the improvements he'd made. She listened and responded brightly enough, but finally when they came to a secluded path that wound around the garden, he stopped and took her hands in his. "What's bothering you, Francine? I can see you're worried."

Francine bit her lower lip and dropped her eyes. "I—I can't tell you, Gavin," she murmured.

He was mystified. This was not the Francine he knew, for there was a strange, unusual restraint in her manner. She was a vivacious, outgoing young woman, the life of any society she entered. Now she seemed pale, and there was something like fear in her eyes as she looked up at him. "Why, of course you can tell me. Now, out with it. It can't be all that bad. Is some of your family ill?"

"My father died last week."

"Oh, Francine, I'm sorry!" They were standing beside a huge

winterberry holly bush, and the bright red berries were large and plump. Honeysuckle vines covered a wall to their left, and their sweet fragrance filled the air. A silence lay over the spot, and Francine seemed unwilling to break it. Finally she lifted her head, and he saw what he thought were tears in her eyes. "I'm sorry to bring my troubles to you, Gavin. I have no right—"

"Why, of course you should come to me!"

"No, not . . . not with *this!*"

Gavin put his hands on her shoulders and demanded, "Francine, what in heaven's name *is* it? Surely it can't be so bad as you make it seem."

"Yes, it is. And worse!" Francine suddenly seemed to sway, and when he put his arms out to steady her, she fell into them, moaning, "Oh, Gavin! I'm so miserable!" She began to weep, holding him tightly.

Holding her soft form, Gavin could only stroke her hair and wait for the storm of tears to end. Her body shook, and she held to him as if he were her only hope in the world. Finally the spasms lessened, and when she was still, he lifted her chin, saying, "Now, whatever it is, tell me."

"I—I don't have any place to go, Gavin." Francine saw the shock rise in his eyes and her lips trembled. "There's no money, and I have no relatives to help."

Gavin could not bear to see the pain in her eyes. "You'll always have a place—with me." He kissed her and she clung to him. "I've loved you since I was a boy, you know that."

"I know, I was a fool," Francine answered, dropping her eyes. "I thought there was plenty of time. I'm older than you, and I thought that might make a difference. And you're of noble blood and my family has nothing. Men don't marry for love, they marry for money and position."

"Not true! My father married Angharad Morgan, and she came from humble people."

"That's why I came to you, Gavin. I was going to—to kill myself! Then I thought of your father and how he married a poor woman for love—" Francine's eyes were wide, pleading for understanding, and she whispered, "I came because I love you, and there's nobody else for me to turn to."

Gavin was still in shock over her news, but as she stood in the circle of his arms, she seemed to possess a sweetness and gentleness he had never seen before. Gavin took a deep breath, then said, "We must marry, you and I."

Francine's body jerked, and she lifted her head, startled. "Why, Gavin, that's impossible!"

"Why is it impossible? I've loved you for years. I'd have asked you before, but you always put me off. I thought it was because you didn't love me."

"Oh, I *do* love you, Gavin! I have for years!" Francine suddenly pulled his head down and kissed him. The softness of her lips and the curves of her body against him shook Gavin. She had never given herself to him like this, and he held her tightly. Finally she pulled back and her eyes were huge. "But your father would never permit it."

"Yes, I think he will. He's never believed in marriage for the sake of gain. Come along, Francine, we'll tell him and Angharad."

"Oh, Gavin, you're so sweet!" Francine kissed him again and then shook her head. "I wish it weren't the way it is. It seems like I'm coming to you for money."

"Do you love me? That's all that counts."

"Oh yes, Gavin, I love you so much! There's no other man in the world like you!" Francine looked up at the young man, kissed him again, then as the two turned and walked toward the house, she smiled.

He's so easy to handle! He's like a child! His father will be harder to fool, and the woman might be clever—but Gavin will have his way!

The next few days were difficult for everyone. Both Chris and

Angharad were shocked when Gavin made his announcement. Chris, of course, had known of his son's interest in the young woman, but had not known it was serious. He spoke of it to Angharad, saying in a troubled tone, "I thought it was just infatuation, the sort young men have."

"I fear not," Angharad said slowly. She had met Francine only once before, but there was a troubled expression on her face as she thought of the newly announced engagement. "I wish they'd wait," she said. "These things sometimes fade away."

"I don't hold much hope for that," Chris said heavily.

Angharad thought hard, then said, "I wish Gavin had married Susanne."

"So do I, but she's Catholic, and he's got strong feelings about that. Besides, they grew up together. He looks on her like a sister." Chris sighed and shook his head. "All the happiness God has given me, Angharad, you and now the child to come. But I have a heaviness when I think of this match of Gavin's."

"We will put it to God."

Chris grinned and drew her close. "You're the prayingest woman I ever met!"

"There is foolish you are!" Angharad said shortly, then she came into his arms, and they stood holding one another quietly. The shadows outside the house were growing long, and overhead the swifts were doing their acrobatic flights, twisting and turning wildly. Finally the pair turned and went inside, passing from the fast falling darkness into the light and warmth of the hall.

Twenty-two

THE WALLS COME
TUMBLING DOWN

All are from the dust, and all return to dust. . . . I am the resurrection and the life. . . . This mortal must put on immortality.' . . . And so we give the body of Sir Vernon Woodville to the earth."

Susanne stood beside the open grave that yawned horribly in the raw, red earth. The funeral had been held in the cathedral, and she had endured the long service with a dull ache. The acrid odor of candle smoke had made her nauseous, and the interminable eulogies and lengthy sermon had been difficult for her to bear. She had not been close to her father, for in many ways he was a difficult man to live with—touchy, easily offended, and unable to express what affection he may have felt. Still, Susanne could remember a few times when he had managed to break out of the shell that imprisoned him, and during the service she had summoned up those meager memories.

When I was six, he gave me a white pony. And when I fell off, he picked me up and kissed me. He said, "Now, don't cry, Susanne, you're going to be a marvelous rider!"

She concentrated on that event, finding that she could remember it as clearly as if it were captured in a painting.

Father was wearing a maroon coat with brass buttons. When he picked me up and wiped my tears away, I saw he had a small scar on his neck

I'd never noticed before. When I asked him how he got it, he laughed and said a bear had bitten him.

The tempo of the sermon changed, and, sensing that the end of the service was drawing near, Susanne thought wistfully, *I wish there had been more times like that. . . .*

But now, standing in the gray drizzle of rain that soaked all the mourners and turned the earth into a glossy, slick mound, she could not keep back the tears. They ran down her face unnoticed, mingling with the raindrops. Glancing at her mother, she tried to read her thoughts, but could see only a fixed expression that hid whatever lay inside her spirit.

They were never close. I don't remember more than two or three times when they ever showed affection in public.

Then the service ended, and she turned away, glad to leave the gloom of the rain-soaked graveyard. She sat silently in the carriage with her mother, wishing that she could think of something to say to give comfort. But her mother sat upright, her face turned to the window, saying nothing at all, just staring at the slanting lines of rain that came down incessantly.

When they reached the house, the two women left the coach and entered the building. "Take your wet things off, Susanne," Frances said evenly. "We can't afford to get sick."

"Yes, Mother."

Susanne waited for her mother to say more, but when she did not, she turned and went to her room. Her maid, Annie, helped her change, fussing over the soaking and trying to offer condolence for the death that had come to Woodville. "What a shame, and him in the prime of life!" She nodded, gathering up the rain-soaked garments. "He was a good man, he was. A bit short with us sometimes, but we didn't mind that. . . ."

Susanne murmured thanks to Annie, and was glad when she left the room. Going to the window, she stared unseeing out at the wide expanse of lawn, thinking how life would be changed without her father. She felt uneasy, for there had been a strange reticence in her mother since Vernon Woodville's death. All of her vivacity was muted, and there was a sober look in her eyes.

Susanne's thoughts so engrossed her that she was startled when a knock sounded, and she turned to see her mother enter the room. "I have to talk to you, Susanne," she said rather shortly. She was wearing a black gown, not of dull ebony, but of a glistening kind of material with fine pearls embroidered around the neck and on the sleeves. Even in mourning, Frances Woodville made certain her clothing showed off her figure and complexion.

"Yes, Mother?"

"Sit down, over here on the sofa." Frances seated herself on a chair opposite her daughter and said evenly, "I don't like to speak of problems at a time like this, but we're facing a difficult time."

Susanne was bewildered. What could be more difficult than losing one's father? But she had no time to question, for her mother's face drew down in a frown. "We're in financial trouble— no, that's not true." She hesitated, then shrugged slightly. "We're ruined, Susanne."

"Ruined? Why—what does that mean?"

Frances Woodville's well-formed lips twisted into an ugly shape as she said bitterly, "I mean that your father made foolish decisions. He never told me, but he mortgaged everything and used the money to support the king. And now the king has lost, and we're penniless!"

Susanne had lived in a world where money was taken for granted. Anything she wanted had been there. Now she tried to imagine what sort of life lay ahead of her, and she murmured, "But surely not *all!* There must be something left."

Her mother's white hands clenched, and her eyes were hard as she said, "He threw it all away, I tell you!" For the first time in Susanne's life, she saw fear in her mother's expression, which frightened her as well. The woman went on, "It wasn't just that—he gambled for high stakes, and he was an abominable gambler!"

"Mother, we don't need all this." Susanne swept the ornate room with a gesture of her hand. "We can buy a small house in the country—"

"Buy it with *what?* The lawyers have tried to salvage something, but even after everything is sold, there won't be enough to pay them off."

"What—what will we do?"

"Susanne, you've got to marry Henry. Oh, I know you don't *love* him, but love's a luxury we can't afford."

"Mother, I-I can't—!"

Anger threaded the tone of her mother's voice, and her eyes glinted dangerously. "You've been fed and clothed all your life. Now it's time for you to pay the bill. Are you going to let your own mother be thrown out on the street? And what about you? Will you scrub floors for your wealthy friends?"

The scene went on for nearly an hour, and when Frances left, she said, "There's no choice, Susanne. We can't beg! Henry Darrow is one of the wealthiest men in the country, and he's wanted to marry you for a long time."

"But it was for our money and for our land! He won't want me now that we don't have those things."

"Don't tell him, you fool! Marry him now, and when he finds out, it'll be too late!"

But Frances Woodville's scheme had no chance of succeeding. Henry Darrow had been wiser than many Royalists, for he had invested the bulk of his money on the Continent, not in support of Charles. He watched many of his friends lose their estates as the Roundheads took over, and he was very much aware of the plight of Frances and Susanne Woodville.

He came for a visit once, but said nothing about marriage. Frances had desperately tried to give Susanne instructions to snare him, saying, "Use your body, girl! That's what it's for! Make him want you so much he'll do anything to have you!"

But such tactics were beyond Susanne, and finally she and her mother were forced to leave Woodville—the only home Susanne had ever known. They took rooms at Oxford, and after a month, Frances shocked Susanne to the bone.

"I'm leaving England, Susanne. I'm going to France."

Susanne had been sewing, mending a slight tear in a dress, something she was not at all good at. Looking up with astonishment, she gasped, "Why—Mother, what will we do there?"

Very few things could cause Frances Woodville to blush or show awkwardness, but she did both at her daughter's question. She licked her lips nervously, then cleared her throat. "I'm going as a companion to the Marquis de Luncford's daughter."

Instantly a warning bell rang in Susanne's mind. She had heard stories of the marquis, none of them savory. He *did* have a daughter, but she was twenty-seven years old and in little need of a companion.

As she gazed at her mother, perplexed, Susanne recalled the words a guest had once spoken to her father regarding the marquis: *"Why, the old man uses her as an excuse for keeping his loose women around. He's bedded down with everything in skirts in France, and now he's here chasing after our women!"*

Susanne had met the marquis when he'd visited their home once, and she had disliked him instantly. He was in his fifties, but there was a lustful air about him, and she had wondered that her mother would invite such a man to their house. He was enormously wealthy and a widower. Her father had said, "If the lecherous old goat didn't have twenty million francs a year and a dozen estates, what a boring old cob he'd be!"

Frances caught the expression on her daughter's face and said coldly, "I know what you think, what everyone will think. But you're wrong! The marquis is in love with me. After a proper mourning for your father, we'll be married." She seemed upset by the grief on Susanne's face and said angrily, "I don't *love* him, but as I've tried to tell you, a woman has to get by in this world. Men have the money and the power, and we have to do whatever we can to survive!"

Susanne knew it would be of no use to argue—she had never won an argument of any sort with her mother—but she did hold her head up and say, "I hope you'll be happy, Mother, but I can't go to France with you."

A slight expression of relief showed on Frances's face, and she said in a more modified tone, "That's up to you, Susanne. There is a small endowment that was not taken by the creditors. It will pay only enough to keep you, and that very poorly. But it's yours if you choose to stay."

"Thank you," Susanne said quietly. She came to her mother, put her arms around her, and kissed her cheek. "You and I haven't been close, but I'll miss you. I hope you'll be very happy."

The gesture seemed to break something in Frances Woodville. Her lips trembled and she bent forward and returned the kiss. There was a tremor in her voice as she said before leaving the room, "I've been a poor mother, but I wish you well."

Two weeks later, as Susanne said the final good-bye to her mother, both women said little and showed little emotion. For a week after the parting, Susanne felt totally miserable. She stayed in the small apartment for the most part, for she had made no friends. But she was in her apartment one Wednesday afternoon when a knock startled her. Going to the door, she found Henry Darrow standing there. "Why, Henry, come in," she said.

"I had trouble finding you, Susanne," he said after they had exchanged rather awkward greetings and she had made tea. "I heard about your mother." There was a sardonic look in his eye, but he said, "I'm sorry she left you here."

"There was no place for me with her."

"No, of course not." Darrow sipped his tea and for a time spoke of mundane affairs. Finally he set his cup down and gave Susanne a rather compassionate look—compassionate for him, at least. "Susanne, I'm in a rather difficult position. . . ." His voice trailed off, and he looked so embarrassed that Susanne could not imagine what was coming.

"What is it?" she asked.

"Well—blast it!" Darrow said with feeling. "I've been worried about you. Should have come to offer help before this, but it was awkward. One never knows how to go about these things."

"I don't know what you mean," Susanne said. She gave him a curious look, and then suddenly it came to her. She could not help but smile as she said abruptly, "You've come to tell me you can't marry me, I suppose."

"Why—!" Darrow's face registered shock and then he laughed abruptly. "You're a quick young woman," he said. "I've spent days trying to find a way to tell you that, and you just throw it right at me."

"I knew you'd never marry me," Susanne said. "The woman you marry will need money and land, I think, to be attractive to you."

A slight shame touched the light blue eyes of Darrow, but he forced a grin. "Know me pretty well, don't you, Susanne? You always have."

"I hope we can be friends now that this is out of the way."

"Of course!" Darrow extended his hand and, holding hers, studied her for a long moment. "You'd never have married me anyway. I'm not 'romantic' enough for you, am I?"

Susanne pulled her hand away gently. She was feeling nothing so much as a sense of relief. She had been pressured to marry this man for so long, and now she didn't have to worry about it! "I don't love you as a wife should love a husband, Henry," she said quietly.

Darrow didn't believe in much, but as he stared at Susanne, taking in her beauty, her steady blue eyes, and the air of quietness that surrounded her, he felt that he was missing something. For one moment he considered pursuing this girl, for there was something in her that he'd not seen in other women. However, he was far too ingrained in selfishness to do more than *think* of such a thing and said merely, "I'll be your friend, and you must let me help you with funds—"

"No! You mustn't do that," Susanne interrupted. "That wouldn't be a good thing, Henry. We can be friends, though, and I'll look forward to seeing you from time to time." She knew as she spoke, however, that she would not, for her new world was as far from his as the moon. She entertained him for half an hour, then he left, with the air of a man who had gotten a difficult and embarrassing task out of the way and could go on to more pleasant things.

And as he left, Susanne looked around the rather worn and poorly furnished room, thinking: *I would choose this, and to be my own mistress, rather than all the fine houses and rich things that Henry prizes. . . .*

<hr />

"It's a fine girl!"

It was early on the twenty-fourth of May, and both Christopher and Gavin leaped to their feet as Dr. Williamson came through the door, his face beaming. They had walked the floor all night and were the worse for wear. He stopped short, then laughed aloud. "You two look as though you've had a harder time than the mother!"

Christopher rushed to the short, pudgy physician, grabbing

him by the arm so tightly that he wrung forth a wince. "How is my wife?"

"Well, if you'll stop breaking my arm," Williamson said, "I'll tell you. There! Now, she's fine. Come along and have a look at your new daughter, and you, too, sir, a fine sister for you!"

The two men moved down the hall with alacrity and entered the chamber, and Chris stumbled to fall beside the bed. His face was pale and he asked hoarsely, "Are you all right, Angharad?"

Angharad's face was relaxed, and she grasped at his hand, smiling beautifully. "Hurting I am only a little, but look what we have, Husband." She drew the white blanket back to expose the red face of the baby. "There is beautiful she is!" she whispered. Looking up she said, "Would you like to hold your daughter?"

"Oh, no!" Chris burst out. "It's been so long since we've had a baby here. I-I'd be afraid to!"

"Are you a rat with green teeth then?" Angharad demanded. "Here." She handed the baby to Chris, who took her and looked about as awkward as it's possible for a man to look. But he smiled and Angharad said, "Gavin, does he look like a proud father?"

"He didn't look so proud when *I* was born, I'll wager." Gavin came over and touched the soft cheek with a cautious forefinger. "Hope. What a nice name!"

The three of them took turns finding new aspects of Hope Wakefield's beauty, and when Dr. Williamson said, "Now, it's time for the mother to rest," Chris and Gavin both bent over and kissed Angharad.

"You did magnificently!" Chris whispered. "A fine gift for your husband."

"A gift from God to both of us."

For the next weeks the center of the universe was found in the child, at least for the parents. And for Amos, who was fascinated by the pink, fat visitor in his world. He insisted on holding her, and nothing pleased him more than to be allowed to lie on the large bed and take naps with her. Angharad laughed more than once at Chris, who fussed over Hope constantly. "You're the most foolish father ever I saw," she said fondly. "But I love you for it!"

The two of them talked for a while, and finally Chris said, "If it wasn't for this attachment Gavin has for Francine, I'd be the happiest man in the world." The young woman had come to stay at Wakefield and had behaved very well. Still, Chris was apprehensive about the match.

"It worries me, too, but I'm praying on it," Angharad said. Then she added, "I have something that's come to me, Chris. I've prayed much and there's something I want to say to Gavin. See what you think of it."

Chris listened as Angharad spoke, then nodded. "I think we'll talk to him. It may mean nothing, but God speaks to you in wonderful ways. We'll tell him after lunch."

Gavin had no inkling of what was afoot, but after lunch Angharad said casually, "Did you hear of Susanne's trouble?"

"Susanne?" Gavin looked up quickly, and so did Francine. "What's happened? Is she ill?"

"No, but she's having a difficult time," Chris said. "I talked to David McCrory. He saw her in London."

"Her mother went to France, didn't she?" Francine put in. "Not a very good thing to do, if I know the marquis."

Gavin's face had grown intent. "What's Susanne doing?"

"Living in very poor circumstances. . . ." Chris described the manner of Susanne's life, then shook his head. "I hate to hear it. She's a fine young woman."

"Why, we've got to do something!" Gavin exclaimed.

"Do what?" Francine demanded at once.

"Why—why—we can bring her here!" The idea leaped into Gavin's mind, and he didn't see the quick glance that passed between his father and Angharad. "We've got enough room for twenty guests!"

"I don't think that would be wise, Gavin," Francine said carefully. "I love Susanne, but once you give charity, there's no end to it."

"Oh, don't be foolish, Francine." Gavin shook his head. He was impulsive and had made up his mind. "Would it be all right with you, Father? To have her come as a guest for a time?"

"Certainly! She'll be good company for Angharad and Hope."

"Yes, indeed!" Angharad nodded. She smiled sweetly at the younger woman, adding, "You two are great friends, aren't you? You'll be company for each other."

Gavin leaped to his feet, demanding, "Where is she staying, do you know?"

"McCrory can tell you," Chris answered. "Take the carriage, Gavin."

Gavin left in less than an hour, and Francine's last words made no sense to him. "Be careful on this trip," she said, after kissing him forcefully.

"Why? It's not dangerous."

"A man alone with a woman? That's always dangerous."

Gavin laughed, then kissed her again. "Don't worry. It'll be fine having Susanne here. We'll go fishing!"

But as the carriage drew away, Francine's face grew dark. *I'll have to keep this thing from getting out of hand. Gavin is a fool where women are concerned.*

❦

Gavin was slightly appalled at the house where he had been directed. McCrory had warned him, "It's not a fit place for a young woman, but it's all she can afford, I suppose."

As Gavin turned off the narrow street to the battered house that had once been rather pretty, he thought, *She can't stay here! This is frightful!* He knocked on the door, and a tall woman in a shapeless dress peered at him narrowly. "Wot is it?"

"I'm looking for a Miss Woodville."

"Ah, go upstairs, first door on yer left."

Gavin felt the stairs give under his weight, and the smell of the house was dank and fetid. He groped down the dark hallway, found the door, and knocked. Susanne's voice asked, "Who is it?"

"It's me, Gavin."

A bolt slid in a rusty chamber, and then the door opened. "Gavin!" Susanne whispered. "How nice to see you!"

"Can I come in?"

"Well—yes." Susanne nodded with a trace of hesitation. "There's not much room." She stepped back, and when Gavin entered he saw that the room was very small and had only a bed, a rickety chair, and a chest. The paper was peeling off the wall, and the single window allowed little light.

"How did you find me?" Susanne asked. She was wearing a plain brown dress, and Gavin thought she looked pale, though it was difficult to tell in the dim light.

"Never mind that," Gavin said. He had planned to ease into the reason for his coming, but his strong distaste for Susanne's lodgings spurred him on. "Susanne, you're coming with me to Wakefield," he said. When he saw her lips part with surprise, he shook his head, adding, "Now, don't argue with me! Father and Angharad gave me strict orders. 'Don't come back without her,' Angharad said, 'or I'll have the bones hot from your body!'"

Susanne stared at Gavin, speechless. In truth, she was totally miserable. The money in the endowment had been insufficient for any sort of comfort. Worse, she had grown afraid of the men who came and went in the house, rough men who stared at her with hot eyes. Day after day she had sat in the single chair, alone and friendless. She was not a praying young woman, but two days earlier, she had fallen into despair. She had wept for the first time since she had come to this awful place and cried out, "O God! Help me! Take me out of this place!"

Now as she stared at Gavin, she somehow knew that God had answered her cries.

"Do *you* want me to come to your home?"

"Why, certainly!" Impulsively he took her hands—and was startled at how cold they were. "You must come, Susanne," he said, struggling against the emotion that filled him. "This is no place for you!"

"You'll do this for me?"

Gavin lifted his hand and stroked her smooth cheek. "If things were reversed, wouldn't you do it for me?"

Tears formed in Susanne's eyes, and she couldn't speak for a time. He put his arms around her, as he had done once before, and drew her close, holding her. She lay still in his embrace, listening to the firm beating of his heart, and a feeling of peace came over her.

Drawing back she said quietly, "All right, Gavin, I'll go with you to Wakefield."

Twenty-three

A MATTER OF PROPHECY

Fall came to Wakefield overnight, or so it seemed. One day the sweltering summer heat burned the earth and the fish came to the surface of the pond, gasping—the next morning a frost laid its hand on the grass, shriveling it into brown blades of dead tissue.

For Gavin it was the best time of the year, for he savored the smell of burning leaves and sound of windblown leaves crunching beneath his feet. He tried to get Francine to go with him on the long rides and treks he made on foot, but she laughed, saying, "I'm for creature comfort. Besides, this wind would turn my cheeks into leather!"

But Susanne loved the outdoors, so she accompanied Gavin on his roaming over the hills and fields and valleys. One morning, when a thin coating of ice glittered on the brook where they'd fished together as children, they roamed far from Wakefield. Leaving the house at dawn, they walked past the bakery, the walled garden, and the stables. As they moved past the windmill, Gavin asked, "Too cold for you?"

"No, I love it!"

Gavin noted the rich color in Susanne's cheeks and thought, *Francine's wrong—this sort of thing doesn't spoil the beauty of a woman's complexion.* He led her a mile to the north, following rutted pathways and tramping over the stubble of the hayfield. They spoke little, for they had found that they had that sort of good relationship that didn't call for endless talk. Once Gavin had said to her after a long, unbroken silence, "I always liked what they said about Roger Bacon, that he could be silent in six languages."

Now as they hurried out of the fields, where two men were sowing winter wheat, and plunged into the thickness of an ancient forest, Gavin said, "Come along, I can't wait for you!"

Challenged, Susanne said with an impudent gleam in her dark blue eyes, "Just try to leave me, Mr. Wakefield!"

Gavin at once broke out into a brisk trot, and for half an hour the two threaded their way between the huge, twisted trunks of ancient yews and oaks. The brambles snatched at their legs and scratched their hands, but when they emerged, breathless and laughing, Susanne was right beside Gavin.

"Well, you can make your way in the woods better than you can cook," he said with a grin. He was wearing a green doublet with rich black fur at the collar and cuffs, and a fur cap covered his auburn hair. He looked young and strong and virile, and Susanne suddenly realized that she was enjoying herself more than she had for months.

He took her hand and suddenly pulled her along, shouting, "Come on! We'll see if you can fish as well as you can run!"

For the next two hours, they fished in the cold stream, using saplings Gavin cut with his hunting knife for poles. He carried lines and hooks in his pocket, and for a time the two separated, Gavin taking the east fork while Susanne wandered down the other.

The air was sharp, nipping at her face, and when she put her hands in the water, they were numbed instantly. She caught three fish, all fat and thumping. She strung them on a sharp branch with a fork that Gavin had made for her, then started back down the creek. She was a fine fisherman, having a good feel for the exact moment when the hook had to be yanked and set. She had learned early the folly of pulling too soon, and too late. Now she knew to concentrate on the line and had made an art out of angling. She thought as she cast her line under the shelf of a rock, *I remember when we were children and Gavin and I would catch fish out of the stream by our house.*

So intent was she on that memory, that when her line suddenly went taut, she was taken off guard for once. She gave the line a tremendous yank—and her foot slid on a slippery rock. With a wild cry, she went over backwards and fell full length into the icy water. It closed over her head, and the shock of it numbed her brain. The water got in her nose, and she came up gagging and sputtering. Flailing her arms, she made her way to the bank, then pulled herself onto the dried grass. She stood up, and the wind cut her like a knife.

Got to get out of the cold! she thought and ran beside the brook until she heard Gavin call her name. She answered and he came to her at once.

"You'll catch your death!" he exclaimed, then seized her arm and pulled her down the narrow path. "The old cabin—we'll have to go there!"

Susanne followed, stumbling as they turned down a path. She remembered the old cabin, for they'd visited it often for picnics when they were children. When they came on it, she was so numb she barely noticed it, for it was nearly concealed by overgrowth. Gavin yanked the door open and pulled her inside. "I'll get a fire going. You've got to dry out."

Gathering a handful of dry twigs that were scattered in the cabin, Gavin pulled flint and steel from his pocket. Quickly he struck them, and a spark fell on the smallest twigs. Carefully he nourished the spark, then, as he blew on it gently, a tiny yellow flame sprang forth, and he grunted with satisfaction, "Good." He fed the growing fire carefully until a full blaze was going. Then he turned to Susanne. "Get out of those clothes."

"No—I can't do that!"

He glared at her impatiently. "This is no time for modesty! You've got to get warm and dry."

"I won't!"

Gavin shrugged off his coat, tossed it to her, and turned his back. "Hurry up!" he ordered.

Susanne knew he was right. Awkwardly she stripped off the soaking coat and dress, then frantically pulled on his warm fur coat. "You—can turn around now," she said in a small voice.

Gavin turned, a grin on his face. "If I'd known threats worked so well with you, I might have tried it long ago."

"Don't waste your time!" she retorted smartly. "I only complied because I knew you were right—and because I was freezing!" With that, she went to lay her clothes near the fire.

"I'll get some more wood, and we can have some of these fish for supper." Gavin left and came back soon with large chunks of wood. When the tongues of flame were reaching high, he gathered the fish, cleaned them, then carefully cooked them over the fire.

An hour later, Susanne was sitting on a wobbly stool, eating a small fish. It was delicious, the white flesh falling apart and smoking hot so that she almost burned her mouth. "It's good, isn't it?"

"I'm just a good cook," Gavin said, clearly pleased with himself. He nibbled at the fish, saying, "Wish we had some fresh bread, but we can't have everything." They ate the fish, unsalted and burned in spots, but both thought it was better than a feast. Finally Gavin asked, "Are you warm enough?"

"Too warm," Susanne said. "Go outside and let me change." When he stepped outside, she quickly slipped into her dry dress, still warm from being near the fire, and called out, "All right, you can come in now." When he entered, she said, "I guess we can go home whenever you're ready."

"We'll have sweets first."

"Sweets? What sort of sweets?"

"These. Gavin held out his cap, which was full of large purple berries. "Sweet and ripe! I found them when I went for the wood. Here, try them."

Susanne put one of the berries in her mouth and opened her eyes wide with pleasure. "Oh, these *are* good!" she exclaimed.

The two sat there in front of the fire, side by side, eating the juicy fruit. Gavin looked at her and laughed, "You've got juice all over your face!"

"Well, so have you!"

"Women are supposed to be neater than men," he teased her.

"They *are* neater. You look like a pig that's been rooting!"

"Is that so?" Mischief gleamed in his eyes, and he suddenly reached over and grabbed her, holding a handful of berries in his free hand. "I'll just smear these all over your impudent face!"

"Oh, Gavin, please don't!"

Suddenly the light in Gavin's eyes changed as he looked at her. They had roughhoused countless times when they were younger, but he became suddenly aware that this was no child in his grasp. Her enormous eyes were the eyes of a woman—and her lips were soft and tender as he lowered his head and kissed her.

Susanne froze for a second, then, as his lips covered hers, she reached up and clasped him to her.

Finally when he pulled back, he seemed dazed, almost as though he was drugged, and would have kissed her again but she turned her head away.

Breathlessly she said, "Let me go, Gavin."

At once he stood to his feet, then held his hand out to her. She took it and stood slowly. For a moment they stared at each other, uncertain and shaken by the passion that had stirred them. "I don't think we'd better be alone anymore," Susanne said quietly.

"Are you afraid of me?" he asked, his eyes searching her face.

"Not of you," she said, then looked up into his eyes. "I'm afraid of me," she whispered so softly that he could barely hear her voice. "Take me home, please."

They did not speak much on the way back to Wakefield, but when they got to the door and stepped inside, she turned to him. Her cheeks were smooth and slightly pale, which made her dark blue eyes seem larger. "You've been so kind to me, but I can't go riding with you again."

"We've done nothing wrong!"

"We could have."

Gavin stared at her. "Suppose I'd been a fool and not let you go?"

"Why, I suppose I would have been a fool, too." She shook her head and turned to leave, stopping suddenly when she saw Francine standing there watching them.

"You've had quite a long walk, haven't you?" Francine said, her eyes on Susanne. "I'm surprised you're not exhausted, as long as you've been gone."

"Why, Susanne fell in the brook," Gavin stammered. "We had to dry her clothes before she got her death of cold."

Susanne's face grew pink at the look she got from Francine, but she said nothing. She simply walked away, going at once to her room.

Francine watched her leave, then turned to Gavin. "I'd like to hear about your little adventure," she said, her eyes narrow as she regarded him. "Come along, and you can tell me all about it."

From that time, Gavin felt strained whenever he was with Susanne, which did not happen often, because Francine made it a point to be with him almost all the time. On those rare occasions when Gavin did see his friend, though, all of the ease and the laughter between them was gone.

The winter came on, and Francine did all she could to make things most unpleasant for Susanne—though she was careful never to let Gavin see what she did. She was continually asking how long Susanne meant to stay, making thinly veiled remarks about the strain on Gavin's kindness and the burden of caring for those who did not belong.

One evening, after a day filled with Francine's barbs, Susanne went to her room, encased in gloom. *I can't stay here a moment longer,* she thought desperately, and her thoughts seemed to flutter like captive birds frantic to escape. She stood looking up at the pale glittering stars, frosty and so far away, yet seeming so close. She remembered her prayer, and how Gavin had seemed to appear in response to it. For a long time she stood there, listening for the voice of God. Angharad and Owen had taught her that God would speak if she would listen.

But nothing broke the silence, and heavily she turned away from the panoply of stars. But even as she lay in bed, determination rose within her and she whispered, "O God, I *know* you're there! And I'll seek you until you hear me. And until you answer me."

All was silent and Owen lay quietly, blending into the silence. The pain had gone now, and he could hear voices from his past all around him. They were thin and faint, like silver bells pealing far away from over the hills in Wales.

His eyes were closed, and he had no desire to open them, but when someone called his name, he knew he had to make one more effort. Slowly he gathered his strength, and when he opened his eyes, he saw Angharad's face, the amber glow of the lamplight forming a corona around her head. "Father, do you know me?" she whispered, and when he nodded, she put her hand on his hair, smoothing it back. "I thought you'd slipped away from us," she said, then turned and said, "Will—?"

And there was Will, his face strong in the lamplight, but his eyes filled with grief. Owen had lost most sensation, so that his body seemed to belong to someone else, but he felt the pressure of Will's hand on his and was able to return the grip.

"A good son you've been, Will, always faithful." He spoke a few words to Will, then turned to Angharad. "Let me—see the child—" Angharad turned to the cradle, picked up Hope, and put her on the pillow. Hope stared owlishly at the face of her grandfather. Reaching out, she touched his face, then laughed, a gurgling, happy sound in the still room.

Owen let his hand rest on the small head, and his lips moved faintly. "You will be the handmaiden of the Lord . . . and your feet will be dipped in oil . . . your life will be demanded, and you will not say no to God's command. . . ."

Gavin was standing back in the shadows, his eyes filled with sorrow. He had come to the cottage with Angharad and his father and now stood across the room from Susanne, who had come with them. He listened as Owen willed away his life, blessing Angharad and Christopher. As Gavin watched the solemn scene before him, he thought, *He'll be with God tonight. I wonder if I could go as quietly and with such joy?*

The light seemed to falter, and Owen felt himself fading away. It was a good feeling, but he caught a glimpse of Gavin and whispered, "Gavin . . . you will taste bitter fruit, but your heart will be pure—" The old eyes closed, and a faint whisper came to Gavin: "Choose ye a woman of God."

The voice trailed off, and the watchers stood quietly. Angharad's eyes filled with the glory of God as she bent over him and whispered, "I'll see you when I come to the King, Father."

"Aye," Will said at once and held his father's hand. "In that morning, we'll join you at the supper of the Lamb!"

Owen's eyes opened once more and he looked around the room, slowly examining each face. He focused at last on his daughter's face, and the light seemed to swallow her. It was as though she grew transparent, and the light finally grew so bright that he closed his eyes.

But the light only grew more intense, and at that moment he heard a sound that he'd been yearning to hear all his life—a much loved voice, calling him home. In one moment, he willed himself away from earth, and then he sighed once and was no longer a pilgrim.

Owen Morgan's death was serene, but even as the old man was laid in the earth, a sinister aura was closing around the king of England. As the army and parliament moved inexorably forward, Charles found himself shut in the candleless gloom of a small tower prison. He said to his wife, "The army m-means to have my blood. It will be their vindication. But the b-blood I s-shed will cry out from the e-earth!"

The army set forth a document, the *Remonstrance,* which was from its inception a vicious paper. It was liberally sprinkled with phrases such as "The king is guilty of all the bloodshed in these intestine wars."

Oliver Cromwell tried to bring reason to those who cried for Charles's blood, but even his power could not stem the tide. On November 20, 1648, the *Remonstrance* was presented to the Commons, taking four hours to read aloud. The decision to try the king came as no surprise to Cromwell, but he still hoped for some sort of milder verdict. On December 21 the king was moved from the Isle of Wight to Hurst Castle on the mainland. The demand for the king's blood grew stronger, and on the twenty-third Charles was brought to Windsor. His trial was set for January 1, 1649.

Christopher Wakefield had not seen Cromwell recently, but he did make a special trip to Windsor. When he gained an audience, he said at once, "Oliver, take care what you do."

Cromwell looked tired and haggard. He had fought two wars

and now faced the most critical moment of his life. Heavily he said, "I am weary of this matter, Christopher, but it must be done."

Chris shook his head. "Why, there is no way under heaven to try a king! He cannot be tried under common law, and as for a jury of his peers, of course a king has none. Surely you remember Mary, Queen of Scots? She was 'tried,' but the nation was never satisfied with the justice of it. Elizabeth herself fought against it."

"I have thought of all that," Cromwell groaned. He put his head in his hands, and his body seemed to shrink. When he lifted his head, despair was written on his face. "I have tried *everything* to avoid this course, but I am helpless."

"But how will you try a king? There is no—no *machinery* for such a thing."

"We will have to create it."

Chris argued for as long as Cromwell sat with him, but in the end saw that it was hopeless. "I wish any other man in the world but you had to meet this crisis."

Cromwell reached out and gripped the hand of his friend. "I say 'amen' to that, but we do what we must."

In the next few days, Chris saw a series of ordinances passed by a parliament that had been "purged" of all not in sympathy with the trial. The ordinances gave parliament the right to do what it had not the right to do under ancient English law: try a sovereign and put him to death.

The stage was now set for the trial of the king of England, and it began on January 20.

Charles entered Whitehall dressed in black, with the Star of the Garter around his neck. He sat down in a chair upholstered in crimson velvet and waited. The charge against the king was read by John Cook. It named the king as a tyrant, traitor, murderer, and a public and implacable enemy of the Commonwealth of England.

When Charles responded, he brought forth his strongest point. "By what authority h-have I been b-brought here?" He glanced around at the purged parliament and said scornfully, "I see n-no lords here to make a lawful parliament and will not answer to it."

"It is by the authority of the people by whom you were elected king!" President Bradshaw insisted.

"Ah, but I was not elected. I was b-born a king." The president flushed, and a murmur ran around the spectators.

During the days that followed, Charles showed a style and grace that had been sadly lacking from his life. Courage and dignity went hand in hand, and Chris murmured to Gavin, "The Stuarts are better in misfortune than they are in prosperity."

But the net closed inexorably around the king. On January 26, the death warrant was signed, Oliver Cromwell's name among the signatures. On January 27 Charles was led in to hear the sentence against him read out. He tried to protest, but was led from the court.

And thus it was that Charles I, king of England, was brought to his tragic end. As Christopher saw the king being led away, he said, "Gavin, if that man is executed, all justice in England will be lost!"

Twenty-four

A ROOM IN LONDON

Neither Gavin nor Susanne were able to forget their fishing trip, for Francine saw to it that they did not. She was clever enough not to quarrel with either of them, but she mentioned it, supposedly in jest, from time to time.

Angharad observed this and said to Chris, "I hope she keeps on with her sharpness about Gavin and Susanne."

"Why?" Chris asked, surprised by the hard edge of her tone.

"It's the one sure way for Gavin to see what she really is. But she'll never do it. She's too smart. She'll keep him on the rack!"

"She's driving him half crazy," Chris stated gloomily. "Well, I'm going to see Cromwell, so try to keep an eye on things."

Angharad said no more to Chris, but one victory had come to her. She had been reading the Bible and praying with Susanne since the young woman had come. At first Susanne had resisted, but little by little, the Scripture had burned into her. Somehow the calm tones of Angharad's voice seemed to echo in her mind, and one morning she said after Angharad had read a portion of the Gospel of John, "I want what you have, Angharad."

"What I have?" Angharad looked up with surprise. "What does that mean?"

"You have such—*peace!* I've never really had that. And God speaks to you, and he spoke to your father." Susanne's eyes were thoughtful and she shook her head. "All I've ever had is, well, *religion*. I want more than that."

Carefully Angharad began to counsel Susanne, and soon the day came when the young woman made a decision. She came to Angharad and said firmly, "I want to change my faith."

"You want to become a member of the Anglican Church?"

Susanne hesitated, then nodded. "As a child, I did what I was taught to do, but now I don't want just a list of rules and commandments. I want—" She hesitated, then tears came to her eyes. "I want to know Jesus as you and Will do, and as Owen did. Our Lord is a person to you, not just a name in a book. Will you help me know him?"

"He longs to know you, child! Suppose we pray right now. You tell him how you long to know him, and he will come to you!"

So the two women prayed, and that was the beginning. Susanne plunged into the Bible, putting herself under the teaching of Angharad, and she grew quickly in the ways of the Lord.

Francine observed this, but wanted no part of the Bible study the two women so enjoyed. Gavin, on the other hand, was happy to see Susanne getting close to Angharad. And he was pleased to see her come into the Anglican Church.

When Francine heard that her future father-in-law was going to London, she began pressuring Gavin to go with him. "We can go pick out my wedding dress, Gavin," she wheedled. "We've been stuck out here in the country so long, I'm bored to tears!"

"Don't you like it here?" Gavin asked in surprise.

"Oh, very well, but I'm dying for a ball, for some excitement. You know how much time I spent in the center of London's busy life. Though I find life here . . . peaceful, it is slow, at times." Francine spoke carefully, being sure to keep the proper balance of longing and satisfaction in her voice. She watched Gavin's response, thinking, *Wait until we're married. I'll get Gavin to buy a house in town—and we can leave this little rural pond to Susanne!*

In truth, she was getting edgy, for all her attempts to get Gavin to move the day of the wedding forward had failed. She had used every enticement at her command to stir Gavin, but merely had succeeded in making him miserable. He had grown a little morose and moody and had staunchly refused to go beyond his parents' request to wait until spring.

It's Chris and Angharad who are against me—but I'll win them over! Even if I don't, after we're married Gavin and I will spend precious little time at Wakefield!

Gavin had been taken aback by Francine's campaign to go to London. He was willing enough, but said, "There's too much to do right now. We'll go next month." She had cajoled him and driven him half crazy with her charms, but he had proved surprisingly stubborn.

Finally Francine had grown sharp, saying, "I'll ask your father to take me. I can choose the wedding dress while you stay here on the farm." She had little hope of accomplishing such a thing, but to her surprise Sir Christopher had been easily persuaded.

"Why, of course," he said at once when she put her request to him. "We'll leave in the morning. I'll get you a nice room, and you can do all the shopping you like. How much money will you need?"

Francine saw this as a victory and congratulated herself on winning him over. When they left the next day, she kissed Gavin, whispering, "I'll buy a beautiful gown for our wedding night, one that you'll like. Now think about *that,* sweet!"

"I can't think about anything but you, Francine," Gavin said soberly. "The poets write about men being driven crazy by the moon when they're in love. I hope after we're married, I won't be so dazed."

"When you have me, that's all you'll need!" She kissed him, then left with a knowing smile.

All the way to London she made herself agreeable to Sir

Christopher, and when he found her a fine room in one of the most expensive inns in London and gave her a fat purse full of gold coins, she kissed him on the cheeks, her eyes glowing. "Oh, thank you, Sir Christopher!" she exclaimed. Roguishly she smiled at him. "It's a good thing I wasn't around when you were Gavin's age. I'd have snapped you up in a second."

After he left, Chris shook his head thinking, *She's beautiful—but she'd drive a man to distraction.* Putting her firmly out of his mind, he drove to his appointment with Cromwell. He found the great leader meeting with the leaders of parliament and waited for an hour before being admitted. Cromwell came to take his hand and ordered food brought. "I haven't been able to eat," he complained. "This business of executing a king takes away the appetite." His eyes were sunk into his head and ringed with dark shadows.

"How is the king taking it?" Chris asked quietly. He knew that it was too late to argue for another course, and his only concern was to keep his old friend from being destroyed by what was happening.

"Better than anyone expected." Cromwell spoke of the confinement of the king, and when servants brought a tray of food in, he nibbled without appetite. "He's never acknowledged the legality of his trial, you know. He's steadfast in that!" Cromwell lifted a piece of cake, then put it down, grief in his eyes. "He seems to have found the peace he's always wanted but never found."

"Peace with God?"

"Yes. He listens reverently to the devotions of the Anglican Church, and he's urged his children to forgive his enemies—as he has." For some reason this appeared to disturb Cromwell. He sat staring at the wall, his thoughts bringing a look of slight confusion to his homely face. He was an honest man and had agreed to the execution of the king only after great internal misgivings. If the king had struck out at his enemies with hatred, he could have accepted the judgment, but the patience and grace with which

Charles accepted his fate had caused him to wonder if he had taken the right course. "It's too late to stop the thing," he muttered sadly, lifting his eyes to meet Chris's compassionate gaze. "But the manner of the king has made me grieve that it's come to his death."

"No chance of a rescue?"

"No, none at all. The scaffold is being built in Whitehall."

"Right across from the king's banqueting hall," Chris murmured. "He loved that place most of all, I think."

The two men exchanged a long look, then Chris said, "I'll be in prayer for the king. And for you."

"I am much in need of your prayers. I am indeed!"

Gavin was sitting in the library, engrossed in reading a brown leather-bound book. Twilight had fallen, and he was vaguely conscious of the soft moan of the doves that gathered outside his window, but he looked up with a start when the hinges of the door squeaked.

"Oh! I didn't mean to interrupt—" Susanne had stepped inside the room, but halted abruptly on seeing Gavin. She turned quickly to go, but his voice caught her.

"Come in, Susanne," Gavin said. "I want to read you something. Sit down and listen to this." He waited until she sat down across from him, then cleared his throat and read aloud:

> "O Sir, doubt not but that angling is an art. Is it not an art to deceive a trout with an artificial fly? A trout is more sharp-sighted than any hawk you have named, and more watchful and timorous than your high-mettled merlin is bold! And yet I doubt not to catch a brace of tow tomorrow of a friend's breakfast. Doubt not, therefore, sir, but that angling is an art, and an art capable of learning: The question is rather, whether you be capable of learning!"

Looking up, Gavin nodded firmly. "There! The next time anyone chides me for wasting my life in such a pastime as fishing, I'll have the weight of the evidence behind me!"

"Whose book is that?"

"A fellow named Izaak Walton. The whole book is about angling. By George, the fellow has a headful of sense." Gavin paused and grinned at her abruptly. "He *exactly* agrees with what I've always said!"

Susanne's lips curved upward into a smile as she teased, "You've always sought every excuse for fishing instead of working."

"Not so! But even if I did, it means I'm an *artist!*"

"You can't even draw a dog—never could!"

"Ah, but that's where this fellow Walton has set the world straight, don't you see? Listen to this:

> "Angling is like poetry, men are born to be so, for he that hopes to be a good angler must not only bring an inquiring, searching, observing wit, but he must bring a large measure of hope and patience, and a love and propensity to the art itself!"

Gavin nodded vigorously, then put the book down on the table beside him. "I'll have you know, then, that I'm an artist, so don't ever let any man or woman insult my art!" He stood up and gave her a half-embarrassed look. "I'm just a fool for fishing, I suppose. Any excuse to fish rather than work is always welcome."

"I'm somewhat the same," Susanne said. She rose and walked to the window, staring out at the evening. "I remember the time we caught the big pike, down below the bridge near the mill."

Gavin hesitated, then came over to stand beside her. "Seems like a million years ago, those days."

"Yes, they do."

"Do you ever wish you could go back to those days?"

"No, not really. They remember well, but the reality was a little harsher."

Gavin glanced at her, admiring her clean-cut jaw and the glints of the sun as it caught in her hair. "I never thought of that," he said quietly, then after a thoughtful silence, added, "It's true enough. Things far away always seem better than what we have. My uncle used to say that the South Sea Islands are beautiful to think about, but the bugs and snakes take away most of the fun."

"Yes, and the past is like that, I think. I think of the good things, but there were bad things too. No, I wouldn't go back." She turned slightly to face him. "What about you, Gavin?"

"Do I pine after the days of golden youth? Well, to tell the truth, of late I'd give almost anything to live in the past *or* in the future." He turned to meet her eyes, and there was a tense quality in his tone as he added, "The present hasn't been so good." When she didn't answer, he flushed, adding, "Not a very good statement for a prospective bridegroom to make, but it's true."

Susanne said gently, "I thought it was only women who were supposed to be nervous about getting married."

"Not true!" A bat suddenly fluttered across the window, snapped up a wandering insect, then, with a shudder of black wings, rose into the lowering darkness. Gavin paused at the interruption, saying, "Those fellows scare me a little for some reason." Then he appeared to be uncomfortable with the tenor of the conversation. "Enough about me. How are you, Susanne?"

"Me? Why, well enough."

Gavin hesitated, then said, "It's been uncomfortable since our last fishing trip. I'm sorry that Francine's been so nasty about it. I've tried to explain, but she's very possessive."

"Yes, she is, but so am I." Susanne summoned up a smile, saying, "If I ever get a man, I'll hang on to him like that snapping turtle that got on your little finger!"

Gavin laughed abruptly, then held up his left hand. "You cried more than I did when that monster caught me. Look, I still have the scar."

Susanne bent her head forward to see, and Gavin was caught by the faint scent of her hair. "I threw up," she said. "Another golden memory of childhood."

"Yes, but I wouldn't take anything for those times we had, would you?"

Susanne said, "Some of them were fine. But we can't live in the past." She was suddenly uncomfortable and said quickly, "I must go now."

Gavin saw that she was not at ease and said stiffly, "If you're worried that I might kiss you again—" He paused, uncertainly, then a light gleamed in his eyes. "Well, I might!"

Her eyes widened in surprise. "No, that wouldn't be right."

The teasing light in Gavin's eyes changed, and he looked at her with glad eyes. "I'm happy to see you doing so well with your new faith. It must have been hard to leave the church you grew up in."

"Yes, but it's been worth it. I—I wanted something real, and Angharad has helped me a great deal. The Lord is with me now."

As she turned and made for the door, he said, "I'm leaving for London early in the morning. Can I bring you anything?"

"No, I don't think so." Susanne hesitated, then asked as she reached the door, "Will you see Francine?"

"Yes. I'm going to help her pick out that blasted wedding dress!" He shook his head with annoyance. "A marriage is more than a dress, isn't it?"

"Yes, but to a woman that's important." Susanne felt out of place with such talk, but added impulsively, "Be patient with her, Gavin." Then she left the room, and for a few moments Gavin stood there, his eyes fixed on the door. Then he uttered a mild oath and left the room with long, determined strides, muttering, "All right, I'll be patient—but for a *dress?*"

Gavin rose early and had breakfast with Angharad, who made him promise to send his father home as soon as possible. "I miss him," she said simply. Then the streak of humor that ran through her surfaced. "When an old maid finally gets a man, she doesn't want to let him go for a second!"

"I'll try to pry him loose from some of those bold young women who always seem to gather around a man like father," Gavin promised. "He always was a ladies' man, you know."

"Go you—I will have them for it!" The two of them laughed, enjoying the teasing, and sat there speaking lightly. But when she rose and went to the door with him, she paused to say, "I love you like you were born of my flesh." At his look of surprise, she said evenly, "Be careful—very careful!"

Gavin took her kiss on his cheek, but then as he rode away toward London he wondered at the terseness of her words. *Be careful of what?* He could not make anything of it, but he had such great respect for the wisdom of this woman that he remained sober as he moved toward the city.

He arrived in London just as night was beginning to close over the city. The smoke of thousands of chimneys lay on the air, and as the acrid smell of coal smoke bit at his nostrils, he grunted, "Don't see why anyone would live in a place like this!" He disliked the city and already could see that a conflict would surface with Francine, for she thought that heaven itself was not so attractive as London.

He got a small room in an inn, then set out for the inner city, hoping to find Francine before it was too late. When he got to the large inn where his father had said he would get her rooms, he asked the innkeeper, "Miss Fourier, which are her quarters?"

The innkeeper, a burly man with a hook for a left hand, waved the shiny instrument vaguely toward the stairway. "End o' the hall, sir. Last door on the left."

Gavin thanked the man, then ascended the stairway. When he reached the door indicated, he knocked, but there was no answer. "Blast!" he muttered. "Probably gone to visit friends."

He moved back down the stairs, then realized he was hungry. The smell of freshly cooked beef caught at him, and he moved to one of the tables at the back of the tavern. "Bring me steak and whatever else is good," he told the stubby waiter who came to ask what he would have.

"Yes, sir, I 'av a bit of kidney pie, would that go down? And taters. A gentleman allus likes taters!"

Gavin agreed and drank a pint of ale while he waited. The room was crowded, and he listened to the talk that ran around. Most of it, of course, concerned the execution of the king, which was to take place shortly. He was a little shocked to find out that the sentiment was against the execution, for he had assumed that parliament's decision reflected the desires of the people. But one red-faced man with a thatch of flaming red hair and a pair of small eyes dominated the talk. "Kill the king," he warned shrilly, "and no man can look for justice!"

"But he was found guilty!" A thin man with snow white hair protested.

"Found guilty by a bunch of guttersnipes with no more authority than this 'ere glass o' beer!" the red-faced man shouted. He harangued the crowd in the tavern as though they were in the square, but his words had their effect on those who sat listening as they ate and drank. Finally he shook his head and uttered a dire threat. "If Charles goes to the block, you'll see England turned into a kingdom of serfs, with King Oliver Cromwell lording it over every man jack of us!"

Gavin listened as he ate his meal, then went back to see if Francine had returned. She had not, so he left the inn for a walk. The fog closed in like a gray overcoat, and the cold bit at his face and fingers. The streets were not lit, and there was no sheriff's force to keep order, only a bellman who patrolled the streets calling the hours. Gavin wandered so long that he was shocked to hear that it lacked only an hour to midnight. He turned and made his way back to the inn. When he approached the door and lifted his hand, he thought he heard voices inside and hesitated. Feeling like a boy sneaking where he shouldn't be, he glanced down the dark hallway. When he saw he was alone, he put his ear against the door. The door was made of thick oak, but still his hearing was good, and he thought he made out the sound of a woman laughing.

Might be coming from another room.

He knocked, but there was no response, and he decided he'd been mistaken. Going back downstairs, he thought, *Which room did the innkeeper say? Maybe I made a mistake.* The innkeeper was still standing behind the bar, cleaning glasses. When Gavin asked, "Which room did you say Miss Fourier was in?" he gave Gavin a peculiar look, then shrugged.

"Top of the stairs—last door on the left."

Gavin stared at the man for a moment then left the inn. He turned and walked down the street, then peered upward. There, in the corner angle of the building, was where he supposed Francine's room would be. The window was outlined in a square of amber lamplight.

For a full minute Gavin stood in the street, staring at the window, as though willing something not to be so. Then, his jaw tight, he turned and made his way back inside, ignoring the stare of the innkeeper. When he reached the door, he leaned forward and listened.

There was no mistake this time. He heard not only the laughter of a woman, but the voice of a man! Gavin stared at the door, and for a long moment indecision ran through him. Then his face grew tense and his eyes narrowed. He didn't knock this time, but gathered himself and hit the door with all his weight. The hasp tore loose and the door swung open under his onslaught. As it did so, Gavin was propelled into the room, thrown off balance. As he caught himself and straightened up, he heard a voice and knew that he had been terribly right!

"Gavin—!" Francine screamed in horror.

But the emotion in her voice was nothing compared to what surged through Gavin when he saw the scene before him. Francine, his fair and beautiful fiancée, was in bed with Henry Darrow. Her eyes were wide with fear as she pulled the sheet up around her.

Darrow was half drunk, but he sobered at once as he saw Gavin standing there. "Get out of here!" he bellowed, but his voice was hollow, as though he suddenly realized he was in a poor position to give orders.

Gavin felt sick. He stared at Francine, thinking of the years he'd spent loving this woman. Now with her features loosed from drink and sex, her beauty was marred by a grossness that repelled him. He remembered how she'd kissed him, allowed him to caress her, then had been coy when he'd tried to press her into greater intimacy. And yet, all that time, she had been giving herself to Darrow.

The sickness in him grew—and with it a burning anger. He drew his sword and stepped forward, moving jerkily.

"No! Don't!" Darrow cried, and at the same moment Francine began to weep and plead. They both realized that they were helpless. Fear shone out of their eyes as Gavin lifted his blade and held it poised before Darrow's naked chest.

"Wait, Gavin—!" Francine begged. "Don't kill him!"

"Why shouldn't I?" Gavin's voice grated. "He's taken what's mine!"

"She was never yours, Wakefield!" Henry Darrow might be a shallow, wicked man, but there was a sort of courage within him. The shock of being suddenly exposed was fading, and now he made a firm line of his lips and stared across the gleaming blade aimed at his heart. He was pale, but said calmly, "Francine never loved you."

"Henry, don't say that!" Francine cried out, thinking that after Gavin killed Henry, she would be his next victim.

Darrow glanced at her, then shook his head. "You never loved anyone but yourself, my dear. I know that," he added cynically, "because I'm exactly the same." He looked at Gavin, then gave a fatalistic shrug. "You will kill me, I suppose, but do you think I'd be here if she hadn't invited me?"

Gavin blinked and the tip of the sword wavered. "You're a dog, Darrow!"

"Oh yes, but then I've always been a rogue, if you'll remember. Just as you've always been a noble sort of fellow. Why is that, I wonder?" Darrow seemed to be studying a philosophical problem and finally said, "I'm what God made me, just as you are."

"No, that's not the way things are!"

"Well, of course *you* don't think so with your views on God, but since I don't hold those views, I'm free to think that men are all more or less puppets. And Francine here, why, you've made her into some sort of pure and chaste thing, but she isn't, Wakefield. She and I are alike, and that is something we cannot help."

Francine saw that Gavin was wavering and said quickly, "I'm sorry, but Henry is right." All her plans to marry into the Wakefield clan had vanished the moment Gavin had crashed into the room, and she knew it. Now she pushed her hair back and added, "It might give you satisfaction to kill us, but I would never have made the kind of wife you want. Now—do what you have to do."

Gavin stared at the two, bitterness in his eyes as the awareness that she was speaking the truth washed over him. Deliberately he sheathed his weapon, then turned and walked woodenly toward the door.

When he was gone, Francine began to weep, and Darrow put his arms around her. He was trembling himself, now that the danger was gone. He knew he had been very close to death, and he had faced it well. For that he was grateful.

"Now, don't cry, sweet," he said and pulled her face toward him. A thought came to him and he smiled. "Who knows, maybe I *will* marry you. I'd probably get bored to tears with some fat, wealthy widow! Now, let's see if we can get the proprietor of this fine establishment to fix our door."

Gavin left the inn, and the darkness of the night closed in on him. He walked along the streets, his mind churning. Shame and rage flowed through him as he relived the scene, knowing that it would take months or even years before he could shake off the memory.

Finally he straightened his shoulders and said, bitterness in every word, "I made a fool of myself over a woman, but by heaven, I'll never do it again!"

Then he pulled his hat down over his face and walked into the fog, the darkness closing around him like an ebony river.

Twenty-five

THE FALL OF THE AX

On the morning of Tuesday, January 30, Charles Stuart dressed for his execution. He wore two shirts so that he would not shiver from the cold and thus be accused of showing fear.

The scaffold had risen in front of the king's lovely banqueting hall, and those who were in charge had stapled ropes to hold the king in case he struggled. They did not know their man, for Charles purposed to leave the world with dignity.

Between five and six o'clock on the morning of his impending end, the king awoke and drew back his bed curtain, saying, "I will get up, for I have a great work to do this day." As his attendant helped him to dress, he said gently, "This is my second marriage day. I would be as trim today as may be, for before tonight I hope to be espoused to my blessed Jesus."

The king walked from St. James Palace to Whitehall and, once there, took a little wine and a little bread. At two o'clock, he stepped forth from the banqueting hall to face the waiting crowd. He was accompanied by his chaplain, Bishop Juxon.

The weather was cold, very cold, and to the spectators the king seemed much older. His beard and hair were silver, and his face was lined with care. When he was asked if he had any last words, he spoke in a high, clear voice that did not falter—and that showed little sign of his stammer.

"For the people truly I desire their liberty and freedom as much as anybody whatsoever; but I just tell you that their liberty and freedom consists in having government, those laws by which their lives and goods may be most their own."

Finally he said, "I die a good Christian, forgiving all the world, yea, chiefly those who have caused my death. I go from a corruptible crown to an incorruptible crown, where no disturbance can be, no disturbance in the world."

He took a small white cap from his chaplain and assisted the executioner in arranging his hair under it. The king raised his hands and eyes to heaven and prayed in silence. Then he slipped off his cloak and knelt down carefully and placed his head on the block. The executioner bent down to make sure his hair was not in the way, and Charles, thinking he was preparing to strike, said, "Stay for the sign."

"I will, and it please Your Majesty," the executioner said.

A deep silence fell over the crowd. Then the king stretched out his hand—and the executioner lifted his ax and let it fall, severing his king's head at a single stroke.

One of the marshals picked up the head and held it high so that the people could see, proclaiming, "This is the head of a traitor!"

But Chris, who was standing in the crowd, sick at heart, remembered all his life that at the fatal stroke, a groan broke from the crowd such as he had never heard before.

Twenty-six

"WHEN THE SUN GOES OUT!"

The execution of King Charles produced a spirit of fear and horror among the Royalists of England.

"They were for a time like those that dreamed," said Anne Halkett, a writer of the time, and another said, "When we meet, it is but to consult to what foreign plantation we shall fly!"

Indeed, the melancholy that resulted from this dark event was to torment the Commonwealth all the days of its existence. They had done what had never been done before. They had put a king to death, executed "the anointed deputy of the Lord," and this fact haunted the land for years, so that even a stout Puritan such as Ralph Josselin wrote in his diary, "I was much troubled with the black providence of putting the king to death; my tears were not restrained at the passages at his death."

A scholar named John Milton was one of the first to publish a defense of the execution of Charles. He published a pamphlet with the mind-stunning title, "The Tenure of Kings and Magistrates: Proving That It Is Lawful, and Hath Been Held so through All Ages, for Any, Who Have the Power, to Call to Account a Tyrant or Wicked King, and after Due Conviction to Depose and Put Him to Death."

The "defense" of the new regime so pleased Cromwell that he had Milton appointed Latin Secretary at the modest salary of 288 pounds per year.

As for Cromwell himself, whatever doubts he may have entertained over the rightness of executing Charles, he kept them to himself. Outwardly he appeared to be cheerful, full of optimism for the budding Commonwealth.

Chris met with him once, just two weeks after the execution. He had been asked to serve in a government post, but he said, "Sir, I must ask your pardon. There are others more fitted than I, and if truth be told, I am greedy of every day with my family. My son Amos is nine now and needs me. And I have a new daughter, you know, and am as foolish a father as you will find in England."

Cromwell's face was lined, but he smiled at his friend's happiness. "I am glad for you, Christopher. Would that it pleased God to allow me to follow that way!"

"Things are going well for you and the new government, aren't they?"

Cromwell pulled his hands across his face, then shrugged. "Things never go well with a new venture. The same men who agitated for a new government are now bemoaning the loss of the old."

"I pray daily that God will strengthen you."

"Thank you, my friend! I knew I could count on your prayers." He cocked an eyebrow, a slight smile at his lips. "But not on your service, eh?"

"If you insist, I will obey."

"No! No! I do not insist. Go to your family. What did you name your new daughter?"

"My wife said the Lord gave her the name of Hope."

Cromwell sighed deeply. "A fine name—Hope. It's the only quality that gives me heart, Christopher . . . hope for this holy experiment we are now engaged in."

Chris left soon afterward, and when he got back home, he seized Angharad and spun her around. "Now—no more war! No more leaving you and Amos and Hope!"

"Put me down!" Angharad pretended to be cross, but she was so glad to have Chris back that she put her arms around his neck and said, "There is glad I am to have you back!"

They kissed, then she took him into the kitchen, where she made him a fine dinner. As he ate, she told him all that had gone on at Wakefield during his absence. When he asked about Susanne, she said, "The lass is well enough, but sad on the inside."

"What happened in London?" Chris asked. "Has Gavin told you anything?"

"It was as I told you in the letter I sent you," Angharad said. "Gavin came back from London and announced that he and Francine had decided not to marry. He seemed very angry and bitter. Since then he's been sullen, keeping to himself most of the time."

"And he won't say what happened?"

"No, nor will he ever tell, I think. It was something so painful you can see it in his eyes." Angharad picked up Chris's hand and caressed it. "But I cannot help but believe it was of God—the breakup between the two. Francine was no woman for our Gavin."

"No, she was not. Still, he was so infatuated with her, I'd wager whatever caused the rift was a hard knock for the boy." They spoke of Gavin for some time, then went to see Hope, who claimed all of Chris's attention for some time.

For three days Chris said nothing to Gavin about his problem, nor did Angharad. They were troubled, and it was Angharad who finally said, "A bitter man is something God cannot honor, and Gavin is on his way to becoming one."

"Shall I talk to him?"

"No, let me do it." She waited for a time of privacy, and it finally came one day when she saw him come in from riding in the fields. Putting on her coat and shawl, she made her way across the yard. As she stepped inside the barn, she saw him turn to her, his face fixed in the perpetual frown that seemed to have taken up permanent residence on his visage. Abruptly she said, "Something to say to you, I have."

"What is it?" Gavin turned from her and stripped the saddle from the horse, which was heaving for breath and trembling with fatigue. That Gavin would treat his horse badly told her how far the young man was from being himself.

"You're acting badly, Gavin. Your father and I are worried about you."

"There's nothing wrong with me," he bit out. He tossed the saddle over on the floor and jerked the bridle roughly from the mare's tender mouth.

Angharad's eyes hardened, and when she spoke, her tone was hard as well. "You deserve a whipping for treating a fine mare like that."

Gavin flushed, for he loved the animal. But he was stubborn and said, "She's my horse, and I'll treat her any way I want to."

"And you're my son, so I'll treat you the same as you treat the mare!" Angharad's hand flashed out and struck Gavin's cheek with a loud report.

Angry red surged into his face, and he raised his hand to return the strike. But when his eyes met her unblinking stare, he froze—and his hand dropped to his side. "I . . . deserved that," he muttered. He reached out and patted the mare's neck, keeping his face averted.

Angharad instantly came to him. She reached up and stroked his jaw, whispering, "Ah, Gavin, a bad bump you've had with that woman! I know it's hurting you are."

He turned, and confusion marred his face. "I'm—sorry, Angharad. I've been feeling low, but I shouldn't take it out on you and Father."

"Do you want to tell me how it was?"

Gavin hesitated, then nodded. "I've got to tell *somebody!*" he burst out. "I think about it all day, then I lie in bed and think about it all night."

"Come you, sit down and say it. My father was a great one for not holding things back. 'Let it out and it won't sour your spirit!' He must have said that a hundred times." She sat down on a pile of hay, pulling him down beside her. As he poured out his tale, she kept her eyes on him. He was flushed with shame and anger, and she thought, *That's got to change—he won't be any sort of man unless he can get rid of those feelings!*

Finally Gavin threw up his hands—which were trembling. "That's the way it was, and what a fool I was for loving her!" He struck his fist into his palm and cried in vexation, "I'll not be made a fool of again!"

Angharad longed to heap advice on him, but now was not the time. She let him rant on about how he'd never care for another woman, waiting for him to run down. At last he did so and sat there silently.

After a moment she said, "You've been spared of a terrible fate. Francine would have made a hell out of your life."

"I know that!"

She hesitated then added, "She was not a good woman, but not all women are like her. There *are* good women."

Gavin was flushed with the turmoil that was going on inside, but he put his hand on hers and managed a smile. "There's one, anyway—Angharad Wakefield."

She shook her head, smiling. "Now you've got your father's charm." Then she sobered and her eyes studied him steadily. When she spoke, her words startled the young man beside her. "Gavin, go from here."

"Go? From Wakefield?"

"Get away from everyone." Angharad nodded. "There are times when every one of us needs to get alone with ourselves and with God. I love you, boy, and God loves you, but you're on your way to ruin if you don't whip this thing."

Gavin sat silently for a long moment, then nodded. "I—I think you may be right." He got to his feet and helped her up. "I'll tell Father I want some time alone. There's not much to do now, and Will can take care of things."

"Good for you!" Angharad said, pleased, then the two of them made their way back to the house. Later, when Angharad and Chris talked about it, she said, "We'll put God onto him. That's the only medicine for a bitter spirit!"

Spring came early to England in the year of 1649. Gavin felt it begin as the icy breeze that burned his cheeks became gentle. He followed the lanes of England, always heading southwest, stopping at small inns or private homes—sometimes sleeping in barns. His mare enjoyed the leisurely days of wandering down narrow lanes.

One day Gavin lifted his head, for he smelled the sea. Lifting the mare to a gallop, he rode until finally the ocean unfolded, spread out before him like an enormous gray blanket. He rode to the shore, then walked for hours, searching for shells. That night he built a fire of driftwood and sat listening to the roar of huge waves as they seemed to hurl stones at the beach. He was overwhelmed by the power and size of the ocean. The next morning at dawn he stood peering out over the water, and a sense of the power of God came to him. *To* make *all this! The ocean and the land and the mountains!* Looking upward, he saw the faint twinkle of stars and thought of the countless multitudes of bodies rolling in space . . . and he worshiped the God who had made it all.

I need to get alone more, out like this, he thought as he saddled the mare. He rode along the coast unhurriedly, coming after many days to Cornwall, which some said had been the home of King Arthur. He made his way to Land's End and sat down on a promontory to look at the sea.

This is as far as I can go, he thought. *Now—here is where I will find God!*

For a week he wandered the jagged shoreline, fascinated by the rugged beauty of the coast. He stayed at a small inn, eating simple fare. The owners of the inn had never been to London, and they begged for tales of it as if it were far-off China. Gavin discovered that they were dismayed by the king's execution.

"No good will come of it!" the host said, nodding. "Mind my words, we'll see hard times. Blood brings forth blood!"

"You may be right," Gavin agreed. He did not want to argue politics, so he turned the conversation to other things. The next day he left and started back down the coast. At last he headed away from the shore, and the first night inland he found the peace he was looking for.

It came so simply that he could not believe it was real. For weeks he had struggled with hatred for Francine and Henry Darrow. No matter how he tried, it was always there. But the days alone had been more productive than he'd realized. He had turned his thoughts from his own problems, first to the magnificent world about him, then to the God who had made it all.

He made a fire and cooked a simple meal, then rolled up in his blanket to watch the blaze. The wind made a soft moaning through the branches overhead, but he could see the stars that lined the heavens like glittering points of ice.

A Scripture came to him, one that Owen had read to him many times—but he did not so much recall the verse as hear Owen Morgan's voice once again, quoting with the ring of reverence: "You are worthy, O Lord, to receive glory and honor and power; for You created all things, and by Your will they exist and were created."

For a long time he lay there, the voice of his deceased friend echoing within him. The words soaked into him, and finally he whispered, "Why, that means *me!* Not just the world and the stars . . . it says *all* things! *I* was created to give God pleasure!"

It was a concept that had never occurred to Gavin, and he lay there struggling to understand. *How could a man be any pleasure to God? Especially such a foolish creature as me?*

Finally realization came to him, not logically, but as an inner certainty—not unlike the way he knew he loved his father without having to convince himself as to why. He got up and fed the fire, then stood looking down at it, and finally he reasoned aloud, his voice startling the night creatures: "God made me to give him pleasure, and all this time I thought it was the other way round. I thought God made heaven and earth for my benefit. But . . . I'm not a pleasure to God. Not like I am!"

He thought suddenly of Owen and smiled. *"You* gave God pleasure, old friend. I don't doubt that. But I'm no Owen Morgan."

The wind rose and fell, and as he stood there, though he heard no audible voice, Gavin felt a truth come to him.

No, my son, you are not Owen. You are Gavin Wakefield—the only one there will ever be. If you do not serve God and love him, he will lose forever something he made to enjoy throughout all time. That's what gives God pleasure, the love and worship of a human being who was made to live with God.

Gavin began to weep, and he prayed through his tears. When it was over, he felt drained and weak—and, he realized with a shock, void of ill will for anyone, even Francine and Darrow!

"Why—it's all gone!" he cried, throwing up his hands with abandon. "God, it's all your doing! Now, don't let it ever come back!" His voice rang loudly, and the next morning as he mounted the mare, he looked around. "This is holy ground, but I can't come and live here. I have something else I must do."

A thought had been growing in him, and it was with a sense of joy and excitement that he drove the mare down the road. He had to return to Wakefield.

A few days later, when Gavin looked closer and saw that the rider who approached him was none other than William Hollis, the miller at Wakefield, he spurred his horse forward.

"William," he cried as he drew near and pulled the horse to a stop, "what brings you from home?"

Hollis was an excellent miller, but his speech was almost unintelligible. His tongue seemed too large for his mouth, the same as King James I, and his speech was such a garble that one had to listen closely. Even then, many could understand almost none of what the man said.

"Aw, Master!" William sighed. "You been gone a long time, and to come back at such a time!"

This was expressed in groans, and Gavin could not grasp it all, but he started at the words. "Is someone dead?"

Again the miller seemed to blubber. "It's Mistress Susanne, sir. She's in a bad way."

"What's wrong with her, the plague?" A coldness came to Gavin, fear clenching like a fist around his throat. He listened desperately, trying to sort out the man's words, finally understanding that Susanne was dying and that Hollis was going to bring the doctor.

"But Lady Wakefield, she says the poor girl can't live—ho, wait, Mr. Gavin—"

But Gavin spurred the startled mare into a dead run and kept her at it. As the trees flashed by a numb desperation filled him, and he suddenly saw himself—and his heart—with a new clarity.

I've been a fool! All the time she's been right there!

The village came into view, and he made straight for the castle, praying, "God, God . . . don't let her die. Not now!"

The road to the castle led beside a field that flanked a line of huge trees. As he flashed by, he caught a glimpse of someone bent over in the tall grass. He let the horse take several strides, then pulled her up sharply. Wheeling around, he kept his eyes fixed on a woman—and then cried out, "Susanne!"

Susanne had seen the horseman go by, but had not realized it was Gavin. Now she dropped the young spring flowers on the ground and just had time to cry out, "Gavin—" before he pulled the horse up and almost fell out of the saddle. She saw his pale face and the wild look in his eyes and cried out, "Gavin, what's wrong?"

But she had no time to say more, for he threw his arms around her and pulled her close, holding her so tight that he hurt her. She gasped with pain and tried to think, but he buried his face against her neck and was whispering her name over and over in a desperate fashion.

She pulled back and was shocked to see tears in Gavin's eyes. "What—what is it?" she asked, but he could only shake his head, unable to speak. His arms held her tight, and despite herself, she felt a pleasure in his embrace.

"William Hollis . . . he said you were dying," Gavin finally managed to say. "I nearly lost my mind!"

A thrill of joy shot through Susanne, but she shoved it away. *He only feared the loss of a friend,* she told herself, then said, "No, no, Gavin, it's *Susan* who's so sick, not me!"

"Susan . . . our cook?"

"Yes, though Angharad says she thinks she'll get well."

Gavin was still holding Susanne tightly, and she said, "Gavin . . . let me go! Someone will see us!"

He only looked down at her and shook his head. He was as shaken as he'd ever been in his life, and he was not willing to give up the solid, living feel of her. That was all he wanted at the moment. "Let them see! I don't care."

Susanne felt his arms tighten, and she looked around wildly, then said, "What's *wrong* with you, Gavin?"

"Nothing's wrong with me—not now!"

"You look so—so *odd!*" Susanne's face was only inches from his, and she felt his arms tighten more. "Gavin, this isn't *right!*"

"Yes, it is," Gavin said firmly. Taking a deep breath he went on, "I've got so much to tell you—"

"Can't you let go of me and tell me in the house?"

Gavin shook his head. "Not all of it, but some. After all, we've got a lifetime for me to tell you things, Susanne. But right now, don't get angry, but I'm going to kiss you."

Susanne didn't get angry. She simply closed her eyes and gave herself up to the embrace. Then, when he lifted his head to say, "Sweetheart, I love you!" she pulled his head down and kissed him!

Then she drew back, and there was wonder in her voice. "I've loved you since I was a child, but I never thought you'd love me. Are you sure, Gavin?"

Gavin nodded. "See that sun up there? When that sun goes out, then maybe I'll stop loving you."

Susanne studied his face, then leaned over and put her face against his chest. Tears stung her eyes and she shut them tightly. She and Gavin stood there in the middle of the field, awash in the glory of newly declared love, secure at long last in their feelings for each other . . . completely unaware that they were being watched.

Chris and Angharad had seen the whole thing from a window high in the house. Now Chris's arm went around his wife and he shook his head. "Well, it looks like we'll have a daughter-in-law after all, doesn't it, Wife?"

Angharad smiled, remembering her father's last words to Gavin, and whispered, "Yes, and a woman of God she is!"

They watched as the two in the field embraced again, then saw Gavin sweep Susanne into his arms and swing her around, dancing wildly among the tall grass.

Angharad slanted a sly glance toward Chris. "You never do that with me, Christopher."

"No? Well—!"

Hope was lying nearby, hitting herself in the eye with one pudgy fist. But she stopped her action and watched with interest as the man who always poked her neck and tickled her cheeks picked up the woman who gave her lunch and began to dance around the room.

Finally she grew bored and began to study her fingers very carefully, only faintly aware of the joyful laughter that echoed around her.

THE END

In addition to this series . . .

THE WAKEFIELD DYNASTY
#1 The Sword of Truth   0-8423-6228-2
#2 The Winds of God   0-8423-7953-3

. . . look for more captivating historical fiction from Gilbert Morris!

THE APPOMATTOX SAGA
Intriguing, realistic stories capture the emotional and spiritual strife of the tragic Civil War era.
#1 A Covenant of Love   0-8423-5497-2
#2 Gate of His Enemies   0-8423-1069-X
#3 Where Honor Dwells   0-8423-6799-X
#4 Land of the Shadow   0-8423-5742-4
#5 Out of the Whirlwind   0-8423-1658-2
#6 The Shadow of His Wings   0-8423-5987-7
#7 Wall of Fire *(New! Spring 1995)*   0-8423-8126-0

RENO WESTERN SAGA
A Civil War drifter faces the challenges of the frontier, searching for a deeper sense of meaning in his life.
#1 Reno   0-8423-1058-4
#2 Rimrock   0-8423-1059-2
#3 Ride the Wild River   0-8423-5795-5
#4 Boomtown   0-8423-7789-1
#5 Valley Justice *(New! Spring 1995)*   0-8423-7756-5

Just for kids

THE OZARK ADVENTURES
Barney Buck and his brothers learn about spiritual values and faith in God through outrageous capers in the back hills of the Ozarks.
#1 The Bucks of Goober Holler   0-8423-4392-X
#2 The Rustlers of Panther Gap   0-8423-4393-8
#3 The Phantom of the Circus   0-8423-5097-7